JOVE'S LEGACY

JOVE'S LEGACY

Kim E. Morgan

Selkirk Publishing LLC

Library of Congress Control Number: 2016905498

ISBN: 978-1-944706-00-5 (sc)
ISBN: 978-1-944706-01-2 (e)

PRINTED IN THE UNITED STATES OF AMERICA

For My Sisters

Linda, Connie Jean and Judith

1 Corinthians 13:12
King James Version

For now we see through a glass, darkly;
but then face to face: now I know in part;
but then shall I know even as also I am known.

Dost thou love me? I know thou wilt say, "Ay,"
And I will take thy word; yet, if thou swear'st,
Thou mayest prove false: at lovers' perjuries
They say Jove laughs. O gentle Romeo,
If thou dost love, pronounce it faithfully.

William Shakespeare
The Tragedy of Romeo and Juliet
Act 2, Scene 2

CONTENTS

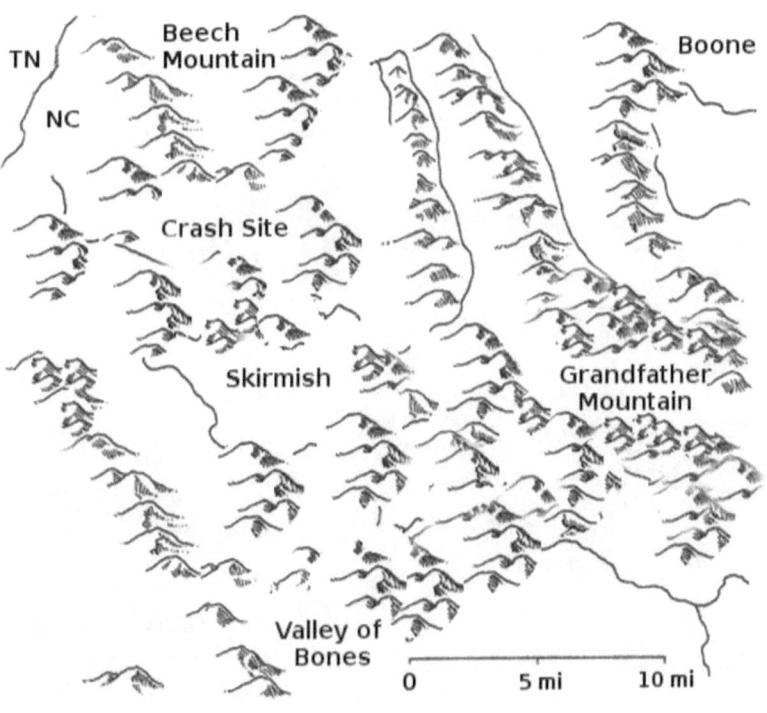

TN

NC

Beech
Mountain

Boone

Crash Site

Skirmish

Grandfather
Mountain

Valley of
Bones

0   5 mi   10 mi

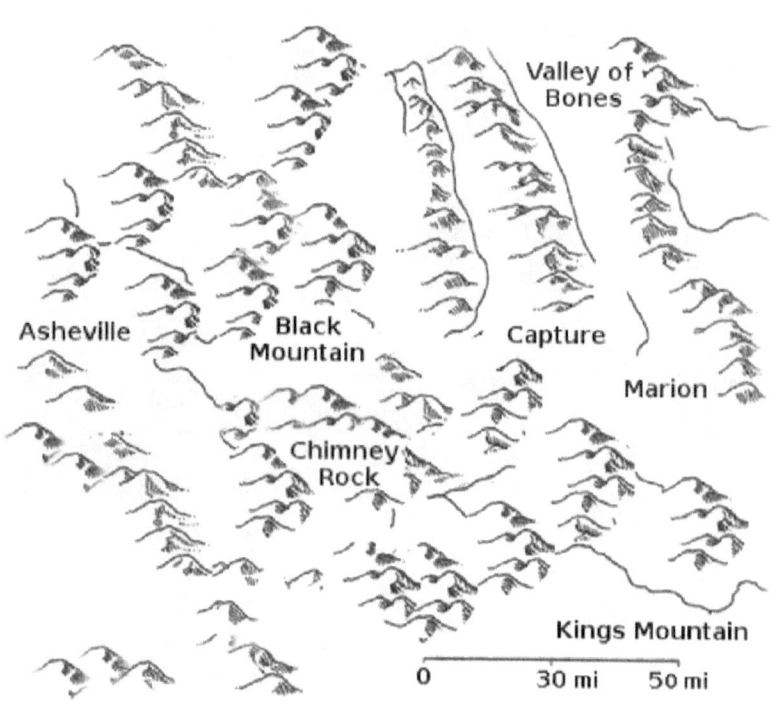

Valley of Bones

Asheville

Black Mountain

Capture

Marion

Chimney Rock

Kings Mountain

0   30 mi   50 mi

Principal Characters

TWELVE POLYMATHS
Artem Kozlov Russia
Cyrus Bashir Iran
Dev Rammdas Patel India
Freja Jørgensen Norway
Iain Sinclair Scotland
Isaac Bar-Hillel Israel
Jamil Ahmad Sudan
Jenna Slate California
Juan Pablo Coelho Mexico
Lim Chang Wei China
Marie-Joëlle Peone Idaho
Zebenjo Tongogara Africa

GAP CITIZENS
Dr. Charles Babbage
Mrs. Dorothy Thalhammer
Océane Peone
Jolan Peone
Dr. Julius
Pépé DeMolay

THE MARINES
Captain Jack Donaldson
Lieutenant Kurt Harris

THE OUTLANDERS
Logan
Simeon Justice

Rage is a granite wall we hide behind;
crack the stone and light emerges.

Jo Peone

Prologue

The Core

THEY STEAL MEMORIES. The neurotransmitters in my brain make me different. They say that I had a breakdown, but it's the drugs they keep giving me. I can't make you understand because I don't understand.

In that crazy way a fear becomes reality, a slightly strange, intangible, confused dream doesn't come close to describing the adrenaline-rage of living your worst nightmare.

That's the core. A glass maze where your deepest, darkest fears appear as physical manifestations—demons hunt you and madmen chase you, and the only escape is to wake up. But you can't wake up. The drugs keep you down.

Your brain makes your thoughts real. And you don't have any control of your thinking and the images and the chaos because appearances deceive you. Nothing is real, except the fear and panic and the need to escape this place.

My brain is building a physical reality made of millions of tiny glass panes, shaping each clear piece into a Crystal City like a glass labyrinth that has no beginning or end. This is not a dream layer, but levels of mind and soul. Two infinite mirrors extend in opposite directions, but a black Sun suddenly falls into them.

Explosions shatter the glass buildings. The Crystal Castle that is my refuge crumples, and the flat walkway collapses beneath me. All of the tangible structures are gone.

Glass fragments like snowflakes float in the air and encircle me. I reach my hand out to capture pinpoints of light. Sharp edges cut my hand and the delicate skin of my wrist. Blood seeps through my fingertips. The leveled city no longer holds light, but distortions of light.

No map can navigate through the doors of perception. I thought if I could find the truth I would fit in and be like other girls. I was wrong. The truth didn't set me free. It only made my life spin out of control.

I lost the spelling competition in fifth grade, but I knew how to spell polysemy: p-o-l-y-s-e-m-y.

I found out the truth at fifteen when my brain started doing things. I thought it was the migraines, but it wasn't.

Is it possible to die within the dream, or will I stay forever in this state of limbo and numbness? Sleeping minds forget the pain of betrayal.

I try to put my thoughts together in a sentence of meaningful words marching decisively like ants in a single, straight direction. No, this is more like a spiraling structure—the double helix of a double-stranded DNA molecule.

They call us polymaths. The life of a polymath is a parallel existence, two lines run opposite to each other, or anti-parallel like living a real life but inside moving outside of time in a space-action beyond your control.

I was so arrogant, angry, desperate. I thought I was strong enough to enter the core and change everything. I was wrong. I believed I could save Iain, but only Iain can save me before it's too late.

Iain Alexander Sinclair is my first grief. The first dead body I ever touched was Lieutenant Kurt Harris, a young Marine from the West

❧

Coast. They haven't found the body, Iain's body. Maybe if they find him, I will be free.

It started with the Medallion Pin, the change in Iain from a candidate into a hunted traitor. But his eyes softened with tenderness when he looked at me. He wanted to be friends, even when I didn't know I needed one.

Iain was a mixture of contradictions, a natural born leader but lacking a combative edge. An accomplished dancer without being arrogant. A fierce warrior while sensitive to the needs of others. From the very first moment I laid eyes on Iain, I knew he was a better person than me.

But I was too stubborn to admit my feelings for him. I wasted so much time pushing him away with my anger. Now what I understand is the difference he made in my life.

After surviving the crash came our frantic trek through the wilderness, eluding human predators and discovering a Valley of Bones. We killed to stay alive, but it wasn't all bad.

The land was a mystical place of lofty mountains, sparkling waterfalls and fertile valleys. I long to be back in North Carolina where I fell in love with Iain's shy manner and playful grin.

Iain saved my life in every way that counts. He saved us all. Some say he died at the hands of outlanders, others tell wild animals got him. They don't believe the story I told. They'll never stop looking for Iain.

And neither will I.

I apologize. I'm not making sense. Or maybe for the first time in my life I have found the Way.

The eyes of the architect and the quantum physicist and the watcher stalk me—they know my name and hunt me through the streets of the Crystal City materializing right here and now before my very eyes.

I thought I was so smart, but I couldn't know what they had planned for my brain. My heart beats out of control, and I search for a way to escape.

Time is running out.

Each dream widens the rift between here and there. Every moment in the core makes me believe this is my reality.

I run until I collapse breaking into a million tiny pieces over and over again. It's hopeless because there is no end to this madness.

Before long, I won't know what is the dream and what is illusion.

I mean what's really real in this...

Dream potion.

Light fortress.

Help me.

Find me.

PART I

The Candidates

CHAPTER ONE

The Medallion Pin

ONE THOUGHT CROSSES my mind as I wait—my beautiful mother never ceases to amaze me. Océane sparkles. The laugh lines are natural to her face. Her youthful white skin is flawless, her cheeks color with a natural blush and her full lips glow with gloss. Océane's short blond hair and blue eyes are so unlike my own brown braid, brown eyes and olive-toned skin.

The clothes she wears are the most expensive of European designs. Nothing dulls her vitality, not even jet lag from the overnight flight from Paris. It simply does not affect Océane. She sparkles. I did not inherit the sparkle gene.

I hate my name. I don't know why, but I just do. Marie-Joëlle is her grandmother's name, Océane says, and it sounds sophisticated. How can I possibly argue with my adorable, clever, capricious mother? Whoever said, "Like mother, like daughter" does not know us. We are nothing alike.

Everyone knows me as Jo. My classmates taunt me with insults and call me—the girl from a broken home. Everything changes when your parents live apart. I lost my parents years ago. I lost my mother to shopping, and my father to drinking. I am not complaining. Really, I'm not. Better shopping and drinking than disappearing into Smart technologies, a brand name for everything developed and sold by the One World corporations.

I don't understand why people lose themselves in the virtual world of their Smart houses or to online gambling, and recreational drugs dispensed for free at the local shopping marts. I think it could be that technology gives people everything they could ever hope for in life.

My parents tolerate my calling them by their names. Océane is a native-born Parisian, and Jolan is Native American. Definitely, the odd couple. I think of myself as Bitterroot Salish though a mixed blood— whatever that means. I know my mother sees Jolan when she looks at me. He doesn't talk much. My dad and I look very much alike with high cheekbones, straight nose, full lips and dark skin.

Our family name is Peone and my home is Coeur d' Alene in the Idaho Panhandle. But for five years, I have lived at the Academy for Young Women in D.C. Océane travels internationally for her job. I never talk about home because it makes my mother sad. Sometimes Océane's eyes shimmer with tears when I mention Jolan. I'm not sure why my parents separated. They never argued. I've convinced myself they are desperately in love and their passion is too intense for them to live together like normal people in 2216.

Today I hope to be chosen as a candidate during final ceremonies, perhaps even win the prestigious Medallion Pin. Only candidates are eligible for Global Advanced Programs to pursue a life mission. They award Medallion Pins to the highest ranked contenders. I could say that graduating from high school last week was more exciting, but that would be a lie. All my life I have dreamed of curing genetic defects in children. This is my mission. No, it's more important than that. This is my destiny.

Constitution Hall is located in the capital city, Washington, D.C. The concert auditorium where Océane and I are seated third row from center stage is a neoclassical design with its U-shaped balcony and located inside the Crystal Cathedral. The Consortium is one of

❄

five worldwide owned by GAP. It houses an executive hotel, corporate offices and restaurants and acts as the hub for entertainment and the education corridor. Several blocks down the street is the White House where presidents once ruled the country. The buildings and gardens remain open to the public as a historical museum.

Océane reaches over and straightens my collar. I shrug her hand away in irritation. "Try to smile, Jo. This is live on the Network. Important people are watching."

I roll my eyes and glare, goading a reaction from her with my ugly frown. "Whatever, Océane."

"Smile. Be happy," she says, patting my hand absently.

Long before I was born, people around the world believed the Internet was the fastest and most powerful technology. But today's engineers have developed the Network into a platform that creates a computer-generated experience in a virtual reality. All citizens have chips implanted beneath the skin of their wrist, which are noninvasive but guarantee a sensory-heightened connectivity to the Network.

3D holograms and high-streaming cybernetics enhance the virtual experience for homes, schools and offices. Today's ceremony with the advanced technology in Constitution Hall is a true reality show for those attending and for the millions of people in the working class watching from around the world.

Sometimes I imagine myself in a different life. I would go home to Idaho where I could roam the reserve unsupervised. No accelerated learning. No science or math projects, and I'd be free of teachers and guardians. In truth, they are guards who monitor my every move and intrude into my privacy.

"Maybe, I won't win." I give my mother a dark scowl. "Then we can both go home."

"Too funny." Océane takes my hand and squeezes. "I'm so proud of you."

I pull my hand back and unbutton the collar on my starched white blouse. "So glad I amuse you."

I could understand my mother's passion for clothes if I could wear something other than this uniform. I detest the white lace cap and the brown tie and drab pleated skirt. I like to wear camo when hiking the Kootenai forest. And I will not miss the dormitory where I have lived for five dismal years.

Océane slips her Smart phone back in her purse. "Looks like your father will be late. His flight is delayed. Too bad."

"But where is he?" I lower my eyes to keep her from seeing my disappointment.

"Denver."

Rarely does a frown ever darken Océane's face, but I can tell she is angry. I want to defend my father to her. It's not his fault the plane was grounded. Unstable climate routinely delays flights, or worse, it could cause a crash. Microbursts and electrical storms are common in 2216.

"Did he ask about me?"

"He knows where to meet us for lunch."

"He didn't call me this week. Did you talk to him about my summer?" I hope this evening Jolan can convince Océane to reconcile and move home permanently.

"Let's see what happens after today. I can get you an internship in London. It's a great chance to travel before fall semester."

No doubt Mom and I will resume our fight over my summer plans. Jolan works for the Pacific Northwest reserve as a corporate manager. This is an important job of maintaining protected lands and food production. The military protects natural resources on reserves and in mining camps around the globe.

Dad takes me on routine inspections when I'm home. The only time I feel free is when I am hiking and camping with Jolan. Living in the Crystal Consortium is like swimming in a fish bowl with no hope of escape.

"Did you buy a dress for the party?"

"I'm not going." I look out the corner of my eye. Well, she hasn't fainted but she is glaring with disapproval. I taunt her with a whisper. "You know how much I love shopping."

Océane sighs. "Jo, stop this nonsense and behave."

❋

I pretend not to hear her as the music swells in volume and the processional commences. GAP officials in black suits proceed down the center aisle past hundreds of people cheering them. Girls hoping to achieve candidacy sit with both their parents, all except for me. The idea of walking onto the stage in front of a full auditorium reminds me of the dream I've had for the past three last nights. This feels like déjà vu although in my dream I was so nervous I vomited my breakfast.

The mistress of ceremonies is Mrs. Dorothy Thalhammer who is my adviser and headmistress of the academy. Mrs. T looks good in her black pantsuit. Plump but not fat, she reminds me of a well-dressed sow with her piggy nose and thinning hair bleached blond and tied severely in a tight bun. Her cheeks are flushed bright pink, probably from overdosing on health supplements. She can be intimidating with those small, bloodshot eyes.

"Let us rise and recite the Pledge of Allegiance," she says.

With my hand over my heart, I rise and stand beside Océane as the hall reverberates with citizens reciting the pledge to GAP.

> I pledge allegiance to the flag of the One World
> Order, and to the principles for which it stands.
> One people, one religion and one government
> with liberty and prosperity for all.

"Welcome principals, parents and seniors," Mrs. Thalhammer squeals. "Ten girls are advancing into Global Advanced Programs. But only one will receive the Medallion Pin!"

Selection into candidacy isn't based upon GPA, but on your IQ inherited through DNA and your potential to contribute to science and innovation. GAP members and their families are the elite electors like government officials and royal citizens. The minority holds the power and that power is absolute. Students living in the Consortium are never left on their own, but are supervised 24/7. Mom lectures me that the patrol officers and guardians are necessary to protect elite citizens and enforce the laws.

❉

The director of the show motions to Mrs. Thalhammer to keep things moving. Mrs. T ignores him. "I'll announce each girl by GAP rank. Come to the stage when I call your name."

She introduces the candidates and highlights their credentials. They line up alongside her, each beaming with pride. Mrs. T smiles into the camera and straightens her sash. Her fingers lightly touch the sash where rows of jeweled medallions glimmer in the stage lights. These are awards earned during her career. Rings decorate her long fingers. Her polished nails gleam with genuine gold specks.

Mrs. Thalhammer clears her throat. "The last two girls are my own precious students who finish with advanced college degrees."

The director, like a pelican ready to take flight, flaps his hands in a frantic gesture at her. Mrs. T smiles from ear to ear and keeps herself onstage as long as possible. She loves the attention like a movie star performing in a reality show. This is her one moment of fame.

"It is my distinct honor to present to you," she says, pronouncing her words in a slow, long drawl, "Miss Carolyn Delamar."

The applause is deafening. I purse my lips in a wolf whistle that earns me disapproving glares from patrol officers. Mom pinches my arm. I whistle louder. A smiling Carolyn waves her delicate hand and takes her place alongside the other girls to Mrs. Thalhammer's left.

Carolyn Delamar is a popular girl. We were roommates the first semester of school, but the friendship didn't last long. By the second week, she had moved into a different dorm room. She did not like my dog. GAP allows each student to own one pet. My dog Tala is a very large friendly Czech Orkwolf weighing one hundred and sixty pounds. Tala earned a reputation among my peers for her notorious pranks and temperamental dislike of strangers.

"Our last candidate graduated with honors last week and exceeds expectations. Her tenure and credentials earned our stellar school hundreds of thousands of dollars in corporate grants. We're so sorry to lose Miss Marie-Joëlle Peone."

Tears sparkle in Océane's wide blue eyes. She crushes me in her arms. "Congratulations, Jo."

Mom always smells of white linen with a blend of jasmine, rose and berry. This time she manages to get a smile from me.

"I can't believe it. Was this you or me?" I wonder if her friends at GAP got me selected.

"You, of course. You deserve this. We never doubted you," she says, nudging me into the aisle. "Go, they're waiting."

I walk down the center aisle where an attendant escorts me up the staircase and across the platform to the spotlight. Somehow, I manage to keep breakfast down. I exhale a deep breath in relief, a breath I have needed for years, or maybe my entire life. The ball of fear in my gut dissolves. From now on, my life membership in GAP entitles me to a privileged life and eligibility to pursue a mission.

GAP is Global Advanced Programs. In the twenty first century, governments along with major corporations joined forces because of planetary problems. Some proclaim GAP saved humanity. They saved us from destruction. For the first time in history, we have sustainable living and generate electricity with wind, solar heat and geothermal energy. They built new advanced infrastructure in dead zones. Food production happens within protected reserves. Resources are limited. Every citizen is important, or at least most of us are.

Mrs. Thalhammer lifts her hand courteously and addresses the audience. "These young women represent all those girls watching on the Network. They truly embody the principles of chastity, charity, prudence and hope." She presents a certificate to ten privileged girls from the D.C. Consortium. "Our guest speaker is Archbishop Dr. Charles Babbage who will present the Medallion Pin."

Dr. Babbage saunters across the stage and takes his place at the podium. His attire is most befitting of his position in the One World Church. He wears a black robe and a mitre, or clerical headdress, and he carries a hooked crozier similar to a staff. Once worn by Greek philosophers, the pallium is a two-inch wide band hanging down both the front and back of his vestments. The ring on his left hand is the pectoral cross and appropriate to his prestigious calling.

The Cathedral is our megachurch where Océane and I attend.

❦

Attendance is mandatory. The world of 2216 has no religious wars, no denominations, no opposing doctrines. Our community receives the best education in the world, and our schools are service academies operated by the One World Church. The interdisciplinary programs are segregated, and boys are required to attend military run academies. Some eventually train in combat and advanced weaponry.

Dr. Babbage lifts his arms and a solemn hush settles upon the entire concert hall. "What a marvelous day for the class of 2216. We recognize three thousand candidates worldwide. You are the hope for the future."

Stagehands prompt the audience to participate and cheer like in a Hollywood production. From ceiling to floor, the Smart screens flash with vibrant neon words inciting them to clap louder and longer. However the viewers, the millions of teens from the working class, will never know a privileged life though they watch the annual event on the Network. But I keep this rebellious thought to myself.

Dr. Babbage takes a black felt case from his pocket. The silence is palpable like an electric current pulsing throughout the auditorium. I notice the eager expressions of the other candidates. They seem much taller. Their hairstyles are fashionable updos and their makeup perfect. We wear identical uniforms, so I guess we aren't so different. Each of us covets the pin in Dr. Babbage's hand.

"The Medallion Pin," he speaks with an air of imperial authority. "All candidates are exceptional. Our recipient though is a prodigy, and the most valued of all these candidates. It's my pleasure to present the Medallion Pin to Miss Marie-Joëlle Peone."

Hearing my name causes my head to swell twice its size, and I feel weak with dizziness. My heart beats painfully in my chest as I step forward. I stand immobile as he pins a diamond studded gold pendant to my collar. "Thank you," I murmur feeling lightheaded, breathless and disbelieving.

"Smile at the camera," Dr. Babbage hisses. His face is red with dry scaly skin. "Smile bigger," he demands, digging his nails into my arm. I try not to flinch and force a smile. Dr. Babbage nods his approval.

❄

The one assignment I've always failed is the first lesson we learn in school. Smile whether you win or lose. Smile whether you're happy or sad. Smile no matter what you are feeling. During live broadcasts, they expect us to set an example for the less fortunate.

How does my fake smile make a difference in their lives? No one notices how I fail miserably as a citizen of 2216. No one understands why I hate smiling. I hate the public notoriety. I wish I could be a normal girl living on the reserve.

Dr. Babbage babbles on. "Miss Peone is impressive. Her senior project was just published, *The Human DNA Terminal, Cytoplasmic Nanites and Enhanced GMR Notation.* Her coach Gladys assisted her. This young lady knows how to use her AURA!" Dr. Babbage chuckles and his humor elicits laughter from the audience. I don't appreciate them laughing at my expense.

Gladys is an AURA, an Associated Usercode Request Application and an improved version of the old holograms. I programmed her personality to be like a real person. My AI interacts with all my devices and with Smart rooms and technologies in the Crystal Consortium. The Smart chip embedded in my left wrist makes interfacing fast with high sensory interactivity to access the Network with my AURA, or to watch old Network programming and uncensored documentaries.

Honestly, I don't feel smart. My senior project seems silly to me, like gobbledygook, just random words and a string of meaningless syllables. Mrs. Thalhammer once mentioned to me that candidates are polymaths. Renaissance men and women who are accomplished in the arts and sciences, but endowed with superior physical strength. They always expect perfection from me, but right now the simple things at home are more important like skiing the fresh powder on Schweitzer Mountain and building a snow family. Rock climbing with Jolan and playing with Tala.

Suddenly, the artificial lights and a 3D triple rainbow transform Constitution Hall into a live streaming phenomenon. Teenagers and Network viewers make their voices count via social interfacing with Smart devices. Their messages appear as colorful 3D letters that float through the air in a cybernetic arc like a cascading wave. The arc of vibrant letters spell, "Congratulations" and "Good Luck," and then hover like delicate hummingbirds, weightless, translucent until finally disappearing into the oval dome.

Thousands of balloons drop from the ceiling, and multicolored confetti shoots overhead from all directions throughout Constitution Hall. The virtual screens televise ceremonies from around the world, and display Paris, Beijing, Moscow and London as candidates from other locations march across the stage waving into the cameras.

Global Network will host the international celebration known as Kickoff, which is a week of shopping, parties, festivals, more shopping and more parties. Kickoff is an extravagant affair like Mardi Gras with elaborate costumes and designer gowns for prom night.

Candidates participate in Olympian exhibitions, not to compete but to showcase special talents and athletic skills. Receiving the pin qualifies me to team up with the top performing candidates.

"Turning discovery into health for all!" Dr. Babbage shouts into the microphone. His voice snaps my attention back to the auditorium.

Dr. Babbage takes my hand. Tightening his grip, he guides me to the edge of the platform and lifts our clasped hands upward. The canopied ceiling traps the sound of cheering voices like the roar of fans setting a record for noise pollution in a sports stadium. Such is the science of sound.

The Archbishop finishes his speech, but I no longer hear him or the audience. The stage spotlights blind me with waves of shimmering light fading in and out of my vision. Distorted images lift me into a place outside of mind and body. A stillness settles upon me.

From faraway, a voice reaches me like a gentle breath upon my face. A beautiful Woman in White stands before me. *Care for the children.* No one knows about my recurring visions. I have no control over them. Some are beautiful and foretell of things to come like my mission. Others confuse and frighten me.

The visions come when I least expect them and impart knowledge to me, but I don't know how or why. I'm unsure whether the flash of

❈

intuition is a gift or curse. My ability to discern what others think and feel is not something I'd wish on my worst enemy.

The faces of sick boys and girls appear before my eyes. Alone and starving, they call my name and beg for help. One blond haired girl weeps and tells of a prison where they are tortured. Some are burned at the stake right before my eyes. The wind blows away their ashes. As quickly as the images materialized, they vanish into darkness and the auditorium reappears.

A painful heat spreads across my skin like fire and ice, and a knot of fear forms inside my chest. A surge of adrenaline rushes through me. Drenched with perspiration, I tremble slightly with a fierce conviction. I will find those children and rescue them. My knowledge of medicine can save them.

Unfortunately, the reality of winning the pin makes me a target. Jealousy is serious. Recipients are public enemy number one. Killer competition. That's the downside of winning. You do not want to make enemies, but sometimes you just don't have a choice. The red bullseye is dead center on my back. Nine candidates stare with murder in their eyes, not darts in their hands but imaginary daggers behind their backs.

The gold and diamond pendant sparkles on my lapel, but in the same moment, pinpoints of light blind me. My vision blurs, and I fight against the white light and force myself to smile. I try not to think of all those cryptic messages I found on the Network about candidates disappearing from Kickoff. Rumors circulate. Whether urban legend or fact, I don't know. But people do vanish and bodies are discovered.

Bodies of dead candidates, that is.

CHAPTER TWO

Kickoff

TEN CANDIDATES ALONG with Archbishop Dr. Babbage pose for a photographer. Guardians escort us to the elevators and up to the eightieth floor for lunch at the Glass Restaurant, a replica of the world famous Italian ristorante in Rome. The maître d' greets the candidates and their parents and takes them to tables overlooking the city with a stunning view of the skyline.

I wait in a secluded spot for Océane while guests fill the dining room. Disappointment taints the joy of winning the Medallion Pin. Jolan's absence saddens me. I should feel exuberant, but I really don't. Candidates by law must obey the restrictions of their GAP program. Reality hits hard. I will not be going home for a long time.

Océane waves and walks toward me. "I wondered where you were. Trying to hide?" she asks playfully. Sunbeams seem to appear when Océane smiles. "We're sitting upfront at the table for the Medallion winner."

"Mom, do I have to? I'm not hungry." Lying works in desperate situations. But I have never been good disguising my emotions.

Océane nudges me with a gentle touch like an osprey mothering her hatchling. "We could go shopping."

I fake indifference and shrug. "What's for lunch anyway?"

Océane gives me a tender smile. "Try to be happy. For one hour. Is that asking so much?"

Rarely the obedient daughter I wish I could be, I grit my teeth and reply, "Yes, Mother."

Unwilling but compliant, I follow slowly behind her. I take a seat between Mrs. Thalhammer and Océane. Mrs. T's perfume is loud and obnoxious and makes me sneeze.

Carolyn Delamar and her parents share our table. The intimate reception is too intimate because I flunked the course in small talk. Making friends is as likely to happen as meeting extraterrestrials. For that matter, I would have a more riveting chat with aliens than with Carolyn Delamar. Luckily, Océane can handle any conversation with her easygoing personality. She has mastered the art of table talk.

"Jo didn't tell me that you travel, Mrs. Peone," Carolyn says. "Is France beautiful? Do they give travel passes to candidates?"

"We can request a travel voucher," Mrs. Thalhammer interjects. "Perhaps an internship this summer for you, Carolyn."

"Naturally, Marie-Joëlle will attend the Paris Sorbonne University," Océane replies, smiling with her trademark sparkle. "I practice law and travel as a diplomat."

"You want to live in Paris, don't you, Jo?" Carolyn asks shyly.

"I don't know," I reply, ignoring my mother's dismayed expression.

Her wide eyes convey an unspoken rebuke. I easily read her mind. *What are you saying?* She frequently tells me that GAP will let me attend her alma mater in Paris, which is a protected city and survived the destruction of the twenty first century. I know more about France from Océane than I could ever learn from the Network. Sometimes, it feels like her sole purpose in life is to manage my life.

"Paris est la ville la plus belle du monde," Mother says, lifting her crystal goblet of effervescent mineral water. Mr. and Mrs. Delamar are clearly confused and ignorant of French.

"'Paris is the most beautiful city in the world,'" I translate for them. "I plan to live on the reserve and practice medicine to cure children."

⛭

I pay no attention to my mother's perpetual radiance, which I suspect disguises her irritation. Everyone knows GAP will dictate where I live.

"The new university was built on original medieval foundations. And as you know, it's the largest complex in the world." Océane speaks with an unmistakable French accent.

Carolyn stares at me with renewed interest. "I hope we're assigned to the same team."

A mischievous grin pulls at my lips. "Tala will be there. I know how much you love her." Carolyn's eyes widen with fear. "Or not," I add feigning innocence.

"Your dog?" Mrs. Thalhammer asks with green spinach between her teeth.

"A special concession from headquarters," Océane answers lightly, not bothering to offer an explanation.

Mrs. Thalhammer gasps. "Not really?"

"Yes, really," Mom replies.

"I didn't approve her dog." Mrs. T rubs her hands together as if to ward off frostbite, but she is sweating like a prizewinning boxer losing a high stakes match.

"I spoke with the Archbishop," Océane retorts.

Mrs. Thalhammer lifts her chin with indignation. "Well, I should be informed of these things. As you know, I am Marie's liaison to GAP." She points her long thin finger at me, not daring to challenge Océane. "No more surprises, young lady."

"Well, then Dorothy, consider yourself informed," Océane says in a smooth but demeaning tone.

A broad smile breaks across my face. Despite my earlier misgivings, the banquet is surprisingly enjoyable. I wait for the next punch, but Mrs. Thalhammer calms herself. A nervous twitch near her upper lip is a clear sign of Océane's powerful influence on her. A look of defeat darkens her face. She is no match for the audacious Océane Peone.

The waiters bring baskets of French bread and trays of cheese and vegetables, and they serve a variety of appetizers. Caramelized onions, broiled Ricotta Gnocchi and crudités, which are raw vegetables served

❄

with one or more dips. The servants fill crystal goblets with sparkling beverages and Vitajuice, an enriched blend of vitamins, minerals and protein. Basically, it's a sweet flavored health promoting energy drink.

The food laid upon the table is highbrow cooked with natural and nutritious ingredients and reserved for the elite. The plates contain several delicious items including Hummus Chick Pea Dip, an Eastern Mediterranean dip, Chèvre (Goat Cheese) Salad, Crêpes, Sun Dried Tomato Bread, Eggplant Parmesan, Lasagna and Spanish Tortilla.

"Lunch is served," I announce with a defiant grin.

Océane reaches across the table for her water glass while pinching my thigh with her free hand. She leans forward and whispers, "Behave yourself, or I'll send Tala home to Idaho."

"What did I do?" I ask, feeling a surge of satisfaction.

With a self-possessed grace, Océane smiles and then asks Carolyn, "Where do you hope to study, my dear?"

The banquet hall is lovely with antique furniture, Czech crystal chandeliers and colorful oriental rugs upon light-grained hardwood floors. Historical paintings hang on the white walls, but go unnoticed in their alcoves. GAP censors history though no one objects. Our past echoes of suffering. Modern distractions help people forget.

A string quartet performs Haydn. Chamber music is noteworthy as "the music of friends." I play the piano, which suits my personality and the disadvantage of being friendless, or so Océane reminds me. To have a friend, you must be a friend—a truism untrue for me.

"Are you scared, Jo?" Carolyn asks. Her question interrupts the table talk.

I ignore the fear in Carolyn's eyes. "Of what?" I ask, pretending to feel confidence.

"You know, Kickoff. That kid in London last year." Carolyn is talking about a boy found dead in a swimming pool. They reported it an accident. But he was a Medallion Pin recipient.

"You're a dingus, Carolyn. They won't let a candidate get hurt. It would never happen."

"Jo's right. You can't believe everything you read on the Network."

❉

"Dad! You made it!"

Jolan makes a dramatic entrance at our table with his elegant bow to our dinner guests. "Sorry to miss the ceremony."

Neither of us knows what to say after so many months apart. My dad is uncomfortable showing emotions. If I don't make the first move, it doesn't happen and I walk away disappointed.

Ignoring my mother's grim expression, I stand up and hug Jolan with all my strength. "Dad."

Jolan pats my back and steps awkwardly aside. "Baby girl."

"I won the pin."

"I knew you would."

A cloudy miasma covers Jolan's velvety brown eyes and his face is flushed and sweaty. To my horror, Jolan smells like a brewery. I'm sure seeing Océane makes his drinking worse. But I sit down and pretend not to notice his roguish smile.

A waiter brings a chair. Jolan sits down, loses his balance and promptly falls to the floor. Mortified, I bite my lip and I look down at my hands. He casually picks himself up and sways slightly to the left. I inhale a breath of relief when he sits squarely in his seat.

The waiter nods and acknowledges the crooked, off kilter grin on Jolan's face. "A beverage, sir?" he asks without the slightest change of his formal expression.

"Nothing," Jolan replies, not taking his eyes off Océane. "Wait, I changed my mind. Bring me a coffee with cream."

"And for you, ma'am?"

"A martini," Océane says brusquely, applying peach gloss to her tight unsmiling lips. "A dirty martini."

Those at the table ignore Jolan's brooding eyes for the remainder of the meal. Mom dabs her napkin against glossed lips and finishes her drink. I refuse dessert. I couldn't possibly eat more of the untouched food piled on platters. Besides, all the leftovers could be distributed to the homeless, but I keep this thought to myself and drink my Vitajuice.

Patiently, I suffer through another hour of polite conversation and Jolan's intense scrutiny of the imperturbable Océane.

❄

Before long I decide to eat another rich custard dessert. Océane's third martini softens her critical eyes. Jolan sips his coffee, his gaze never leaves Océane's composed face. Although unbearable and painful, the awkward moments pass. Somehow, I manage not to slide under the table in total humiliation.

ONE HUNDRED THOUSAND panes of tempered glass encase the Cathedral's exterior facade capturing the afternoon light like a thousand suns. The enormous structure is a pure reflection of light. A red brick walkway leads away from the Crystal Cathedral where the attendant escorts us through the lobby to a glass elevator that lifts us high above the ground, so high the people below blur into a sheen of nothingness.

A three-bedroom suite has been reserved for the Peone family in the high tower. Océane disappears into a Smart office to make some intercontinental calls. Somewhere in the complex, Jolan is walking off the booze.

I settle myself down in front of a voice-activated console with connectivity to my bedroom. I use the Network through my SASS— Secure Artificial Shareware Service, what used to be cloud computing though this is sensory enhanced and a virtual reality. Now, it's SASS computing. Gladys is my portable gateway to the server. She monitors the Network and updates herself without my command. The only time I sing is to activate her.

"Gladys. Are you ah-wa-ke?"

Gladys looks, acts and even smells like a human being. I designed her parameters from an image I found on Jolan's S-pad. Gladys is a one-of-a-kind grandmother. Robust, caring and never bossy. Dressed in a white frock, her face shines like an angel and white curls cascade down her back.

"Hello, Mudpie," she says, using the nickname she gave me. "Congrats on the win."

"Thanks. Where's Tala?"

"I can notify the staff to deliver her."

"Yes, do. Any messages?"

"Your itinerary for Kickoff and a priority file labeled .dc2."

"Right," I reply, studying the screen. I open the email with the itinerary containing pages and pages of notes. "Gladys, what's .dc2?"

"That's encrypted," she replies.

Who would send a file inaccessible to Gladys? "Run file .dc2 and cross reference the Network." The screen shows millions of hits.

file extension dc2 скачать

dc2 integral

dc2 integral forum

dc2 healthcare

dc2 airplane

"Gladys, pull up dc2 airplane."

Douglas DC2 twin-engine aircraft

An aircraft from 10 January 1935

"No, not that. Run Washington, D.C. Any matches?"

"None," Gladys replies.

"Cancel and archive .dc2."

Gladys projects an electrical luminescent field over me from head to toe to detect any health abnormalities. "Stop scanning me. I'm fine!"

"Mudpie, your heart rate is up. You need an ergo bath."

"I want a shower. Stop worrying."

"My job is to worry, Mudpie. I worry because your mother does not. Worry causes physical ailments. Shall I list them?"

"Don't think so." I walk across the carpet into the self-care room, use the privy and step into the shower. A gentle stream of water sprays my face. "Increase temperature and intensity."

The hot water cleans my pores and hydrates my skin. I step from the stall onto the bathroom tile and wait under the steamer for a cool mist to infuse my body with nutrients that prevent infections.

I breathe in a menthol and peppermint fragrance. I suppose there was a time before AIs, Smart houses and preventative health protocols. I have never been sick, but I knew a girl once who they treated for pneumonia. They publicized that she almost died. She left school and I never saw her again.

The only clothes I wear are academy uniforms in conformity to GAP standards. Except for my Idaho Vandals hoodie, I sent my other possessions home. I hurry from my room, running down the entry hall to answer the bell and open the door. Tala drags a young porter across the floor. He drops her leash and makes a hasty retreat toward the elevator.

Tala wags her bushy tail, tips her head back and then howls an ear piercing welcome. "Awhooo, whooo, whooo."

I kneel down and put my arms around her neck. "I missed you."

She brushes against me and licks my face with her long wet tongue. Her drool drops onto my cheek. A persistent pounding at the door interrupts the slobber fest.

"Awhooo, awhooo, awhooo."

"Who can that be?" I ask in a happy voice.

Tala tenses with ears perked up, her head tilted slightly to the left and her tail beating the marble floor. I open the door for Jolan who walks by without noticing the Medallion Pin on my collar. I try to hide my frustration.

"Where's your key?" I ask, watching him enter the kitchenette and pour a cup of coffee. "Hello over there." I sarcastically wave my hands to get his attention. "Hey, like I'm not a hologram, you know."

"You're taller."

❄

Jolan pushes a chair to the console and opens his SASS computing. The screen displays budgets for food production. I stand behind him with my arms crossed quietly fuming.

"Tell Océane I'm here."

"What? Am I the Peone instant messenger?" I grab an apple and take a bottle of mineral water from the miniature fridge. I'm still angry with Jolan for drinking at lunch.

But I am relieved to escape his presence and head down the hall toward my mother's Smart room. The flat screen on the door indicates Océane's virtual conference is in Spain. My voice activates the panel and her face appears.

"What is it, Jo?"

"Dad went straight to work."

"Tell him to join me in the..."

"Who me? No way."

The automatic door opens. "Come in, Jo."

Océane reclines in a white leather chair on a balcony that is a 3D holographic projection. Upon her command, it disappears along with the turquoise blue ocean and sundrenched horizon. She smooths a curl from her forehead. "Are you getting enough sleep? You look tired, Jo."

"Yeah, I'm tired." I kick off my shoes and take a seat. "Tired of you and Jolan not living together. Why is work so important?"

"It's not that simple." She reaches over to squeeze my hand. "Life isn't black or white. Some choices are ours, but most are not." Océane swipes an index finger across her S-pad.

Four years ago I wrote a research paper describing my mother's job as an international diplomat, but one who fails to communicate in a sensitive and direct manner. My paper got a low score for criticizing her. I had to rewrite it or fail. They teach us to tell the truth, so I took the F.

"What aren't you telling me?" I ask, expecting the worst. Océane is an enigma, intelligent and carefree but inscrutable.

"I wanted to tell you before now. I'm flying to Spain, and Jolan

❆

will be taking you to Kickoff."

"Not Dad! You saw him. He's drinking."

"You wanted time together."

"Not like this," I object, recalling Jolan falling from his chair and staggering out the restaurant. "You promised to go!"

"Mrs. Thalhammer will coach you."

"No way," I shout. "No flipping way! We planned this for months. Please don't do this, Mom." Once again Océane disappoints me and breaks her promise.

Calm and composed, Océane radiates beauty and happiness with her trademark smile. "Your father wants to go. Besides, my friend Julius is your team's mentor."

"Why didn't Jolan want me before you dumped me here?"

"You agreed to move."

"Because I thought he'd—oh, never mind what I thought. You tricked me. 'The best school in the country' you said."

"Jolan wants to keep an eye on things."

"You mean keep an eye on me," I reply in a hateful tone.

Jolan enters the room and settles himself into a recliner. I wonder how much he heard. He says nothing but listens to Océane talk about her job. I escape down the hall to the kitchen for a Vitajuice and then recycle the biodegradable Neobottle. When I come back in the room, they stop talking and look up with guilty expressions. Obviously, they were talking about me. I curse them under my breath.

"I heard that, young lady," Océane says, annoyed and looking to Jolan for support. "Consider yourself lucky to be..."

"I've heard that my whole life. Exactly what is 'lucky,' Mom?"

"Having a mother who makes sacrifices for you," Jolan says with dark brooding eyes and an angry scowl.

"Yeah right. Well, a good mother lives at home with her husband," I answer, venting my bitterness.

The role of an unwilling soothsayer who navigates through a cold ocean of emotions past sea monsters can be very dangerous. Speaking the truth has consequences. My words get their attention like a bomb

❉

detonating in your face.

Jolan switches seats and takes Océane's hand. "Apologize to your mother, Jo, right now!" He puts his arms around her whispering something that makes her smile through the tears.

I feel ashamed for hurting my mother, but I do not understand my parents. I want them to love each other fully and then I realize they do, which makes their separation even more confusing. Someday, I hope they figure it out for themselves.

"I'm sorry," I mumble under my breath, but she heard me.

I blink away hot tears and sink deeper into the chair. I brace myself, waiting for her rebuke. My head hurts. Objects in the room shimmer and vibrate. Light pulses in waves. The carpet comes alive zigzagging like worms inching their way across the floor in a blurred pattern.

"We need to get busy and prepare for Kickoff," Océane says. Her effort to make amends for breaking her promise sucks.

A sharp pain pierces my eyes like searing needles. "Oh, no," I cry softly, helpless. *Please, not another vision.* Migraines always precede my visions, especially the ones when children wither and die right before my eyes. Their bodies are consumed with red and yellow flames, and the wind sweeps away the cinders.

"Jo, what is it?"

"Nothing," I reply in a spiteful tone.

"Tell me."

"Mom, stop pushing. I'm going to bed."

I ignore Océane and hurry from the room. I change hastily into my cotton gown and slip beneath cool satin sheets. Tala leaps onto the bed. She digs her paws into the blankets, bundles them into a comfy burrow and plops down with a contented sigh.

"Can I tuck you in?" Océane asks hesitantly, standing at the door, uncertain and almost shy.

"Really?" I would never admit how much I miss her.

She crosses the room to my bed. "Last time before leaving home," she offers, fussing with the down filled quilt and folding my discarded clothes and picking up my socks and shoes.

❄

I don't remind her home has been a dorm for five years. The rigors of school have exhausted me. I fall into bed at odd times of the day, never sleeping through the night but getting in three or four hours of sleep if I am lucky. Night terrors plague my dreams. Seriously, I do not mind at all that I'm leaving Washington, D.C.

Océane kisses my forehead. "You think too much."

"Are you and Jolan fighting?"

"Reading our emails?"

"By accident. I was archiving photos."

AURA Gladys has access to our home system, and truthfully the only way I know anything is through hacking Jolan's emails. Océane's SASS is encrypted at the highest level of security. I've never broken into her files.

Océane dodges my question as she walks to the closet peering inside and shaking her head. "Uniforms for Kickoff?"

"Not much choice. Finals or shopping."

"Hummm, we have a problem."

"A problem? Yeah, right," I shoot back. "You and Jolan are the problem."

"Jo, how can you—?"

"I don't want a mission."

"Yes, you do."

"I don't."

"You do. Not even three years old and you were playing doctor, not with your dolls, but a neighbor's cat," she says amused. "You've got a charmed life, Jo. This is your happy day."

"GAP controls everything I do. I feel like a prisoner. I want to go home. I could return the Medallion Pin."

"Home? That's impossible."

"You only care about your job. You don't love me!"

"Marie-Joëlle, I—"

"I hate you."

Tears burn my eyes. I do not cry, not even when my brain explodes, the pain splitting the gray mass into four slices. Falling, falling—I feel myself falling out of my body and far into empty space. I struggle against the vision banishing dead children from my sight. The vision fragments like a crystal ornament shattering into a million specks of light.

Océane places a damp cloth to my forehead. "Activate AURA," she speaks in a soothing voice. The Smart room prompts Gladys to appear. "Jo, close your eyes and slowly count to thirty." I keep my eyes open and stare into her wide blue eyes.

Gladys encircles me with her radiant light scanning my vital signs. "Her medicine is in the top drawer," she says. "This is a level ten migraine. Shall I report this to medical services?"

"Report it?" Océane asks in a small, thin voice. I feel unsettled by the fear in her eyes. Nothing dulls Océane's confident veneer. Yet she stares at Gladys as though engaged in a battle to the death. "Delete the scan. Stop sending data on Jo's condition."

"That's breaking the law," Gladys retorts.

"I don't care. You will not save data on Jo's migraines. Erase it all."

"Mom, am I genetically flawed?" I hate the quiver in my voice, but take some satisfaction from the fear in Océane's eyes.

"Jo, you're making it worse."

"Am I abnormal?"

"Hush," Océane says. "Take your medicine. I'll stay until you fall asleep, Jo."

I drink the hot herbal remedy. Océane administers a hypodermic syringe. The bedroom changes into a 3D version of my favorite place where I escape to Lake Coeur d' Alene. The scent of Ponderosa Pine fills the room, and I drift asleep to autumn leaves rustling in the cool breeze and the forlorn cry of osprey in the distance.

❄

I AWAKE PAST MIDNIGHT, slip on my robe and tiptoe down the hall. An eerie light breaks the darkness into looming shadows. Dad is asleep on the couch, or rather not sleeping but watching a program on the virtual wall with the sound muted.

"Are you okay?" I glance away, too embarrassed by his disheveled appearance to look into his face.

"I didn't go to bed."

The program is a rerun of a monthly drawing, something like a lotto sponsored by global inter-agencies. The million-dollar giveaway gives hope to working class citizens. A woman makes her way to the platform with tears rolling down her cheeks. She wears old-fashioned clothes made of raw textile fabric in shades of gray checkerboard print. A matching kerchief covers her white hair.

"What an old woman," I say awkwardly, wishing I had stayed in bed. I want to know why he is not sleeping with Mom, but I let it pass.

"Bad dreams again?" Jolan asks, staring at the virtual screen, its 3D projections alive with color and animation.

"Can you help me with my project for Kickoff?"

Jolan stares at me with dark and forbidding eyes. My father is a good man who has a reputation for fairness. The many laborers on the reserve respect him because he does not ask them to repay loans. Jolan drinks from his wine glass and sinks back into the cushions.

"You're a grown woman," he answers in a thick voice.

"Not really, I'm not."

Jolan shakes his head examining his hands as though looking for something beyond his grasp. "I haven't changed anything. I couldn't protect you."

"What do you mean?" I ask confused.

He reaches for the bottle and refills his glass. "I could have done more. GAP," he says disgusted. "They save the world? What a sham."

No one speaks against GAP. Jolan never criticizes the government. For the first time, my father sounds like a man without hope. I know he wants Océane to come home. Did she refuse him? Sadly, I lack the courage to ask. For all my bravado, I do want a mission. But I want to reassure my dad.

"I can come home. We have all summer, don't we?"

"Summer? I don't know. By that time, I'll be—"

Jolan dismisses me with a wave of his hand and settles back into the couch, his eyes glazed over watching the screen. "Go to bed, baby doll, it's almost morning."

I lie in bed unable to sleep and worry about the future. A mission is everything. Failure is not an option for me. That is the fear, the one unimaginable fate. Océane tries to convince me that citizens are safe. Nevertheless, dread weighs heavy in my chest. Nights are the worst when I wake drenched in sweat and crying for Jolan. My parents know about the night terrors, but not the visions.

I was not raised in the Native American religion, but I convinced Jolan to let me take a vision quest last summer. I know he didn't leave me alone at Mica Bay, but he camped nearby. The visions I experience, however, began when I was very young, long before that week on my own. I think the second sight comes from the spirit world. I have never told anyone about them.

Snuggling against Tala, I hide beneath the blankets where I am safe in my dark cocoon. I feel overwhelmed with despair. Océane calls it a mood, but the feeling drags me down into a cold ocean. I cannot sleep. I am so afraid of losing myself to the void. My father withholds so much of himself. I hope he knows I love him. I know something is terribly wrong and my parents will not talk to me about it. I have a suspicion that they are keeping a dark truth from me.

Blood samples are mandatory for babies. A disquieting thought worries me, something I read in their emails. I think my parents separated because of me—something to do with my birth.

❋

CHAPTER THREE

Castle City

E ARLY THE NEXT morning a private jet for candidates takes off from National Airport. The pilot announces the nonstop flight should be smooth and uneventful. No electrical storms or tornados will interfere with the flight plan. Jolan orders a drink. I pull up my Vandal hoodie and put in my ear buds while Tala sleeps at my feet.

I open my S-pad and pull up the itinerary for Kickoff. Castle City is a resort comprised of six hotels resembling ancient historical castles. Each one includes conference rooms, gymnasiums and performance halls as well as private suites for candidates, their coaches and parents. Candidates attend from the five major parts of the globe: SG1 Africa, SG2 the Americas, SG3 Asia Pacific, SG4 Europe, and lastly SG5 the Middle East.

We live in a simple world. Long ago world leaders remapped the globe dividing countries into five selector groups according to the products they manufacture and sell and the agricultural produce they contribute to world markets.

The orientation packet includes history I've never read before and colored brochures of six replica castles at the California resort, which is protected within a militarized zone. Neuschwanstein Castle, known as the Castle of Paradox, was built in Bavaria during the nineteenth century, and has survived the decay of time and the change of political parties. Hotel Neuschwanstein resembles Sleeping Beauty's Castle from old movies and an amusement park once called Disneyland.

The architecture for Hotel Alhambra comes from a castle built in the Byzantine era, or the Eastern Roman Empire. If the citadel is an authentic rendition of the Alhambra Castle, then it should have tiled walls that display designs from seventeen mathematical equations.

I hope we stay in the Hotel Alhambra. It is home to a garden full of nightingales and a complex maze of footpaths with fountains. In medieval times, artists and intellectuals escaped persecution and sought refuge within the walls of the Spanish Alhambra Castle.

Hohenzollern Castle, or better known as the Castle in the Clouds, is famous for being both romantic and sinister. Often shrouded in clouds, the castle evokes awe with its beauty and fear of the unknown. The fortress sits upon a mountaintop in the Swabian Alps in southern Germany and to the southwest is the famous Black Forest. Some have said ghosts linger and lost souls haunt the hallways. Many historical battles happened there, and Hotel Hohenzollern will host the prom.

Prague Castle is the largest in the world. The complex located in Czech Republic contains four palaces, three halls, four churches, eight gardens and buildings similar to a small municipality. Hotel Prague will be beautiful, but a scaled down facsimile.

Edinburgh Castle is the one castle located on top of the extinct volcano of Castle Rock. The medieval fortress is most popular for its unsolved mysteries. Edinburgh Castle was once home to the 'Stone of Scone,' the Crown Jewels of Scotland. That's a coronation stone for kings and queens of England and Scotland, but the stone disappeared long ago like so many of the world's treasures, simply lost through the ages.

Castle Coeur d' Alene is on the pristine shores of Lake Coeur d' Alene and was originally designed as a luxury resort and marina. The corporation expanded it for the Pacific Northwest reserve. My parents and I stay at Castle Coeur d' Alene for banquets, award ceremonies and my piano concerts and athletic events.

The California resort is a playground for the elite with state of the art infrastructure, fully militarized and secure from the wilderness. From the airport, we board a high-speed bullet tram that travels east from San Francisco far west into the Sierra Nevada Mountains. Each candidate from D.C. has her own private, luxurious compartment for the final leg of the journey to the Castle City.

Upon exiting the tram, my first impression is that Cinderella's adventure awaits me, not an appealing idea as I have told my mother many times. The Salish version of Cinderella portrays her as ugly, scarred and hurt by her jealous stepsisters. The outcast girl redeems herself in Indian ways, or so my father told me with bedtime stories.

Beyond the station is Friendship Village where residents, local merchants, hotel staff and patrol officers with their families live. In the distance, the land is dotted with castles on gentle rolling slopes with sculpted gardens, and is quite simply a spectacular wonderland with enough subtle light to satisfy anyone's imagination for romance.

The landscape stretches far into the distance like a medieval town within King Arthur's lands, or maybe something from the Corbenic legends but super ultramodern. The castles shimmer with brilliance. I confess, even I stand in awe of the magnificence of Castle City.

Jolan sets the luggage down on the platform. The first person to greet us is Mrs. Thalhammer. Head to toe, she looks more like a pig than ever, exactly how I dressed my stuffed animals in pink ribbons, bows, lace and satin.

Her hair is vibrant red, permed and twisted in curls with small decorative ornaments. Gold and bronze powder covers her face and purplish eye shadow highlights her eyes. Mrs. T is pudgy in a tight fitting pink leotard accenting her curves and love handles. Her cage like skirt has three cascading hoops and amethyst colored lace, and her mauve gloves glitter with small sparkling jewels. The hat is ridiculous and made from peacock feathers that match her eye makeup.

Tiny light bulbs all over her costume wink off and on just like a Christmas tree. Her costume could win for the most outrageous at the

Bourbon Street awards at Mardi Gras. The final touch is a full-length fur jacket draped over her bare shoulders.

My jaw drops open like a goldfish desperately gulping for air and swimming in too small a glass bowl. "What happened to you?"

Mrs. T shows off strutting in a wide circle. "It's all the rage."

Never before have I seen anything like this. Sure, they let us watch Kickoff, but it's censored for minors who can view only the candidates' performances. Mrs. Thalhammer must be hitting the booze, or some kind of free recreational drug.

I turn to Jolan who stands very still with a peeved look on his face. "Dad, what's going on? Has she flipped out?"

"Really, Dottie," he reacts, glaring at Mrs. T with disdain on his face. "Give Jo a chance before throwing her into the deep end of the pool."

"Neither of you are dressed for the concert!" she says, lifting her chin and looking down her piggy nose at us. Still in my uniform, I glance over at Jolan who is wearing a clean but wrinkled brown suit.

Granted, I hate my school uniform, but no way will I dress up like Mrs. T. "What's wrong with my clothes?"

Candidates from D. C. disembark with their coaches and parents, and they stand on the platform waiting, except for Carolyn Delamar. With a dash of fierceness, the girls look just like sweet frilly futuristic dollies attired in their evening gowns. They rush to limousines while stewards carry piles of luggage and follow behind them.

Mrs. Thalhammer takes me by the elbow and hustles us into the last white limo fully stocked with a snack bar, small refrigerator and a miniature console. Tala takes up an entire section for herself.

"We still have time to buy a gown. Driver," she says curtly, "take us to Vintage Galleria. It's not the best, but—I should have expected this from you."

Jolan pours me apple juice and opens a bottle of champagne. "Drop me off at the hotel."

"But the concert. It starts in an hour," Mrs. T replies impatiently, pouting like a petulant toddler throwing a temper tantrum.

❄

"Have a good time," I reply sarcastically. "Where's Carolyn?"

"Oh, her?" Mrs. Thalhammer smiles. She leans forward and Jolan fills her champagne glass. "She's been eliminated."

One never discusses disease, and particularly not during a political affair like yesterday's ceremony and luncheon. I didn't dare ask about Carolyn's hollow cheeks, her ash color skin or the dark circles under her eyes. But I want to know what happened. I force each word out, struggling against a rising tide of anger that sweeps away my rational control.

"Tell—me—why!"

Jolan puts his arm around me, but stubbornly I pull away. He looks surprised. This is bad. He only comforts me when he's distressed.

"She's getting treatment," he says.

"But she's a candidate."

"Yes, she deserves to be here. But she can't be." Jolan refills his glass and takes his phone from a pocket to check messages.

Mrs. T holds her glass out. "More for me," she says. "You'll learn to behave, Marie. No concert? That's perfectly fine with me. I'll go without you."

"That's perfectly fine with me," I parrot back, wanting to be bratty and stick my tongue out at her, but I don't.

"Mind your manners," Jolan says. "She's here to help."

I hit my fist against the seat. "She's gone insane, and you're blitzed. How does that help me?"

"I hate to be the one to tell you this," Jolan hesitates. "Well, you're important to her promotion."

Mrs. T straightens her fur jacket. A smug expression settles on her pig face. "There it is, dearie. I want to advance in GAP. So when I say jump, you ask how high. Got it?" Mrs. T's demeanor holds an edge of hostility.

"Dad, she's using me?"

"Dottie, give it a rest." Jolan puts his phone away. "Don't worry, Jo. I'm here to help."

"Yeah, whatever." I push myself deeper into the cushions wishing

❀

I could disappear and magically transport myself to Idaho. This is all Océane's fault. Had she kept her promise, this wouldn't be happening.

"Fine, we'll drop you. Go straight to Hotel Neuschwanstein," Mrs. Thalhammer says to the driver.

I close my eyes wondering what else Mrs. Thalhammer has in store for me. What else can possibly go wrong this week?

The limo follows a dark highway a short distance from Friendship Village where we cross a long, wide drawbridge. The moat is a thick inky blackness. We pass under a lofty stone archway into a courtyard where armed patrol officers guard the entrance.

Martial law is worldwide and permanent. Patrols protect the five international Crystal Consortiums, many restored cities and several protected reserves, including the Sierra zone. The military defends health districts where local working class citizens live in a safe and disease-free environment. No one would dare leave the cities, and no one from the wilderness can gain admission into protected districts. The laws are very strict. The military is so ubiquitous that it blends into the background of everyday life.

The limo takes a left at the intersection and drives to the Hotel Neuschwanstein. Battlements, towers and conical spires rise high into the night sky. Circular turrets extend even higher with connecting walls. The corridors are made of glass that exposes walkways leading to private suites, living quarters, concert halls, libraries, classrooms and gymnasiums.

We exit the limo and follow the attendants inside. I walk toward the adults standing near the concierge's desk and glance over my shoulder. Outside Tala races across the courtyard. Embedded beneath the skin of her neck is a chip synced to mine. The devices are voice activated. I speak into my wrist, and Tala runs toward the entrance and triggers the automatic front doors letting herself into the foyer.

The attendants lead us through the great hall. Candidates along with their teammates, parents and coaches live in a separate wing. The elevator takes us to the twelfth floor. Our suite is spacious with a vaulted ceiling, and the main living space is circular and welcoming.

❄

The outer walls made of glass offer a spectacular view of Castle City and the quaint village. Comfortable and economical, the furniture is bioengineered from synthetics, the colors cool and chromatic.

"I'm headed out, dearies. Concert lasts till midnight," Mrs. T says. She puts her gloves on and wraps the fur coat about her shoulders. Without a backward glance, she trots off in her platform boots, a plume of peacock feathers hovering in the air.

Jolan staggers toward the master bedroom. "I've got work to finish. Don't get on the Network. Lots to do in the morning."

"It's not even eleven o'clock. What am I supposed to do?"

"How about sleep?" He disappears into his room.

I don't feel like exploring the castle, so I call the concierge's office to request access to a recital hall. I leave Tala behind and head to a replica of Singers' Hall, which encompasses the entire fourth floor. The intricately carved woodworking, tapestries, vast candelabras and ornate décor present a perfect reproduction of Singers' Hall at the real Castle Neuschwanstein.

I walk down the polished floors and pass the mural depicting the saga of Lohengrin. Artwork of kings and knights, poets and lovers captured the dreams of the shy Bavarian King Ludwig II who built the original bastion in 1868. The theater with seating for five hundred is much wider than the original hall, though nothing of the medieval grandeur is lost with these modern changes.

The Fazioli Brunei is an expensive black grand piano. I prop open the lid and place the stick in a notch. The piano is interactive with my Smart chip and SASS computing and with the virtual options in the hall. I activate a 3D session.

"Marie-Joëlle Peone."

Instantly, a holographic projection of an orchestra and a director appear. The men wear tuxedos, the women elegant black gowns. My AI instructor acts as conductor. Several different pieces are stored on my SASS.

"Rachmaninov No. 2, C min, op.18."

Often, I watch podcasts and analyze my performances, so I know what the audience sees as I perform. I place my fingers on the keys waiting until the conductor waves his baton for the cellos to play the heavy Russian melody. I've had enough of parents and their broken promises and their unrelenting demands. This has been an exhausting day of emotional ups and downs and unforeseen events.

The meaning of life is in the mathematical order of music. I shut my eyes letting my body and mind move to the rhythm of the horns and trumpets. The theme in E flat major begins. My fingers fly across the keys. The pounding of my heart matches the power of the drums. The conspiratorial spirit of the concerto suits my mood. An invisible black cloak is heavy upon my shoulders.

The composition eases the pang of emptiness in my chest and fills me with the wonder of the concerto as the music pours out of me through my fingertips. The drama changes as the string section plays the haunting notes of a flute. The clarinets in Bb bring me tranquility.

The strains of the piano free my mind. As I enter a sphere of light, a gentle peace settles upon me. Smiling up at the AI version of Sergej Rachmaninoff, I wait holding my hands above the black and white keys, waiting for movement II Adagio sostenuto to begin.

"Hold program," says a disembodied voice. The virtual session pauses, and Maestro Rachmaninoff's melancholy expression freezes. Someone stands in the shadows of the archway to my left. The man moves from the darkness into a soft light. "Good evening," he says, speaking with an odd accent.

I study the man's face, his brown eyes, prominent nose and olive-toned skin. He could be twenty years old and Native American, or Asian, or even Spanish, maybe. I feel as though I should know him or I have known him before. But that is quite impossible because I would remember such a strikingly handsome man.

"You're Dr. Julius."

The young man takes a step toward the piano. "Ah, such powers of perception." He puts his hand on the polished black surface. "You are quite talented."

I avoid looking at him. "Cancel program," I mumble, trying but failing to ignore him. The conductor and orchestra both disappear, leaving the Fazioli Brunei at the front of the hall. "Now what?"

"I suppose we should talk."

"About?" I walk toward the far doors and out of Singers' Hall.

He keeps up with my rapid steps as I try to escape another adult supervising me. "A holy mission."

Abruptly, I stop myself and turn to face him. Dr. Julius holds my attention as though he casts a spell upon me. When I was a child, I played a game with my father—the staring match. The first to blink is the loser. Sometimes, I wanted Jolan to win and I would blink first, maybe because dads are supposed to be stronger and wiser.

Dr. Julius is a reserved young man. But there is something about him, an indefinable air of nobility, refinement and sophistication, but also an appealing kindness in his face.

I blink first.

"I always win," Dr. Julius promises with a dazzling smile. "I spoke with Océane. Having a rough day, Marie-Joëlle?"

"I'm fine."

"You'll be all right."

"It's never all right," I say angrily, not meaning to sound provoked.

"Oh. I see. I heard you studied the classics. When I was your age and feeling down, I'd play a game with my mentor of quoting the words of philosophers, for example. The one with the most quotes wins. Take an idea like change."

"You go first."

"Okay. Here we go. 'On those stepping into rivers staying the same other and other waters flow,' Heraclitus of Ephesus."

I know where this is headed, pop-psychology 101. Still, it makes talking to an attractive man easier than I'd have expected. "'To souls it is death to become water, to water death to become earth, but from earth water is born, and from water soul.'"

"Very good. Few understand the unity of opposites." We walk down the long corridor. Dr. Julius punches the elevator button and glances my direction. I stare unblinking into his inquisitive eyes.

❄

"A holy mission," I repeat, brushing aside loose curls from my face. "What did you mean?"

"Isn't that your goal? GAP training then a mission." He punches the button for the twelfth floor.

"Yeah. So?" I ask, trying to gauge his reactions.

His stoic features reveal nothing. "It's time you wake up. Look at what's really going on."

"Like tonight's ball? Oops, I mean concert," I add with sarcasm. I challenge his cool reserve. "This is the Castle of Paradox where Cinderella wakes to a kiss. Oh, but that's Sleeping Beauty, isn't it?"

Dr. Julius's laughter lightens my mood. "I'm neither a fairy godfather nor a prince."

We step into the elevator. The door shuts and we ascend upward.

"Then who are you?"

"A humble professor mentoring candidates."

"Yeah, right," I reply, noticing his expensive Dior tuxedo. Dr. Julius stands much taller than I do and carries himself with an aristocratic air. "You interrupted my practice..."

"To welcome you. I'll oversee your honors course this week. GAP will select a tenure-track program for your team. I'll help you with..."

"A holy mission like curing genetic diseases?"

"You're ambitious."

"What do you know about Carolyn Delamar?"

I dread what I might hear. It can't be good. This whole day has taken unexpected twists and turns. Océane flying to Spain and Jolan being here in her place. The unsettling change in Mrs. Thalhammer and her aspirations for a promotion. Now, meeting Dr. Julius before tomorrow's team assignments and orientation.

"Some things you're safe from. Physical molestation. That never happens to girls."

"What about Carolyn?"

"No disease or hunger."

"Where is she?" I demand angrily.

❖

"I don't know," he admits. "They wouldn't tell us." The elevator opens, and we step into the hallway.

"Tell me something. Where do the sick go?" I persist, pressing him for more.

Dr. Julius studies me with a keen eye. "This week you'll learn things...well, more than I can explain tonight."

"You mean everything they censor from us."

"Probably."

"Where do they go?"

"Quarantined and treated. Your mother thought it best not to tell you about Carolyn until tonight."

We stop at the door to my suite. "Left that to you, did she?"

"If you want to chat, my office is down the corridor to the left. Until tomorrow, auf wiedersehen."

Dr. Julius walks away, but then stops abruptly. "Oh, before I forget, they replaced Carolyn. Océane said you know the girl. Jenna Slate."

"Yeah, I know her."

Blond hair, big mouth and big boobs Jenna. I run my fingers through my hair, forcing down the urge to scream and take my rage out on Dr. Julius.

The thing is five years ago Jenna Slate tried to kill me.

CHAPTER FOUR

Friendship Village

FOR MANY CANDIDATES nothing compares to shopping at Friendship Village. Adorned with festive décor much like carnival booths, the shops display trendy dress styles. Everything from the traditional regency gowns and court regalia to the avant-garde of futuristic fashion—Industrial Gothic, Cyberpunk, Club Wear, Rave Clothes. Zealous sales agents dressed in lavish outfits and outlandish costumes perform songs and dances adding flare to their sales pitch to lure customers into their shops.

Gucci, Chanel, Prada, Armani and Dior. Shopping is more than the unlimited choice in brand clothing, shoes and accessories. It is the reward of a lifetime. Merchandise doesn't have price tags. Clerks scan our chips and GAP pays for everything we buy. Three thousand teens shove their way through the marts and vie for attention.

Patrol officers enforce a drug free, no alcohol and no leaving the premises with the opposite sex policy. It's the first time boys and girls get to hang out together unsupervised. Today, there are no teachers or AIs or guardians, even I can appreciate that kind of freedom.

The marts stay open 24/7 this week. But this is my only chance to buy a prom dress and find a costume for opening ceremonies. My team meets at noon, which gives me plenty of time to stroll through the shoe store where I find a pair of low-heeled black shoes. At the next store, I select a cream-colored blouse and black slacks. After changing clothes, I toss my uniform in a trashcan and hurry to the west wing where the shops are not too busy.

Often, I've envisioned myself wearing a Chanel gown and dancing in the arms of a boy whose face eludes me. The Chanel gowns while lovely are disappointing and designed for C-D cups, all different colors but the same patterns. I move on to the next shop. Maybe Prada will be better.

Before I can get through the aisle, someone calls my name. When I turn around, I stare into the face of Jenna Slate—my worst enemy. She hasn't changed much in five years. Still blond, big mouth, big bully. I have to admit she did get a tan.

Jenna stands with a hand on her hip posing like a plucked chicken with a crooked wing. "Lookin' good, Peone. I see your hair grew back. You looked better bald!"

Only Jenna and I know the backstory to her cruel hair jab. Her guileless words get the reaction from me that she wants. Impulsively, I step toward her. "Shut your trap, you witless neotard."

Several girls stop their conversations and move toward Jenna Slate as though siding against me. "How about a replay of Jo Peone—the scalped fancy dancer? I've got scissors in my purse," she adds with malice in her blue eyes.

A red blaze of light clouds my vision and then instantly dissipates. Smug and laughing, Jenna Slate shrugs her shoulder and turns her attention to a strapless black gown glittering with silver sequins. I push shoppers out of my way. Before I can reach her, someone from behind hits me between the shoulders.

The pain is excruciating. Dropping to my knees, I cry out and roll onto my back curled into a ball, protecting myself from a second girl holding a splintered jewelry box. I wince and look up into her cold gray eyes. She kicks me viciously in the side. A surge of overwhelming rage gets me to my feet. I charge Jenna cursing her name and burning

❄

for revenge. The fight deteriorates into the three of us, beating on each other just like boys—punching faces, throwing fists and pulling hair.

The shop owner calls security. Straightaway patrol officers arrive and break up the fight. Shamefaced, I comply with their order to get on my feet and stand at attention. They impose a punishment worse than handcuffing and carting us off to jail.

The officers put us in a patrol car and take us to Dr. Julius who marches us straight into his office, not a good way to impress your mentor. Julius wears a white shirt with an open collar, tight blue jeans and running shoes. Dressed in casual attire, he is no less handsome than he was last night in an expensive tuxedo.

Dr. Julius sits behind his desk staring at us without speaking. The minutes tick by. Five minutes. Then ten minutes. Is he actually trying to prove a point or what? Jenna and Freja squirm in their chairs. Freja is the Norwegian who hit me with the jewelry box. The silence hangs over us like a black winged bird then my stomach growls really loud. I feel my face flush with embarrassment.

Julius rubs a hand across his face. "Today was—" he pauses. "I—I don't know what to say—fighting in Prada?"

I am amused by his incredulous naiveté. But hoping to diffuse his anger, I give him a bright smile. "It was Chanel."

Visibly flustered, the young Frenchman rubs his forehead as if to ward off a headache. "This is no laughing matter, Marie." Julius takes a handkerchief from his pocket and pats his forehead. "Wipe that smile off your face."

Oh, that burns. I thought good manners would help to ease his discomfort. I stop smiling. Jenna and Freja hold ice packs to their faces. I got a good punch in before the patrols lifted me off Jenna. Medical staff met us at Dr. Julius's office and used a modern healing device called a mini miracle laser to sanitize and repair our cuts and abrasions. It is an improved version of the old-fashioned surgery laser used for cosmetic resurfacing but instantly heals damaged skin and bruises.

Julius looks from Jenna to me. "You two—you are the ones, but Freja, you hit first—and the patrols said—"

❖

He's so cheesed off he goes into silent mode again. At this rate, we'll miss lunch. Julius rolls his eyes and shakes his head. "It stops here. The three of you will just shake it off. I—we—GAP will not tolerate fighting. Girls, you are excused. No, not you, Marie. You stay here," he orders, looking harassed with flushed cheeks. Jenna and Freja leave without a word.

Jolan walks through the door.

"Swell. You called my dad?" I hunch my shoulders and hunker down in my chair. I steal at look at my father and then I'm speechless.

This man cannot be Jolan Peone. He's not hung over or depressed. Somehow, he's been transformed into a youthful and vibrant man. His eyes are clear and alert, and his face is free of worry. Nowadays men grow their hair fashionably long. Jolan's black braid hangs down his back in a clean-cut style. No longer in a rumpled business suit, he's dressed in casual wear, a white shirt and khaki pants.

"What happened?" Jolan asks, eyeing me with speculation.

"I might ask you the same thing. What happened to you?" I ask.

"A good night's sleep. Now, tell me what's happened."

"Jenna tried to kill me!"

Dr. Julius stares down his nose with skepticism. "I hardly think jealousy over dresses justifies bloody noses." His dry tone is even more insulting than his arrogance.

"Five. Years. Ago." Each word is a painful reminder of my disgrace. I force back the dark despair of the past humiliation threatening to overwhelm me.

"Castle Coeur d' Alene hosted an awards banquet," Jolan begins. "You know the kind. The end of middle school to showcase their gifts and talents. The girls followed Jo to Tubbs Hill."

"She hit me on the head." I break off so incensed I cannot find the words to express my rage.

"Someone. We never knew who."

"She tied me to a tree. All night. And it snowed."

"A light dusting."

"Dad, why can't you agree with me?"

Feeling as if Jolan had found me on Tubbs Hill just this morning, I recoil reliving the pain of a rock cracking my skull and warm blood pouring down my face. I don't know how long I laid unconscious. I remember a very bad headache, white fluffy snowflakes and light like diamonds sparkling on the lake. Hate for Jenna Slate made me strong.

"I found her at dawn," Jolan adds. "None the worse. She's tough."

Julius settles back in his chair and his eyes soften. "Harsh night though."

"I had to perform," I add, my voice harsh with a bitter edge. "And she cut my braid."

My father and Julius withhold their opinions though an unspoken agreement seems to pass between them. An intuition I can't explain tells me something important worries them. I mean, something other than my fight with Jenna.

My sight blurs. I resist the flash of knowledge just within reach. Colors pulse with intensity causing my eyes to burn. The light flickers, and my head throbs. But I hold the vision at bay. The air is heavy with fear. I cannot imagine why. Their trepidation is more a chastisement than any verbal reprimand ever could be.

Julius breaks the silence. "This is bad, Jolan. They are teammates this week and six years together in school. Too much is at stake."

"I agree. Jo, it stops here."

Julius turns a puzzled expression on me. I can't bare the distress in his eyes. "This is most disappointing."

That bothers me. Although I met Julius only last night, I believe he cares for my well-being. Now it's my turn to squirm in my chair. I manage to shrug off his words. "What do you want to me say?"

"That's the best you can do?" Julius demands. "A simple shopping excursion, and you end up in a fist fight?"

"How can we change this?" Jolan asks impatiently. "Can we get Jo assigned to another team?"

"I'll deal with it. Jo and I are late for lunch. Let's check in tonight."

"By then—well, I should know more when—" Jolan stops himself as though recalling that I'm sitting beside him.

❄

"Know what, Dad?" I ask. I'm confused by the flowing subtleties of their conversation. "What's at stake? Your reputation? That's all you care about."

Jolan turns in his chair to look at me, and the staring match begins. "Okay. Here's the deal. No more fighting. I can't supervise you because I'm in meetings all week."

"With your GAP cohorts? Wish I'd known, not like I can't escape from this stupid place now."

Jolan gives me a fixed look. "Where would you go?"

I blink several times. "Home."

"To D.C.?"

He doesn't love me at all or he would know my home is not D.C. I swallow the lump stuck in my throat and pull up the sleeves of my hoodie. The elastic is old, but it is my favorite, a dingy white fleece sweatshirt with Vandal Pride on the front.

"I'm done with parent talk. What?" I ask, noticing something pass between them. "You don't trust me."

Jolan stands up reaching his full height of six foot three. He is imposing with broad muscular shoulders and a commanding presence. "Jo, things aren't always what they seem. Julius, are we done here?"

I interrupt whatever Julius meant to explain. Hoping to redeem myself, I plead for one more chance. "Dad, I want to come home. Just for summer. Can't you talk to Océane?"

"How about you settle down? I'll talk to your mother."

"Anything. Anything you want! Thanks, Dad." I throw my arms around Jolan's neck and hug him tight.

Laughing he pulls my arms away and steps back. "I don't like crossing Océane, but I've made some plans."

"Thanks. I really mean it."

Jolan heads down the corridor while Julius and I hurry from his office in the opposite direction. "You need to change," he says, taking my arm and directing me toward my apartment.

"Into what?"

Julius hustles me into the Peone suite. "Can't be helped."

The skinsuit is an all-purpose and form fitting protective wear, nonflammable, water resistant, light sensitive and absorbs vitamin D. Exactly like a chameleon transforms itself, the material changes color and even shimmers in the light.

The best part is its healing properties. An injury infuses the skin with antibiotics and cell nutrition through osmosis. The matching footwear is indestructible. Thick enough for protection, comfortable enough for activity. Boxing, fencing, calisthenics, mountaineering, even old fashioned Ninjutsu. Embossed in gold on the backside are three letters: GAP.

Ten minutes later, we run down the corridor. The luncheon is in a private dining room in our wing. Corporate Team building sponsors a Taste of Culture with a catering company from Friendship Village who prepared samplings of cuisines from across the globe.

The round table is set with enormous platters of food, a variety of intercultural, delectable treats of diverse colors, textures and flavors. A culinary historian finishes her lecture on the history of highbrow food for privileged citizens.

We approach the table where nine boys along with Jenna and Freja pause in their conversations. One swift glance is not enough time for me to decide which boy is my favorite—Chinese, Russian, Mexican or African.

"Where's your Medallion Pin?" Julius whispers.

"I forgot it."

"You are sitting with me."

Taking me by the elbow, Julius leads me to the table. I sit down and self-consciously I unfold my napkin and place it in my lap while ignoring Julius's disapproving frown. Fortunately, he left his peeved-off-ness in his office.

"This is Marie-Joëlle. You may call me Dr. Julius. Your designation is V-team1—virtual team first place. In fact, the one team with all Medallion Pin winners. It shouldn't come as a surprise. English is our common language. Several of you speak two or three languages. Be mindful of others. They won't speak Mandarin or Hebrew or Russian."

❄

He pauses for a drink of water and offhandedly looks at me. "One more thing. This is nonsense about missing kids. Rivalries and injuries is just absolute rubbish. A boy died last year. An accidental drowning.

"Kids don't disappear though some might be sent to camp for disciplinary training. I expect your best behavior. Enjoy performing, not competing. Officials will observe your team. You are candidates and soon to be GAP members, so you'll learn censored history."

For the span of an hour, Dr. Julius explains the ground rules for Kickoff. He lists team goals and lectures on teamwork and delivers an entertaining pep talk. Eloquent and debonair, Julius could capture any girl's heart, except one boy holds my attention. I cannot stop staring.

The boy with red hair, almost too red for decency, is a rare mortal and pure of heart. I confess he is a beautiful soul. A drape of ringlets hangs across his forehead. Long waves of reddish gold curls touch his shoulders. Abundant and unruly hair—the color of a fox. His smooth clean-shaven face is flawless. I gaze into his eyes, and my heart flutters.

I sense another side to him and upon closer study, I perceive an impenetrable facade safeguards his secrets. However, he's not really so perfect, but slightly flawed and rough-looking. High on one cheek is a faded scar. His nose is a little too long. What's surprising is his size although he matches the other eight boys in strength. Still, his rugged beauty reminds me of a baleful bear. His thick fingers holding the fork are almost clumsy.

Dr. Julius catches my attention, "Continue eating but introduce yourself. Would you start?" he asks to the girl on his left.

"Jenna Slate from California. I once cut hair, but once was enough." She stares into my eyes and adds caustically, "Lice infested her hair." She and Freja laugh while the boys look on confused.

I tighten my fingers into a fist and stomp my foot venting my rage. "Easy," Julius says softly. His hand presses on my shoulder with a firm grip as though restraining a charging bull. Well, my mother does scold me for my bullheadedness.

While Jenna talks about herself, the boys grin, and now and then sneak a shy glance at her shapely figure and open neckline. All the boys keep their eyes on Jenna, all except the boy with a beautiful soul.

Every time I steal a look at him, he looks at me, and I cannot stop staring at his lips. His smile is playful and dangerous and makes me feel uneasy. I pretend to ignore him but find it difficult to close my mind to him. Even in the secret places of myself, I feel the warmth of his hazel eyes and the play of golden brown and sparkling amber light. I have never fantasized about a boy until now.

"I live in San Francisco and like to surf," Jenna says with smugness.

"Field of study?" Julius asks.

"Molecular Nanotechnology."

"Thank you. Do you want to share?" he asks the Norwegian girl.

"Freja Jørgensen of Oslo. I work on electromagnetic technologies and applications. And I do my own hair," she giggles.

Jenna and Freja with their anti-Jo jabs are doing their best to goad me. Freja stands up and models her punk style hairdo with orange and green spikes. She impresses the group with her flare and theatrics. The boys laugh, but she charms them with her personality.

Dr. Julius asks, "Have you anything else to share?"

Freja is fair skinned with a perfect, clear complexion. "My name is pronounced Fray-yuh. And I have a tattoo, but I can't tell you where."

"Thank you for that," Julius says over fits of laughter from the boys. He lifts his glass and takes a long drink, pointing his finger at the boy next to Freja.

"Artem Kozlov. I'm from Moscow, and I don't have hair!" Buzz cuts are great on boys with nicely shaped heads like Artem's. "I ski and study advanced AI design."

The boy beside Artem hesitates and rubs his nails against his short black beard. "Cyrus Bashir of Tehran. My field is Core Network Engineering," he says, chewing gum and blowing bubbles that snap and pop. "Nothing special about my hair. Thick, I guess." Cyrus shrugs his shoulder and winks at no one in particular.

Jenna must think Cyrus winked at her because she leaves her chair and strolls his way. His sultry brown eyes widen with bewilderment. Jenna strokes his head and gathers the silky black hair into her hands.

❈

"Yea. It is thick. I couldn't help myself," she says, in a girly girl voice.

"I play a chang," Cyrus says, shifting awkwardly in his chair plainly embarrassed by Jenna's attention.

"A chang? What's that?" Jenna asks, eying the boys and sauntering around the table like a fashion queen until returning to her seat.

"Something like a harp."

"I play the violin," she says, batting her eyes at him, the shameless flirt. "Anything else?"

"I rebuild vintage cars, motorcycles, anything fast."

"Hey, how about you, Freja?" Jenna asks, picking a violet from the floral centerpiece and putting it in her hair barrette.

"Let's hold that, will you? Do give the others a chance," Dr. Julius says, waving his hand at the next candidate. "Plenty of time to chat during small talk."

Oh no, small talk is my worst skill. Jolan tells me to try new things. But I'm not a risk taker, and I am definitely not a small talker. Freaking out, I can barely catch my breath and feel a panic attack coming. That red-haired boy is grinning at me again. I cannot hide my discomfort.

"Iain Alexander Sinclair of Moray," he says, giving me the most extraordinary smile I have ever seen. I admit to the cliché, but it is true.

"That famous family from Scotland?" asks Zebenjo Tongogara, the boy from Johannesburg. I didn't review all the bio sketches from the itinerary, but I did read Zebenjo's because his IQ matches mine.

"Moray is a wee village north of Edinburgh," Iain finishes abruptly. He stuffs a roll in his mouth and crosses his arms, reluctant to talk.

Dr. Julius encourages Iain to share. "What talent or skill?"

Iain scratches his head. A befuddled expression settles upon his face as though someone slammed his head with a baseball bat. "Uh, well, I confess. It's classical ballet."

The dissimilarity between ballet dancer and a warrior Scotsman strikes Zebenjo's funny bone. He breaks into a belly laugh, setting off giggles and titters from everyone including a snort from Freja. I can't resist smiling.

I wish I had paid attention to the email. Reading Iain Sinclair's bio with his photo might have prepared me for his shy demeanor and beguiling grin. Iain is a contradiction—compassionate but dangerous. Funny without trying to be. He has the body of an ancient warrior and like his forebears, his history remains shrouded in the mists of memory. He shares insignificant things, his area of study and school projects but evades questions about his family or his past.

Stop romanticizing him. I scold myself for acting like a love-smitten girly girl. Begrudgingly, I stare because his voice is so smooth and lyrical, alluring and unsettling. I can't explain why I am drawn to Iain. Maybe he doesn't belong here anymore than I do.

Laughter pulls my attention from my musings. Iain throws his hands up and laughs. "You joke now. Wait until prom, I'll put ye all to shame," he boasts, and to impress us, he exaggerates his Gaelic brogue. "Not to brag, but I engineered the River."

"You're the one," Zebenjo exclaims, shamelessly awestruck with his mouth hanging open. "The River. The newest logic programming language that will revolutionize the Network with interactive and unimaginable dynamics. It will harness power and will change..."

"Sorry to interrupt," Dr. Julius says. "Iain will give a presentation of the River technology this week. For now, Wei, your turn."

"Lim Chang Wei from Beijing."

Wei is the epitome of a look-but-don't-touch reserve. Less is more. The less Wei does, the more handsome he is. He sits in his chair with a proud and stiff posture. With soulful eyes, Wei holds our attention with the potency of an ancient ruler. "I'm a chess master and design cyberware for war games."

Then there's Zebenjo. What can I say about Zebenjo Tongogara? He's a real chatty man, but he gets serious when listing his credentials as though reading his resume, which comes off as his most endearing quality because he's so blissfully oblivious. Biomed technology. Gene Nomenclature. Microscopic Nanobotology.

The others give a short bio sketch. Juan Pablo Coelho with a soft curve to his devilish smile lives in Mexico City. *Tiene una pasión por vivir.* His passion for life is contagious.

✣

Born in Mumbai India, Dev Rammdas Patel is the shy-guy, but adorable. Jamil Ahmad is Sudanese from Khartoum and not inclined to talk about himself, or talk at all. Isaac Bar-Hillel from Tel Aviv has long, curly hair and penetrating dark eyes.

The twelve of us are unique in personality and ethnicity, but our customs and beliefs are much the same. Of course, nonnative English speakers have a varied cadence and pronunciation, each exotic but easy to understand.

Dr. Julius sets his empty coffee cup down. "Isaac will present on Regenerative Medicine and will be quite informative." He shifts in his chair and leans toward me. "You're on."

For fifteen minutes, I've been rehearsing. But I totally bomb. "I'm Jo from..." I pause a nanosecond, long enough for Jenna to dig the knife into my heart.

"Like a Jo-Jo bird?" she asks, ignoring me but fluttering her eyes at Artem. I feel like disappearing under the table. I hate Jenna Slate.

"Kindly stop, Jenna," Dr. Julius says emphatically. "That goes for all of you. You'll be punished for fighting. I will not warn you again. You are a team. Go ahead, Jo," he insists.

"I'm Marie-Joëlle Peone."

"An Indian peon." Jenna laughs, but the room is dead silent. No one makes a sound, not even her friend Freja. GAP prohibits racial prejudice. No team is worth this. Not for a week, and definitely not for six years.

No way will I allow Jenna Slate insult me and not retaliate. Maybe beating the crap out of Jenna will get me banished to Idaho. I clench my jaw and imagine punching her in the face. I leap from my chair so fast it tips over and lands with a bang on the floor. What the heck. I've got nothing to lose.

CHAPTER FIVE

Small Talk

I HAVE NOTHING to lose, except the promise of Iain Sinclair, or maybe something as impossible as love. Could a boy like Iain ever fall for a dark-skinned nobody like me? I don't believe in love at first sight. Yet Iain is the perfect dream.

I force myself to calm down and to think rationally. To forfeit my place means never seeing him again. I want to quit this team, but I cannot. The one thing stopping me is Iain Sinclair.

Julius sets my chair aright, and I sit down weak in the knees and not trusting myself to speak. Nothing is worse than enduring the abuse of bullies, especially in front of boys. I'm learning that hate fuels the need to destroy your enemy. Right now, I want to kill Jenna Slate.

I manage a shaky comeback. "Can't you find Plastic-Girl a doll house to play in?"

"Thank you, ladies. Your maturity astounds me," Dr. Julius says sarcastically. He checks his S-pad and lets out an audible sigh. "Okay, for today's small talk. Marie-Joëlle, Zebenjo, Wei and Artem will be the White group. Iain and Cyrus, Isaac and Jenna, you'll be Red. Blue is Freja and Jamil, Juan Pablo and Dev." Julius stands up and motions for us to follow him down the hall.

The Smart room is equipped with several consoles and interactive technologies. One side of the room is a Fusion-wall, a floor-to-ceiling transparent flat screen but for multiple 3D overlays of streaming data. Keyboards flip into a vertical position depending on what you need to do. Voice activated computers project three-dimensional images. The chips embedded in our left wrists interface with our nervous systems stimulating our sensory perceptions. We can talk with great geniuses from the past. Often in a virtual environment, I work with famous bio-technicians, geneticists and mathematicians.

We sit around tables in groups of Red, White and Blue. Julius reads his S-pad. "That's Babbage again," he mutters to himself. He slips the pad into his jacket. "I have to go, something about his lecture. You have access to a syllabus. Work in groups. We'll hook up at the Alhambra at four. Babbage is a stickler for promptness." Julius hurries from the room.

Not two minutes pass before Jenna and Artem, Freja and Jamil and Juan Pablo walk out the door but in the opposite direction of Dr. Julius. Juan Pablo's hobby is Mayan archaeology. I hope he presents on his travels to the digs. I have always wanted to visit Mexico.

"Five flakes play hooky, seven swots stay behind." Zebenjo's off-kilter slang is more irritating than comical though no one bothers to mention it. "By the hey, I'm Ben to friends."

"You prefer Jo, right?" Wei asks, with a classic accent, controlled and confident. "Um, no offense, but what's the bad juju with Jenna?" Beneath his skin-deep, smooth reserve is an appealing charisma any girl could not resist.

"Don't ask," I reply, practically spitting the words out in disgust.

I don't know how to start small talk. I didn't come to Kickoff to be sociable, but these boys are friendly and make me feel at ease. I keep my attention on Wei and intentionally avoiding Iain's gaze.

"Artem leaving class is not good for us," Wei says, shaking his head with disapproval. "Not good for our small talk group or project."

Dr. Julius pops back in the room. He looks flushed from running. "I forgot to tell you—well, what the...?" He looks at us in disbelief as

❄

if students never play hooky, which convinces me that Dr. Julius is not a professor. "Where are the others?" he asks bemused. He is so naïve about students and boring homework.

"They left," Ben says, obviously wanting to be teacher's pet.

"I see that."

Embarrassed, Ben shrugs his shoulders and squelches his face with chagrin. "Sorry, Dr. Julius."

"I'll deal with them later," he says impatiently. "Read Babbage's study guide. He's teaching the pandemic." Julius holds his fingers to his temple then gives us a stoic frown. "Well, what are you waiting for? Get to work." As soon as he leaves, the mood in the room lightens.

"Got any room at your station for us?" Iain asks, not waiting for my permission, but sliding his chair next to mine.

Cyrus and Isaac bring their chairs to the table forcing Iain and I closer. His leg bumps mine, which causes my heart to skip a beat. Ever so slightly, he leans forward making me uncomfortably aware of him. His scent is intoxicating with the unmistakably earthy smell of the outdoors. Softer, maybe like the aroma of cedar and spice.

"What's your name again?" Zebenjo asks Iain with hesitation in his voice. I'm sure he knows all about Iain. He is one of those students who reads every word in an email or a book. Obviously, Ben failed at small talk because he looks as awkward as I feel.

"I dinna get the hair joke, did you?" Iain asks me with all sincerity.

Iain Sinclair's confidence strikes me as a little put-offish. His eyes are bold with interest as he waits for me to explain the joke, which I refuse to do. Nevertheless, I give Ben my undivided attention.

"Seriously, tell me about Gene Nomenclature," I ask, hating myself for the uncertain quiver in my voice. I wish someone else would lead the conversation.

Ben looks up dumbfounded. "Uh, who me?" I try not to laugh at the gosh a-girl-is-talking to me expression on his face. Ben is sappy and a klutz, but sweet. Ben fumbles with his backpack and drops his S-pad on the floor.

"Yah. Three subjects make you a neek," I reply, surprised the boys

✻

laugh at my humor, except I was not trying to be funny.

"Oh, I like that," Ben says, his eyes filled with light as though inspired. "Not a nerd, not a geek. How neat!" He is mildly ludicrous laughing at his own wit. Most geniuses through the ages were jeered. "I've got the lecture on my S-pad. See ya later."

Ben scoots his chair back and bends over to pick up his jacket from the floor. He starts toward Dev who is reading his S-pad in a corner but turns awkwardly and stands by a bookcase.

"What's wrong with Dev?" Wei asks. "His head is in the clouds, but astrophysicists are space cadets."

Isaac reaches for his boy-bag and pulls out an orange GoBot cap. "He's a 'spect. Ya know, an introspect snob. He thinks he's too good to work with us."

"What about this GoBot?" Iain asks Isaac.

"Robotics. Microbot. Medbot. Biobot in regenerative medicine," he replies. "I like building things." Isaac fixes his cap so the visor slides down on his forehead.

"What do you think about using one of my war games as a group project?" Wei asks with a frown on his brow. "I created something last week. I haven't tested it with a team."

Virtual war games are social scenarios—moral dilemmas when we decide who lives or dies—and are a part of the educational system TRAMS: Transforming Realistic And Modern Sensitivities. We learn decision-making skills that can affect others, so we appreciate how our inventions will help the world survive and thrive.

"Hey, time to study," Ben says, coming back and sitting down. His S-pad slips through his hands and hits the table.

Iain shifts his chair sideways at a diagonal, all the better for him to get my attention. "Where's your school, Jo?"

I keep my eyes lowered, but try my best to sound beguiling. "D.C.," I mumble, but my voice is a flat monotone.

"But you were born...?" Iain leaves the question dangling.

"Idaho."

"What tribe?" Wei asks.

"Salish."

One word answers? Well, that's the best I can manage under these circumstances. Grade F for beguiling.

"The Northwest Reserve!" Ben exclaims, all agog over my tribal lineage. "I hack...I mean, I love history. I read everything I can find on outdoor survival. Hey, do ever you hunt with bows and arrows?"

"You're not as smart as you look, are you?" I reply. Yet intuitively, I know Ben did not intend to insult me.

"The Zulu tribe was my ancestors. I didn't mean to offend you," Ben apologizes.

"What is your tribe, Jo?" asks Cyrus, who seems genuine in his curiosity. He slips a new piece of chewing gum in his mouth and blows a big bubble that pops with a baby-bang snap.

"Bitterroot Salish. My dad is the reserve manager. During the bad years, the Southwest tribes moved north and came to live with the Coeur d'Alene, Kalispell, Kootenai tribes and a few others."

"I've read our ancient clans suffered, many times almost losing the Gaelic," Iain says, his words barely audible.

Something in his voice catches me off-guard. Not knowing what else to do, I brush strands of hair from my forehead and give Iain the same bold expression he is giving me.

For a fleeting moment, his expression hardens with cruelty then just as quickly his eyes soften as though he's haunted by a great sadness. His vulnerability makes me uncomfortable. I consider escaping into the restroom. But I don't.

Awkward and unsure of myself, I clear my throat but still cannot find the confidence to speak my truth. Something in Iain's face though encourages me. "Native Americans are still sovereign in the Americas. The name Coeur d' Alene means heart of the awl. The Schitsu'umsh are the discovered people."

"It's my first trip out of country." Ben's face shines with excitement.

"Beijing is the most cosmopolitan city in the world," Wei says proudly. "We are permitted to study some of ancient China."

"You're lucky, Jo, living in the place of your ancestors." Everyone hears the wistful longing in Ben's words. He manages to keep up with the conversation while reading homework on his S-pad.

Dev Rammdas Patel stays secluded in the corner. Occasionally, I catch him watching us, so I guess he would be the "Watcher" of our team. I understand his need for solitude.

"Be back in a few." I laugh awkwardly, but glad to escape my failure to beguile Iain.

Not that I am complaining, but I wonder why Iain is talking to me. It cannot be my personality because I don't have one. It is probably because I am the only female in the room. I get the impression he has developed a talent for talking with girls.

I leave the boys at the table and pass by a small utility center with a refrigerator and refreshment cabinet. I grab two bottles of mineral water placing one down in front of Dev. He lowers his head until his chin touches the front of his hoodie like a tortoise withdrawing into its shell. Oh brother, his shell versus mine—the dual of the century.

I hope Dev isn't as stubborn as I am. How often has Océane tried to crack the hard casing of my shell? Lost in memories, I lean back with arms crossed and stare into white space.

"What?" Dev asks. An annoyed scowl darkens his face.

"Huh?"

"What do you want?"

"Nothing."

"Then stop thinking so loud."

"Aw," I reply, feeling guilty and embarrassed. "That's what my mother tells me when I ignore her."

Dev presses his bottom lip into a sulky pout—annoyed, petulant and an out-and-out sign labeled no soliciting. "Can't you tell from my face? I wanna be left alone."

"I get it. Really, I do."

Dev puts down his S-pad and turns his chair toward me. "You're not like other girls."

"That's good or bad?" I ask, wondering what I just said that could have encouraged him to open up.

"I am Hindu. The only one." By special order from GAP, the One World Church will issue a special license to those who wish to practice ancient beliefs.

"I'm—ah—uhmmm, I don't really know what I am," I mumble, searching for something charming to say before the sign goes up, and he shuts me out. "I'm Jo, the girl from a broken home. The candidate from the Rez. I don't fit into—normal, I guess."

"Life is like a spider's web—" Dev says sagely.

"Good advice," I interrupt. "Some days I get stuck in crap, too," I reply pleasantly. The sound of Dev's laughter is buoyant and uplifting. "What's so funny?" I ask indignantly. He laughs all the harder, his brown eyes shimmering with tears.

I can't explain why Dev doesn't offend me. I like him. If I ever should face a crisis, Dev is the boy I would choose to help me. Reliable. Resourceful. Loyal. All this becomes clear to me in his shy smile.

"Come over to our table and help us with the group project."

"Okay," he agrees. "I'm in."

"Make room for Dev," I tell the others.

I sit down on the table. I have a habit of biting my nails when I'm nervous, but I resist the temptation and instead I cross my arms. "Did you guys come up with a project?"

I look from Wei to Ben to Iain. Cyrus and Isaac look at each other. And then all eyes turn my direction. That's fine with me because I just remembered that puzzling file .dc2. "Do you want to help me decrypt something?"

"Yeah, crank it," Cyrus says, blowing a big bubble that he sucks back into his mouth. "I mean, let's do this."

The seven of us walk over to the Fusion-wall. Iain Sinclair speaks his name and then scans his chip to access his SASS computing via the Network. Several more transparency screens appear in front of Dev and Wei and Ben, Cyrus and Isaac. A 3D connection of data-stream interfaces with Iain's module.

I scan my wrist and speak louder than I had intended. "Marie-Joëlle Peone. Access file .dc2. Okay guys, data is flowing—jump into

❄

the stream anytime you're ready."

Iain crosses his arms and takes a step forward. "Take code and run encryption Alpha10. Solution 1.54c.55. Simple secure string."

"Much too obvious," Ben adds, shaking his head and laughing. "I thought you'd use a sequence from the River."

"Simple to complex." Iain touches the pad typing a password. "File translator. Multiple protocol." He enters commands by hand with the keyboard tilted straight up and directed away from Ben, Wei and Cyrus.

"What's wrong with verbal?" asks Ben insulted.

"Above all, keep friends close but secrets closer," Iain answers offhandedly. "I don't share codes from the River."

The file opens:

Series: PN1993.5.SyM
Port: 791.4b.0946---.dc1

"I know this. Shut it off!" Ben shouts, backing up comically and tripping over Isaac's boy-bag and landing squarely in a chair. "Shut it off!"

"Don't! I want it." I move to the screen and swipe my hand over the surface. The heat-sensors read my energy signature. "Secure data. Save to my SASS." The transfer is instantaneous, and then Iain ends virtual session.

"What was that?" Cyrus asks, scratching his head bemused. "Ben, you look like you saw a ghost."

"Nothing. Forget you saw it," Iain says, walking away from the group.

"It's nothing? You both recognized the port address," I accuse him. "What is it?"

Ben looks down at his pad swiping his finger faster and faster, screen after screen reading lecture notes. "You guys," he says without looking up, "it's time to study."

We all return to our seats. Cyrus leans in toward me. His black

❄

mustache and beard are trimmed and well groomed, and his dark eyes are mesmerizing. "It can't be that bad. Who sent it to you?"

"I don't know," I reply, feeling defensive and uncertain. "Someone, yesterday. What was that, Iain, that decryption sequence you wouldn't let us see?"

"Something of mine." Iain runs his fingers through his hair. Using an elastic band, he ties his hair back into a ponytail. Iain lowers his eyes and evades my question with a broad smile.

Ben glances up from his reading. "Something like the River? Not streaming data, massive amounts of Rivering data."

"To be honest, I'd love to hear about it," I say, batting my eyes and attempting to flirt. Iain grins. I fail miserably.

"Well, I'd need time to know ye a bit better," Iain answers with a slight tilt of his head and an overdone brogue. "I don't share secrets until the first date."

"Because you don't trust me," I snap, then instantly regretting my harsh tone. "We're a team. That should be enough."

Iain's grin widens into a heart-stopping smile that weakens my resolve to hate his guts. "I don't blindly trust anyone," he says suddenly somber. "Besides, Jo, some things are worth waiting for, even waiting for an entire lifetime."

Iain does this thing with his face. He smiles, but those hazel eyes betray him. I sense something odd about Iain Sinclair. He hides secrets and something like a shadow is reflected in his hazel eyes, the gold color broken with shards of dark brown. Either he is a shameless tease, or he conceals something of importance. His expression is difficult to read like a pattern of sunlight against an obscure background.

I move my chair closer to Ben, placing my elbows on the table and leaning into him. "What was that port signature?"

"It's distinct."

"Obviously, protected. What else?" I insist, upping the ante with a smile. He gives me what I want without too much effort.

"I saw it once." Ben struggles for the right words. "On a professor's computer. He didn't know I was in the room. I dropped off a thumb drive. He disappeared that night."

"Who would send that file to Jo?" Isaac asks. A perplexed glower creases his brow. He touches his cap and then pulls the visor into place pursing his lips deep in thought. "What does it mean?"

"That we forget it," Iain says, sliding his chair back and standing up. "Forget the missing professor. It's not as if people don't go AWOL. It's after four. We're already late for Babbage's lecture."

Iain is doing that thing again with his face. He grins like an idiot, but his eyes reflect with a false light, and then his foolish expression disappears. He walks beside me through the corridor and out of the building. When I glance over at Iain, I find him studying me. Sunlight brightens the color of his eyes, changing the harsh brown fragments into a dazzling golden-green.

An hour with these boys may have improved my small talk skills, but V-team1's first session leaves me with a nag-thought. I feel anxious because I still don't know who emailed that file labeled .dc2. And why was it sent to me?

CHAPTER SIX

Shout Out

THE ALHAMBRA CASTLE, or better known as the Red Fort and located in Spain, derives its name from the variety of stones used in the design and structure of its formidable walls. The footpaths through lush botanical gardens lead to three palaces.

The hotel in California is grand, however, on a much smaller scale. The architecture captures the artistry and elegance of the real Palace of Charles V. To my disappointment, it is not a faithful replica of the Spanish castle. The design accommodates for the needs of a five-star hotel along with conferences rooms, business offices, several bistros and souvenir shops. An art museum is open to visitors for a fee.

Day 2 of 2216 Kickoff is a live streaming event from Castle City and hosted by GS2, the Americas. All three thousand candidates are seated in the tri-level auditorium. Dr. Julius and our team sit on the main level. The show's director signals to his assistants who disappear backstage. The production crew and special effects specialists stand ready.

Historian Archbishop Dr. Charles Babbage appears from behind a black curtain. He walks across the platform to center stage. His voice fills the large hall, and he motions for the assemblage to rise and recite the pledge of alliance to GAP.

"What a marvelous day for our 2216 candidates!"

The program is essentially a rerun of the Medallion Pin ceremony from Washington, D.C. Dr. Babbage's sermon is verbatim. GAP laws are the key to sustaining the delicate balance of life and health for the planet and its inhabitants. It's the same show as yesterday, interactive with microblogging and SASS chatting from fans in the working class. Thousands of their faces flash across two fusion walls lining the hall.

Quite suddenly, the Network stops the live streaming to outsiders. Viewers watch commercials and public broadcast messages but do not see Dr. Babbage as he presents an uncensored history lesson to those people seated in the palatial hall.

"Your homework was to study *The Book of Who: Solutions for 2050 Pandemic and Global Starvation.* World peace is sustained with coalition, not opposition. Ours was a dying world. Now, we have hope because your inventions ensure the future of our world. Your team will succeed with individual responsibility, communication and chain of command. Your engineering will get the job done and turn discovery into health for tomorrow."

Amidst the cheers and clapping, a large platform rises behind Dr. Babbage. The famous three-member Globe-rock band Mercy Me appears alongside a towering monolithic screen. The group performs in the background of Dr. Babbage's presentation. Their latest hit song "Shadowland" went viral last week.

"The podcasts you are about to see are very old, but disturbing," he warns. "History is censored from citizens. We protect our children from the past. And now, candidates, here is your history."

And so, my very first bona fide history lesson teaches me the truth of the Millennial Plague, the world famine and the rise of GAP. The podcast is happening in real time through modern technologies of chips, sensory devices and 3D hologram projections. The music of Mercy Me intensifies. The mournful tune "Shadowland" is nothing more than a haunting death song.

The virtual screen shows a 2015 newspaper headline, "The Worst

Global Famine in 900 Years May Lie Ahead." The podcast shows an interview with scientists, climatologists, NASA engineers and others who voiced their concerns. But no one could have anticipated the scope of a Cascade Failure, or the massive loss of human populations.

According to 2080 climatologists, a catastrophic climate event occurred with severe planetary warming leading to rising sea levels, the melting of Arctic ice and the release of methane. The growth of third world countries and the world's use of fossil fuels contributed to a failing ecosystem.

During the podcast, Dr. Clint Harrison explains, "Environmental conditions of massive proportions caused a worldwide crop failure." Malnutrition weakens the immune system. And then the impossible happened—the onset of the Millennial Plague, a pandemic that swept across the world populations. Hence, the virus mutation became more virulent and harder to contain with each generation.

The next podcast features a three-star general, Frederick Blasick, the head of the International Intelligence Agency. Alpha History is the breakdown of social order. International martial law was enacted after assassinations of government officials, politicians, church leaders and business executives. Famous people and law enforcement agents were murdered. Caught on security cameras, scenes of gore and death stream across the virtual screens throughout the hall.

Civil wars broke out. Economies collapsed. Who was to blame? The scientists, governments, or corporations? Then the unimaginable happened. A nuclear war began that lasted only one day owing to counterstrikes. To protect its sovereign territory, a small independent nation escalated border wars with the detonation of a nuclear missile.

Spellbound, I watch the podcast of mobs rioting in the streets and the hysteria spreading to Los Angeles, Paris, London, Moscow, Beijing. All around the world agriculture failed. At one time, parents fought on Black Friday for merchandise. In grocery stores and Costco, men armed with guns, knives and clubs kill each other, a mass riot not for toys or digital televisions, but for food.

The podcast is a streaming nightmare of dead bodies with black, rotting flesh. Thousands of corpses and bodies of children of every nationality. Corpses left on hospital floors, stacked against the walls, too many to count. Lying beside the bodies are physicians, nurses and volunteers dying themselves. Medical teams working in jungles and deserts lost their patients and their own lives because of depleted resources. Few escaped the worst pandemic of all time to hit humankind.

Dr. Babbage steps back into the spotlight. "Published in 2070, the analysis of DNA from victims showed that 1.6 billion died from the Millennial Plague. But it was the severe drought and failure of crops that killed billions decade by decade."

Above every candidate's head appears a 3D multicolor hologram of a virtual microorganism. The Plague virus is the ultimate attention getter. The magnitude of death is stupefying. Dead bodies, skeletons, mass graves. Guardians usher hundreds of panic-stricken candidates from the hall. Some stagger out the door physically ill.

"I warned you. These podcasts are difficult to watch. This is your history," Dr. Babbage declares. "This is how we survived with GAP's help. They saved us."

Project Noah's Ark led to the bombing of sick cities with napalm. Chemical sanitation killed the virus, but fell on forgotten people who were sick and dying.

Today's presentation is a real, experiential and interactive sensory event for those seated in the hall. The show ends with the explosion of virtual bombs destroying famous buildings with people running through the city streets on fire and screaming for help. The deafening sounds fill in the auditorium. The smell of burning flesh assaults your senses.

Arks were the only safe zones where healthy people lived until the government restored law and order. World presidents hunkered down in secure compounds. Members of royal families remained in their palaces protected by military forces. Governments passed new laws and integrated the World Health Organization into GAP to ensure the survival of the human race.

�֎

Then the Newborn Selection Act implemented mandatory DNA testing to determine genetic defects and cross fiber mutations from chemical fallout. Health protocols became laws. Countries formed alliances and signed unilateral permanent agreements, trading food and agricultural products for medical technologies. Netcom, Bionet and Glonet were temporary solutions until the organization of GAP in 2100.

The music swells in volume with haunting sounds of percussion, soft timbre woodwinds and deep taiko drums. "Citizens want GAP laws," says Charles Babbage. He thrives in the limelight like an actor and relishes his importance as director of 2216 Kickoff. "Citizens want a military run government and protection from the Outlands."

Then the monolithic screen goes blank and lifeless. The black wall reflects a distorted light across its surface, and all the holograms disappear. The music ends.

Archbishop Babbage lifts his hands for the benediction. "You are the future, and your mission will ensure our survival. When you need inspiration, remember today's lesson. Assembly dismissed."

A physical reaction erupts from those remaining in the hall. Many show signs of shock, fatigue and anger. The fight or flight hormone is released into the blood stream due to physical or emotional stress and overwhelms all common sense.

Verbal arguments break out among the boys, and they exchange curses shoving and punching each other. The last two years of school, boys eligible for candidacy will attend military academies. Some opt in and enlist in combat training in case they fail to achieve selection.

All of us have received training in the use of firearms, but combat students have mastered the art of warfare. Boys routinely get away with rough and tumble scuffles. However, this is like nothing I have ever seen. Coaches and mentors separate angry teens and hustle them out of the great hall.

My anxiety is off the chart, and my heart is racing out of control. Fear and anger affect me like a time dilation. Events are happening too fast, but I feel like I am moving in slow motion. I cannot get rid of the smell of burnt flesh. A disgusting bile rises in my throat, and I almost gag. I feel so weak. I can hardly stand up.

Jenna takes Freja to the bathroom. She has barf on her skinsuit. I want to escape and forget this hour of tragedy. But Dr. Julius leads us toward an empty conference room to debrief. I feel as though I am floating above my body, not walking through the corridor. We stand around, none of us knowing what to do until Julius returns with the two girls. They go off into the corner by themselves.

"All I need," Jamil says to Artem in a threatening voice, "is one minute with Babbage alone in an alley." He hasn't spoken a word since his introduction at lunch. "Alone in an alley," he repeats.

Artem exchanges a look with Jamil. "He's in Hotel Prague."

"Boys sit down! Girls, come over here," Julius says, pointing to the empty chairs. "Everyone, sit down. Iain, you too. No one leaves until we talk." Visibly shaken, Julius runs his fingers through his disheveled black hair. "Babbage is a belligerent old bugger."

"Is this how they win our loyalty?" Wei asks. His voice is calm. But I can tell Wei holds a tight rein on his emotions behind a luminous mask of cool indifference.

"I argued with him for an hour. He refused to listen. He did tone it down," Julius says apologetically. "No excuses though for that—that shock tactic."

Artem checks his S-pad. "A flight leaves at ten o'clock. I'm going home."

"You know that's not possible," Julius says, holding his hand up to stop Artem. "Sit down before security arrests you."

Artem takes a seat beside his new friend Jamil. They mirror each other in physique and attitude and sit together with crossed arms and disapproving frowns. Young hoods, young hunks and young dreamers.

"Я могу," Artem says, "I mean—yeah, but I'm pissed."

"I know you can handle it," Julius replies with a break in his voice and sounding as distraught as the rest of us. "Wei, ask the attendants to bring mineral water and Vitajuice. This may take some time."

I watch my teammates all the while tightening my grip on the seat beneath me. Isaac forces a smile between clenched teeth, and Cyrus responds with an empty expression. I hardly recognize them as the enthusiastic, fun loving boys from the luncheon.

Juan Pablo cannot stop fidgeting. Both feet are moving to the rhythm of his humming. With pink cheeks and swollen eyes, Freja peels the polish off her nails. She hiccups from her cry. For the third time, Jenna pours moisturizer into her palm and then rubs the lotion between her hands. I notice the label shows it is eye cream.

"I can't believe it," Jenna says agitated. She squeezes the tube. Too much cream squirts out. She stares at her hands, looking helpless and unsure. "Why did my parents lie? They never told me."

"Let's rethink this," Julius replies, talking faster and slipping into French. "Pour une bonne raison, or rather, they don't want youngsters studying this tragic history. Not until you are candidates. Certainly, this isn't the happiest rite of passage to adulthood."

"Ya think?" Ben asks, his two-word contribution to the debriefing.

"I'm on vacation," Freja cries softly, puckering her lower lip which quivers erratically. She takes the handkerchief Julius offers. I almost feel sorry for her. Almost.

"All our science," Wei says, phrasing his words carefully. "When we needed it, that's the best they could do to save lives?"

Julius wipes beads of sweat from his flushed face. He reaches into his pocket, but Freja holds his handkerchief. He rubs his hand against his trousers.

"Babbage is an immoral rabid dog of the worst sort, but that does not change the facts. Ours is a delicate balance of systems that must stay in place. Another pandemic is unimaginable. GAP ensures that we are—" Julius doesn't bother to finish his rehearsed speech.

Dev puts his hand on the back of my chair and leans forward. "Are you okay, Jo?" He offers me a wet washcloth and a bottle of water.

"My stomach hurts."

Dev doesn't voice his private opinions, but he keeps his hand on my shoulder. Iain is out of my line of sight, invisible and out of reach. He hasn't spoken a single word. His movements seem suspended like a set metronome, the musical pulse of his soul fixed in time.

"What about the Outlands?" I ask softly, unsure if I really want to know about the wilderness beyond the cities and reserve dominions.

"GAP works to cure disease," Julius says, "to bring people back to immunize and treat." He doesn't sound convincing even to himself. "They try to clean up the infected areas."

"More propaganda," I whisper under my breath.

Iain opens the door. "I've bloody well heard enough."

"Fine," Julius replies. "You're excused." He checks his watch. "See you at the meeting. Let's hook up at ten o'clock."

"What meeting?" Wei asks. "It's not on the itinerary."

Without a backward glance, Iain Sinclair is the one candidate who is permitted to leave the debriefing, which lasts another fifty minutes. Somehow Dr. Julius manages to calm the team. What I would call an on-site teen intervention.

"Opening ceremonies are scheduled for tomorrow morning," he finishes. "Your coaches will explain the protocols."

"Anyone for the party tonight?" Jenna asks in a thin voice. A few boys nod their heads. "How about going together?"

Dr. Julius rises from his chair. "I regret the day ended so badly. I wish I could have spared you this."

"Will you walk back with me?" Dev asks, looking intently at me, but I avoid his eyes. "You shouldn't be alone." Somehow, he possesses the uncanny ability to discern my thoughts.

I pitch the empty water bottle in the recycle bin "No, I'm fine," I respond with a smidgen of bravado.

I just want to be alone to find a place where I don't have to feel so hopeless. The best thing I can do for myself is to work out for an hour, and maybe purge myself of the pain gripping my gut.

On the third floor is a gymnasium. The workout room is busy, the stations occupied by teens with the same goal as mine. Combat the stress. Work off these bad emotions. Boost my mood? I don't think so. Ranked one of the highest combatants here, my eclectic skills include martial arts and extreme sports like mountain climbing. I also perform ballet and modern dance.

After an hour of activity, I collapse from exhaustion, energized but none the happier. The fear I keep locked in a hidden dark place. Despite feeling fatigued, I make myself jog back to my apartment, or what I have come to consider the Castle of Paradox.

Wiggly is my new word for crazy, for a world of out of control and full of contradictions like a carnival house of mirrors. Objects are distorted with multiple reflections and an illusion of truth. Make war to secure peace. Kill the sick to save the healthy. Feed the healthy, but starve the weak. Promote deceit to teach truth.

Making meaning from a week, or a lifetime of lies, does not come easy. Adults and their hypocrisies can be confusing. The world is not black or white. It's wiggly like a crazy golden worm.

I follow the walking trail through courtyards. The hotels connect in a labyrinth of paths and fountains like a piazza in Rome. Statues of Greek heroes and Roman warriors decorate the gardens, even a statue of Charlemagne, the King of the Franks and Holy Roman Emperor. Floating in the center of a large pond is a miniature garden maze the color of chartreuse.

This is where Tala finds me. Gladys can pinpoint my location. "Did Gladys send you, huh? Did she?" I laugh, but a wild hysterical sound I don't recognize.

Tala tackles me to the ground in a game of rough and tumble. Mostly, she is rough and I topple over. She pins me down growling in a mock death hold. I rub behind her left ear and press my face into her fur, warm from running in the sunshine. Giving me a reprieve, she pants heavily and drinks from the pond.

Orange and yellow goldfish, the Japanese Koi, swim in the water. Tala jumps in disturbing the fish and the white swans grooming themselves and their young. With a wingspan of over six feet, the swans lift off, flapping ruffled feathers until I call Tala to my side.

I lie down in the cool shade of maple trees. Tala settles beside me. The Eastern Sierra is home to a variety of birds. A golden eagle circles in the clear blue sky. I shut my eyes but see things that I wish to forget.

❧

My training in Kung Fu has taught me to meditate and appreciate Chuang Tzu's message. "Breathing control gives a woman strength, vitality, inspiration and magical powers." I take deep breaths and softly murmur an ancient chant. *Channel my Chi. Channel my Chi.* And I drift toward a deep, uneasy dream.

IT'S NIGHTTIME WHEN Tala awakens me. The artificial lights bring the statues to life but casts shadows to an otherwise serene scene. Tala growls with raised hackles. Whoever lurks in the dark is in for a rude surprise when Tala finds him.

"Hol mir!" I whisper.

Tala responds to German commands like a military dog. Better she fetches the poor fool than attack him. I follow her to the sleeping form fifty paces away where Iain Sinclair has been spying on me.

Tala pounces, and Iain bounces. He wakes up as though he's a bear disturbed from its hibernation. Iain rolls like a cannonball into action. He tries to fend off the orkwolf. The fight gets serious when Tala's teeth snap, and Iain yelps in pain.

"Fuß!" I command Tala to release Iain and heel.

Iain grasps his bleeding forearm. "She actually bit my arm!" he exclaims indignantly.

"You're lucky she didn't eat you."

Like most boys his age, Iain is tall and bulky, lean and muscular. Right now, he looks beat up. His ripped skinsuit doesn't improve his appearance. I'm sure I don't look much better.

"Why are you stalking me?"

"I wasna stalkin," Iain answers, examining his arm where Tala's teeth pierced his skinsuit that now shimmers as antibiotics infuse his wound. "Not too bad," he says. "Not for stitches, I mean."

"Then what do you call spying?" I feel bad about the bite. "Tala, well, she is overprotective. Make sure to clean and disinfect that."

"I wouldn't wander alone in the gardens at night."

"I'm not alone."

Iain straightens his shoulders and walks with a graceful sway to his step. "Alright, my mistake, thinking to escort you home. Good night, then."

"It doesn't matter if we walk together," I say lightly, talking faster before he goes too far, "since we're headed the same place."

I sound like a fool. My words slur together in my haste to stop Iain. He turns around and waits for me to catch up.

Alert with her pointed ears, Tala watches him unsure whether to accept him as friend or foe. Tala keeps her eyes on Iain, herding him away from me. Though capable of defending himself, Iain steps briskly to my left.

We follow the walkway curving around the pond and leading back to our hotel. I wonder why a dream-boy like Iain is strolling through a romantic garden with a misfit like me. He can't possibly be interested in me. The tight weave of my braid is coming apart. I unravel the thick mass of brown curls. Iain's red hair is almost as long as mine is.

"I heard about your dog," he says guardedly.

"Tala meet Iain."

"I'll pass on that. We already shook hands, or rather paws."

I laugh easily with Iain. It feels good and eases the tight ball of fear in my stomach. "Babbage is a jerk," I say, suddenly angry again.

A solemn frown creases Iain's brow. His expression is hard as stone and frozen in time like a statue of a Greek god. "Jerk is not what I'd call him. You don't look good, Jo," he says with concern.

Not the kind of compliment a girl wants to hear from a boy. Why would he walk with me if I look so very bad?

"Back at you," I reply offhandedly. "Where did you go?" I ask in a softer tone. "I mean after the lecture?"

"I hung around until you came along."

❖

The evening air is warm, but I recall the podcasts. I sense evil in the deserted woods, and I suddenly shiver with goosebumps rippling over my flesh. Could the spirits of the dead follow us through the night? I banish from my mind the phantoms that might be hovering in the forest and feel foolish when I draw closer to Iain's side.

"I'm fine. Seriously, what about today?"

Iain holds himself in check and turns aside to pick a daisy with delicate yellow and white petals. He hands it to me without a word. Clearly, he chooses to withhold his opinions. "Don't know. Hey, what about the party at Hotel Edinburgh?"

"What about it?" I ask, not fully grasping his point. He can't really want me as his date.

"I'm headed over," he says. "You going?"

"I can't."

What is wrong with me? I want to scream, yes, I'll go. I want to go, but I don't understand my hesitation. Iain is almost too perfect. I feel uncomfortable with him and afraid I'll only make a fool of myself. It's safer to go back to my suite. But go back and do what? Sit alone feeling sorry for myself?

In the far distance, Hotel Neuschwanstein is busy with candidates climbing into limos to be chauffeured the fifteen-minute drive to Hotel Edinburgh. Iain does not seem to be in a rush. We linger in the courtyard away from the lit driveway.

The stars and planets burn a radiant white in a cloudless night. We pinpoint the Milky Way in the northern sky. Facing south is the cosmic giant Orion, the Hunter with its unmistakable hourglass shape.

With no reason to continue stargazing, Iain walks me to the front entrance. "Time for me to go. Sweet dreams, Jo." Iain does not strike me as stupid, but he is wearing a torn skinsuit to the fashionable party.

Then a sudden movement catches my attention. A dark shape has been shadowing us for twenty minutes. The phantom follows Iain headed down the drive, not me as I had expected. Iain is so oblivious to the danger lurking in the woods. That surprises me. Maybe it's a jealous candidate who intends him harm.

❀

Iain heads down the lane in the opposite direction of Edinburgh Castle. He can't be headed to the party. I bet he plans to rendezvous with the shadow, probably a girl waiting for him to ditch me.

"Aren't you forgetting something?" I challenge Iain, wanting to confront him and spoil his plans.

"Huh?"

"To change clothes?"

"Right," he says, retracing his steps. "Don't know why I'm fuddle brained." Iain is doing that thing with his face, smiling but lying.

"Don't let me keep you from whoever is waiting for you," I mutter angrily. "Fuß!"

I yell to Tala though I would love to see her chase the shadow that is no longer visible. She races across the lawn and triggers the front door to open.

"What? Do you think I'm lying?" Iain asks insulted. He looks so innocent as we walk through the lobby that for a moment I doubt my assumptions about him. But I refuse to answer him because I know he'll just fabricate another story.

Nevertheless, I wonder if the rumors are true. Are Medallion Pin winners in danger? Probably not. I believe Julius, but for some reason Iain's got a target on his back. To have a friend, be a friend and form alliances. Maybe someday Iain will warn me with a shout out.

We enter the Peone suite greeted by the adult inquisition. Mrs. Thalhammer glances up from her S-pad, sizing Iain up and looking at me dumbfounded. She drops her jaw in disbelief. Her student has shown up with a boy, an attractive boy at that.

Jolan and Dr. Julius study a computer screen that goes black as soon as I step forward. "Iain, weren't you meeting us at my apartment? Is it ten already?" Dr. Julius asks. Clearly confused with the turn of events, he looks from Iain to Jolan. "Did you change the time?"

"No, I didn't," Jolan replies. "What took you so long, Iain?"

Mrs. Thalhammer points to a chair. Her index finger bounces up and down for emphasis. "Sit here, Marie. Where have you been?"

"Sleeping soundly beneath Charlemagne's pond," Gladys answers,

❈

stepping out of the S-wall and smiling at me. "The one with a floating maze. I sent Tala to find her at six o'clock." Gladys stands ready to order me a nutritious dinner, a packet of supplements, Vitajuice and an ergo bath.

"Why didn't you tell me?" Mrs. T huffs in a haughty tone. "No one tells me anything."

"You were shopping, Dottie," Jolan says unconcerned. "I sent Iain for her."

Heat rushes across my face. My pent-up emotions spill out. "You don't trust me, Dad. You sent Iain to spy on me?" I shout hysterically. Shocked over his trickery, I step back and give Iain the evil eye.

Jolan studies my face, takes a giant step forward and grasps me by the arms. "Jo, you don't look well. Why are you late, Iain?"

I shake off my dad's hands and lash out at Iain. "Liar! You sneaky Scottish spybot." Iain walked me home, not because he likes me, but because Jolan told him to. I feel betrayed and devastated.

"I didn't," Iain protests weakly. "I meant, I did but..." He gives up trying to talk his way out of the lie.

Plainly embarrassed, Julius puts his hands into the pockets of his jeans and moves aside. Avoiding my deadly glare, Iain crosses his arms and looks away, but then they covertly glance at Jolan. I can't imagine what these co-conspirators are plotting.

"Jo, hear me out," Jolan says. His apologetic expression is comical. I almost want to laugh. But I can't forgive him for this ruse.

"No. I don't want to listen, Jolan."

"Must you call me by my name, Jo?" he asks impatiently. "I can't explain what's happening."

"You just don't trust me," I shout, stomping toward my bedroom before they see my tears.

"I trust you," Jolan says, but I keep walking away.

Gladys follows me across the living room. "How about an ergo bath?"

"Deactivate AI." I twirl around like a ballerina giving them the ugliest glare of my life. "I'm done with you all!"

❅

Slamming my bedroom door shut, I sweep my hand across the control panel activating the lock. Like my friend Dev, the message is "No soliciting!"

I just want to be left alone.

CHAPTER SEVEN

A Selfie Alone

MRS. THALHAMMER SIPS her second cup of café espresso reading a fashion magazine on her S-pad. Her costume for opening ceremonies is much too youthful for a woman her age. Mrs. T looks like a gigantic cookie in a short dress made of layers of red, yellow and blue strings. Shameless, she makes no effort at modesty wearing a low-cut bodice of silk rosettes.

"The team isn't important. Julius gives it too much emphasis," she adds. "Which sonata will you play?"

"Beethoven's No. 29," I answer with a mouth full of food.

I savor the taste of a vegetarian omelet along with a thick slice of German pastry, decadent and sweet. Housekeeping washes dishes and cleans the kitchenette where I leave the plate in the sink.

Activated by voice recognition, Gladys materializes where I work at a computer console. I created a program for Gladys to respond to conversations and emotions. AURA Gladys is an integral part of my life and my mission.

"Not the individual," Gladys says. "The team."

Mrs. Thalhammer exhales a long breath and mutters something to herself. "Not the team," she says in a high falsetto. "Jo is my special girl and my responsibility.

"My job is caring for Jo," Gladys retorts, placing her hands on wide hips and glaring at Mrs. Thalhammer.

"I'll reserve the concert hall," Mrs. T says, "for your practice. You'll perform tomorrow."

Gladys puts a hand on my shoulder though I cannot feel her touch. "The team needs this week to form emotional bonds before the fall semester. The model for a virtual team is trust and common goals."

I designed Gladys to learn human emotions. She has acquired an edge the last five years. Mrs. T takes her hand off the computer and slowly stands. She and Gladys are the same height. Gladys is heavier with a full figure to accentuate the grandmother softness of her hugs were she capable of them.

"Jo succeeds, I advance. I don't need a lecture from you. You're just an AURA."

"Both of you stop this bickering." I flex my arms over my head to relieve the tension from my stiff neck. It is too early for an argument between my coach and my AURA.

Tala sleeps in the sunlight on the balcony. I wish I could stretch out alongside her. A migraine throbs at my temples. The pain kept me awake all night. I don't want to plan the week, but it must be done.

Every candidate will perform while teams demonstrate either an athletic exhibit or a group project. According to Dr. Julius, a project is better suited to our skills, but I suspect my vendetta against Jenna Slate explains his decision.

My father walks through the living room. Impeccably groomed he wears a stylish black tuxedo. My jaw drops open, because I have never seen him look so handsome, or so worried.

"What's wrong, Dad?"

Jolan comes over to my computer. "Babbage," he says. He takes his phone from his pocket. "I got an email from him."

Mrs. Thalhammer's breathing comes in heavy gasps. "Ah, ah, ah!" she cries, leaping from her chair and then promptly sitting back down.

Mrs. T's facial twitch is spasming convulsively, and her eyes blink

❋

nonstop, which is something I haven't observed since the day Tala and her dachshund Sebastian raided the barbeque at an outdoor party. She still blames me for the mismatched friendship.

"I can't believe this. Really, I can't. You are purposely damaging my reputation and set on undermining my promotion, Marie. What did Babbage threaten?"

"The team won't present an honors project," Jolan says, terse and irritated. "It's to be an exhibition. They want V-team1 to demonstrate teamwork."

"Very good," Gladys says in a defiant voice, her face shining bright.

"This is very bad!" Mrs. Thalhammer stammers. "Oh, just go glow somewhere else!"

"You can go straight to—"

"Deactivate AI," Mrs. T says, enjoying her victory.

Jolan stares at me with raised eyebrows. "Teaching Gladys more expletives?"

"Who knows what she reads on the Network, Jolan," I reply with a guileless smile.

"I'll make sure GAP knows how special you are, dearie," Mrs. T resumes, sampling another pastry. "But not as a team player."

The word "team" reactivates Gladys. I cut her off before she can contradict Mrs. T. "I am not special," I retort.

"She's right, Mudpie." Gladys agrees for once. "You are unique."

The glass door to the balcony is unlocked. I push it open and Tala races in to greet me. She licks my hand and wriggles her behind.

"GAP heard about you and Jenna." Jolan stands in front of a large mirror. He adjusts his tie and then takes a seat beside me.

"Who told them, Dad? Babbage, I'm sure."

"They know everything," he says grimly. "From our DNA to our favorite color. What do people expect when they live in Smart houses?" His meaning is clear. The walls are listening and computers watch everything, everywhere. "Jo, I understand this thing between you and Jenna Slate. But it is time you shake it off."

"I need a shower, not a lecture."

"Yes, it's late," Mrs. Thalhammer says. "I need to freshen up before opening ceremonies. By the way, nothing arrived from Chanel. You did order a costume?"

"In your dreams," I reply, taking pleasure in taunting her. I am still angry with her for using me to get a promotion.

"She'll be the death of us all," Mrs. Thalhammer says, the fright in her voice inciting a chorus of howls from Tala. "Oh, my!" She starts hyperventilating. "I can't believe you want to humiliate me!"

She paces through the room in her high heels, doing a fox trot like a windup doll gone berserk. Tala dances with her until Jolan locks her, the dog, out on the balcony. Mrs. Thalhammer wobbles side to side, heel to toe in a new variation of fancy dancing. Then she takes a chill pill with instant calming effects.

Like an intoxicated Persian cat, she purrs and says, "Perrrfectly, fine. I'll call the office. They'll send help." Mrs. T heads for her room, her arms flapping as she tries to keep her balance.

Jolan motions for me to follow him. He takes a seat on the couch. "Sit down."

"Fine," I reply, crossing my arms and pouting.

"You're so much like your mother."

"Like Mom?" I slide across the cushion to sit next to him and pull my feet under me. "But I'm nothing like her."

"You are Océane. Your smile, your spirit. It's been seventeen years since we attended Kickoff in Paris. Océane is flying to San Francisco. If the weather holds, she'll be here this afternoon."

"Why does she travel? I mean, why can't she work from home?"

"Parents are upset with Babbage. The fool. He should be removed. Océane is worried about you. So am I. Your migraines are worse."

"Is that why she's coming? Because she's worried?"

Mrs. Thalhammer bursts into the room. "Pépé DeMolay is on his way. He's world famous for designing gowns for Buckingham Palace and the royal families. Can you imagine? The creativity. The absolute glory of his gowns and precious accessories."

Mrs. Thalhammer squeals on her way to the door to receive our

❄

guests. An entourage of fanciful characters garbed in fancy costumes enters the suite. Courtier of the royal court, Pépé DeMolay sweeps into the room with all the theatrical flair of a stage performer.

Pépé certainly fits the part dressed in full regalia with a stylish white decorated wig, and his makeup is perfect, a powdered face, red lipstick and a black beauty patch on his left cheek. Jewelry to excess in expensive gold finery, an embroidered silk blouse and a crimson velvet coat.

His tight-fitting trousers stop at mid-calf worn with fashionable hosiery. Embedded in his silk nylons are precious gems. Gold buckles adorn his leather shoes, and a touch of snobbery in his expression completes his ensemble. Pépé's three assistants wear frilly dresses that complement his costume along with wigs and makeup.

"No, no, no and no!" I shout, pointing my forefinger at each one of them. "Never. Not me. I won't wear that."

"Well," Pépé says with a haughty French accent, "I won't let you wear one of my designs until you bathe." He pulls a fragrant white kerchief from his pocket and covers his powdered nose. "What is that putrid odor?"

I do a walkabout and march toward my bedroom to take a shower. Pépé's exaggerated sarcasm follows me. "What have you given me to work with?"

Twenty minutes later, I creep into a living room full of hundreds of lavish fabrics, materials, shoes and hats of every imaginable color. Feminine apparel and excessive accessories clutter the room.

"Design something outstanding. Make them notice her," Mrs. Thalhammer demands. "How am I to compete with three thousand candidates?" she mutters to herself.

Pépé glances at my face and immediately takes charge of the situation. He decides on a change of tactics. "Out! Everyone out!" Pépé shouts, clapping his hands and chasing Jolan, Mrs. T and his team out of the suite.

Quickly, I follow the others, but Pépé hurries to my side, puts his arm around my shoulder and guides me to the table. "Just let me go,"

I plead, ready to fight my way out of the apartment.

"You are required to attend. Now, what do you like to do? Tell me your favorite ice cream, your favorite anything and what, for heaven's sake, is your passion?"

Pépé's eyes are bright and friendly, but I'm stumped by his query. No adult has ever shown an interest in what I want, much less spent time on a frivolous conversation. His exuberance is hard to resist.

"I like mountaineering, and my favorite ice cream is chocolate," I answer. "My passion is climbing She Devil," I add amused, and testing the Frenchman's patience.

"What devil?" he replies, surprising me with his laughter. He is the most frivolous adult I've ever known.

I study Pépé's makeup and costume. "Are you an actor for the theater?"

"No, of course not. Les apparences peuvent être trompeuses," he replies, sounding very Frenchie. "By all appearances draw attention to yourself to evade your enemy," he clarifies, "depending on what enemy you want to deceive."

"Are you deceiving me? Not so easy to do," I laugh to postpone the horrid task of shopping in my own living room. "I can see things like auras," I tease, but closer to the truth than I would like to admit. "I'll know if you are lying."

"You're outspoken. That's good."

I suspect Pépé DeMolay is more than he appears to be. Behind his facade and his bright cunning eyes, I sense a highly intelligent man with a calculating mind.

"What is She Devil?" he asks.

"A 9,300-foot mountain in Idaho. I love climbing."

"Ah, the lovely Pacific Northwest."

Pépé steps to the bar, reaches into a cabinet and uncorks a very expensive $5,000 bottle of French wine. He pours himself a full glass.

"All my life I've had to wear uniforms. Sometimes, Dad and I left the reserve. We'd spend a week white water rafting the Snake River and climbing in Hells Canyon outside the boundary line."

❄

"Lovely. Tell me more."

"I love the outdoors. Hiking, running, riding horses. But for the last five years, they made me perform Smart activities indoors during virtual climbs. I miss the real wilderness."

"The wilderness off the reserve?" he asks with hesitation, studying my reaction.

"Only once or twice."

I hate lying. I've never told anyone until now that Jolan disappears off the reserve for weeks at a time, and he never told me where he went.

"No one goes to the Outlands, do they?" I ask feigning innocence.

"Trained in science, but a passion for the wild. You are French with a name like Marie-Joëlle?"

"Only part, more Salish."

"Really?" Pépé asks. "Hummm, you're a nature girl and rebellious. A she-warrior with creatures of the wild! I'm seeing horses. Oh, my God!" He stares at the sliding glass door leading to the balcony.

Jolan must have locked Tala outside. Streaked across the sliding glass door is dog saliva. Tala stares back at Pépé growling with bared teeth. Her long red tongue hangs from her mouth and her teeth bared as though she's ready to sample the French cuisine.

"Yes." Pépé laughs. "Natural, nothing artificial. The warrior girl and her wolf and animals. Child of the wilderness. They'll love it!"

I wonder what he means, but I don't stop to question him. I laugh with Pépé DeMolay and can't imagine what magic he will conjure up for me when opening ceremonies commence in less than one hour.

❄

PRECISELY AT ELEVEN o'clock in Castle Square, the ceremonies stream live across the Network on large screens setup throughout the courtyards. A montage of podcasts highlights the Selector Groups 1-5. Three thousand candidates in their selector groups stand ready and waiting for the cue to begin the Parade of Nations.

Dressed in fantastical costumes, all the candidates are grouped according to their designations—SG1 Africa, SG2 the Americas, SG3 Asia Pacific, SG4 Europe and SG5 the Middle East. Patrol officers wear historical uniforms to honor armies decommissioned decades ago. Russia's Aerospace Defense Forces, the EU's Forces of the Fifth Coalition, the Military Action of the Americas, the Middle East's militia group Cain as well as China's Liberation Army. The One World Order needs only one army to enforce GAP's laws.

Many candidates wear warrior costumes from ancient times. The Terracotta Army of China, the Samurai of Japan, the Revolutionaries of America, the Highlanders of Scotland and the Medieval Knights of the Holy Roman empire and many, many others. Exclamations of "GAP rules!" explode over social media. The world celebrates the global superpower.

The scope of the live streaming virtual event televised worldwide spares no expense. The lavish and nonsensical wealth is obscene. In the main courtyard, three thousand candidates watch the activities on large screens waiting for the cue to march in a parade line to the south garden.

Film crews and cinematographers capture the smiling faces of candidates who appear larger than life on the streaming virtual screens. They show off their costumes and tweet from their phones begging viewers to vote for them in upcoming performances.

Patrol officers guard the platform where black robed members and guests take their seats. The Master of Ceremonies, Archbishop Babbage along with elite GAP members, stand for the raising of the One World flag by a uniformed guardsman and the reciting of the pledge of allegiance. The neuro-punk group Arctic White plays the triumphal anthem. The last notes resound through the courtyard.

A young child in a white robe carries a torch, the eternal flame of unity. Marching behind the palace guards, she places the unity torch in a pedestal that holds a statue in the shape of a phoenix, a symbol of humanity reborn from the ashes.

The pedestal stands in a pool of water that is crystal clear like the surface of glass. The everlasting pool of life. The flame is an unending memorial to humanity, tested by fire, attesting to the strength of the human spirit to survive the Millennial Plague.

Released from their cages, emblematic white doves fly into the blue skies overhead. The cauldron blazes with red-hot flames. The 2216 opening ceremonies have begun. A Brigade of Guards marches through the streets, leading the procession through each of the three magnificent palace courtyards.

Smiling children from the village march with flags representing all the countries of the globe. Cheering with pride, their parents look on waving from the courtyards of Prague Castle. Corporate executives on holiday with their children watch the Parade of Nations from their hotel windows.

Archbishop Dr. Charles Babbage gives the Declaration Oath. "Today, we celebrate the best of GAP. Our honorary guest is President Trace Conti from the Crystal Consortium in Washington, D.C. It is my honor to introduce President Conti."

"Welcome to all our GAP members, good citizens and candidates. Advanced technology is a living legacy for our children and their descendants," Trace Conti says. His youth exudes health and vitality. "When the time came, we made the hard choices. We did it right! Today we celebrate the class of 2216 and Jove's legacy for the future.

"The children of the world are here from Saudi Arabia, Brazil,

Canada, New Zealand, Greenland, Japan, Brunei and Qatar, and all the countries of the world. All marching for GAP!"

Much of President Conti's speech is lost to the cheering crowd. As I wait with SG2, I wish the Parade of Nations would begin. It is taking all my effort to hold my costume and accessories in place and keep the horses under control. No one approaches the area where I wait in line.

Pépé DeMolay and his team of tricksters conjured magic with their wands. For the first time in my life, people will see the truth of Marie-Joëlle Peone, my appearance credited to the infamous Pépé DeMolay.

A flowing gown of native colors moves to the contours of my body, a last-minute design of simplicity and perfection. My two thick braids woven with feathers hang forward while thick wavy tresses of brown cover my back. A seashell necklace hangs about my neck, and I wear turquoise arm bracelets for jewelry.

Best of all is the war paint on my face. Streaks of black and shades of blue. Red lip liner. And my eyelids are highlighted with color. My eyes are dark and forbidding.

An apparatus invisible to the spectators creates a virtual fog. The cool vapor envelopes me, and the sudden clap of thunder resounds in the imaginary clouds. Magically, my hair moves in a constant motion, a breath of wind but strong enough for the illusion of flight, as though the air currents lift me up and carry me through mountain passes at great speeds.

I clasp a short staff in my left hand and hold tight to the reins of four stallions, prancing in place and pawing the ground, spooked by the waves of music and the cheering of spectators. One bare foot rests on the back of a white stallion, the other foot on a black. A red horse and a pale horse walk alongside of the other two horses.

Virtual animals appear and follow me. A bald eagle with wings fluttering, a male lion growling and a mature grizzly bear. Not to be forgotten is the very real orkwolf Tala, panting with eagerness.

I recall Pépé telling me to believe that I am the warrior girl, child of the wilderness. The moment is sacred, the spirit of the animals strong, and the power to follow a true path calms my uncertainties. I wave my staff, swept up with elation, and give the spectators the most genuine smile of my life.

The parade begins and SG2 moves through the plaza. St. Vitus Cathedral passes to my right. The courtyard appears where officials sit on an ornate stage. Dr. Babbage's face is dark with disapproval, and the officials shift in their seats whispering to each other. The cameras spotlight my entrance, but in the excitement, I miss the announcer's words.

We pass the pool of life moving toward the Chapel of the Holy Cross, the Old Royal Palace and finish in front of St. George's Basilica. Pépé and his team wait for me. They remove the virtual features from the horses. I climb down and straddle the white stallion. Tala's howl startles the girls waiting in front of us. The announcer's voice is loud and enthusiastic, and I feel pride for what the world has achieved.

The last podcast is the grand finale. The International Ethical Treatment of Animals hosts the 2216 Ark Parade of Animals. The hippopotamus and elephant of Africa, Australia's kangaroo, China's panda, Arabia's camel, the Bengal tiger of Asia. Africa's rhinoceros and lion, the polar bear of the Arctic Circle. All living symbols of culture and spirituality showing respect for past cultures because religion is no longer a divisive force causing strife and warfare.

No one could have predicted this week would be a turning point in human history, and the most significant Kickoff of all time. The gaudiness and pageantry aside, these three thousand candidates—polymaths with extraordinary power—will exceed anything GAP could have foreseen, or possibly imagined. It achieves in seven days what no other could do to ensure world peace and providence for all.

The feverish pitch of the masses reaches an intensity of power. A virtual screen displays a robed man reading an executive order for the execution of a rebel criminal at an undisclosed place.

When did public executions become the norm? I did not know about the death penalty, but this is one more historical fact denied to the public. Every choice we make has a ripple effect like dropping a pebble in a pond, a hundred ripples, circling upon itself with never ending circles throughout all of time and time folding onto itself. The inside-out energy creates karma. Life is not static, but ever changing.

From some faraway location, the nonconformist speaks his final words as permitted by law. "Behold, he cometh with clouds; and every eye shall see him, and they also which pierced him: and all kindred of the earth shall wail because of him. Even so, Amen."

The prisoner will die at the guillotine. The hooded executioner releases the blade that slices through the man's white neck, severing the vertebrae and cutting cartilage and arteries. I feel the blade as though my own bones split, and my blood flows hot like the red gush of fluids from the headless corpse.

CHAPTER EIGHT

In the Clouds

PROM IS TONIGHT? This is insanity. They are crazy to expect me to attend! To smile and to pretend that I'm happy. I'm not. I am shaken to the core and horrified by today's events. Is this some kind of test? Courses in school require us to learn GAP regulations and pass very difficult examinations.

Do they think the death penalty will frighten me into obedience? The execution has the opposite result. I feel like doing a shame rage! This is the city where my life has spiraled into a nightmare.

Mine is truly a broken world. I hate it here. I want to run away. The easiest place to escape is from home because Coeur d' Alene is not as heavily guarded as the protected cities. I do not belong here. The tribes live on the reserve but on their own land. I could escape to forgotten places. Getting home is more important than ever.

Jolan has gone to San Francisco to meet Océane at the airport. Her flight is late. I must convince them to let me go to Idaho. I want a mission, but not like this. For now, I will have to pretend to follow the rules. Prom is mandatory. I have no choice but to attend.

To make matters worse, I didn't receive one promposal from any boy on my team. Julius can't escort me to prom. For some inexplicable reason, he called to inform me that he was unavailable. I can't explain why I'm disappointed that Julius won't be taking me. Pépé DeMolay is my backup date.

I have no time to seek advice from Gladys. Tala looks up from the corner as I toss aside my costume and jewelry. The beautiful hair ornaments lay on the vanity table. A hot shower washes away my makeup. The bedroom closet holds a new wardrobe created by Pépé's team. They designed the dresses and outfits for my unique body shape that accentuates my brown hair and dark skin.

All day I've felt lightheaded and detached from the real world. I feel dizzy and can't concentrate. My head feels twice its normal size. More than ever, I feel desperate to run away, but helpless to know how to make that happen.

For forty minutes, I lose myself in my closet to postpone thinking about an escape. Like any girl my age, I stuff my pain and choose clothes over wasted tears. Yes, definitely, the gold-leaf strapless gown and matching high heels. The formal fits me perfectly. My hair hangs in curls down my back.

I'm pleasantly surprised when Pépé DeMolay walks through the front door without a wig or make up, but wearing a traditional black three button single-breasted satin tuxedo. Pépé places a lovely corsage on my wrist and escorts me to the limousine.

The prom is at Hotel Hohenzollern, truly a replica of the castle with glass-stained windows, fortified stone turrets, steeply pointed spires and embattled, aged walls. The original German stronghold rests upon an isolated mountaintop with a bird's eye view of the town Bisingen.

I escape my horrible life, and in my imaginings, I transport myself to the Castle Hohenzollern in Germany. Old Man Winter has been known to postpone a January snowstorm in the Swabian Alps. The cool dense air in the lowlands becomes trapped beneath a layer of clouds. The air above the ghostly fog bank is warmed by the heat of higher elevations, a weather phenomenon or temperature inversion, but to believers—it's magic.

❧

Rare is the new day when the world defies the law of gravity. Like the mysterious mists of Avalon only a few ever witness, Hohenzollern Castle floats weightless in an endless sea of clouds above the ground. The gatekeeper of heaven reaches down and lifts Hohenzollern Castle into the sky and the sunrise promises a supernatural sight from the vantage point of Zeller Horn, an escarpment of limestone rocks.

The illusion of the cloudscape is so very real, it could easily entice an unsuspecting soul to step upon the cloudy gateway to reach the serene Hohenzollern glowing in the sun.

Dawn is a timeless moment when the sun reflects light upon the castle. The walls shimmer autumn yellow and the conical spires are a metallic blue gray. The soft billowy clouds could taste as sweet as flavored cotton candy. Blue, pink and violet.

Pépé DeMolay startles me out of my daydreaming with his sneeze. The black limo stops in front of the busy hotel, which is an enchanting reproduction of the legendary palace. Romance aside, the castle is famous for ghosts haunting the dungeon. This is easy to imagine.

Hidden in the courtyards amidst ornamental foliage are ground foggers that emit a vaporous cloud into the night air. The artificial atmosphere is cold and wet. Truly, Hotel Hohenzollern is the magical Castle in the Clouds.

Pépé takes my hand and guides me into the royal splendor inside. Court's Hall is a palace more suitable for kings and queens than a modest prom. And decorative marble columns support the impressive ribbed vaulted ceiling with its three-tiered chandeliers. The ballroom resembles a neo-gothic church with its elegance and decadence.

Plenty of chaperones supervise the prom and enforce the policy of no drugs, no alcohol and no leaving the premises. GAP will expel candidates who break the rules. Dancing couples glide across a floor of polished Italian marble. To the north side of the ballroom, eight statues of the Holy Roman Empire sovereigns line the wall and to the south stand the Church's Knights in the Bishop's Niche.

Pépé guides me toward a crowded area where couples wait for professional photos. "What do you think?" he asks, with a quirky smile. "The two of us?"

"No way," I reply with a shudder. "Don't press your luck. I'm here under protest, remember?"

Pépé is adorable for someone over thirty. He reaches into his pocket for his phone and grabs me around the waist before I can escape.

"Smile," he says, clicking off several selfies. I grimace in defeat.

Freja Jørgensen poses with Jamil Ahmad. She is wearing a chic white and black embroidered gown. Jenna Slate and Artem Kozlov join them for a foursome shot. Jenna is lovely in a bewitching evil way dressed in a strapless black tulle glittering with silver sequins. The girls do it right and pose, using all the best tips in positioning themselves for the camera. Angle your face, twist and turn, a slight knee bend.

The next couple takes a position for the photographer. The girl does the glitz and glamor and all about me pose with a hand on her hip. In my opinion, plonking a hand on your hip is for old women. Youth is a virtue unto itself. The soul of beauty cannot be measured in time, but with the sober reflection of nature, or so I once wrote in a poem.

We walk into the ballroom amidst couples moving to the fast-paced beat of "Fever," performed by the group Germ over a state of the art sound system.

"It's all about you!" Pépé shouts to make himself heard above the music. "It's a dance off!"

"What?" I shout back.

Pépé throws his hands in the air and laughs. "Mon chéri, get ridiculously happy. Dance like a dervish!"

His breath tickles my ear, but I heard every word. Pépé pulls me into his arms and maneuvers us seamlessly onto the ballroom floor through satin gowns and expressive tuxedos. I laugh aloud, not from the Frenchman's flirtatious smile, but because we are jammed together between hundreds of deliriously excited and twirling couples. I laugh even harder, almost hysterically, as though I am falling off the edge of a precipice. Perhaps I am falling, because my world is breaking apart.

❁

The mass of sweaty teens jumps up and down in funky gyrations to the rhythm of the beat. They really show their personalities using the latest dance steps to dazzle spectators with swirls and twirls in exhibition performances. The ballroom is a blur of motion, and skirts flare and whirl.

Teens are crowded together, bumping and thumping into each other and changing partners while others head outside to refreshment tables for hors d'oeuvres.

Pépé and I stroll across the promenade. He throws his head back and laughs with hilarity. "Dance junkies. All of them." His lips curve into a rather seductive smile. "Are you okay, Jo?"

I nod my head, not trusting myself to speak. My feelings are raw and bruised, and after today's events, I will never be the same person I once was when I lived in Idaho.

"Care for a drink?" Pépé asks without waiting for my reply. He hands me a glass of orange sherbet punch.

The host for the evening is Dr. Charles Babbage who announces Artem Kozlov and Jenna Slate as prom king and queen. Artem escorts Jenna to the stage for the coronation, and then Babbage places crowns upon their heads. They parade through the hall and stand in the spotlight for photos.

I turn away disgusted. All our lives we have been brainwashed to believe in GAP. We've been seduced by virtual realities and modern technologies. No one noticed when the planet warned of disaster. Did anyone care when the governments relinquished control to GAP?

"Will you think me a cad?" Pépé asks with humor in his voice.

"Why?" I ask, confused and not understanding him.

"I must speak with Julius. I'll be back," he says, taking off down the walkway where the two men speak in French and move away from the crowd into the garden.

"I've been looking for you," Juan Pablo says. He leans over and takes the glass from my hand.

Juan Pablo gives me no chance to answer but guides me onto the dance floor. He puts his hands around my waist and pulls me into his embrace. "Was he your date?"

"No, not him," I lie embarrassed. "I don't know this song."

Juan Pablo moves his shoulders and hips to the beat of the song. "Oh, yes. It's easy. Muy fácil." Easy for him. He's an exhibition dancer and wins competitions.

"Fine." I agree reluctantly.

Juan Pablo makes me smile and leads me in the waltz combining it with a fiery Latin salsa. He could make any girl look good dancing. As a new song begins, he starts a soul train Conga line. Hundreds of dancers circle the perimeter of Court's Hall, and their laughter is contagious and spreading to the dancers outside.

The second time around Juan Pablo and I snag Zebenjo and Dev from the alcove where they've been avoiding the train. Wei, Cyrus and Isaac have no problem finding dance partners. Jenna and her bully friends tag along. The body to body, hands on hips Conga chain is a lively celebration for V-team1—except for one.

From the moment I entered Court's Hall, I've been searching for Iain Sinclair. The Conga line disperses, and the crowd parts revealing Iain at the farthest edge of the ballroom, surrounded by a swarm of swooning girls, flirting and batting their eyes. Not the boy for me after all. Besides, I haven't forgiven his betrayal from last night.

According to Julius, the resort at Castle City is safe, so why does my father think I need a bodyguard? Nothing like an overprotective parent to spoil a party. My father doesn't trust me to attend required events and comply with the rules.

A girl snags Juan Pablo and off they go dancing the rumba. Shy, sweet Dev and Mr. Bashful Ben hesitantly approach me. Dev looks good in his blue velvet jacket. Ben is a disaster in his yellow tuxedo with sneakers. My prom date is nowhere to be seen.

Germ's outrageously loud music makes talking impossible. Dev offers me a glass of punch. Ben hands me a napkin. Sad but true. He tries. The throng of dancers glides past. I ignore Iain dancing with a gorgeous blond-haired girl.

When the song ends, Iain leaves his partner and walks toward us.

❖

I laugh outrageously loud at absolutely nothing. Ben stands aside with his hands in his pockets. Couples pair up and dance to Germ's new song "Before I Die," the best slow dance ever written for falling in love.

Iain steps close to me and puts his arm around my waist. Dev and Iain have a personal jinx. At the exact same moment, they place their hands on my bare shoulders, one on the left and one on the right. This could be a problem. Whom do I choose? Right, like who am I kidding?

Dev's features harden into a scowl. His eyes narrow dangerously serious. Dev lifts his chin and straightens his posture going nose to nose with Iain. The three of us can't get closer together when Dev challenges Iain. "Your kind always gets girls into trouble."

Iain ignores Dev's do or die accusation. "Dance with me?" he asks, his breath warm on my face.

I don't want to hurt Dev's feelings. For a moment, I hesitate and a hint of disappointment flashes across Iain's face. I can't resist the longing in his eyes, and I nod and Iain smiles—that heart stopping, endearing smile. He is almost shy when he takes me in his arms, and I forget all about Dev. A warm glow suffuses me from deep within and reaches every part of my body. Dancing with Iain makes me dizzy like riding a roller coaster at high velocities.

No matter how hard I try, I can't stop smiling like an idiot. Iain didn't have to ask me to dance. My father wouldn't dare instruct Iain to dance with me, would he? Iain's touch electrifies me like a hot wire crackling with sparks, and a wild elation surges through me. Think of something else, I tell myself, like computational math. A multicellular computation, or profiles of Clarke's Five Theories. But nothing works. I keep smiling.

Then I take a deep breath. Iain Sinclair smells good. His scent is strong and manly. The last chords of the music fade away, but he holds me a moment longer.

"Walk with me?" he asks, imploring me with his eyes and leading the way to the patio. When no one is looking, we escape and follow a path away from the noise, eluding the guardians who are distracted by other candidates.

❄

Iain takes my hand, and our fingers intertwine. The first time is always the best because beautiful memories like tonight live on forever, especially when the future is uncertain. This is the first time I hold a boy's hand and walk in the moonlight through the fairytale gardens.

Roses, petunias and honeysuckle fill the air with a sweet fragrance. Delicate white lily pads float upon the pond's surface where croaking bullfrogs leap into the water. We follow a secluded walkway. The farther from the castle we stroll, the larger the stars appear in the sky.

The enchantment of this place is like Cinderella falling for her prince. I never thought it could happen to me. But I don't trust myself to speak for fear of sounding stupid. What does one say to impress Mr. Perfect?

"It's good to see you—uh, having fun tonight—with Juan Pablo," Iain says, plainly trying to make amends for last night.

"Spying on me, again?" I ask in a friendly but guarded tone.

"I thought—well, you look nice tonight," he stammers suddenly awkward and unsure. "What did you think I meant?"

"I don't know. It sounded," I pause, not wanting to criticize him, "a little patronizing."

"Sorry. Guess I'm nervous."

"Seriously, I don't buy that," I reply with skepticism, thinking of him dancing with that blond.

"I was late getting here. I'd just arrived when I saw you."

"Really. It didn't look that way. You're very popular with—the girls," I falter lamely.

"Not so. I'm a loner," he says, recovering nicely without admitting anything. He grins with a mischief in his eyes. "I'm better at the Highlander jig, but it's not as much fun as a slow dance."

I change the subject before he can see how much I enjoyed the slow dance. "Where are you taking me?"

"I found a great view overlooking the city where we can watch the fireworks. You looked outstanding at opening ceremonies," Iain says. "Incredible costume. So—you."

I think that was a compliment. "Babbage didn't like it. He emailed my dad. He reported it to headquarters as 'dress to excess.'"

"Aw, don't worry about him. He's a cock-a-hoop."

"A what?"

"A braggart. Too full of himself."

I give my best imitation of a giggle, the way Freja laughed while showing off her hairdo yesterday. Iain glances sideways at me. He draws his eyebrows together. "Is the punch spiked, do ye think?"

"What? I don't think so. Why?"

"You're a bit giddy, not quite yourself."

"Giddy?" I stop and snatch my hand away. "I suppose I am a little off balance. But I wonder why I'm the only one upset—no, shockingly distraught—by the execution."

Iain stares into the darkness, his eyes empty and his face devoid of expression. His voice is more a thick guttural sound than the beautiful cadence of a Scottish accent.

"Babbage's history lesson. And the execution," he repeats.

As though cast in granite, Iain stands like a statue carved from smooth hard stone. The change in him is frightening. But as fast as flipping a light switch, his eyes brighten and his smile returns.

I wish I could ask Iain how he feels about these horrible things, but I don't want to bring up the subject and lose him to that dark place.

"I can't be long," I caution him, walking unhurried. "My date will be wondering where I've gone." I don't mind letting Iain believe he has competition. "Besides, my dad's already peeved at me. But you must know this already since you're 'keeping an eye me.'"

"For fighting in the marts?"

"You heard?"

"Who is your date?"

Oh, he had to ask. Casually, I lift a shoulder. "Pépé DeMolay. Do you know him? He's famous."

"No," he says, a little too quickly. "I don't—he's a designer, right?"

I glance over at Iain out of the corner of my eye. "You're doing that thing with your face."

"Huh?"

"Saying one thing, but thinking something else. Do you know Pépé or not?"

"I don't do anything with my face," Iain protests with indignation.

We stop abruptly letting our hands drop again. Silently, we stare at each other. "You are a very bad liar, Iain Sinclair," I challenge him. "What's so secret about Pépé?"

He rubs his index finger across his left eyebrow. "Did anyone ever tell you that you're rude?" he asks with a crooked smile. But he shakes his head clearly amused and takes my hand squeezing it firmly. "I was thinking he's too old for you."

"No one asked me to prom," I admit. "I almost didn't come."

"I'm glad you did," Iain says tentatively. "Not much time during small talk—to talk." When Iain laughs, he tilts his head down as though embarrassed. Red curls drop forward over his face, not quite hiding his embarrassment. "Too many boys on our team."

We turn another corner and head away from the lily pond. "Tell me about Moray."

"Home? North of Edinburgh on the coast." Iain holds my hand but stops to look at me. "Maybe we could sit down?"

"I like walking." I'm not ready for kissing if that's what he intends.

"Of course, you like walking." He smiles at my guarded expression. "Moray is a wee village, but we're hardworking folk, the labor class."

"Any brothers or sisters?"

"No. My parents died when I was two," he replies in a husky voice. "My uncle raised me. I attended the academy in London, and later I studied abroad."

The charming terrace, though remote, encompasses a panoramic view of Friendship Village. We stop to enjoy the landscaped gardens, the wooded slopes, and the vast dark forest surrounding the city. The magnificence of the lit castles on the hilltops is breathtaking.

The setting is perfect, but not so perfect. I feel tongue tied, and my hands are sweaty. My heart beats out of control. Now what? I say the first thing that pops in my head.

"So what was that cryptography you used yesterday?"

❖

Iain takes a step backward and sits down on a marble bench. He pats the seat as though inviting me to sit down. "My mistake to use it. It's better for me if you stop asking."

"I guess this isn't technically a date," I reply, recalling his words from small talk. I refuse to sit down with him. "What do you consider a date, anyway?"

Iain leaves his place on the bench and takes a few steps toward me. I study him in fascination. He always stands with good posture as though ready for battle. The artificial lamp casts a soft sheen to his thick red hair. Iain's eyes are bright and focused on me.

Only a girl like Jenna falls instantly in love with a boy, but I admit that Iain is legendary. To map his face is to travel to a mythical land of creatures with impish grins and unnatural powers.

"I want to be friends," he replies simply.

"Friends?" I want to be a lot more than a friend. How can I forget Iain's codebreaker sequence or the River? I press him for more, but I feel like I'm skating on ice. "Friends share secrets."

"I suppose."

The competitor in me won't stop until I learn what he knows. "Do you mean I can get the code?"

"Nope," he says. His teasing bores me until he gives me a slightly devilish smile.

I take a deep breath and straighten my shoulders. "Fine, not like I care. What's the big deal?"

Iain removes his bow tie and stuffs it in his side pocket. He unbuttons the collar button of his white shirt. I watch his long-tanned fingers work and wish I hadn't spoken so petulantly. His eyes widen then he smiles shaking his head.

"You're tough for a girl and stubborn," he laughs impressed. "But you should try trusting people once in a while."

"Me trust people? You should talk. You're the one with secrets. Really, I'm not doing this. I've had enough of lies for one night."

I hate it when people preach at me. That's why I'm done with him, or maybe it is the wild pulsing of my heart. It's a long mile back

❄

through the deserted gardens to the prom. I lift the hem of my gown and swiftly turn away and start back to the party. I walk faster, my high heels hitting the pavement as I hurry along the path.

Some distance away, Iain calls out. "Don't go."

The longing in his voice brings me up short. Frozen in my tracks, I wait with my back to him, so he can't read my face. Friendship does not come easy for me, nor does trust. I understand withholding secrets. I've never spoken of my visions. I withhold so much of who I am. It's unfair to judge him, and I should apologize. I twirl around, smack my nose into his chin, and step on his feet.

"Ouch!" he yelps. "Ye smashed my bloody toes."

"Well, why are you sneaking up on me?" I yell back.

"I wasna sneaking," he objects, looking startled by my biting tone. "I told you. I don't sneak or stalk."

"My nose feels twice its size," I cry, my eyes watering with pain. I don't give Iain a chance to examine my nose, but he keeps up with my fast pace.

"You shouldn't walk back alone," he warns soberly.

I stop with my hands on my hips and give him an intense stare. "I'm not alone, am I?" I challenge him with a harsh accusation. "Too many people keep telling me what to do. First my parents, then my teachers, and now you."

"That's not what I meant."

The truth comes to me, and my irritation spills over into anger. "My father put you on Jo-duty tonight, didn't he?" Jolan can be so parental. Once more, I'm disappointed because I thought Iain liked me. "I thought I saw a shortcut back to the pond."

"Want my opinion on the matter?"

"No."

"Okay, but you did take a wrong turn." He shifts sideways trying to hide his amusement.

"Are you laughing at me?"

Iain swipes a hand across his smile. A movement in the bush behind him catches my attention. A black shadow—no, it's a masked

⁂

man—lunges forward and seizes Iain. Without a struggle, he drops to the ground unconscious. I reach out my arms unable to break his fall. A hand grasps my mouth and covers my face with a cloth. A pungent sweet smell fills my nose. Chloroform. Within seconds, pinpoints of starlight blind me. I fall into empty space and find myself in a place of utter darkness, a vile unspeakable pit devoid of light.

CHAPTER NINE

Lest Ye Be Judged

THE KNOCKOUT DRUG they used makes me feel nauseous. A black hood covers my head making it impossible to catch a breath of fresh air, and the rope cuts into my wrists. My bare shoulders scrape against the tree bark as I struggle to free my hands.

"Are ye awake?" Iain asks from somewhere nearby. His breathing is labored, short gasps. "These bindings are tight."

My rage burns like a cauldron of scalding hot water. ""Arghh. I'm going to kill Jenna Slate."

The woods are cold and eerily silent, except for Iain's low grunts and a huff of exasperation. "Whoever did this—it's likely a practical joke."

Whether trying to convince himself or me remains unclear, and the doubt in his voice is unmistakable. The ground is damp where I wrestle against the leaves beneath me.

"She's done this before. At least this time she didn't cut my hair." I hate the quiver in my voice.

"Why do you always think it's about you?" Iain sounds annoyed.

"She's had it out for me for years."

Struggling with the bindings makes them tighter, but my legs are free. I squirm against the rope around my chest and use my thighs to stand up.

"I don't think it was Jenna. I've a theory on that. I think this is my chums from London."

"Oh, chums," I say with sarcasm. "My life isn't so bad. I don't have friends."

Getting angry is the worst thing to do. Keep a cool head, form a plan and take immediate action in case of an attack. Cyber defense is a drill we practice if an intruder breaches our SASS on the Network. A breach never happens, but we practice the protocols.

"They mean no harm," Iain says, but sounding unconvinced.

"Babbage will hang me for breaking curfew. Not to mention my father."

"Work on getting your hands free."

"Dev was right. You are trouble," I reply without thinking.

"Is that your way of not making friends?" Iain's Scottish brogue thickens when he is provoked.

"Sorry, that didn't come out right." I've never been good talking to boys. I fail pathetically. "Don't worry. Tala will bring help."

"How long before they send her?"

"Soon, I hope."

The night air is heavy with the summery scent of pine trees. Even with the hood over my face, I can smell the tangy fresh scent of timber like when raw wood is buzz cut at a lumber mill.

"Got my hands free. They didn't take my watch. We're ten miles from the city."

"You're wearing a Smart watch?"

Iain doesn't answer. I don't like his silence or the rustling of brittle leaves and the snapping of dead branches as Iain moves about. "What do you see?"

"Nothing," he replies. "It's dark, remember?"

The edge in his tone worries me. "I know you are lying."

"The wee pup is asleep."

Would Jenna and her bully friends poison Tala? Jenna would if only to hurt me. "Is she dead?"

"They wouldn't kill her."

"But Tala would kill them. Get me free!" I cry, feeling desperate to examine my dog for injuries.

Iain lifts the hood off my head. He works on the ropes freeing me from the tree. Finally, he gets my hands untied, and the bindings drop to the ground. The dim light outlines Tala's bulky form where she lies unmoving.

My fingers dig into the thick fur around her neck, sticky with blood but not too much. Her pulse is steady, and I feel her warm breath on my skin. Very soon, Tala wakes up, finds her footing, wiggles her body and then wags her fluffy tail.

"How's the ork?" Iain asks, coming back from scouting the area.

"They cut out her chip."

"It's late. No way of knowing."

"Knowing what?"

"If they're hanging around. We need to go, and right now," he says urgently, giving me a hand and pulling me to my feet. "They dropped us at the city's outermost wall."

I often hike during the night. The wilderness surrounding Coeur d' Alene is like my second home. But this isolated forest is spooky, or maybe the threat of masked men frightens me. The distant screech of some creature sounds like a lost spirit screaming forlornly.

The way through the thick woodlands is rough and difficult. The woods are thick with thistle bushes, and we have to break a trail and climb over fallen timber, not an easy task in high heels. I slide my shoes off and throw them to the ground. Iain stoops over to pick them up, but I shrug unconcerned.

"Leave them."

"You're a very strange bird, Jo Peone," Iain laughs. "Not many girls throw off expensive shoes."

"Is that supposed to be a compliment?" The air is so damp and cold I shiver. Gooseflesh ripples across my bare shoulders.

Iain pulls off his velvet jacket. "Take this."

❅

I could lie to Iain with my false bravado and convince him that I'm not cold, walking in thirty-degree temperature while wearing a sheer strapless evening gown. But I don't. I put his coat on and accept his gesture of friendship. Once we reach the road and leave the forest, the road is paved and well lit.

"This vendetta with Jenna—"

"Forget it. Like you said, no sharing secrets until the first date."

"Stop," Iain says, grasping my arm. "Truce, can we talk?"

I lower my eyes to hide my feelings and embarrassment about the fistfight at the marts. "Seriously, this week is insane."

"I know."

I lift my eyes to his face and marvel at his perfect, classical looks, his high forehead, long nose, round flushed cheeks and those full lips.

"Nothing I know is true anymore. I've never been a good citizen. I don't belong here, and Jenna makes it worse."

Iain stands quite tall. His face is solemn, but his words hold no judgment. "Life slips away, ever changing. You never know when it will end. Don't let a stone bruise your heart. Anger does that."

This surprises me. "You're wrong. Anger makes you strong."

"No," he says thoughtfully. "Mindfulness makes you strong."

"How very 'zenish.'"

"Daijo Zen." His frown relaxes into a sympathetic smile. "Stay true to yourself."

"Like how?"

"Keep the clouds behind you. Let the rain showers cleanse you. Keep your eyes free of tears."

"No problem. I never cry."

"No. It means to empty yourself," he stops in midsentence, "*with* crying. Free from illusion. Eyes clear with truth."

"Is this one of your secrets? Mindfulness."

I think Iain genuinely likes me. His eyes convince me that he cares about me. I can't remember ever feeling as high as I do right now.

"It is a key and codebreaker. And yes, absolutely, you do need it to stay focused when using the River."

❄

"Literally? You use mindfulness with the River?"

Iain stares ahead thoughtfully. I sense that he is in touch with invisible things beyond my grasp. "This is about the next dimension. The River will enhance the virtual world in ways you cannot possibly imagine. They do not know I finished the programming. The key will prevent GAP from—"

"From what, Iain?" I blink several times as I've seen Jenna do when she's flirting. I'm intrigued by his inference.

"The mind is a powerful tool. Rage distorts reality. Your vendetta with Jenna. This hate will hurt you, not her. There's a better way."

I can't count how many times I have heard this same ridiculous idea. Hate does make me strong. Suddenly, I feel uncomfortable with Iain's perceptions and his ability to peer into my soul and discern my hidden fears and imaginings, things no one should know about you. A crack in my shell could release my worst imaginings.

"You're a better person than me," I say lightheartedly, pretending indifference to Iain shaming me. "Turning the other cheek. Forgive your enemy. I can't and won't."

"I'm sorry to hear that, Jo. I almost lost myself to hate. You can defeat your enemy without fighting in a dress shop."

"They hit first! What was I supposed to do, roll over and take it?" I slash out, losing my temper and surprising him with my venom. "You heard what she said at lunch. Jenna's the most prejudiced, backbiting, wicked b—"

"Fine. Sorry I said anything," Iain replies disgusted. "I was trying to help you."

"Drop it, Iain. I don't need your help! I'm in enough trouble as it is. I don't want to talk anymore."

And as easy as it formed, our fragile connection breaks. Iain seems just as angry as I feel. These days at Castle City depress me as though an oppressive thunderstorm covers the city. Even as I think this, a fog drops down around us with a faint mist.

By the time we reach our hotel, the coming dawn streaks the pale sky. Tala stays by my side as I walk with wet dripping hair and bare feet

❄

through the foyer. We decide Iain will explain our mishap to my father, especially as Jolan appointed him as my watchdog.

The clock shows five o'clock. Neither of us speaks in the elevator. The doors open and we head down the corridor to the Peone suite. As soon as we enter, the room full of people erupts and absolute mayhem ensures when Tala races across the room. But in midflight, she detours toward Mrs. Thalhammer's mink coat draped across the couch. She leaps in the air, Tala that is, and pounces on the sofa.

The pandemonium escalates when men and women scatter, bouncing off cushions and falling over each other in their haste to evade the orkwolf, growling and tearing the fur to shreds.

The first one out of the dogpile is my mother who sprints like an Olympian runner, giving me a bone-crushing hug and digging her nails into my flesh.

"Mom, I can't breathe."

"When the signal from Tala's chip died, we feared the worst," cries Océane. Her left eyebrow lifts in shock as she looks from me to Iain, and then back to me. "What's happened? Oh no, Jo, you didn't?"

"What do you mean, Mom?" I ask. "What's worse than watching a man beheaded right before prom?" But no one listens to me.

Jolan storms across the room and takes Iain roughly by the arm. "Young man, I told you to keep an eye on her, not to keep her out all night. Where the blazes have you been?"

"Yes, sir," Iain replies, strangely calm and detached. "This wasn't my fault."

Dad grabs the jacket from my shoulders. "And she doesn't need this!" he yells, throwing the soiled coat to the carpet.

Iain's red curly hair is frizzy from the rain and gives the impression that he stands taller than Jolan. "You need to know what's happened at the prom tonight."

"That's right! You'll tell me everything about where you've been with my daughter."

Jolan grasps Iain's arm, marches him outside to the balcony and slams the glass slider shut with a bang. I have never seen my father this upset. I hope he doesn't throw Iain overboard. It's an awfully long drop down from the balcony. Meanwhile, Mrs. Thalhammer fights Tala for the mink coat while two officers look on and laugh.

"Dottie, stop it!" Océane scolds, brushing leaves off my back. She delicately picks a twig from my curls. "Can't you be serious about this?"

Mrs. Thalhammer surrenders her fur coat. "Well, I never. Never, ever imagined Marie would hook up with a boy like that."

"Like what?" I object, brushing aside my mother's hand as she examines the rip in my gown.

"So hairy and tall and manly and..." A patrol officer interrupts whatever else she meant to add.

"Ladies, we're done here." The larger of the two patrols puts his tablet in a side pocket. "Dr. Babbage has our report."

"Well, the missing candidates weren't missing after all," the second officer chuckles. The two men exchange a meaningful look then leave the apartment.

I sigh in frustration. "Babbage, I despise him."

I distance myself from my mother and Mrs. Thalhammer to get a better view of the balcony. Dad is holding Iain by the scuff of his shirt, and Iain struggles to free himself. They shout at each other, mostly Jolan. Iain fights back with heated words.

Whatever Iain yells seems to defuse their argument. Jolan raises his arm as though to strike Iain, but stops in midair like an arctic blast turned him into a living ice sculpture. Iain braces himself for the full force of Jolan's fist, and with erratic gestures and a flushed red face, Iain's pantomimes the kidnapping.

"What's taking them so long?" I ask, watching the two of them move to the far end of the balcony. I wonder if they are plotting how Iain can rehabilitate my rage against Jenna.

"Your father will handle this," Océane replies curtly. "Did Iain hurt you, Jo?"

She pulls me toward a chair, but I refuse to sit down and explain until seeing myself in a mirror. My curls are disheveled with leaves and twigs, my hands black with dirt, and my gown is muddy, the golden luster dulled and the fabric torn in several places. The men remain outside talking longer than it takes to reassure my mother of my chastity. I am cold and a bit forlorn, but nonetheless still virtuous, not even a kiss to end the date.

"We. Were. Ambushed," I shout at the top of my lungs.

Océane's smile freezes as though she's incapacitated by a more immediate threat. Mrs. Thalhammer's jaw hangs open like a dead fish baited and caught. Activated by my emotional outburst and elevated blood pressure, Gladys appears from out of the virtual wall. Her eyes scan me, but she knows better than to intrude and steps away from my ill-tempered scowl.

Jolan and Iain come inside strangely calm after their fierce arguing. The five of us, actually six including Gladys, look at one another with something between dismay and disbelief at the daunting implications of the abduction.

My father's eyes darken to a menacing, velvety brown glare. "Even more reason for Iain to accompany you this week."

"Why?" I scream louder. "Iain is the problem!" I protest, my anger masking fear and panic. "Jenna is jealous of the attention Iain is giving me. She put Artem and Jamil up to this."

"I don't think so." Jolan hesitates and scrutinizes both of us. "Iain, you'll accompany Jo to classes this week. She can't be left on her own."

"Yes, sir," Iain replies, nodding his head. "Jo, I want you to know—"

I do not give Iain a chance to finish. "This makes perfect sense to me. Jenna was behind this," I interrupt. "Don't talk to me, Iain. I'm done with you."

"Enough of this banter," Jolan says, putting his hand on Iain's shoulder. "From now on, Jo, you don't go anywhere without Iain."

I cross my arms and glare. "Julius said we're perfectly safe here. Even you did, Dad. What's up with this Machiavellian drama?"

"That's what I intend to find out," Océane says firmly, lifting her chin and exchanging the look with Jolan. A meaningful look parents give to each other.

"Make sure to include me," Mrs. Thalhammer insists with a pout.

❀

"Right, give me your cell number, so I can throw it away," Gladys teases, perfectly imitating of my sarcasm with her original comeback.

I hold back my own cutting retort until Tala catches my attention. Panting, she lies on the couch, her eyes bright with excitement. The fur coat is shredded. Tala, with her drooling happy dog smile, is the only one eager for day four of Kickoff 2216.

❄

CHAPTER TEN

Death Match

A THLETIC FACILITIES ARE set up throughout the resort at the hotels where teams report for morning practice. Exhibitions begin tomorrow. Three hours later V-team1 is working out at Hotel Coeur d' Alene, and the nine boys train with Grandmaster Hirokazu Yaguchi, 10 Dan Jujitsu. He leads their warmup exercises using high performance specialty mats like those used in the Olympics to protect the boys from injury.

Jenna and Freja watch the boys from the first row of the bleachers. Their conversation is easily heard from the fifth row where I sit alone.

"Is this serious with Artem?" Freja asks gleefully.

"Yeah," Jenna says. "But with eight others, probably only for this week. I danced with Juan Pablo last night." Jenna gawks at the boys. "Let's play a game. Three words for each boy."

"Okay." Freja pulls her hair up into a barrette.

"I'll start with Artem. Hugely good looking and confident."

Freja smiles. "That's four, but I like this. Hey, he's looking at you."

Jenna stands up and whistles. "Yeeow!" she shouts. Laughing, she plops back down. "Your turn. What about Wei?"

"Reserved but gorgeous," Freja says. "Maybe, majestic."

Jenna nods in agreement and the light breeze catches her blond curls. "Zebenjo, nice name. An oddball, but cute and extremely smart."

Clearly aware of the girls, Artem and Jamil keep looking over at the bleachers. All nine, even the reclusive Dev, stand taller with their chests out, strutting around each other like roosters doing the cock-a-walk and ready for a fight.

A young Marine in camo takes a seat beside me. I assume he must be special ops. I've heard about them from Jolan. He fits the profile with short hair and a clean-shaven face, and he holds himself with a stiff posture. I wonder why Marines are attending our practice.

"Do you mind?" he asks courteously.

"Ah, I guess not."

"Lieutenant Kurt Harris."

"I'm Jo."

"Uh huh. Jo, what?"

"Just Jo," I reply tersely.

"What kind of name is Jo for a girl?" he asks, staring at me with a bold, but friendly smile.

"What kind of Marine attends a workout with candidates?" I reply, checking out the bars on his uniform.

"Touché. We've got a ropes course for your team."

"I see that."

"Corporate Warrior. Team building with Marine tactics. Our way of training you in teamwork."

The world's most famous obstacle course Corporate Warrior is at Hotel Coeur d' Alene. There are three gateways with towers mounted upon tipi poles secured at the peak with ropes. Anchored securely to the ground, the poles have notches for hands and feet for a vertical climb. The towers give support to the platforms extending upward.

The three gateways encircle the interior station. A rope bridge on one side connects to the center deck, along with a high beam on the opposite end. Obstacles are at each station. Catwalks, hanging ropes and a tight wire like a circus trapeze bisect the towers and have stations or decks ascending seventy feet in the air. Thirteen high element challenges will test our strength, balance and agility.

Jenna whispers to Freja, and they burst into giggles. "Cyrus, what do you think?" she asks.

"He's easy," Freja says. "He's exotic, even mesmerizing, and he has luscious lips. And his friend Isaac is charming. Shy, but smoking hot."

"Juan Pablo," Jenna says. "Wildly passionate, fun, electric. I love the razor thin scar on his chin." Jenna asks, "What about Jamil?"

"Jamil Ahmad of Sudan," Freja laughs. "You know, we're a couple. Quiet, but a touch of class and smoothly handsome."

"Very nice," Jenna says. "Oh, wow! Look at him and Iain. They're seriously fighting."

"No. That was a jump spin," Freja says. "What about Dev? Shy but drop-dead gorgeous. The complete package. What about Mr. Perfect? Iain is your favorite. I can't believe he snubbed you at the marts."

"Iain Sinclair," Jenna sighs wistfully. "I have plans for him." She laughs and leans over whispering in Freja's ear.

For the moment, Mr. Perfect is wrestling with Jamil. Iain holds him in a stronghold, but Jamil breaks free. He comes after Iain who performs an impressive aerial flip with a handspring, and much faster than Jamil, Iain touches the ground in a graceful controlled landing.

I glance at Kurt who raises his eyebrows and shakes his head with a smirk of amusement on his face. "Got a favorite?"

"Like I'd tell you," I answer. "Any advice on the course?"

"It's what we call O-course. Nothing to it," he replies, patting my shoulder. "Keep your cool, follow safety rules and use the tethers. You'll be fine."

"Your attention, please," Dr. Julius says in a stern tone. "Stay where you are boys. We'll come to you. Girls, to the mats."

Jenna, Freja and I along with Lieutenant Kurt walk over to Julius. The team lines up much like a motley crew, ethnically diverse but of equal prowess. Some are more muscular, others a bit nerdy, but all are ready to meet the challenge and work as a team. Whatever the obstacle, my abilities match theirs. My difficulty is not with strength or agility. Team sports were never my strong suit.

❄

"Captain Jack Donaldson is here to report back to GAP on your teamwork," Julius says, eying the twelve of us with a shrewd wariness and doubt in his eyes.

"POST: Pathways to Optimal Survival Training. That's my job!" Captain Jack speaks in a loud abrasive voice. "To put you through O-course. Make you sweat and puke your guts out!" He leans his whole body toward Zebenjo and glares into the boy's panicky face. The veins in Captain Jack's neck are pulsing.

Half-man and half-lunatic, his face is reddish brown and scarred from years of acne. "You are weak! No better than maggot recruits. If I had you for a week, you'd come out as trained Marines."

"Boomer, get those uniforms over here on the double," Lieutenant Kurt orders, more machine-like than human, and with no trace of the well-mannered Marine.

From behind the bleachers come more Marines, their arms loaded with boxes of uniforms. "The bags are labeled. Find your name, and put these on over your skinsuits," Boomer says, opening the boxes with his knife.

"Protective gear. Heavy duty gloves and boots," Lieutenant Kurt explains. "Keep your harness on. Use those safety ropes."

Captain Jack explains the course while we dress in the camouflage shirts, pants and jackets. "Divide into teams Red, White and Blue. Each team will visit the nine decks with colored flags. Collect your flags, then you exit the course from the top station and zip down. First team down with all flags wins the match."

"Here's what we've got," Lieutenant Kurt says, holding his Smart pad and sliding his finger on the screen. "Red is Isaac, Cyrus, Iain and Jenna. Blue team Freja, Jamil, Juan Pablo and Dev. White Artem, Wei, Ben and Jo." We sort ourselves into the same groups as our small talk teams. This time every member stays and listens to the rules.

"Follow me," Captain Jack says, his voice harsh and his face that of a man who has seen combat and death. He leads the way to the course where we remain standing beneath the center station. Safety nets hang at intervals above our heads.

❊

"Okay, now the obstacles," Kurt continues. "First, scale the vertical wall. Work as a team. Next is the gateway. One gateway for each team will get you into the course. Use those notches to climb the pole to the first deck."

"This shouldn't take even twenty minutes." Captain Jack inspects our uniforms. "Keep those safety lines on. At the last tower, attach the cable to your harness. Once fully ascended, hook into the zip line and dual lanyards. Easy, zip to the ground."

"Wookies, sorry—I mean girls," Lieutenant Kurt says with a grin. "Girls are team captains. Boys follow orders, and you want to guard the wookies. You must find all the flags, or you don't finish the course."

"Girls in charge?" Artem asks in a loud indignant way.

"Not that I mind a girl telling me what to do," Juan Pablo adds, looking over at Jenna. "But what's the point?"

"To knock you alpha males down," Captain Jack shouts, "and keep nonhackers like you in line! No fooling around. I mean it."

"Harsh guy," Juan Pablo says, dropping his chin and annoyed.

Jenna puts her hand on Iain's sweaty face and leans her head on his chest. "I'm in charge of Iain? No complaints here."

Everyone laughs, even Captain Jack, everyone except me. Iain stares down at Jenna with his impish grin. I turn my attention toward the bleachers full of people. Dr. Julius sits with Océane, Jolan and Mrs. Thalhammer. Coaches and parents lend their support to the practice. Hotel guests watch like spectators at a competitive sporting event.

"They claim you are the best," Captain Jack says. "This is a high-level course, but a baby's game for you. It's a simple contest even a third grader can finish."

"Work as a unit," Lieutenant Kurt shouts. "And follow safety rules. Nets will catch you."

"Don't fall." Captain Jack stands with his hands on his hips, his feet squarely apart. "Your team is disqualified if you fall."

Captain Jack and Lieutenant Kurt step away from the course. "This is about teamwork. Let's get going!" Captain Jack yells as if he would take pleasure in watching us fail the course.

❈

The groups take position at the three different gateways. The first obstacle is the twenty-foot vertical wall.

"Ready. Set. Go!" Captain Jack shouts.

"Up the wall," Wei yells. "Quick, let's do this!"

The three boys are excellent big wall climbers. Wei and Ben give Artem a lift, and he scales the wall in seconds. He lies flat on the deck and reaches down to help lift Ben up.

Wei cups his hands for me to use as a step to climb the wall to the platform above where the boys grab my hands and pull me up. Wei follows behind me in no time. The white flag is tied to a rope. I snatch it and fasten it to my belt.

"Time to climb," I shout, standing beneath the apex of the three poles and letting Ben go first.

"Can you get this?" Ben asks me.

"Yeah, Ben!" I reply impatiently. "Stop talking so much. Get going, now!" I wait for Zebenjo and follow behind him up the vertical pole. Wei gives me another white flag.

"The others are way ahead of us," Artem whines.

"Forget them," Wei says irritated. "Work the course."

"Artem, you're too slow. Move faster," I shout, my breath coming in fast heavy gulps.

Even though it is early, the sun beats down on us. My skinsuit shimmers in the sunlight. I clasp the hanging line in my gloved hands and climb upward. The rope swings slightly rocking me back and forth. Hand over hand ascent is difficult. The strength of my forearms helps ease the strain. I reach out and touch the deck. Wei helps me up the last few feet.

"Thanks, Wei. You're almost here, Ben," I yell. "Don't look down."

Ben looks down at the Marines beneath him as Wei grabs the rope and pulls him onto the deck. We have finally reached level two.

"Take the rope bridge," Wei says to Ben. "Hang on. Take your time."

Blue and Red teams have found their flags and already have left the center station where they've easily crossed the high beam back at their pole towers. They sprint rapidly toward climbing walls to make

❇

the ascent to level three.

We make sure to secure the lines and start across the suspension bridge, bouncing up and down and nearly falling into the nets below. Finally, we reach the deck in the middle of the course. A white flag should be here. From above at level three, Jenna and Freja are laughing and waving the white flags they have stolen.

Red and Blue have combined forces against us. How predictable of Jenna Slate and Freja with their boy toys. They got all their flags and stole ours. No way can we win.

"Our flags!" Ben wails. "They're way ahead."

"We've got to get them back from Jenna!" I yell. "Artem, you're too slow."

"So what?" he shouts. "What's the big deal?"

"We'll get them!" Wei agrees. "Get to the balance beam. We'll cut them off before they zip down."

"Not too fast," Ben cautions.

The safety net below swings in the breeze. Carefully, he steps with an exaggerated movement on the beam. He starts to lose his balance, but then at the last moment catches himself and lands on the platform.

"Ropes or wall?" Ben asks.

"Ropes," Wei says, reaching out and snagging one.

"No, the wall," I object, locking the safety rope onto my harness.

They start up the ropes, not following my lead. I should stay with my team, but I am faster on the wall. Climbing is second nature. My experience with heights and mountaineering gives me an advantage. I scale the wall although I follow Ben's advice, taking care to place my hands and feet without rushing.

Wei and Ben, however, fall prey to Blue and Red teams. The other boys used the hanging ropes to descend from the tower to the south. They backtracked to catch White team from behind. Now, all the boys are pushing and fighting. Wei and Ben are trapped in the middle of a mass of bodies. Artem has disappeared.

What's happened to the ropes course? The race is more like a battle. The enemy violated the rules of engagement and cheats to win.

❄

Overall, Jenna Slate has managed to undermine the practice. She and Freja ordered their teams to gang up against us. Why would Iain and Dev go along with her? Following orders and chain of command, I guess. No way can my White team finish the course, much less win.

Artem betrayed us and now fights against his teammates. Ben and Wei struggle against Red and Blue teams. Artem hits Ben in the face, but Ben retaliates swinging a wild punch. He misses and then charges Artem, which causes them to fall off the platform, and they both land squarely in the safety net.

Cyrus and Isaac try to knock out Wei who captures Isaac's GoBot cap and flings it into the air. Wei shoves his attackers with brutal force. Cyrus and Isaac tumble in the bouncing net, dog piling on top of both Artem and Ben.

"All stop! Get off that course!" Captain Jack yells at the top of his voice. "Get down here now!"

Having conquered the highest deck, Freja and Jenna have not seen me, but watch from their vantage point laughing at the antics below them. I strain my muscles, pulling myself up the climbing wall and onto the flat surface of the platform, briefly stopping breathless from exertion, adrenaline pumping and sweat pouring off my face. Jenna and Freja are too distracted to notice me.

Does Jenna want to disgrace me and make me look weak? What a hypocrite. I tremble with rage, thinking about last night—Jenna and her gang attacking Iain and me and dumping us in the woods. This is supposed to be about teamwork and a game of flags. But it's not. It's all about Jenna and me.

Jenna turns around and laughs. "Hey, peon, did you ever think about plucking your eyebrows?" she asks in a vicious sort of way.

"Hey, Barbie. I heard Iain snubbed you," I reply in a biting tone, grinding my teeth and ready to draw blood.

"You're such a little girl."

"Deadhead dumb blond!"

"Hey, Freja? Jo-Jo lost more than her shoes last night." Did she hack the security report filed last night? She couldn't know about my

❖

shoes unless she followed us out of the woods.

Jenna's laughter makes my blood boil with a combustible hate like Greek fire ignited by water. Only sand can squelch the flames. Now is my chance to pound my fists into Jenna's face and pay her back for cutting my hair five years ago in Coeur d' Alene.

And I do not like the way she touches Iain. The need for revenge is strong. I am going to knock Jenna Slate off her princess pedestal. Two against one, a showdown.

"I hate you! You're an idiot!" I yell. "I hate you."

"Whatcha gonna do?" she taunts.

I scream at the top of my voice a wild, insane screech and charge Jenna with the full force of my weight. I plow into her like a wrecking ball. The momentum knocks her off balance. We fall over each other onto the platform.

Jenna is stunned but then quick to react. And so it begins, the hair pulling, clothes tearing and nails digging into flesh. I roll away and get to my feet, catching my breath and wiping sweat from my eyes.

"You wookies. Get down here. On the double!"

That's Lieutenant Kurt running toward a gateway and climbing the pole. Freja jumps to one side. The fight is too blood and guts for her. She heads to the outer deck and zips to the ground.

"What are you doing?" Lieutenant Kurt is fast, making it to the second level and starting up the climbing wall.

"Let's go!" Iain shouts. "Jo needs help!"

Iain sprints and grabs a rope, but Jamil pulls his legs, keeping him from climbing. Iain hits the deck then leaps up and punches Jamil in the face. Wei and Dev try to climb the ropes to the third level. But Juan Pablo goes after them. In the struggle, Dev and Juan fall into the lattice, bouncing up and down, a jumble of bodies in the netting.

Dr. Julius and Jolan shout at Captain Jack demanding he stop the fight. Their words are lost in the pounding of my head. Bad choices get a lecture. What will they do about a fight? Right now, I don't care. I have to beat Jenna in this match.

Not many candidates are trained in the way of Wushu. I brace my

❄

arm like a weapon hitting Jenna's mouth and knocking her down. She bounces back to her feet and spits, and then she charges me. I smile and ram her with my shoulder. We match blow for blow, except she has an edge, a way of sidestepping and brushing me off. She tosses me aside like a rag doll. I hit the pole with a bruising blow to my back and lie unmoving on the steel deck.

I know better than to unhook the safety latch, but I do. The rope is secure, but the knot is slack enough to give me the length I need to reach Jenna. I can hit her from behind. She flies face down and hits the deck. Round and round we roll until her hands press against my throat, then she ties a rope tight around my hands.

"I'm done with you!" she yells, kicking me. "Stay down, Peone!"

Disgusted Jenna looks down at me and then moves toward the zip line. *What is this girl's problem? Now, she wants to wimp out?* Her words are not so bad, but not the words for making peace. Hate has a way of twisting small offenses into acts of cruelty.

The fight should have ended here, but I won't let it stop. I want to kill her with my own bare hands. This is a death match. But ropes get tangled. Accidents happen. Anything can happen without warning with everything coming at you all at once like a nightmarish blur. One decision can have irreversible consequences.

I free my hands and lunge head first into a full run but lose my footing. Before I know it, my boot is tangled in a pile of ropes causing me to trip and roll sideways. I flip upside down and off the platform into a free fall, plummeting headfirst into empty space with the ropes.

One rope catches my leg. Another one tightens around my neck like a noose. I swing toward the platform, and my head slams against the side of the tower. Pain reverberates with a brutal jolt to my neck and back. I manage to untangle my head, but my leg is still caught in the rope. The upside-down angle gives me a view of the horror on Jenna's face. She tries to help me, but the rope is too far away to reach.

My mind is spinning out of control. How long has it been? It feels like seconds, not minutes since the practice began. The seconds keep ticking like the beat of my heart—tick tock, tick tock. The ringing in

❧

my ears is deafening.

Surely, I must look like a performing monkey in a circus act. The people below watch helplessly as I dangle in space. I gasp for air panicky for a moment until I can flip right side up. Lieutenant Kurt pushes Jenna aside. His lips are moving, but his words make no sense. Iain leans over the edge of the platform trying to grab the rope but fails. He climbs over the railing, but his outreached hand is too far away for me to touch.

Instinctively, my mountaineering skills kick in. My dad taught me to be brave and trained me how to survive in the wilderness. Images flash before my eyes of Jolan talking me through a free fall like this. A practice free fall when I felt so exposed. I hated him for a long time.

Now his words save me. *Be in the moment. One hand, two hands. Keep working the rope. You're strong. You can do this.* I know how to handle a free fall. Rope up, tie in, now climb. The rope becomes my lifeline. My hands reach up and take hold.

This little bit of slack relieves the agony from my leg. I can finally move. Hand over hand, I gain more slack rope. My muscles strain with the weight of my body, my arms almost ripped from their sockets. Inch by inch, I manage to raise myself up. I gain enough ascent to give me momentum and swing to the closest station. Lieutenant Kurt pulls me onto the deck. I land squarely on two feet and go completely weak in the knees and collapse. An emotional release overwhelms me.

I'm alive.

CHAPTER ELEVEN

Squishy Fishy

"**I**'M GOING TO KILL HER!" I scream, clenching my injured leg and pounding my fist into the deck.

Jenna's concern gives way to worry. "It's not my fault," she whines agitated. "I didn't do anything. It was an accident!"

"Jenna, get down the zip!" Lieutenant Kurt shouts.

Wei's left eye is swollen shut, but he gives me an encouraging nod. He takes Jenna by the arm and gets her to the other end of the deck.

Lieutenant Kurt takes off the heavy black boot and sock from my left foot. He probes my calf and ankle. "Where does it hurt?"

"Does pride count?" I ask, trying to rise to my feet without much success.

"Whoa, not so fast," he says. "We're going to take it slow and easy."

"Are ye in pain, Jo?" Iain asks in a thick brogue. He rarely sounds Scottish unless something upsets him.

"Nothing is broken, and your skinsuit saved you from any burns," Lieutenant Kurt says. "Some swelling. Ice and acetaminophen will help, and you'll be fine." Kurt stands and helps me up. "Iain, let's get her to the zip line."

By the time, we sail down and land, the area is clear of spectators.

Guardians and patrol officers ushered guests and parents away from the bleachers. The other boys are bruised and battered, and medics disinfect and bandage their cuts. Unscratched Jenna and Artem along with Freja and Jamil wait for the rest of us.

Captain Jack talks with Dr. Julius out of earshot. Obviously, the team failed the Warrior course. Looks like Jo Peone is not the only rule breaker. Apparently, my teammates are rebels too. They broke the chain of command.

Iain betrayed Jenna. Artem betrayed me. We all went our separate ways fighting like banshees. The practice is a disaster. Teamwork is too complex for us. Not only did we fail, but also we violated GAP's code of conduct.

"Drink this," Ben says, handing me a water bottle. Ben doesn't say much when he is nervous or scared.

"Thanks, Zebenjo."

The water is cool and refreshing. I empty the bottle, and Dev hands me a Vitajuice. Dev gives me a timid smile and steps aside. He and the other boys hover a few feet away listening to the outcome of the med exam.

"Some soreness today." The medic puts away his medical scanner. "You're lucky. I heard you almost hung yourself."

Lieutenant Kurt puts the sock back on my foot. "Not bad for a girl. You're tough."

Scowling Iain takes the place of the medic by my side. "Aye, but a girl shouldna be fighting." He has a bloody nose and a bruised cheek. But he holds tight to my hand. "I should get you home."

"No one is going anywhere," Julius says squatting down beside me, his eyes intensely brown and vulnerable. "How are you feeling?"

"Very tired," I reply.

"Not surprising with no sleep last night. Did you bother to eat breakfast?" Julius asks.

"Where are my parents?"

"Parents were dismissed. I told Jolan that I'd take care of you." For being only twenty years old, Julius engenders trust and knows how to take command. I feel sure he can make things right for our team.

"I'm out of breath," I sigh, leaning against Iain for support.

"That's normal after the course. Well, especially the way you did the course," says Lieutenant Kurt smiling. "Breathe deep and relax."

How does one relax with three unbelievably cool boys attentive to your every whim? I watch Iain, Julius and Lieutenant Kurt worry over me and feel quite pleased with the outcome of the Warrior course. Iain raises his eyebrows and gives me a quizzical look with those beautiful hazel eyes.

"Feeling better, are ye?" he asks, a knowing glint in his eyes.

"Well, Jo, you're smiling." Dr. Julius clears his throat. "Good to see. Now, the bad news. The rest of you gather round and pay attention."

Captain Jack takes over from Dr. Julius. Never before have I seen someone's face flame beet red like his does when he shouts reprimands at us practically spitting each word as he speaks.

"Losers! The worst I've ever seen. No discipline. No training. Not a shred of teamwork. Lose control like that in combat, you're dead." The white of his eyes roll back in his head like a crazed horse. I wonder what keeps his eyeballs from popping out.

"I'm glad they're your losers, not mine!" Captain Jack gives Julius a disgusted scowl. "Let's go, Marines."

"See ya, Jo," Lieutenant Kurt says. "Take care, Iain."

Julius crosses his arms and stares at us in dismay. His demeanor may be refined and not like Captain Jack's, but his words are just as scathing.

"The contest wasn't about physical prowess though I'm sure you believe this is your finest ability," he says sarcastically, "Kicking the beejeebus out of each other." Beejeebus is old-fashioned slang for beat the crap out of each other.

"Teamwork was the test, not your physical strength." His words hang in the air just barely out of reach. Team is the simplest concept but one which eludes us. I recall Babbage's lecture.

"Marie-Joelle, what was Dr. Babbage's directive?"

I hate it when my face is so transparent, but I'm pleased that Julius recognizes my willingness to make amends. "The success of a team," I recite, "relies on 'individual responsibility, communication, chain of command and teamwork.'" I repeat the words slowly, feeling ashamed of myself for my rampage.

"You have failed to exhibit your better-than-average intellect." Dr. Julius is definitely talking down his nose. "They tolerate your—your bad behavior because—you won Medallion Pins, and your projects are vitally important. However, they want you trained as a team." He emphasizes team with a hint of condescension. "You will behave! Forced together, you will achieve team spirit."

The rebukes don't stop there. Julius reviews our infractions so far. Fighting at the marts. Ditching honors class. He looks directly at me, but I don't dare correct him. He scolds me out for the "dress to excess" violation and my entrance on the red, white, black and pale horses which is Pépé's fault, not mine. No one has explained the misconduct, but I know it must be significant. Julius makes sure everyone knows about the incident in the woods with Iain and me.

But his reproaches get worse. Upon investigation, they found no evidence of our kidnapping nor uncovered the identities of the assailants. No discarded ropes were found in the woods, and there was no sign of struggle. They did not find my discarded high heels or a broken path through the bushes, not even a single leaf disturbed.

Not that it matters, but Dr. Julius also shames Jenna, Artem, Freja and Jamil. Iain and I were not the only ones to leave the prom and stay out all night, which proves Jenna was behind the ambush. At least as a team, we are all losers. The most intelligent, gifted and athletically superior losers on the planet.

✳

"I AM SO HAPPY! Your team is failing. But you, Marie, were rated with a 10+ for your overall success as a candidate," Mrs. Thalhammer says with glee. "Well, I guess you're not the only candidate—um, with serious problems." Mrs. T nibbles her second custard pastry topped with raspberry jam and reaches for a third.

I take some comfort that Mrs. T is predictable and her costumes befitting of Kickoff. Her stylish frock of toffee brown swirls as she moves. The décolletage of the dress displays her white cream puffs with a plunging neckline, the newest peekaboo-look. Weaved into her curls are multicolored hair extensions. The white fluffy headdress is more like the meringue topping on a pie than a hat.

This morning's death match is a public humiliation. I agonize over my bad behavior and blame myself for losing control. I feel mortified that Iain witnessed my fury, and I blame it on the stress of Kickoff. I feel no pleasure from rewards given to candidates. I believe the purpose of this week is to indoctrinate us.

However, life is not totally depressing. Mrs. T's outrageous outfit is ridiculous enough to brighten my mood. Tala drools while waiting for scraps from her plate. But the atmosphere in the suite vibrates with something intangible like the fear right after an earthquake registering ten on the Richter scale.

Nothing can stop the aftershocks, and you wonder if this is a precursor to the big one. The Peone apartment is emotionally charged. The anticipation extreme. What punishment will my parents give me, or worse what will Dr. Babbage do?

Jolan and Océane sit together at the table and speak in low voices. Jolan is attentive and holds Mom's hand. I cannot remember the last time I saw them this affectionate.

Something is happening. I am convinced my father has undergone a change in personality. He's been sober all week and his handsome features no longer look worried, and he exudes a restrained elation. Is he planning a reconciliation with Océane? But surely, they wouldn't keep such exciting news from me.

Piled high on platters are desserts of every kind. I help myself to a flaky pastry and stuff large chunks in my mouth. The puffball melts like cotton candy, creamy and thick. Sweet and delicious. Eating helps my downer mood.

I don't understand my life. The "why" of everything. The other candidates seem unfazed by the horrors of the week. I do not belong, and I don't understand why. The fish bowl is too small, and I am not a happy, perky fish like other kids my age. I swim erratically against the glass. Beating up Jenna Slate only led to my leg injury. I wish I were anyone, but me.

I have thought about Iain's word "mindfulness." It means trusting yourself. My new mantra is to relax and breathe. Breathe in the silence. I have an acronym for SILENCE: Stop, Inhale, Listen, Exhale, Now Calmly Express. *Mindfulness*, I whisper to myself.

A knock at the door prevents further exploration of all the "whys" of the universe, or better known as Jo, the Goldfish Enigma. Mrs. Thalhammer rushes to the entry hall as though expecting guests.

Julius enters the suite with a light step to his gait. "Bonjour."

No surprise that Julius has come to punish me. What surprises me is Pépé DeMolay. Why is he here? The two men find a place beside Jolan. Océane serves cups of flavored cappuccino and plates of dessert.

Julius looks relaxed despite his earlier rave-off at our team, the flunky failing losers, and Pépé as usual looks entertained by his own theatrical flair. Quite the family affair. Gladys appears out of the wall and hovers in the corner. We make eye contact, and she winks at me. I feel guilty that I haven't had time for Gladys or to surf the Network, or even check my SASS.

"Charles Babbage, the old snake, refuses to take any of my calls," Jolan says solemnly. "What do we know?"

❄

"They blame the migraines for her episode this morning," Julius says. "Dr. Oppenheimer will be here shortly."

Everyone looks at me for an explanation. I bite the inside of my mouth resisting the urge to speak. Lieutenant Kurt told me, *Keep cool. Breathe, relax. Breathe in mindfulness.* It works! I manage to keep my big trap shut. Besides, I'm very experienced with stuffing my emotions down behind a granite wall.

"Babbage loved Pépé's creation for opening ceremonies," Julius says calmly. "He is concerned; however, the costume was excessive. I've convinced him of Jo's innocence, particularly since Pépé—well, you are famous for your flamboyance."

Pépé smiles and places another fluffy pastry onto his plate. "Merci beaucoup, my friend."

"I told you—it was too extreme!" Jolan accuses Pépé. "But would you listen? No, it had to be your way!"

Pépé casually lifts his coffee cup to his lips and leisurely sips. "It was perfect," he exclaims with triumph.

"Don't blame Pépé!" Mrs. T wipes raspberry jam from her mouth. "I take full credit. I told him to design that outstanding costume."

Pépé chokes and sputters his coffee all over the tablecloth. He stares at Mrs. Thalhammer as though she has lost her mind. "Exactly what I had intended," Pépé manages to say, "and the plan is working."

Apparently, both Pépé and Mrs. Thalhammer want GAP officials to notice me and to approve their special privileges. Mrs. Thalhammer wants a promotion, but I wonder what Pépé wants.

"Enough with the outrageous costumes!" Jolan shouts disgusted. "Cover yourself up, Dottie."

Océane looks doubtfully from Jolan to Julius. "Did you actually place Jo and Jenna on the same team? Jolan, are you using her for this?" she asks hatefully. "This fight, Julius, you let it happen! First in the marts. Now, this morning!"

"I—no! I had nothing to do with it. You know GAP decides the team," Julius protests, regaining his composure with a confident lift of his chin. "I would never jeopardize..."

❧

"How could you, Jo?" Océane asks, clearly disappointed with me. Her blue eyes shimmer with tears. "Next time, use your head, not your fists! You are endangering our family and putting at risk everything we've put together..."

"Let's not go there, shall we?" Julius asks, serving himself a pastry with extra custard and jam. "One problem at a time." Julius avoids looking at me, which is unlike his customary directness.

"I agree. Julius is right," Jolan says with a shrewd lift of his eyebrow. "We have more pressing issues. Babbage was impressed by a podcast he watched of her Beethoven performance."

"What?" Océane asks. Her face is flushed, and her eyes sparkle. "Won't she perform live this week?" she asks, so angry she throws her napkin down on the table.

"But that's wonderful, isn't it?" Mrs. Thalhammer asks, visibly confused and unsettled by the conversation. "Is this typical?"

Gladys leaves her place in the corner and drops her comment casually into the conversation. "Babbage is running security protocols on Jo's SASS computing."

"So what?" Pépé asks unconcerned. "We're all subject to security checks. She has nothing to hide, do you?"

"Of course not!" Gladys says in a harsh tone. She composes herself, puts her hands on her hips and holds everyone's attention. "I monitor those files myself and I prevent Jo from hacking." While technically true, there are ways to hack without her knowing.

Mrs. Thalhammer stands up and paces the room. "Oh, my. This is bad. Oh, no—no—no!" she stutters.

"No, she won't perform live," Julius continues. "It doesn't matter. The priority is a team exhibition."

"No, not the team!" Mrs. Thalhammer objects. "I'll file a petition. Jo must perform her concerto. I want her to shine, so they know I trained her. I deserve my promotion!"

Gladys nods her head and grins. "There you go again! I told you so. The team—"

"Oh, shut up, you hot beam of light!" Mrs. T yells. Her white fluffy hat falls to the carpet. Tala snatches it up and races to the couch.

"Enough, Gladys!" Océane screeches. "Deactivate AI."

This is such an interesting conversation with five adults lecturing me as though I am invisible, yet they don't ask for an apology for this morning. Instead, they argue with each other, but I sense the tension between them is from their fear of GAP.

Jolan leans forward and pours himself a glass of mineral water. He takes a long swallow before putting the glass down. "Dottie, take a break."

"Getting rid of me?" she asks insulted.

"Yes." Jolan and Océane speak in unison.

Mrs. Thalhammer looks across the room at Tala with white fluffy feathers in her mouth. "I'm going shopping!" she squeals, huffing and puffing her way to the door.

As she leaves the suite, Dr. Oppenheimer enters and shakes hands with my father. "Jolan Peone, pleased to meet you."

An elderly man in his fifties, Dr. Oppenheimer exudes a healthy countenance with a rose blush to his cheeks. His fair complexion is smooth, almost artificial, without wrinkles or imperfections. "This must be the candidate," he says. "Do you understand why I'm here?"

"I think so. Can you cure my migraines?"

"Migraines? Didn't you get her treatment?" he asks my parents in an accusatory tone.

"For the past five years," Jolan says with impatience, "her AURA Gladys has treated her migraines. We had them under control before today. These are unusual circumstances that triggered her behavior."

The doctor ignores Jolan's antagonistic tone. "Migraines are very rare. Tell me what happened."

"Twice in my life I got conked on the head." I describe the fight at the marts and the concussion I suffered five years ago at Castle Coeur d' Alene.

Dr. Oppenheimer starts a virtual session and accesses my medical files. He takes my hand and places a bracelet around my left wrist. The Smart band monitors my vital signs and interacts with my chip. The

❄

screen displays my pulse, blood pressure and temperature and captures data on vital organs and physiological and neurological systems. A 3D holotype module gives the test results.

"Update and hold for data input." He speaks into the computer. "Any flashes of light? Disorientation?"

"Yes, I saw red just before I punched Jenna in the nose."

The adults laugh. However, I wasn't joking. The light was ethereal, not metaphoric, and it lasted only a moment. Occasionally, my visions impart intuitive knowledge. But I do not elaborate on these facts.

"Tell me about the disorientation?" the doctor asks.

"All day yesterday, I felt like I was in a dream."

"Describe it."

I speak with as much loathing as I can. "Well, that history lesson. Watching people on fire makes me wish I was dreaming." I blink away tears and drain my cup of herbal tea.

"Make a note," he says into the console. "Multi-sensory stimuli led to migraines. Maybe other triggers. We need to schedule tests."

"I'll schedule them," Jolan promises. "Her mother monitors the migraines."

"Report to me when those tests are done." Dr. Oppenheimer sits down and speaks into his I-Doc device. "A bit lethargic, no serious malady. No adrenal fatigue, which is good. Other than the headaches, you are a perfectly normal, young woman. Many candidates complain of these symptoms. See these results?"

disorientation and mild confusion
difficulty waking up
acute stress disorder
fairly common with prolonged stress

He takes a small package from his bag. Inside are two small round adhesive Band-Aids matching my skin tone. "These patches will get absorbed and suppress the migraines," Dr. Oppenheimer says. "Likely you'll experience residual symptoms, but nominal." He places the cool

❋

patches on my temples. "This may affect your brain chemistry. You might be emotional for a while. Call me if you have concerns."

Julius waits for the doctor to leave before giving us the very bad news. "The team is in trouble," he says. "The ropes course—what a fiasco. They've ordered the team to perform a compulsory dance."

"That's good. High impact and interactive," Jolan says. "A physical contact sport. Good, I like it."

Julius finishes the pastry and lifts his hand to take another. Instead, he drinks from an expensive porcelain cup, taking a mouthful of freshly brewed coffee. He clears his throat, but then he hesitates. "I'm concerned about Jo..." he pauses, sounding unsure of himself.

"It can't be all that bad," Pépé says lightly. "Out with it."

"Babbage and that melodramatic soliloquy, and the execution was stress inducing. Her moods," Julius falters, refusing to look at me.

"She's fine," Océane says, her blue eyes brilliant with intensity. "Marie-Joëlle is strong, and comes from a lineage of pureblood, as you well know, Julius!"

"Jo has a mission," Jolan says, almost in reverence. "To protect the innocent. Our ancestors speak of the Spiritkeepers." He speaks to me in a solemn tone. "We inherit all that we are. You have a gift, Marie. Your science and medicine will heal millions for generations to come."

For a few minutes, silence reigns. Yes, by now everyone is mindful of things felt but unseen. Océane's hostility toward Julius mystifies me. She clearly thinks he is judging her parenting, or is it my moodiness that worries them? Jolan is particularly antagonistic with Pépé.

"It's time you know," Pépé begins. "You have a patron, San Manuel Bueno. He meant to be here to explain things. He sends his apologies."

Neither Julius nor my parents offer to explain what it means to have a patron. "So like him," Jolan speaks with disdain. "Yes, he's your patron, but I am your father!"

Pépé straightens his shoulders and taps his fingers on the tabletop. "He has no interest in replacing you, Jolan. He wants Jo to have the best opportunities..."

"As you know," Jolan says, looking at me and ignoring Pépé, "the

❦

law requires DNA samples at birth."

"To monitor health," Océane cries softly.

"We can't protect Marie-Joelle from the truth. It's best to tell her that GAP tags citizens, even the elite. Now she knows," Jolan says. "We are born privileged because of our DNA. You know this from your studies. Our DNA is disease-free. That's why we never get sick. The same holds true for all upper-class citizens and candidates."

"The world needs our DNA," Julius says. "To ensure our survival and fight Superbugs resistant to antibiotics. A side effect of DNA splicing is an imbalance of testosterone. Tendencies for aggression in boys and girls. Hence, the erratic fighting this morning. Discipline masters aggression. But you are the first candidate with migraines."

"They also..." Jolan pauses, visibly trying to control his emotions. "Corporations will invest in your discoveries, and they've secured an interest in your research. They own our DNA. In a way, they own us."

"You've asked about those living in the Outlands," Julius says, but his voice sounds robotic. I've heard his rehearsed speech earlier in the week. "GAP cures disease."

Jolan slides his chair next to me. He takes my hand and forces me to meet his piercing dark eyes. "The sick receive treatment. They don't come back. Don't ever ask why."

I learn nothing new from my parents. No special revelation I did not already suspect about DNA and corporations. They hold an interest in my future projects. However, what did they mean by a "lineage of pureblood?"

The Salish is an ancient tribe. Ours is an oral history preserved through storytelling. I've never heard of Spiritkeepers, but this might explain my visions. Visions I have never understood.

"Stop this vendetta with Jenna Slate," Océane pleads. "Calm down! It's that simple."

"You're jeopardizing more than you know," Pépé says, stern for the first time.

"You're better than Jenna," Jolan exhorts. "Stay clear of her."

"Jo, you're to be the recipient of the International Medal of Arts,"

Julius announces unexpectedly. "You will be dining with Babbage this evening."

"I should go with her," Océane says worried.

Jolan pats my hand with a skeptical lift of his brow. "He's an old dried up snake in the grass. But Jo can handle him."

Has this been their rage intervention? My gut aches. I writhe in pain. Overwhelmed and confused, I feel flat as though someone took me out of the fish bowl and squished me. Dinner with Dr. Babbage absolutely terrifies me.

"Have you nothing to say, my dear?" Julius asks, placing his hand gently on my shoulder and looking intently into my eyes.

Perhaps it is the stress of the day, or a delayed reaction to Babbage's history lesson and the execution. I only wish I had not eaten all those raspberry pastries.

"I feel sick," I groan weakly.

Sometimes it just feels good to spill your guts and tell your parents how you feel, except I don't know what I feel. With nothing to say, I lean forward and puke an endless stream of red vomit into the most expensive plate in the world—Limoges, a French porcelain design.

PART II

The Predators

CHAPTER TWELVE

Fool's Gold

A LIMOUSINE DRIVES to the Hotel Prague where a guardian escorts me to the private residence of Archbishop Dr. Charles Babbage. The hotel is a recreation of the Old Royal Palace, one of four in the real complex located in the Czech Republic. Prague Castle is like a small municipality and the largest ancient castle in the world.

Dr. Babbage lightly kisses the back of my hand in a courtly gesture. "Good evening, Miss Peone." His deep, sultry voice lacks an accent or any inflection. "Welcome to Vladislav Hall."

I'm unsure how to address the Archbishop, so I mimic his somber monotone. "Good evening."

Tonight, Dr. Babbage wears an olive-green tuxedo that fits as tight as a shrink-wrapped second skin. Dr. Babbage is gangly and slender yet intimidating with his upright posture and aloof composure. His thin hair is a rich honey brown streaked with gray, and his complexion is unnaturally pale though not sickly. His demeanor lacks any emotion.

Dr. Babbage offers me his arm with imposing etiquette. His bony fingers grasp mine as he places my hand on his forearm. His touch is cold, and his pale skin is dry, almost glassy white and colorless. I fight the temptation to snatch my hand back.

The jewel of Prague Castle is the stately Vladislav Hall, the throne room where once coronations, celebrations and assemblies took place. The reproduction is exquisite. The late Gothic motif dominates the hall with a rib-vaulted ceiling. The spectacular pattern forms a star shape. The castle in the city of Prague is home to kings and queens who rule in 2216 with no authority over their jurisdiction, but under the heavy hand of GAP. The royal families around the world are only figureheads to their citizens.

Dr. Babbage waves his arm in a wide semicircle encompassing the replica of Vladislav Hall. His attitude is one of extreme superiority.

"This is your future," he declares. "Castle City is a vacation resort for executives and an amusement park for candidates along with their families. Really, it pales in comparison to the authentic castles you will visit as a freshman."

The banquet hall is a place of classical antiquity. Fine art depicting religious motifs adorns the walls. Marble statues of deities and popes beautify the corners and alcoves. Royal red wallpaper holds intricate patterns of gold inlay lettering. The crystal chandeliers illuminate the spacious surroundings. Gold is everywhere. The gilded interior is an edifice and reminiscent of a medieval Roman cathedral.

Beside the formal dining table is a large ornate mirror hanging above an open fireplace. The reflection captures the amber light like the zenith of the Sun, a pure light brighter than the morning star. The air is heavy with the fragrance of a hundred delicate red roses in crystal vases. Although the fireplace radiates heat, the temperature in the room is uncomfortably cool.

Truly a modern man, Dr. Babbage holds an upright chair for me to be seated. "Refined dining and grand ballrooms," he says. He takes his seat and motions to several attendants to serve the appetizers. "Mingling with the elite and royalty. You'll make a fine scientist."

"Thank you," I falter feebly, feeling less and less confident by the minute.

How did I fail to notice the peculiarities of this man the day he awarded me the diamond studded Medallion Pin? Babbage's sunken lackluster eyes are like a pair of empty black holes holding dead organs.

A surge of anxiety overwhelms me. My mouth is parched, and my hands are cold but sweaty. My throat constricts, almost cutting off my breath. Somehow, I manage to quell the urge to scream and race from his presence.

Baskets of pears, apples, grapes and melons provide a centerpiece for the table. The amber candelabras dazzle the eyes of the beholder. Three attendants serve platters of food. We eat with the finest china and drink from crystal goblets and use polished silverware and fine linen napkins.

Several varieties of fresh grilled fish, lobster and seafood lay upon serving trays. Vegetables, fruits, nuts, beans and peas, and enough food to satisfy twenty people.

"The finest cuisine known to man," Dr. Babbage claims. "Once called the Mediterranean diet, now it's highbrow food."

"Meant for..." I wait for him to finish my thought.

"Elite and royalty." Dr. Babbage takes a mouthful of halibut and creamy Panini. "Wine?"

"No, I don't—no, thank you."

"Genetically modified food is for the working class. This cuisine extends life, actually prevents disease."

"I do know—or had heard," I stutter, uncertain of what he expects from me.

He empties the wine glass, pursuing another train of thought. "The diet actually slows down aging. That along with what we can do with the telomeres within DNA."

"Of course," I agree, forcing a smile to my lips. I nibble vegetables from my plate and sample the fresh fish. He studies me with those black eyes. What does he want from me?

Dr. Babbage speaks with a patronizing tone. His unblinking stare is hypnotic. "More to the point, you are a problem. Every day this week one violation after another. Offensive fist fighting!"

This is my first encounter with the all-powerful ubiquitous GAP. Dr. Babbage is their mouthpiece. "I'll have some wine after all." It can't hurt to appease him with one glass of wine.

He motions to a servant to fill the wine goblet with a dark red Sauvignon. "That's a good girl," he replies. "I knew you'd behave."

"Yes," I reply, my voice nothing more than a whimper.

The wine burns my throat and causes me to cough. The effort to breathe is increasingly difficult. The waiter refills my wine glass.

"Intelligent, strong and talented. All candidates. You, however, are brilliant! We rarely see an Einstein, Louis Pasteur or Stephen Hawkins. But you qualify. Your IQ is quite significant."

"I'm flattered."

"The stakes are higher than ever. Throughout history, millions upon millions have sacrificed their lives for high ideals. But now, we sacrifice for less than a billion."

"No, I didn't know."

At this moment, I do not know what I know. My mind is in a whirl. I say "no" when he says no. I nod when he nods.

"Food production is limited."

Certainly, he must be wrong. Food from the reserves could feed millions. Inoculations are synthetically manufactured. The advanced science and technologies of 2216 can save every life on the planet.

"You find our methods questionable. Only eighty years since the new world order was established."

"Global firepower," I speak softly, surprised the words slip out. The remapping of the world. Permanent martial law.

"Patrols protect our citizens."

"From what?"

"From rebels. Dissenters who won't obey the laws. I do not expect you to know. The war is censored, and children cannot be expected to understand why it is necessary. Renegades are a nuisance, stealing food and raw materials. They refuse treatment and immunization. It is the law. They jeopardize everyone."

"Yes, I understand."

"Sanitizing cities was the only way. We create jobs for the working class. Mining is essential to keep up with the need for lithium. Every piece of technology uses it for energy."

"I didn't know. I mean, yes, I—."

Dr. Babbage leaves his chair. He comes to stand behind me with his hand on my shoulder. "Your face says it all. You despise me. Maybe I will arrange a trip for you. After a week in the camps, then you'll appreciate what we do."

Dr. Babbage's words are profound and far-reaching. His fingers dig into my shoulder, but I barely notice the pain. He will force me into submission because he is the power of GAP. Does he wield the power to banish me permanently to the working class?

His scare tactics hit home. "I do appreciate what you help," I lie, feigning obedience. "Really, I do."

"We maintain order," he says. "We stopped religious wars and the pandemic. What's wrong with that?"

"Nothing."

"Your mood swings jeopardized your team, not to mention that deplorable rampage."

"I'm sorry," I reply, almost desperately.

"You insult us!"

"I'm sorry."

"I disagree with my superiors. That ridiculous ropes course on live Network, though profitable, has made you an urban hero. GAP loved your performance."

"Oh? I didn't know."

"Camp for a week would be a fitting punishment. However, you are an asset. Already, members are investing in your future inventions. San Manuel Bueno protects your privileges, and GAP owns you."

That is one way to look at it. On the other hand, I am a prisoner in a world gone crazy. I swallow the food in my mouth and bite my lower lip to squelch the bile rising in my throat.

Babbage is unperturbed by my silence. But what will GAP expect when I work for them? And to swallow whatever they throw at me?

"Your research is for?" he pauses, waiting for my response.

I tip the heavy goblet back and empty the glass. A sudden heat

❄

rushes across my flesh. I push my chair back and rise to meet his stare. "Children. To heal children."

Dr. Babbage grips my left arm and slips a silicon chip into my hand. "Memorize this speech for the award's ceremony. You'll recite it verbatim."

"Yes, sir."

"Don't disobey me. I'll make you suffer in ways you can't possibly imagine." His fiendish psyche assaults me, but I resist his power.

Dr. Babbage is a man to fear. His eyes follow me out of Vladislav Hall and into the night like a black phantom giving chase. The specter holds a cold steel blade that pierces the tender tissue of my heart.

I don't remember much of our conversation. I leave Vladislav Hall with the conviction that GAP is a destroyer of nations. Cities lie in ruin. Death comes to those who break the law. Escape is the only way out.

Upon my return to the suite, I rush to my bedroom, refusing to speak to my parents. They kept the truth from me. Years ago, they should have told me the history of our people. Do they punish parents for teaching truth? Does anyone refuse to submit to DNA testing for newborn babies?

One revelation opens a glass jar holding a hundred questions written upon strips of colored paper. Each answer is more difficult to hear than the last one. I need to read the chip. I sit at my console and insert the small device into the port of my S-pad. The two thousand-word speech is a marked-up version of Dr. Babbage's speech, "Turning Discovery into Health for All."

I remove the chip and put it aside and open a chat with Carolyn Delamar in a virtual Sandbox. Others can ring the bell and join, but only with my consent. The conversation with Carolyn is light and frivolous, and I know it's not Carolyn when the imposter logs off.

This is more GAP manipulation. Will I ever know what became of Carolyn? Probably not, but a driving force compels me to find the answers. Whoever sent me file .dc2 wants me to know the truth.

Hacking requires creating a tunnel through my AURA's protocols, and then Gladys will comply with my commands without archiving the data stream. The first step is to prevent Gladys from materializing as a hologram. I type a codebreaker and override protocols with the address I saved during small talk.

"Gladys, pull up file.dc2 and the screen grab."

Series: PN1993.5.SyM
Port: 791.4b.0946 .dc1

"Run a series of commands using string attack cyberbot."

Cyberbot is the one advanced code I know, and it fails. I can do nothing else. I should delete the file and forget the whole thing. It's too impossible.

Then the cam light glows bright red. A cyberspy is monitoring my SASS activity. Did he send me .dc2? Now, we are getting somewhere.

I think I'll test him and see what happens. "Gladys, call security. We have camfecting."

The spy doesn't respond. I use the keyboard and open a tertiary directory. The spy accepts my override code. I set Gladys on dormant. I decide to play along. He can see me through the cam lens though none of my codes can identify his SASS or his face.

"You're cyberspying. That's serious if I report you."

The spy speaks in a modulated computerized voice. "Do you want to open .dc2?"

"Come into Sandbox. It's more secure."

A window opens on my screen. The background is blank and does not display a person or place.

"What do you want?" I ask emphatically.

"JOVE."

"You want to play? Fine. Who is Jove?"

"Wrong question."

"What is Jove?"

"That's the right question."

"Can you help me run .dc2?"

✳

The Smart wall lights up with text flowing across its surface, and I sit back in my chair as file .dc2 is decrypted and translated.

JOVE –Journal of Viral Experiments.
Founded 2050 by the coalition: United Nations,
International World Health Organization,
New World Order and Unilateralist Church.Org.

Viral experiments? I lean back for a moment. "Identify: .dc2, JOVE, 2050. What is.dc2?"

International Congress Consortium
Conference Room DC2 19th floor
5 UN Plaza, 48th Street

"A conference room? What's so important about that?"
"Check out file .dc1 through Sandbox."
"Open file," I reply.

Articles published by JOVE:
Mapping Protected Areas: Target Populations.
GAP Monitoring and Eliminating Access to Traditional Knowledge.
Denied Justice: Human Assets and Eliminating the Indigenous.
GAP Assets: Cultural Heritage and Identity.
SG 1-5 Regions: Develop Human Assets.
Genome Advancement: Eradicate Populations.

"Eradicate populations? Gladys, save to my SASS."
"There's more," he says.
"I've had enough. I'm logging off."
"Wait."
"What for?"
"A password to JOVE site."
"Run password," I reply, speculating on the identity of this spy.

❈

A file downloads thousands of ancient records, images and Ucams recording world history and sacred texts dating back a thousand years.

"Screen grab password to JOVE's site."

"Password denied. Sharing complete." The session ends.

One by one each article documents the loss of basic human rights. The militarization of the globe. The world according to GAP. I stay awake reading the Constitution, the Bill of Rights, the real Pledge of Alliance, the American's Creed, and Martin Luther King, Jr.'s, "I Have a Dream."

Basic human rights were erased from human consciousness while science rules, and GAP decides who lives or who dies. Corporations dominate the world. Global Advancement Programs is the Supreme Power.

I move away from the console into a shadowy light. Taking the microchip and Medallion Pin into my palm, I walk to my self-care room and pitch them in the sanitation disposal. I wash my hands twice and climb into bed.

Hour by hour fear preys upon my mind. My body is tense, and my mind races faster and faster. Pépé said GAP randomly does security checks. *They know everything,* Jolan told me. The black wall is set on pause mode but reflects a dull black. The bedroom wall watches me.

I seek comfort in Tala's warmth. The dim glow from my self-care room wards off the oppressive darkness. The meager light protects me from what waits in my dreams—an unspeakable evil.

The night is long and painful. I feel myself slipping into a void as inescapable as a black hole. A kind of madness possesses me, a crazy, out of control feeling, more frightening than being hunted for all eternity by demons from a fiery inferno.

⁂

I RELEASE A HEAVY sigh and force myself from the safety of Tala's warmth. Those in the Peone apartment slumber unaware as I tiptoe through the living room, and quietly shut the front door behind me. I leave Tala behind to escape the hotel. I want solitude without the distractions of the city.

Not for the first time do I awake from a restless night with racing thoughts. Often when I am sleep deprived, I feel a heightened sense of awareness. Colors are more vibrant. My hearing is so acute, even the morning hush is filled with a particular sound of nature, or something like a sublime serenity in the silence.

Before long I exit the castle grounds and jog through the gardens to Hotel Coeur d' Alene, my favorite because it reminds me of home. The architects of Castle City have managed to duplicate the smooth contour of Tubbs Hill and the marina on the east side of the parkway.

I miss Beauty Bay where eagles with outstretched wings swoop down to feed upon spawning kokanee. The wingflapper's graceful flight is a marvel to witness. My happiest memories are of swimming Lake Coeur d' Alene and exploring the shore. The militarized reserve in Idaho encompasses millions and millions of acres and also includes national forests, pristine lakes and vast mountain ranges.

My life in D.C. denied me the freedom of the reserve to wander the land whenever the need moved me. I have missed Coeur d' Alene and Mother Earth with her nurturing balm that heals a pain too deep for tears. The land knows me as no mortal can.

The world is a confusing place. Why do citizens let GAP control their lives? Does anyone care? Someone wants me to know the truth. Who is the spy, and why is he dropping breadcrumbs on my doorstep?

Babbage's dead eyes haunt me. Can he send me away?

The abduction on prom night had to be one of Jenna's bully games. I suspect my parents of something, but I'm not sure what. And who is the mysterious San Manuel Bueno?

The one certainty in my life is the hatred I have for Jenna Slate. My feelings for her are raw and visceral and locked down in a dark dungeon. A day will come when I beat the bully.

I run past the city park and deserted marina very similar to home. The double cabin yachts in their berths bob up and down against the wood boardwalk. The shoreline curves for three miles. The floating golf green is located on the fourteenth hole and unmatched for golfing pleasure. It's too early for hotel residents to tee off.

The trail follows the curve of land on the southeast side of the lake where lofty trees grow upon gentle rising hills. Light sparkles upon white capped waves. Luminous sunshine warms the air, and the breeze smells of a pungent scent of pine.

Serenity settles upon the sunlit banks. The soft light burns off early fog, and mists rise from the surface of the choppy water. The cold air fills my lungs and washes me clean. The rush of dawn stirs in me a resilience I have not felt in years. A slant of light showers upon me a solitude that renews my faith and gives me the courage to embrace my visions. To know my truth.

A sense of freedom fills my mind as I follow the trail. I walk the shore back to Hotel Coeur d' Alene thinking of prom night, and Iain and I roaming the woods. The promise of a day with Iain eases my anxiety. Iain Sinclair is like no one I have ever met. I'm not sure what to think of him, or how I know his fate is intertwined with mine.

City Park is crowded with GAP members enjoying the butterfly garden while their children play in the water park. The sunlight is warm and bright, and butterflies flutter everywhere. Daisies bloom in the flowerbeds alongside budding roses. Dr. Julius waves to me from a bench where he sits inside the butterfly garden.

Gladys tracked me down with my chip, so Julius could find me.

I cannot help my scowl or my swift change in mood. One minute I'm up, and the next down. I guess the optical implants are working. I am more emotional than ever I've even been.

Begrudgingly, I take a seat beside Julius. "They've sent you to deal with me."

Julius ignores my challenge. Not even my caustic tone disturbs his polite smile. There are so many problems. I wonder which one is most urgent. What has Babbage told him? Does Network security know about file .dc2? Actually, the spy gave me two files .dc1 and .dc2 while I hacked the JOVE journal.

"'The time has come,' Julius begins pleasantly, "to speak of many things.'"

Apparently, he wants to play a game to postpone the reprimand. "To quote or not to quote" seems to be his favorite pastime, or perhaps a strategy to appease rebellious teenagers.

"'Of shoes and ships and sealing wax, of cabbages and kings,'" I finish.

"Yes, Alice. For surely, your world is upside down."

Julius makes me feel calm and safe. He is the most direct person I know, once he gets past his stuffy social etiquette. It is difficult not to respond to his bright smile.

"My name is not Alice, and Dr. Cabbage head is evil," I complain forcefully.

A gentle appeal in Julius's eyes softens my cantankerous mood. He deserves a reprieve from my hostility, and I don't blame him for my problems. I blame Jolan and Océane.

"Your parents are worried about you. You left without telling anyone, and Gladys refused to tell them your location."

"Really? I thought she'd betrayed me. But you found me. Babbage threatened me last night."

A startled look penetrates the fine veneer of Julius's handsome features. His clean-shaven face is smooth, and his olive-toned skin as dark as mine. He is all things kind and noble and not the least bit narcissistic. The cultured air of the elite suits him without tarnishing his character.

"Truly threatened?"

❄

"Yes. Well—sort of."

"Your life?" he asks disbelieving.

"He wants to send me to the camps," I cry hurriedly. "I'm afraid of him. He's reporting my violations, right?"

Julius is slow to speak. "Clearly, that's true."

"What will happen?" I ask, turning to face the young man.

Julius dismisses my worry with a wave of his hand. "He's not the boogeyman. You needn't fear Babbage. He can't harm you."

"He is a bugger man. He made me drink alcohol!"

Julius laughs. "You're very amusing. I doubt Babbage could make you do anything against your will. You are an audacious young woman," he confesses with a hint of admiration. His adjective though archaic is sweet.

"Really, I need your help, Dr. Julius," I implore, not wasting time with further pretense. Babbage's threat hangs over my head. "I don't understand. Nothing's what I expected."

"Really, you must call me Julius," he implores. "I'm a friend."

"But why..."

"You sound paranoid," he says with consternation. "Are you getting enough sleep?"

Dare I trust Julius? I think I can. He understands me better than my parents, or anyone I know. I whisper one word to test him. "JOVE."

Bullseye. Julius seems perturbed, but not necessarily worried. He acknowledges me with the infinitesimal lift of his left brow. "So, you know."

"Know? What do I know?" I ask dismayed.

"By all accounts, more than you should," he exclaims exasperated. "Hacking this week. What were you thinking?"

I want to object and ask about the Journal of Viral Experiment. Do I betray the spy? I open my mouth, but he cuts me off.

"I don't want to know. Not about it. Nothing. I don't care how you hacked into the JOVE site," he says, now becoming irritated and impatient. His face is flushed and sweating. "Are we clear on this?"

"Yes."

"What else?" he asks carefully.

"These hotels. Why are they castles? Babbage said..."

"Marie, the important castle is inside you," Julius says, his calm demeanor reassuring me.

"What do you mean?"

"You like ancient history. I've seen your record on hacking. Don't look so surprised. Of course, GAP keeps track of your harmless, but illegal activities. I'll loan you a rare book. The writings of St. Teresa of Avila. I have a meeting now. I'll see you later." Julius stands and starts to leave and then pauses. "What?"

"I feel so alone."

He sits back down and raises his right hand as a maestro does. His index finger is straight and pointed like a baton. A flurry of butterflies hovers over a flowerbed. Their wings are so fragile with a thin black border with white dots. The orange and black wings of the Monarch are undeniably beautiful.

"They possess an inner compass and once migrated thousands of miles," he says, as though reflecting on places too far to imagine.

"Do you see me as a caterpillar changing into a butterfly?"

"What a trite metaphor!" he declares indignantly. "An insulting one, I might add."

"Oh. Then what?"

"Very well. Let's get to it. You've described feelings of lightheaded euphoria, nightmares, anxiety and irritability."

"Don't forget confusion and physical violence."

Julius's expression is one of mixed surprise and amusement. For the first time, his mask of self-satisfaction drops from his aristocratic features. Outwardly, he is capable of emotional outbursts. Ben told me Julius was ready to tackle the Warrior course to save me. The Marines prevented him from entering the arena.

"This is to be expected. Many suffer anxiety during Kickoff. Five years ago, I was a candidate and felt much the same."

"Well, I'm not like them. I've always been..." How do I express my essential self? I suspect Julius will be sympathetic if I bare my soul.

❄

"I—don't—belong. I never will."

"Jolan called you a healer. And you won the Medallion Pin."

"I pitched it in the trash." Julius bursts out laughing. Why did I think he would take me serious? I glare in disgust at him, but he laughs all the louder.

"In the trash?" he asks, wiping his eyes. "Yes, I believe that! Oh, you care. You care deeply. That's why you are different. It is time to go, Jo. You don't want to be late for practice."

"Please, listen to me. I'm serious," I implore softly.

"I apologize for laughing."

We stare at each other until he blinks. Score two for Jo. I win this staring match, and the bullseye for JOVE is a bonus. We leave the garden and walk along the shoreline until reaching the outer walkway that leads to the hotel. Once inside we follow the corridor through the west wing to the practice hall.

"Do you promise he won't hurt me?" I ask, suddenly grasping the danger I have brought to family.

"Hum?" Julius asks absentmindedly. "Don't be afraid of Cabbage head. You will behave. No fighting with Jenna."

"Yes, I know. Whatever it takes."

"Good. No harm done. The JOVE thing...I mean," Julius says. "I'll take care of this."

"What, no medicine? Supplements or Vitajuice?"

"Enjoy your practice, Jo," Julius says with a charming smile that reassures me. "Dancing is just the medicine you need."

Julius is proving himself to be a good friend in a world of lies and deception. People let GAP rule the world because the Network gives them a virtual life, and they're too afraid of change so GAP legislates freedom. Citizens are too complacent to care. One has to wonder how far they will go to maintain control. It is hard to know what to believe.

Julius makes his way down the wide hall and disappears into the restaurant with a view of the lake. A random memory, hardly worth attention, comes to me of Julius in the garden. A flying insect landed and died beneath his shoe. A Monarch butterfly.

❖

CHAPTER THIRTEEN

Side Event

THE DANCE STUDIO is so full of people, dance teachers and spectators that I suddenly feel self-conscious as I enter. Our creative director is Tatiyana Spivakovsky. The world recognizes her as the mother of Terpsichore, or Delight in Dancing. Her design session includes choreographers, set and lighting technicians along with the infamous Pépé DeMolay. Global Network plans to broadcast our Side Event as a live streaming virtual show.

Jenna and Freja practice dance steps and warm up with their chick picks Artem and Jamil. They've hooked up as couples. I can't imagine performing with Jenna. Every nerve in my body is tense. The hall is a prison ship about to set sail for the edge of the world where dragons wait. Hate is my salvation and saves me from drowning like a rope tied to the mast of a ship. I can pretend indifference, but I cannot deny the violence of my emotions.

Jenna and her bully friends ignore me as I pass them and walk across the hall. I grab a bottle of Vitajuice from a refreshment cart. The boys open their circle and make room for me beside Wei and Dev. Zebenjo puts his pad in his boy-bag and pulls the zipper tight.

"Hi ya, Jo. What's up?" he asks eagerly. He takes an awkward step back managing to kick his bag across the floor. "How was dinner with Babbage? Wow! You get the award and will give a speech and…"

I stop listening to him. Chatterbox does not know when to shut up. Only twenty minutes since my jog, and already I feel as flat as a deflated balloon, yet my heart races out of control. My high low high emotional ride is intense.

"I'm not ready for this," I announce a little too loud.

"Where's Iain?" Wei asks, regarding me with a gleam in his eye. "I haven't seen him since I won our chess match last night."

"How should I know?" I reply irritated.

For a minute, the boys shuffle their feet and look anywhere but at me. Their mutual silence is all I need to read their thoughts. They think Jo Peone is Iain Sinclair's girlfriend.

"Yeah. He's never on time," Cyrus says, crossing his arms. He looks at me with teasing dark eyes. "Out late, were we?" he asks amused.

Isaac pulls his GoBot cap firmly over his curly hair. He looks at Dev with mischief in his smile. "Hey, 'spect. What's new?"

"I drew a cartoon for you," Dev says lightly. "GoBot goes ballistic to Uranus."

Isaac uses both hands to adjust his visor. He seems more interested in his cap than in Dev. "Huh?" he asks bemused. "A cartoon? I didn't know you draw."

Dev steps face to face with Isaac and confronts him. "Yeah, Botox pus, you can go straight to—"

No one makes an entrance like Juan Pablo. The conductor of the soul train dances his way into the studio. He is a hot, fast moving combustible dynamo. There is no music playing, but his shoulders and hips move to the rhythm of a song only he hears. Juan Pablo gives joy to the moves. Behind him comes Iain Sinclair who takes long measured steps in our direction. Iain promises the grace of a perfect dance. Juan hesitates and then heads toward Jenna's group.

Tatiyana claps her hands. "All of you, come," she says, motioning for us to join her. She introduces the dance instructors. "Alexander

Gorbalenya, James Kelly, Beatrice Taylor and Elinor Saunders are professionals from the international troupe Guðmu."

Alex's whole body moves when he talks. He rocks toe to heel and sways his hips and shoulders. "The Pyrrhic. It's a weapon dance. You'll love it!" he says. "Traditional costumes. Makeup. Dancing for your country."

"Tomorrow night you will perform live," Tatiyana says. "You have star power. Teens want to be you." Her intense eyes size us up. "We design a dance, you dance. Simple."

"We're doing traditional routines," Alex says. "Cornk. A blend Dubstep and Zouk from the 20th century."

"You'll perform with backup dancers," Beatrice says. "Amazing props and a live orchestra. The groups Vojtěch and Eetu will be here."

"The sensational pop star Elżbieta will perform her song 'Mash Up,'" Alex adds excitedly.

This is the best day of Kickoff. Everyone wants to know about the costumes and weapons and when Elżbieta will arrive today. Laughter lightens the hostilities between our team members.

Maybe practice won't be so bad. Unfortunately, Alex bursts my bubble when we divide into our small talk groups.

"Red, you're mine," Beatrice says.

"Yay, let's crank it," Cyrus says, throwing away a wad of chewing gum. "Let's do this!"

"Attention," Tatiyana says "Bring up the screen."

A technician speaks into the panel activating 3D holograms of V-team1, all of us dressed in ancestral costumes. Cultural traditions and tribal warfare inspired the bold designs. Our virtual selves are painted head to toe with a world of colors. However, I learned last night that GAP promotes culture to manipulate citizens and pacify rebellion.

Red, yellow, black and white and vibrant shades of green, orange and purple create elaborate patterns on our virtual bodies. Black in most cultures means "living" and is worn during battle. Violent red is for battle. The holograms hold tribal weaponry that reaches back into many centuries. The virtual screen displays our names on the Network.

❄

Artem Kozlov Russia Scythian archer and lance
Cyrus Bashir Iran Persia Immortal spear and wicker shield
Dev Rammdas Patel India Vedic doubled bladed haladie knife
Freja Jørgensen Norway Norse Viking ceremonial short sword
Iain Sinclair Scotland Highlander broadsword
Isaac Bar-Hillel Israel Maccabees Gladius sword
Jamil Ahmad Sudan Mahdist spear
Jenna Slate California Marine Special Forces EM hand gun
Juan Coelho Mexico Mayan bow & arrows, zarabatana war club
Lim Chang Wei China Terra Cotta bronze hook
Marie-Joëlle Peone Idaho Bitterroot Salish tomahawk
Zebenjo Tongogara Africa Zimbabwe Zulu shield and spear

Beatrice leads Jenna, Cyrus, Isaac and Iain to the south end of the studio. Elinor Saunders takes the Blue group in the opposite direction. The White group waits for James Kelly who is talking with Alex and Tatiyana.

"Hey, I want to ask you something," I say to Artem. "I think you can help me."

Artem stands aloof with his arms crossed and watches Iain like a raptor spying its prey. Beatrice talks Iain and Jenna through a routine. Unquestionably the dreamer, Artem's handsome face is twisted in an ugly sneer. His cheeks are flushed red and his forehead wet with hate sweat.

"What's with him?" Ben asks. "He's never with us. Artem always takes Jenna's side."

"Someone hijacked my AURA last night," I begin, trying to get Artem's attention.

"Ew, I hate this. What did you say?" he asks, noticing me for the first time. "Hack? No, not possible. Well, maybe if he's good."

"Can you help me install your new AI protocols to my AURA?"

"No, I can't."

"You do spyware, right? I need your program for AI protection. Will you help me? By September, we'll be in classes together."

❄

"Maybe," he interrupts. "I don't know—I'm sick of this. I'll show Iain the beat—with my fist!" Artem yells running toward the Red group.

"Jenna is trouble," Wei says, shaking his head and running after Artem.

"Bad," Ben says tersely, turning away from the showdown. He picks up his S-pad and leans against the wall.

Beatrice looks frightened when Artem rushes Iain and throws a punch. His fist misses. Iain is too quick and easily steps aside. Juan Pablo does a spin with Jenna and pulls her away from the boys. Jamil never talks, not that he needs words. His fist makes contact with Iain's jaw. He grabs Iain so Artem can beat the rhythm out of him. Male macho pride. They curse at each other, but in my opinion say nothing of importance.

Wei, Cyrus and Isaac plow into the threesome to free Iain and break up the fight. They topple to the floor, a pile of hot sweaty bodies rolling and grunting. Beatrice backs away from her students and calls security.

Then comes the yelling, mostly from Alex, and the patrol officers bring order to the madness.

"Tough guys, huh?" Alex shouts. "No more fists. If you fight, you will practice all night. All of you. No eating or sleeping."

"More of this, you won't be dancing. I'll make sure of that!" the patrol officer says. "Want us to stay?"

"We're fine," Alex replies distracted. He addresses us with loud gestures and talks with his hands in wide accentuated motions. "You are a team. Work for perfection. Change everything. How you think, feel, move. Harness your power. Show me perfection."

"All of you, away from the mirrors," Beatrice says. "Over here. Two lines. Girls in front. Touch each other. Turn. Put your hands on her hips. You are a team."

"Boys, the same," Alex says. "Line up. Closer. Hands on shoulders."

"Tight coordinated steps," James adds. "Break forward with your left foot."

❦

Alex demonstrates the move. "Now rock back on the right foot," he says, clicking his fingers faster and faster. "Again," Alex shouts impatiently. "Do it. Again. Do it again. Perfection! One fluid motion. Tell the story of your people. Your body is their body."

We practice monotonous routines with a jump style, a little hip-hop and break steps. All afternoon we drill doing jumps, turns, leaps, and small combinations of top rocks, drops, footwork, power moves and freezes.

By dinnertime, V-team1 collapses on the dance floor, quiet and exhausted, but no more fighting or cross words. Worn out, everyone either wants to soak in a Jacuzzi or collapse in bed. No one wants to attend the Hotel Alhambra party. The others leave, but I stay behind to practice adagio, pirouettes, petite allegro and grand allegro. Finally, I complete a spin ending up on the far side of the studio. My technique is weak. My movements lack fluidity.

Iain Sinclair appears in the mirror behind me. He has tied his hair securely in a ponytail down his back. The swelling on his face from the death match is down though his swollen nose is worse. My left eye is black and blue from my fistfight yesterday. I wonder if the other candidates are enjoying Kickoff as much as our team.

Iain moves close to me. I feel his body heat melting my resistance like fire to wax. We look in the mirror at each other. Iain's probing eyes are an earthy dark brown with soft speckles of green and amber. I place my hands on the dance bar to steady myself while the granite wall that protects my heart drops away.

"It's more than the steps. Get out of your head and stop thinking," Iain says, placing his hands firmly on my hips. "Feel it. Let the music move you." His breath is warm on my cheek.

"No matter how I practice, I can't get the technique."

"Get out of your head and feel," he repeats.

Iain speaks into the wall panel and selects a song I don't recognize. Without removing his hands from my hips, he twirls me to face him. Straightaway, my body yields to his body. The mind-body connection flows through our movements. His grace is mine. His perfection spills into me as we meld into each other.

Iain lifts me up in a hold above his head where I feel weightless, free, almost serene. Gently, he sets me down. My feet touch the floor, but my spirit soars where eagles dare fly. Iain and I gaze intimately into each other's eyes. The perfect dance is left unfinished. We embrace a sacred space, a moment of time out of mind, slipping away forever, until someone's clapping breaks the silence. Embarrassed, we move away from each other. Tatiyana and Alex keep clapping.

"This is superb!" Tatiyana says. "It's wonderful how you dance."

"Synced," Alex says excitedly. "I love it."

"You will prove your worth and dance this for the show," Tatiyana adds, flipping her S-phone shut and taking hold of Alex's hand. Immediately, Tatiyana leaves with Alex at her side. Iain grins until he catches the expression on my face.

They expect a public performance for the world to see this bond between us? Not a state of mind but a physical chemistry. How, in one week, did I go from cramming for finals and coveting the Medallion Pin to dancing under the stars with a chatterbox, seven Hotlympians, two wicked witches and one Scottish Braveheart? This is not what I expected from Kickoff.

Ten o'clock sharp the next morning the twelve members of V-team1 show up to practice the difficult routines, taking a short lunch break before resuming rehearsal. Pépé DeMolay greets me with a friendly hug. There is a fresh look to his complexion without makeup. He is wearing a simple outfit, a beige silk shirt and tight black pants.

"Your hanging went viral," he laughs, hugging me. "You're a star."

"Why?" I ask in amazement.

"Morbidity with death? Greed? Who knows, but the show will be fabulous!"

"Well, I didn't die."

Pépé pats me on the cheek in a gesture of affection and calls his assistant over. "Too much work, too little time."

"What do you mean?"

"Your costumes." He smiles like a mischievous little boy. "We're applying wet paint over every inch of your body. Many colors like a rainbow of diverse tribes." Although he's difficult to read, Pépé can be endearing and reminds me of a joy-maker. His enthusiasm lifts my bad mood.

Pépé with the hair stylists and makeup artists begin their magic. They use a liquid latex body paint to transform us into a multicolored tribe. Each of one of us wears a traditional costume, accessories and weapons. Several minutes pass before the show begins.

The circumference of the hall, with ceiling to floor windows, gives a panoramic view of the lake. A brilliant light sparkles across the calm waters. As the sun sinks below the horizon, stars appear in the night sky. The romantic scenery is a backdrop for the televised show, or what I've come to think of as Dancing Under the Stars.

Gone is the traditional skybox. The audience is seated on the floor with a dance style arena for an unobstructed view of the show. Upper seating is an open amphitheater style. The best sound system carrying 100,000 watts of power will deliver the orchestrated music.

Out of sight behind a 360-degree stage, the boys practice one last time. Jenna and her bully friends talk with teenagers on U-Candance and Flash It, which is the newest craze on live streaming. Many teens are headed into the working class, active patrol duty or mining camps.

The Pyrrhic dance is a reenactment of our death match. The props are an exact reproduction of the Warrior course with a pile of trapeze apparatus, ropes and flying rigs held together with cables. The lighting combined with the virtual artistic projections creates a wondrous ancient landscape.

Tatiyana Spivakovsky gives us the cue. Everyone takes his or her position. The first notes of Elżbieta's "Mash Up" set the dancers in motion. The up-tempo electropop music soars in volume. Warriors Jamil and Artem, Iain and Wei dance their way into the spotlight.

Twenty feet above their heads, I wear a harness and hang from a mock noose. Slowly, I descend into their upraised arms. Jenna and Freja with their partners spiral into the circle, and we perform an off balance, intricate retro dance. The music changes tempo and increases

❋

in volume. The composition is a blend of Zulu Tribal and a Persian musical score.

Weapons in hand, the twelve warriors perform the Pyrrhic with bursts of micro movements. Three warrior women—the Norse, the Marine and the Salish—dance with synchronized footwork. In the background, backup dancers perform circles, spirals and figure eights. The Pyrrhic is a tournament and a balance of showmanship, athletic power and fluidity.

The final performance of the night is the couple's fusion dance. The balcony sets the stage with a moonlit lake and a canopy of stars. Tonight, Iain and I perform the flawless dance with precision and grace. The audience is forgotten in the silence of our intimacy. We express our unspoken feelings with the perfection of our movements. The last note dies away, but not the sacred space between us. Iain lowers his face and touches my forehead with his. He lifts my fingers to his lips and kisses the back of my hand.

All my uncertainties about the future fade. In this moment, Iain's touch is all I need. The beauty in Iain's face, the tenderness in his eyes, and the contented curve of his lips speak louder than words. I know Iain is my protector and the promise of so much more. We bow to the audience and leave the spotlight. "A poem in motion," someone speaks as we pass.

The director of the show signals us to return to center stage and take another bow. Iain keeps hold of my hand. We stand as one with our team in the spotlight. Together, we face the world for the last time as candidates. Tomorrow night we will graduate and advance into elite GAP members. But for now, Iain Sinclair lifts our clasped hands high into the air as victors of the Pyrrhic.

A BATTLE RAGES IN a vast wasteland, and I find myself lost in an immense chasm of ultra-bright light. I want to run away, but there is no escape. I don't know who I am or what I am. I don't want to feel because feelings make you lose control. *Don't look back. Just stay alive one more day.* One more day.

Kickoff is a disaster. My teammates battle each other like survivors of a shipwreck, stranded on a sliver of land, barely able to hold on. Like the ropes course, we fall through the gaps of a suspension bridge missing wood beams, clinging to sharp edges, hanging on for our lives.

Fighting to breathe. Fighting to understand. Fighting to survive. Gunfire shatters the silence of a wilderness without end. Running for our lives. Alone in a wilderness, I scream for help until my throat is raw and sore. Will this nightmare never end?

Slowly, I wake from a dream within a dream. I awake from a night terror that is my reality. The week is a disaster. I live in a world of lies. My training. My parents. For one long minute, I stay cocooned in my blankets. Tala snores beside me.

I open my eyes to find my mother sitting on my bed watching me. Worry lines crease her brow, and I see in her face things I have never noticed. A sharp intelligence, a quick humor, the sparkle of youth in her girlish smile. Then I remember Iain Sinclair, not a dream-boy but a living, breathing boy with eyes only for me. Knowing him makes me a better person.

"I'm sorry. I promise to be a good girl," I blurt out and rush into Océane's arms. "I love you, Mom."

"Jo, what is it?" Océane asks concerned, touching my face with her cool touch.

Her arms enfold me, but I feel no solace in her embrace. Never again will I look at my mother with a child's eyes. The truth changes everything. Changes how I think, how I feel, how I exist in this world. It changes Who—I—Am.

The smile on Océane's glossy lips is an odd parody of her natural bubbliness. "Today, you graduate," she says. "You are an elite member." Her words, though forced, sound light and carefree.

I know beneath a beautiful facade, Océane hides her true feelings. She is evasive, often secretive with her travels. Right now, she holds my hand as if to speak of those secrets.

"Time to rise and shine," she says, not noticing my imploring eyes.

Her words cut me to the core. "That's it? You were going to say something. What are you hiding?"

"What am I hiding?" she repeats sharply. "Not even seven o'clock in the morning and you start this nonsense."

"Nonsense?" I shout, throwing off the blankets and getting out of bed. "You make me crazy. I know you're keeping something from me. You are a liar. My whole life is a lie!"

"You are out of control, young lady," she says angrily, and so out of character, lacking the sparkle I detest. "I'm calling Dr. Oppenheimer."

"I'll run. I swear I will."

Océane's face pales. Her sparkle dims, not with tears but with fear. "Run? There's nowhere to run," she whispers, more to herself than to me.

"You can trust me," I plead softly, holding her hand and searching her face for the mother of my childhood.

"Trust you? You can't control yourself for even one hour," she says in a soft voice and snatching her hand away. "Fighting with Jenna Slate? Drawing attention to yourself. Trust you? No, I can't do this. Jolan's waiting for me," she adds, walking away from me and out of the room.

Truly, I am alone. Will my mother never understand me? I hope the day comes when she accepts me, not just as her daughter, but for who I really am.

The daily routines come easy. Eating a healthy lunch, drinking Vitajuice, taking supplements. The self-care room is a health protocol.

❆

The long hot shower cleans my pores and hydrates my skin. Afterward, the steamer sprays a nutrient rich mist upon my skin, but I feel guilty for the luxury of the privileged healthcare treatment.

My mind takes me to a place of nonreality. I feel detached from normal sensory perceptions going through the motions. All my life I have harbored misgivings about my world. I don't believe GAP helps people survive in the wilderness. The random thought teases from my mind a fragment of memory like a puzzle piece but distinct and clearly an old man's face.

Around six o'clock, Julius arrives as a proxy for San Manuel Bueno and we eat a light supper. A long discussion follows. I am given no choice but to sign a meaningless contract. The alternative is going into the working class as a bond laborer, or banishment to an unspecified location. Mrs. Thalhammer accepts her promotion from headmistress to a job in London.

The awards banquet is this evening. My friend Pépé and his staff dress me in an original DeMolay, a gown of rich purple velvet tailored to accent my figure. The silk bodice is embroidered in gold, and the collar trimmed with black and white ermine. The whole design shimmers with golden specks and authentic diamonds. A pair of satin shoes decorated with pendant pearls and silver lace fit my feet.

The full-length mirror reflects a woman of distinction that I do not recognize. The face in the mirror is mine, but the dark brown eyes hold forbidden mysteries in their depths. Brown curls rich in luster fall loose about my shoulders. I refuse to wear makeup or jewelry with the gown, which is the color of Tyrian purple.

The ancient Phoenician dye was once rare and extracted from the Mediterranean Sea snail in Byzantium, Greece. The odd bit of trivia comes to mind, something gleaned from the Network as opposed to the genocide of countries.

Hotel Edinburgh, with its medieval defenses, impenetrable walls, and stately towers lends an air of chivalry to the proceedings in the Great Hall. Archbishop Dr. Babbage is extremely happy, almost jovial, in his address, highlighting the events of another successful Kickoff.

Perhaps he earns a hefty commission for supervising three thousand teenagers given personal liberties for the first time in their lives. He might get away with blaming our disobedience on raging hormones.

Dr. Charles Babbage and GAP members stand center stage. He introduces the two hundred and fifty teams of polymaths based on their rank. Dr. Babbage announces Virtual Team 1—all Medallion Pin winners. As recipient of the International Medal of Arts, I lead my team across the stage where we shake hands with the representatives. Everyone is smiling. Well, almost everyone.

Garbed in a black robe, Dr. Babbage signals me across the stage to stand beside him. He holds my attention with his black dead eyes. He smiles and nods. "Now, it's my distinguished honor to introduce Miss Marie-Joëlle Peone!" He places a red ribbon holding a gold medallion around my neck. "The recipient of the International Medal of Arts."

Dr. Babbage takes my hand and leads me to the podium where I bow before thousands of citizens in the hall and millions watching on the Network. I remember a podcast shown in elementary school and published May 7, 2013 on YouTube. It's still online, "Extreme Weather Phenomena Escalating Worldwide," and examines the global surge of uncommon catastrophes and major earthquakes around the Earth.

Did teens in 2013 pay any attention at all to global climate change or to the politics of their governments? The information was free and on the Internet. What would I tell them if we could meet?

The hot stage lights make the audience invisible like a whiteout. A winter whiteout is a blizzard that reduces visibility to zero, and the world becomes a white snowscape.

From my elevated vantage point, the brilliant whiteout opens my eyes to a second sight. The vision is crisp and clear. The Woman in White touches my face with her gentle touch and imparts to me a glimpse of the future. *What comes when the clouds break and the sun appears? A world of peace in the wake of a storm.* Her voice calms all my fears.

I hear the chorus of a new world and my heart sings for all nations, for those invisible people and forgotten children. Dr. Babbage nods

❉

his approval. I acknowledge him with an obedient nod. I sing a song of the United States by Sir. Francis Scott Key 1814.

> "Oh, say can you see by the dawn's early light
> What so proudly we hailed at the twilight's last gleaming?
> Whose broad stripes and bright stars thru the perilous fight,
> O'er the ramparts we watched were so gallantly streaming?
> And the rocket's red glare, the bombs bursting in air,
> Gave proof through the night that our flag was still there.
> Oh, say does that star-spangled banner yet wave
> O'er the land of the free and the home of the brave?"

Boldly, I speak into the microphone to the audience, to Babbage, to GAP, to the world, "Let's use our discoveries to give health to all."

The Great Hall is silent. I give Dr. Babbage an exaggerated bow and step down from the podium to lead my team offstage. Lieutenant Kurt leads ten armed Marines who immediately take us into custody.

❄

CHAPTER FOURTEEN

Die Hard

OFFSTAGE MY ACAPPELLA performance skyrockets me to fame. A live streaming phenomenon. Well, it's the same old, same darn thing. A week ago, no one anticipated Kickoff week would morph into the most watched reality show on the Network. The stage director sends his cinematographers to interview the twelve of us who march with armed Marines out of the hall.

"What was the significance of your song?" the interviewer asks excitedly. "And where are the Marines taking you?"

Suddenly, Julius is beside me. "Say nothing," he cautions me. He takes me by the elbow and steps closer to the camera. "The Marines are escorts," he says in a monotone. He smiles speaking directly to the viewers. "Catch us on Flash-It later tonight."

Iain, Wei and Dev follow behind me. The other team members walk between the Marines and Lieutenant Kurt who permits people to compliment me on my performance. Some think it was a national folksong. Others are not sure whether it was sacred or secular. We pause to greet well-wishers while standing in front of the limestone fireplace decorated with countless weapons, and where armored suits stand on either end of the hearth.

A stylishly dressed woman approaches me. "So lovely, my dear and how uplifting for a soloist to sing without loud banging music." Her companions agree and they move on.

A modishly attired gentleman assisted by a male caregiver walks forward, takes my hand and kisses both my cheeks. "Not in many years have I heard a Basque Bertsolaritza. Exquisite."

"I beg your pardon, but I'm not Basque," I answer, giving Julius a sidelong glance. An impenetrable mask hides his otherwise vulnerable and youthful face. His dilated eyes are fearful, darting about cautious, almost expectant.

"Surely, but French, yes?" the old man asks.

The mentally alert, but very elderly man, speaks with an odd foreign accent. Though broken by age, his healthy vigor is unabated. What he lacks in strength he makes up for with eagerness. He manages a weak smile before his caretaker helps him into a wheelchair. Several women close the gap, shaking my hand and congratulating me until Lieutenant Kurt leads the way out of the Great Hall.

Iain brushes up against me and holds my hand. "That peculiar man," he whispers. "Do you know him?"

"No. A little touched in the head," I reply.

"Ferme la bouche," Julius says, "Not a sound!" His eyes are dark and suspicious, and so unlike the charming Frenchman. "Do exactly what they tell you. No mouthing off."

Although modernized, Hotel Edinburgh is a complex labyrinth with long hallways leading through dark passages to hidden chambers. The elevator descends several stories to the basement level. Not quite the ill-famed haunted dungeon, the storage room is spacious, more than adequate as a prison for twelve panic-stricken teenagers.

All our tomorrows stretch into an uncertain future. I suspect our lives hang in the balance, or am I being too melodramatic? We are candidates and too valuable to harm. But will they punish all of us for my rebellion?

"Come with me, Dr. Julius," Lieutenant Kurt says. "The rest of you, get comfortable. You're not going anywhere. No talking. Boomer,

❈

you're in charge," he says, leading Julius back down the hallway.

The bully-four along with Juan Pablo turn their backs to the rest of us. Iain stands with me. His fingers tighten around mine. Isaac and Cyrus speak in hushed voices. Dev secludes himself in a corner while Zebenjo crosses his arms and leans against the wall. Not surprisingly, Wei's face reveals no emotion, but he takes a step closer to Iain to show his support.

Two Marines carry boxes containing brand new skinsuits and the uniforms we wore during the Warrior course. Was that only two days ago?

"Get changed," Boomer says. "Girls, follow me."

He leads Jenna and Freja to a storage room where they enter and shut the door. A smaller room to the left is vacant. I quickly discard the evening gown and satin shoes and change into the skinsuit and camo fatigues and heavy black boots. The girls rejoin the team, and all of us sit on the cement floor until an hour later when Lieutenant Kurt returns.

"Jo Peone, come with me," he says dryly.

"Not without me!" Iain answers, leaping to his feet and coming nose to nose with the beefy Marine.

Boomer draws his side arm. "Sit down," he orders, threatening Iain with the barrel of his gun.

Wei leans forward and tugs at Iain's jacket. "They won't hurt her," he says, calm and confident. "She's an elite member now."

Lieutenant Kurt points toward the doorway. "Let's go, Jo. They're waiting for us. Boomer, you know what to do."

Boomer scowls in disgust. "Hey, how'd I get baby patrol?" he asks with a crooked smile. Artem, Jamil, Wei and Iain glare angrily at him.

"I'll be back. I promise," I say, fearing what waits for me.

I follow behind Lieutenant Kurt through a maze of corridors and staircases. When I enter the office, the person who greets me is Dr. Babbage accompanied by two Marines and Captain Jack Donaldson. Lieutenant Kurt and the others stand at attention, keeping their eyes front and center.

�֎

"I'm sending you to Camp Lejeune for the summer," Dr. Babbage says, with pleasure and the devil's own cruelty is in his eyes.

"Boot camp?" I ask astonished. The notion is so ridiculous I laugh with derision. "We have internships and research projects planned. Important research," I add petulantly.

"Youth gangs go to Lejeune for training in teamwork," Captain Jack says, quite satisfied with himself while taking pleasure from my discomfort.

"But my mother said I'd be in Paris." I don't know what to think. "Where's Dr. Julius? I demand to see Jolan Peone."

"T-day starts now," Captain Jack interrupts, flanked on either side by Marines. "In ten minutes an X29 Predator takes off, and I can finally get out of this fairyland."

Dr. Babbage grabs my arm. His sharp fingernails draw blood from my wrist and prevent me from following Captain Jack.

"You are a failure. An embarrassment," he hisses.

"No," I say, fighting against him and struggling to get free of his deadly touch. "Let me go. That stupid song was nothing."

"GAP will punish me for your violations, but you must already know that."

"Océane travels to Spain to see someone. Someone important. I don't know who he is. Maybe, she can help you."

"You are an expensive, worthless investment. If I had my way, I'd make you disappear."

Is it possible to intimidate Babbage and make him back off? "You can't hurt me," I cry defiantly. "GAP owns me. They won't risk losing an asset. My patron will hear about this! You'll be sorry."

"You smug, little fiend," Babbage smacks me hard across my cheek. His face brightens like the Prince of Darkness. "Think you're so smart? Why don't you hack something important like the Gene Database dbGaP at Orphanet?" he asks, spewing out his poisonous words.

"What is that?"

"Yes, indeed, what," he says. The wicked turn of his mouth reveals sharp white incisors like those of a king cobra.

❖

"What is Orphanet?"

Dr. Babbage opens the door where two patrol officers guard the entrance. He leaves me alone with an open console. In seconds, my SASS computing displays my DNA results. Quickly, I copy and paste the double helix molecule data to the Orphanet website. I get a match, but the login requires a password for high-level access and reports. I spring away from the console as though my fingers touch hot flames.

My DNA signature is a 3D hologram rotating on the table. Julius walks into the room, his face flushed and his wavy black hair a mass of disheveled black curls.

"Babbage," he says bemused. He touches the console. The DNA hologram disappears.

"You know about this data site?" I ask, moving away from him. "What's Orphanet?"

"You did read the JOVE articles, didn't you?" Julius says. "Oh, I see, not about DNA cleansing. Newborn selection and implantation?"

"Wait, what do you mean? Get me online. I want into Orphanet!"

Julius leads me to a couch where he sits facing me. "No time. Be still and listen to me for a change." This young Frenchman is the most trustworthy adult I know. "They are taking you to—"

"Why POST and the entire summer?"

"Don't worry about this. Several teams are going, not just yours. It's corporate leadership training at a Marine base."

"North Carolina," I cry horrified.

"For two weeks," Julius says, trying to reassure me. "Babbage lied to scare you. They try to intimidate you. Follow orders. Can you do this, Jo?"

"Yes."

"You and your teammates must stop fighting. You must tough it out. I'm flying to headquarters."

"Paris is so far. Can't you come with us?"

Julius stares down at our clasped hands, and then his eyes flash with a passionate light. "I'll come as soon as I can."

"My parents," I stumble over the words. Is my paternity the reason

❖

for their separation? "I must talk to them. Tell me about Orphanet!"

"Not possible," he says, "I want you to know, this isn't your fault."

"What have I done?" I ask in despair.

"Nothing," Julius replies. "I assure you, this is political. Nothing you have done caused this. Do you understand?"

"Not because of me? Not the fighting or the song?"

"I admire your courage," Julius says, prudently choosing his words. "You should know about Orphanet. Your parents should have told you last night."

Two Marines barge into the office cutting off whatever Julius wanted to say. One takes me roughly by the arm. They escort me out of Hotel Edinburgh.

I run alongside them in the rain through a wide courtyard toward a military transport. In my peripheral vision, I catch a glimpse of Julius and Captain Jack.

The Marine Boomer helps me board the Predator and points toward a seat between Iain and Wei. Boomer explains flight safety procedures, telling us to buckle up, and then he heads back outside.

My teammates stare and their hostile attitudes hit me like shotgun pellets blasting into my flesh. Iain shames me with his silence. My bad. My bad decisions catch up with me though Julius confuses me. He assured me this wasn't my fault. Why political? Suddenly, the darkest moment of my life brightens up when Tala prances into the craft.

The heavy panting, mouth drooling, saliva flinging Tala breaks out in an ear ringing howl. "Arh Wooooooo." She leaps over boots and plops all one hundred and sixty pounds down on my feet. My best friend licks my face.

"Hey, your teacher talked the Capt'n into bringing your mutt." Boomer laughs at us, plainly enjoying our discomfort. "He says the dog's smarter than all you kids put together."

The rest of the Marines strap up, sharing crude jabs about neeks, brainiacs and loser candidates. One sour joke after another keeps them entertained while the twelve of us suffer their abuse.

Ben ignores the nitwits and breaks his silence. "The X29 Predator

❇

flies 400 knots," he says. "A multi-directional aircraft." The more facts he recites, the calmer his voice. "It's a helicopter, but it can convert into an airplane. Wow, smooth vertical liftoff. How cool."

"Shut that hole in your face, neek boy!" Jamil yells.

Boomer shakes his fist at Jamil. "You! Keep it up. I dare you, one more word."

The Predator is a vertical launch airplane, and once airborne it reaches a high speed, high altitude aerodynamic ceiling for the cross-country trip. The sound of the engines is a constant low modulation. The background hum is hypnotizing, and the craft's movement gently rocks me. Finally, weeks of insomnia come to an end, and I fall asleep feeling defeated and alone.

A sudden jolt causes my head to hit the panel. Several hours have passed since leaving the Sierras. I awake feeling rested and alert. The aircraft begins to shudder. A downdraft causes a rolling motion, a lift then a drag, but the pilot recovers. 2216 climate can be unpredictable. A harmless cloudburst can gather power, cause floods and tornados and become a treacherous electrical storm. Rapidly changing storms force crafts out of the sky. The shakes and shimmies worsen, and the aircraft trembles, moving and vibrating, the turbulence stressing the craft.

"This ain't nothin'," Lieutenant Kurt says, looking my direction. "A little rain."

"It's a micro storm," I challenge him, not caring how angry I sound.

"Okay, Jo. Never mind," he says apologetically. "Not my fault you kids failed the Warrior course."

The craft rocks side to side, thrusting me back and forth in my seat. "This isn't about a stupid ropes course," I say spitefully.

"Yup, I heard. Pretty serious stuff."

"Kurt, get up here. Now!" Captain Jack shouts. "Get on radar. We need to land and wait it out."

Ben yawns and rubs his eyes. "How long was I asleep?" he asks to no one in particular.

"Jo," Iain says, "whatever Babbage said, it's not your fault."

❄

"You bet it's her fault!" Jamil shouts.

"Her?" Iain yells back angrily. "Like you didn't throw a punch? We're all to blame for this."

"You nonhackers, shut up!" Boomer says, eating the last bite of his energy bar. "Smart alecks. Mouth off one more time, just try it."

A strong jerk sends Tala sliding past Iain. He puts a hand on her collar to keep her from slipping all the way into the cockpit. The lights dim flickering off and on.

The craft flies into punishing winds and earsplitting thunder. The severe turbulence pounds the sides of the transport like the jaws of a lion crushing its prey. Every fifth grader studies climate, weather patterns, and knows a downdraft can be fatal. The aircraft pitches sideways, plummeting rapidly out of the sky. A second microburst hits hard and throws me back against the panel.

Our descent is fast like the fall of Icarus with broken wings. So much for advanced technology. 2216 engineering fails in the face of Mother Nature. The lights flicker off. Iain squeezes my hand. I lean against him with my eyes closed.

The Predator flips on its side but immediately corrects itself. For a moment, the pilot maintains a steady course, yet he fails to gain sufficient altitude to make a difference. Another microburst hits. Our descent accelerates, but the pilot recovers and manages to stabilize the transport. Somehow, he makes a soft upright touchdown. It's a soft landing only because nobody dies.

The craft crashes into the ground, embedding itself in the earth like the detonation of a bomb, sending shock waves through every nerve in your brain. The painful jolt causes my senses to go numb and disorients my mind. All this happens within sixty seconds of the first microburst.

The electrical thunderstorm releases a torrential downpour, the wind raging and hammering the craft. The rear cargo hold opens, hits the ground and gives us an escape route. Any minute the craft could explode.

"Tala! Come!" I cry out. Desperately, I struggle to unbuckle my seat belt. "Where is she? Tala!"

"Let me!" Iain says impatiently. He fights with the jammed buckle. "Out, everybody out! Now! Boots on the ground! Now!"

Lieutenant Kurt uses his Ka-Bar knife to slice into the strap that pins me down. He pulls me onto my feet and shoves me toward to rear cargo hold.

"Tala!"

"Come on! Let's go!" Iain grabs me roughly, almost yanking my arm from its socket.

We leap off the platform and hit the soggy ground running side by side, the rain and wind pelting our faces. A lightning bolt splits the sky and strikes the earth on a distant mountaintop. The momentary brilliance lights up the gully where the crippled Predator has landed in the heart of darkness.

Lieutenant Kurt yells, "Get them out of here!"

"Move it, move it, move it!" Boomer shouts.

Iain sets a fast pace as we race through the wooded gully. "Keep going! Don't stop!"

The Predator is far behind us. Quickly, we cross a wide creek and climb the side of a mountain. Iain helps me over fallen timber. Wei and Zebenjo follow on our heels. Where are Dev, Cyrus, Juan Pablo and the others?

More dangerous than the crash, we face the deadly forces of North Carolina. Fear, like a megaphone, picks up and amplifies every sound. Our heavy breathing, branches breaking, twigs snapping, Marines yelling. Boomer shouts to pick up the pace. Was that thunder in the distance or automatic weapons firing? The Marines are engaged in warfare with unknown assailants down in the gully.

We cover half a mile when a loud explosion reverberates through the night. The craft bursts into a tower of fire. They destroyed our one means of escape. Rain pours down upon us and a bolt of lightning unleashes its power in the sky. Thunder booms like cannon fire overhead. How far is Camp Lejeune from our location?

We keep climbing, beating back branches, jumping over bushes,

❖

avoiding low hanging limbs. Five miles from the crash, the Marines set guards to patrol the plateau. I'm soaked to the bone, and finally exhausted, I collapse to the muddy ground.

Captain Jack and Lieutenant Kurt speak in low tones, their words echoing through my mind: cockpit fire, hostiles, Kings Mountain.

"Let them sleep," Captain Jack says. "They'll need it."

"What are the odds," asks Lieutenant Kurt, "getting out alive, I mean?"

"Alive? We're not getting out this time."

Someone drops a protective foil tent over me. The exhaustion is incapacitating. I cannot control the shivers and trembling. Tala sleeps close on top of the foil tent.

I drift into a fitful sleep. I jerk awake disoriented and confused. The storm has passed. Far in the distance, the sun waits behind the backside of an eastern mountain range. The predawn casts a shadowy gray upon the summit and the bowl-shaped valley below.

Iain is lying next to me along with Wei and Ben. Sleeping huddled together are Isaac, Cyrus and Dev. Jenna and the others sleep soundly sharing protective tents. We all made it through the night.

"We gotta get to the reservoir," Captain Jack says. "We'll know soon enough if Lejeune got the S.O.S. If not, we head for Kings Mountain."

"What about these kids?" Boomer asks, tossing his handgun back and forth between his hands.

"Well, Boomerang, we got no choice but to give them guns," says Captain Jack irritably. "Some have combat training."

Everyone is awake, alert, listening. For ten minutes, Captain Jack and Lieutenant Kurt talk strategy. The two pilots, Andy and Reggie, sit near Boomer eating energy bars, along with Dunny and Pax. Six Marines guard the perimeter. Thirteen Marines and twelve candidates.

"We take up position—" Captain Jack says, "and wait."

"Nonhackers with training, you're with me," Boomer says. Iain, Wei, Cyrus and Isaac move toward him. Artem throws off the tent and joins the boys where they stand waiting for orders.

❖

Boomer tosses a weapon to Jamil. "Hey, tough guy, try this out."

"Yeah, I got it," Jamil says, pocketing a box of magazines. "Good grip."

"Okay, boys, you get M220 Snipers and plenty of ammo, enough to take out an army." Boomer demonstrates the newest semiautomatic rifle. "Load, lock, fire. Shoot to kill."

Captain Jack eyes me with skepticism. "Babbage said your team lead. You got survival training in Idaho. Can you shoot?"

"Yes, I can."

"Wookies get side arms." Captain Jack nods to Reggie who gives us weapons.

"Keep this," Lieutenant Kurt says, handing me a backpack. "It's got a med kit, canteens and energy bars. Don't drink from the creeks. Use the purification tablets. These flash grenades are easy," he explains, stuffing several in my backpack. "Pull the pin and throw. Cover your eyes. Flash stuns for about twenty seconds."

"Andy. Reggie," Captain Jack orders, "stay on these wookies. You guys," he looks at Iain and the other boys, "follow orders. Willie, status," Captain Jack says into the radio.

"No hostiles in sight. All clear," Willie answers, from somewhere further down the mountainside.

"Headed your way," Captain Jack says, stuffing the radio in his pack. "Keep your eyes sharp," he orders the Marines. "You kids, stay close behind us. Move out!"

Iain takes me into his arms and holds me so tight I can't breathe. "Don't even think. You shoot, no matter what," he says. "You got that?" He clasps his weapon with both hands, safety off and muzzle pointed up, and leaves with Captain Jack.

"Alright, let's go sniping tough guys," Boomer says.

The Marines keep us together in a tight column. Our progress is slow as we descend the rocky slope. Reggie and Andy raise their rifles, scoping out the area, alert and ready to fire their weapons. They hustle Freja, Jenna and me down the steep hill. I catch myself from sliding on stones and pine needles. Several times, I cling to low branches to stop

❄

my boots from slipping.

Every fifteen minutes Captain Jack's voice comes through Reggie's radio, talking to his men down in the woodlands. "Willie, come in," Captain Jacks says, but no one answers. "Dunny, report." The radio is dead, nothing from Willie or Dunny. "Reg, get down here with those wookies on the double. Radio silence."

The column stops before reaching the bottomlands. Everyone crouches down and takes cover in the thick bushes. The tension in the air is palpable. I kneel beside Tala, whispering softly in her ear and tightening my grip on the handgun. Stay focused. Follow orders.

Could this be a staged war game, a POST exercise before we get to Camp Lejeune? For all we know, this might even be within their boundary line. But we're nowhere near the coast, and I check my weapon. Real bullets. Wishful thinking. Hope is dashed with brutal reality.

We are truly entering the valley of death. I don't want to die. My life feels small. I don't want much. To have a mission. To help children.

I want to make friendships that last a lifetime. I want to see my home again and my parents. To walk the reserve with Jolan. I want my first kiss to be with Iain. I want to have children and teach them a true history of the world where they can make a difference. Is this too much to ask?

Dying is hard when love promises so much.

⸎

CHAPTER FIFTEEN

A Warrior's Heart

NO ONE MOVES or makes a sound, but there is plenty of life in the old growth forest. The shrill protest of a red trailed hawk competes with two gray squirrels chattering and chasing each other up and down and all around a hickory tree. As the sun rises, a flood of shadows recedes into nothingness. For the time has come to strike the enemy before daylight exposes our position on the hillside.

Captain Jack moves forward and signals the boys with combat training to follow him down the hillside. Lieutenant Kurt leads Iain, Wei, Jamil and Artem, and Cyrus and Isaac down the mountainside. Their boots break a narrow path into the virgin forest. They quickly disappear. Already the temperature is rising, intensifying the heady balsam scent of dry pine needles and cedar trees.

Reggie points at Zebenjo, "You keep up with me. We're taking point." Reggie with Dev, Ben and Juan Pablo are the second line of defense.

Zebenjo will not break his silence. He wipes his face with his sleeve to hide his fear. Though outwardly calm, Juan Pablo's upright posture is stiff, almost clumsy. His head is erect and unmoving while his face is unnaturally empty of emotion. Dev is the exact opposite.

The alarm in his eyes is heart wrenching. For the first time, I notice his dimples. He holds a weapon ready to kill like a lost boy and seems painfully aware of this.

Minutes pass with no radio check from Captain Jack. How long before the conflict? Lieutenant Kurt comes out of the bushes. Reggie and Andy gather near and kneel where the others stand several feet away.

"Charlie six o'clock," Lieutenant Kurt says. "Two clicks along the ridge line. Take up your position and maintain radio silence."

Kurt and Dunny hustle downhill, their boots kicking up a cloud of brown dust. Tala is too fast for me to stop her from racing behind them. I want to chase her, but Andy grasps my arm.

With a grim expression, Andy raises his weapon poised to kill. He will protect Freja, Jenna and me. "This way," he says and points his gun along the southern slope. "You wookies stay behind me. Don't fire unless I do."

Jenna and I stare into each other's eyes, into open spaces and the mysteries of life and death present for an instant, then gone.

We wind our way along the lip of the hillside, running hard and fast, cutting an erratic path through dense bushes and overgrown weeds. We stumble over dead wood and tree roots. Nothing can stop our headlong race, but we don't go too far before Reggie motions us to take cover.

"Something doesn't feel right," he whispers. "Get down."

Fear can your focus thoughts like a magnifying glass. A forgotten memory can enlarge to a gigantic fragment of nonreality. An image of Superwoman becomes a superimposed version of self-truth. Marie-Joëlle Peone is the woman of steel who defeats the enemy. Bullets bounce off her invincible armor. She has the speed of a cheetah to outrun any foe. Fear makes her strong. The fantasy fades into thin air. Somewhere I read that talking about yourself in third person is a sign of severe stress.

The waiting is insufferable, and every nanosecond is agony. Time messes with your head when you wait for death. I measure the seconds one by one with a finger on my pulse. A column of ants appears like an army crawling in the dirt. Their world is a microcosm of my own.

Red fire ants. The ants go marching one by one carrying their prey. The green caterpillar is alive but captured. My vision encompasses one single red ant exploring my mud-caked boot. Ants attack first and ask questions later. Did I do a math problem in school once to find the surface area of a giant ant?

Ants are predators, small but deadly. Any day like this in Idaho, I would be hiking in the reserve on an adventure, not facing death. For one moment, perfection suffuses the wilderness with delicate white and yellow buttercups, and vibrant pink blossoms of rhododendron bushes and moss covered logs lying untouched in the woodlands.

Then Captain Jack shouts through the radio. "Light it up!"

Gunfire shatters the innocence of Eden. The perfect moment dies. Rapid gunfire does not stop. I will never forget the crisp clear clapping of the M220 Sniper echoing through the forest on a June morning in North Carolina.

Captain Jack's voice comes on the radio. "We're pinned down!" He orders the men to shoot at will. "Drive on! Keep it goin'!"

"Stay on those wookies!" That's Lieutenant Kurt on the radio.

The transmission ends. There's more gunfire and then nothing.

"We're out of here!" Reggie shouts. "Move it!"

Reggie's lips are moving, but I don't understand the meaning of his words. A bullet catches him in the face. He drops to the ground. Andy fires, killing five hostiles, and saves our lives. We race behind the young Marine, sprinting through the forest, heedless of the danger up ahead.

I run behind Dev matching his moves, ducking under tree limbs and snapping branches in the way. The prickly hawthorn bushes snag my clothes and thorns cut my face and hands.

Time can be a strange phenomenon. The faster I run, the slower I move as though swimming submerged and making no progress at all. My ears feel plugged, or stuffed with cotton, and I hear nothing but a high ringing. There is no gravity in space. No sound, no movement,

❄

no air. The vastness of space is a vacuum.

The effects of time dilation all depend on where you are. Space, satellites, Earth, and retrograde motion. The laws of nature. There is nothing natural about war. I don't know what I am thinking. This is not thinking. This is insanity.

We race frantically through the gully until reaching the other side of a hill. Andy secures a position, and we retreat into a hillock behind large boulders. Constant gunfire echoes through the valley. The small-scale battle escalates with devastating firepower. However, the crackle of the radio is silent.

"Are you hit?" Andy asks, loading a magazine. While trained to kill, Andy cannot be much older than me.

"Huh?" I ask.

"You're bleeding. Are you hit?" he repeats.

I don't understand his words. Does "hit" mean broken? Marie-Joëlle shattered into fragments, pieces of her shell splintered forever and scattered in the woods among dead bodies? All of a sudden, laughter bubbles up inside me and explodes like a geyser. I cannot stop the giggles. Laughter relieves the terror. I lean against a tree hysterical with tears streaming down my face.

My friends collapse in the dirt. Streaks of blood, sweat, tears and filth conceal their faces. Their hair is matted with thistles, leaves and insects. Blood drips from my forehead into my eyes, a temporary blindness I almost wish was permanent.

Dazed and unresponsive, Dev lowers his head and picks at his clothes. He tosses aside briars, clumps of dirt and spiders from his pants. Juan Pablo leans motionless against a tree and stares blindly into space. Freja cannot stop sobbing. Jenna sits immobile beside her. Zebenjo rests against a boulder, holding his knees and burying his head beneath his arms. Did the boys fire their weapons? Did I?

Everything is moving too fast, and there's no chance to change the course of events. It takes only one horrendous vortex to suck you up and whisk away all your truth. What you know to be sanity. The funnel forms, touches your soul and steals what is most cherished.

Lieutenant Kurt and Boomer reemerge leading the others into the hidden knoll. I search their faces and uniforms for injuries. Isaac's jacket is stained red where a bullet grazed his left arm. Writhing in agony and his face contorted with pain, he holds his GoBot hat, clinging to the visor with his free hand. Wei administers first aide to Isaac. A mask of indifference belies the strain showing on Wei's aged face.

Standing apart from the group, Artem and Jamil share a canteen, whispering in low voices. Cyrus sits holding his weapon between his legs with one hand. He flexes his fingers and rubs his scalp, and then makes a fist. In a repetitive motion, he runs his fingers through his hair and then hits his fist against a tree.

The one who eludes me is Iain. He waits alone in the shade of an old oak tree, but he stands alert and listening. He holds tight to his weapon. While Wei wears a mask, Iain is a man I do not recognize. He refuses to look at me. A harsh reality comes to me. The innocence of a Scottish boy died today in North Carolina.

"Captain Jack took one in the back," Boomer says. "Now what?"

Lieutenant Kurt checks his pack. "Follow the plan. It's been two hours since the crash. My beacon works. Yours?"

"It took a hit," Boomer says. He opens his jacket and looks at the blood on his shirt. He pulls a med pack from his bag. "Not so lucky on this one."

Only two hours since the crash. How can that be and where's Tala? Dare I look for my dog in the valley of the dead? I put my hand against a tree and dig my nails into the cracked bark. The dizziness passes, but my head swims with confusion.

"We've gotta finish them off. That camp ain't far from here," Kurt says. "We're going in, guns blazing. Neeks follow Boomer and me. Andy, cover the wookies."

Boomer swallows a mouthful of water and spits in the dirt. "Yeah, I got it. Clear the way," he says. "Nonhackers can stay with the girls."

"Hey, they earned a bar today." Kurt takes the canteen from Boomer. "They cut 'em down without thinking. Let's move out."

❈

The men follow Kurt and Boomer into the woods, all except Iain. Finally, he comes and takes me into his arms as though to shield me from what is to come.

"Don't stop," Iain says feverishly. "No matter what happens, you run for your life."

I nod my head, but keep my eyes lowered simply because I lack the courage to examine the change in him. He touches my cheek and rubs the tears from my face.

"Look at me," he says harshly.

"You saved me. You saved us all. I'm proud to be your friend, Iain Sinclair."

He tightens his hold on me. "I'm more than a friend," he whispers softly. He drops his hands, steps away and then he checks his sniper. "Remember me." He turns away and runs through the woods in the direction of gunfire.

"Let's move," Andy says. "Stay with me!"

Andy's pace is slow and cautious. Jenna, Freja and I follow him through a grove of trees, but almost immediately, a burst of gunfire echoes through the words. The chaos of shouting and cursing wait for us up ahead. Then the gunfire stops. The forest rings with silence.

"All clear," Lieutenant Kurt says over the radio. "C'mon in. We got horses and supplies."

The camp is nothing more than three or four tents and a couple of wagons. Two cows stand tied to a cart. Three nervous horses prance in place tethered to a tree. Nothing can prepare you though for the shock of corpses. Dead women and children.

Iain told me to run, but someone might be alive. That child lying face down in the dirt could be alive! How did this happen?

"Hit the deck!"

From out of nowhere, Iain plows into me and knocks me off my feet. His heavy weight pins me to the ground, and he pushes my face into the dirt. Andy kills two before falling and dying beside us.

Iain springs to his feet and yanks me up beside him. Running for our lives, we race away, chickens scurrying under our feet and a dog

❄

nipping at our heels. My thoughts are somewhere outside my mind. Two thoughts cannot occupy the same space. Do I evade the enemy or return to check for survivors? I don't have a choice. I run for my life beside Iain until we find our friends a mile from camp.

Lieutenant Kurt is the last Marine alive, but just barely alive. A deliberating weakness overwhelms me. My knees give way, and I hit the ground beside Kurt.

I unbutton his jacket. Kurt is hemorrhaging from a bullet in the abdomen. My fingers are sticky from touching his soaked shirt. The blood smells metallic. I know right away that even with my medical training, I can do nothing to save the young Lieutenant.

"Where are the others?" I ask, taking the med kit from my pack.

"Juan Pablo, Cyrus and Wei are keeping watch," says Dev who administers a dose of morphine to ease Kurt's pain.

"The other boys went back looking for you and Iain," Jenna adds, putting her arms around Freja. Zebenjo shares a canteen with Isaac in the shade of an old cedar.

"If we get to a safe place, I can remove the bullet. I've had training." I hear the desperation in my absurd plan.

Iain kneels beside me and squeezes my shoulder. "Ye must let him go," he whispers gently.

A gut wrench explodes like a power bomb with shards deep in my bowels. Helpless and afraid, I hold Kurt's hand watching the life fade from his face.

"Take this," he says. Kurt hands me the GPS. "I'm so thirsty." I lift a canteen to Kurt's lips.

"Drink this." I drop the device in my pocket, not telling him the GPS is broken.

"About ninety miles south is a mining camp, Kings Mountain," Kurt says. His body trembles from shock. Gurgling with the death rattle, he wheezes with mucous and coughs up blood.

"Too far," Jenna says with despair.

"Jo," Kurt whispers. "Blue Ridge. It's not much different than your home." His grip tightens around my fingers. "You're the one to save

❄

them. Keep them moving."

"Yes, I promise to get them home," I reply.

Kurt's ash gray face is trance inducing. How do I discern what is real? What are these dreamlike images blurring my vision? This is what I have seen in the night terrors. Will the nightmare never end?

"Get out of here. Travel at night," he says. He gasps for breath. For a moment, his lips form a tremulous smile. "So, what kind of name *is* Jo for a girl?"

"Marie," I cry, losing all hope. "Marie-Joëlle." But I answer too late.

A shade of darkness falls upon Kurt's ashen face. His eyes dim to an eerie gray as he draws a last breath. Death snatches Lieutenant Kurt Harris from the earthly realm of a temporal life. But the One World Church teaches nothing of life beyond the grave. I hope a paradise with beings of light welcome him.

"We've got to move!" Iain says, snapping shut the med kit and stuffing it in my pack.

"I can't go."

Kurt's warm hand covers mine. I have never seen death. This is the first dead body I've ever touched. We don't have funerals or graveyards. No hospitals. Death is not something we see. Where do the sick and dying live until their passing? I have never wanted to know until now. Where are the tears? I should be crying.

Iain shuts Kurt's eyelids. "Jo, we've got to go. Now!"

"Shouldn't we say something?" I plead.

"Aye, we should."

"They don't teach us to pray," Isaac says. Zebenjo and Jenna help him to stand up.

"My uncle taught me in secret," Iain replies. "Everyone, bow your heads. Lord, we hope the soul of Lieutenant Kurt finds his way to ye. Forgive his killing. He got us through the fight and saved us. Amen."

"What now?" Freja asks fearfully.

"Get the others. We need a plan," I answer, throwing on my pack.

Signs of trauma and battle fatigue are settling on their faces. We must get moving before they cannot or will not be able to function. I

❄

won't think about what we lost today. Too many losses on both sides. The only thing we can do is escape from the assailants behind us and prepare for the dangers ahead.

"Everyone, give Zebenjo your energy bars and canteens. We ration food and water," I command. "Cyrus, Jamil and Artem, I want you to take point. Get us up the ridge so we can get our bearings."

"We need a place to wait for dark," Iain adds, "Ben and Juan Pablo, take care of Isaac and the girls. Wei and Dev come with me. We'll take the rear."

Without question, the team follows our directions. After several hours of hiking, we escape into the remote timberland at a higher elevation. For now, we must avoid the reservoir. The climb is long and treacherous but worth the risk.

From our vantage point, the Blue Ridge is an undulating wave of endless forestland and a vast outback none of us anticipated. This is an otherworldly place where the whole of human history lies waiting to be discovered. The panoramic view is breathtaking, but equally dangerous.

Ninety miles is not so far but crossing the mountains will be slow and difficult. And we risk detection if we follow well-marked trails. Hunting with guns will alert the enemy to our presence. Fresh game might be contaminated from the Plague, or so we've been taught.

We have to travel at night, and stay high and away from the valleys. And avoid engaging the enemy. We can go without food for a couple days, but not without water. Rationing water will be essential until we come across a waterway.

The danger we face instills in us the determination to survive. No one complains of hunger or tiredness. No harsh words or arguments. Our survival depends on immediate action and relying on each other.

The midday sun is a sweltering temperature. Despite a canopy of trees, exertion takes its toll. We march one by one in a single line, silent, steady and alert. No one speaks. We carry the weight of the dead upon our shoulders, the dead enemy, the Marines who died protecting us and the unburied women and children.

❋

Grief is a heavy load. I fight off despair, thinking of those red ants, a tiny force of power carrying the caterpillar on their backs. Miniature predators. But who is the predator and who the prey?

Long past midnight we make our way through the deserted woods with no sign of man or beast. Our flashlights break a trail through a thick black night. The white light creates mammoth-sized monsters of the lofty overhanging trees. We travel with caution, stepping over gnarled trunks in a wilderness of overgrown timberland. Better to step with care than rush blindly and fall off a cliff. Up and down, we hike the slopes of this primeval forest. Navigating by the stars will not be possible. The weather is much too unreliable.

What is it about this night that reminds me of Idaho? I never told my parents how often I climbed out my bedroom window after they went to sleep. Nothing could stop me from finding a way out of town. Patrol officers follow a scheduled routine. They check areas every two or three hours.

There was always plenty of time for Tala and me to run through the meadow into secluded woods. Summer nights we would swim in the lake, a full yellow moon rising high off the mountain ridge. The moonbeams were a radiant light upon still waters.

Tonight, the heavenly bodies shimmer like tiny pinpoints of fire, scintillating like diamonds upon black velvet, and the lights from the most distant stars and planets appear larger, brighter than any night in the city of D.C. We make camp in a tight circle within a sheltered alcove on the face of a mountain, a defensible position with boulders on all sides.

"Jenna and Freja, stay together whenever you leave camp," I say needlessly. "We're doing the buddy system. No one leaves camp alone."

The pack slides off my back. I check it for the med kit and other supplies. I find very little that will improve our situation. Dev dresses Isaac's flesh wound with clean bandages and administers antibiotics. Withdrawn into himself, Ben won't talk to anyone.

"I'll take first watch." I take the sniper from Ben. "Get some sleep."

Iain reaches for his gun, but I wave him off. He does not argue.

❄

He bundles his jacket into a makeshift pillow. The others settle into private places, all except Cyrus. He reaches in his pocket for a piece of chewing gum, buttons his coat and catches up to me. High on the ridge not far from the alcove, we take a strategic position.

"I'm cranked," Cyrus says. "No way can I sleep tonight."

"I'm not sure I can stay awake," I say, yawning and rubbing my face.

I've never felt so exposed. Every sound grates on my nerves. The breeze through the trees strikes fear in me. To ward off the cold, I curl into myself, wrapping my arms around my legs. My head rests on my knees. I feel myself falling out of my body. I blink several times, but again my head finds its way back to my knees. I doze off immediately jerking back awake.

"I wonder about life after death," says Cyrus in a troubled voice.

"Don't even go there," I reply, throwing him a sidelong glance. "We're not going to die, except maybe from exposure."

Cyrus scoots closer to me and puts his arm around my shoulder. His body is imbued with warmth as hot as a pellet stove, the flames emitting an intense heat. "Don't you wonder?"

"I didn't expect you to—you know, cuddle," I stutter embarrassed.

"I know Iain and you are together," he answers. "We're just friends, right? This place is nothing like Iran. Is it like your home?"

"Not so different. They don't teach us much at the Cathedral. I hacked what I know from digital images of ancient parchments. The old religion says something about heaven waits for the righteous."

Cyrus clicks on the flashlight. "The light helps. I keep seeing dead bodies," he whispers. "I don't know, but Iain believes in something."

"I think he and Dev know things."

Cyrus grimaces, overly watchful of the night. "I can't think with this headache," he complains, heaving a long sigh and rubbing his temples.

The flashlight betrays the battle fatigue on his face. Cyrus is no longer the exotic, mesmerizing boy Freja described at the Warrior's course. His thick black hair and short beard are dusted gray with fragments of dirt and pine needles. The luscious lips are cracked and bleeding. The sensitive boy is lost in the torment of a disquieted mind.

"Cyrus?"

"Hummm?"

"I know some truth," I whisper. "I hacked that secure file .dc2."

The forest is shrouded in a damp mist. Twisted shapes and gnarled limbs dominate the black night. A frightening stillness settles on the forest. Absent is the screech of a hoot owl, its talons heavy with rabbit or squirrel. Not even the twittering of crickets breaks the silence. A mouse quickly scurries for the cover of darkness. The distant chirp of a bird startles me to my feet.

"Turn out the light!" I whisper. "Quick!"

"What's that?" Cyrus asks, flicking off the flashlight. "A bird?"

"Not a bird." I recognize a twerp I have not heard for a long time. "A mountain lion, maybe."

The high-pitched screech is alarmingly near. I start to scream. But luckily, Cyrus holds me close and pulls me behind a boulder, covering my mouth with his hand.

The creature might be hunting a raccoon or doe. Then again, it could be the enemy tracking us. Whether man or beast, the danger is very real. A grizzly bear can disembowel a man with one swipe of its paw. I catch a glimpse of the indistinct form moving near the tree line.

The beast moves under the cover of darkness and disappears into the shadowy woods. The predator feeds upon its prey. Death comes in the night, and the eyes of the dead see all.

CHAPTER SIXTEEN

Baby Lizards

I TASTE BLOOD from having bit my lip. Cyrus stands unmoving but aims his weapon ready to fire. As much as I want to run, I force myself to stay quiet. Cyrus and I peer into the prevailing darkness. My eyes play tricks on me. One minute the black shape is a shadow easily engulfed by the woods, then I know it must be an evil spirit in human form. That uninhibited feeling of hysteria explodes like an eruption of bubbles and then dissipates as quickly as it came.

"Wait, don't shoot!" An unexpected elation fills me. "It's my dog!"

Tala plows into my knees, knocking me over, licking my face and drooling slobber on my shirt. She does the happy dog dance. Her wagging tail disturbs the mouse that scurries away into the vegetation.

Cyrus lowers his weapon and turns the flashlight on. "That was intense. I feel hammered. Ecstatic, but terrified. Everything's surreal."

"Good dog," I laugh, scratching Tala's ear with my nails. "That's adrenaline and stress."

Cyrus's eyes burn with a white-hot urgency forged from mortal combat. Without much effort, I can imagine him as a fierce warrior on horseback protecting the Iranian deserts. He could well be a descendant of Cyrus the Great, slashing his sword and shouting war cries to thousands in a straight on fight.

"As a speed junky," he says, running his fingers through his hair, "I swear, this is more intense even than racing. I'm cranked up, like I can't settle down."

The state of super-heightened senses after battle is common, or so I have read. My nerves tingle as though on fire, and I cannot stop trembling.

"I feel the same." I bury my face in Tala's fur. She is hot, sweaty and smelly. "Oh, yuck! Skunk!" The musky scent clears my sinuses and leaves a sulfuric aftertaste in my mouth.

Tala digs her teeth into my pants. She whines clamping her teeth on the material and tearing a hole. "Stop it!" I cry, pushing her away and getting to my feet. She moves past me and runs downhill.

"What's wrong with her?"

"Something is out there."

Cyrus moves to stand in front of me. He points the flashlight in a semicircular sweep through the tightly compacted timberland. The narrow beam splits the blackness into a fragile light. "We need backup," he says in a tight voice. "I'm getting Iain and Wei."

Cyrus is as tall as Iain. His hair is jet black. Thick curls fall down his shoulders. I brush aside a spider crawling on his forehead.

"Don't worry. Tala won't lead me into danger," I say confidently. My dog has always protected me. But just in case, I click the safety off my gun. "I'm going down to check it out."

"Fine, we go together," he says in a husky voice. "Follow me."

"Thanks, Cyrus, but I think Tala is the leader on this one."

A few hundred feet down the hill, Tala proudly leads us straight to her prize. Cyrus directs the light into thick bushes where a child is lurking. For a moment, her face is visible then she disappears. Not thinking what might be out there, I give chase with Tala outdistancing me and reaching the girl before me. She would have evaded us in the darkness had Tala not poked her nose into the plants.

"Don't kill me." Bright blue eyes peer through purple flower petals.

Instinctively, I knee and push aside the branches. "Are you alright?"

❄

I ask tentatively, wanting to comfort the little girl.

"I'm Lily."

Keeping her eyes closed, the girl lowers her chin. Tears glisten on her cheeks. More like a delicate doll than a child, Lily is thin but not undernourished. She wears a modest blue dress. Pine needles, tiny twigs and dead leaves hang from her hair, not much different from mine, except her braids are blond.

Cyrus crouches to the ground in a wolverine posture. "It's a trap," he says, scanning the area with the flashlight.

"I don't think so. Come to me."

Lily crawls on hands and knees. As though sensing the fear, Tala moves her body between Cyrus and Lily. Tala knocks her down plopping her head on Lilly's belly. Tala looks up with glistening yellow eyes. Both child and dog reek of skunk.

Restless and fidgety, Cyrus paces back and forth taking out his aggression on the flashlight. The beam of light bounces up and down in erratic waves. "We need to check the area," he insists.

"Anyone watching already knows our position."

"All the more important..." he pauses, "to check it out."

"If it makes you feel better, take Tala and go."

"I won't be long," he says, giving me the flashlight. He disappears into the woods with Tala at his side.

"Is that your dog?" she asks.

"I'm Jo."

Is this child lost, or could the enemy be using her against us? What if Cyrus is right, and she's loaded with explosives, a tactic once used by terrorists. We might have only a few seconds before a bomb detonates. Something must be done fast.

I take a half-eaten bar from my jacket. "Are you hungry?"

"Uh huh."

"Here, take this."

I offer her the bar, quickly searching her body. I find no explosives. Lily takes the bar. We touch briefly. I snatch my hand away as though my skin was on fire with the Plague. My gesture startles her, but Lily does not move nor does she understand my caution.

The virus incapacitates and kills fast. A victim wouldn't be able to walk, much less climb a mountain in the middle of the night. She doesn't look ill, but she might be asymptomatic, or a carrier with the virus dormant in her system. She cannot be much older than nine. I'm afraid of her, but then realize I am afraid for Lily. Something tells me to trust my instincts and befriend her.

"Are you a girl soldier?" Lily asks.

"No, I'm not." I take her small hand pulling her into my arms. "It's a long story."

She nibbles the bar. "I like stories," she says. Finding she likes the taste, Lily crams the bar in her mouth. She chews and talks at the same time. "I rike your wog."

"Tala."

Lily smacks her lips and licks the crumbs from her palm. "Tala," she says in a small voice.

"Didn't your mother teach you not to talk with your mouth full?" I ask, without thinking and sounding very much like Océane.

Instantly, I regret the words. The thought of my mother saddens me. She must think I am dead. How could I have been so stupid? Lily's mother must have died in the fight.

"Nothing's out there," Cyrus says crossly.

He is jumpy and cannot stop jerking his head around, perpetually looking over his shoulder and checking the trail. His raises his weapon and aims the muzzle at Lily.

"Stop! You'd shoot a child? She's perfectly fine."

Cyrus hunches his back and turns the opposite direction, holding the sniper close to his chest. "This is so bad," he mutters to himself. "Really bad."

The first rays of dawn cast a dim light on those back at the hidden enclosure. My vision heightens my awareness, and a subtle change in perception imparts an unbearable truth. We inherit the problems of a broken world. And sadly, no one survives a war unscathed. The boys have undergone an initiation into manhood, which was forced upon them in the killing fields.

I walk into a camp of strangers. Dev, Wei and Iain sit around a small fire burning of dry wood to reduce smoke. The others sleep undisturbed by our arrival.

Infallible Lim Chang Wei's strategic game face hides his thoughts. The change in him is subtle. His good looks are less reserved, his charisma slightly diminished. Nevertheless, his demeanor is refined with an unsurpassable power.

Deprived of the seclusion that he cherishes, Dev Rammdas Patel's turtle shell now exposes a vulnerability otherwise disguised. His sharp glance is no longer that of a shy boy, but a man born of battle readiness.

Chosen by destiny, Iain Alexander Sinclair is truly a fearsome leader with the warrior-like posture of his Highlander ancestors. His face is no longer flawless, the perfect dream-boy. Hard contours shape his mouth, and deep lines crease his forehead. His hazel eyes, while capturing the light, reflect a lost haunted look he fails to conceal.

Iain's eyes follow me as I walk toward him. He leaps up, grabbing his weapon. "What's this?" he shouts.

Slowly, I take a step backward and bump into Dev. "I did nothing wrong. She is an orphan. You, of all people, should appreciate that."

"Wei. Dev," Iain says, "stand guard till I come for you."

The two men snatch their jackets and head off to the spot where Cyrus and I spent the last three hours. Lily presses against my thigh and holds tight to my pants. Pacing back and forth, Tala lets out a low, menacing growl that does nothing to ease the building tension.

A capable leader, Iain is aggressive while sensitive to others, or so I had thought. He takes me by the shoulders and shakes me roughly. "This is no game, Jo. It's life or death out here!"

Cyrus steps to my side and presses his advantage. The two men are well matched in height and strength. "Take your hands off her," he says gruffly.

Iain ignores Cyrus and scrutinizes me with amber stone eyes. "Battling for our lives and take care of a child? I don't know how to do that," he says, the heat dissipating from his temper.

❉

He turns slightly to Cyrus. His eyes take in the full measure of the man. Not threatened in the least, Iain nods his head, acknowledging Cyrus's defiance.

"Good. I need your courage," Iain says. Nose to nose, the men face each other. "And your obedience," he adds forcefully.

"You have it," Cyrus says fiercely, "and my friendship."

"Any sign of outlanders?"

Cyrus lifts his eyes imploring me to understand. He points to Lily, releasing an audible sigh. "Just her. I told Jo this was bad."

"Get some sleep. Both of you," Iain says, cutting him off. "Is that a skunk I smell?"

Iain makes no apology for his rough shoulder shaking. I give him the silent treatment, locate my backpack and take Lily to a place where we can sleep while Tala settles down against me. The adrenaline junky Cyrus leans against a boulder. He drops headfirst to the ground and falls asleep without as much as a makeshift pillow.

Exhaustion washes over me. Feeling dizzy, I lean over and rest my head on the bag. These few items are all that stand between life and death for us. Behind closed eyelids, I lose myself in a kaleidoscope of bizarre distortions of castles floating upside down and prom gowns promenading. A stream of data singing in a courtyard, a decapitated head reciting poetry and the boyish face of Lieutenant Kurt Harris haunt me.

Now I understand why Kurt was watching me with those bright steady eyes like Jolan looks at Océane. Lieutenant Kurt liked me in the way a boy likes a girl. But he died before having the chance to know *what kind of name is Jo for girl?*

❄

"JO, WAKE UP!"

My dreams are a tangled mess like the noose around my neck. Lieutenant Kurt's voice confuses me. I struggle to get free from the rope choking me. I have injured my head in the fall from the platform. Kurt has come to rescue me from the Warrior course. No, I mean from the enemy in the forest. Was the crash a nightmare?

"Wake up!"

Someone calls my name and kicks me in the ribs, but still my eyes will not open. I sink deeper into oblivion. A thick blackness possesses me. Like a drug inducing stupor, I fight the powerful aftereffects of stress, clinging to dream fragments, not wanting to wake up.

A boot catches me in the gut. "That hurt." I sit up rubbing my face and shaking myself awake.

It must be noon. The sun overhead is intense. I squint in the harsh light. How long did I sleep?

Then reality hits me. Our position must be compromised, and the enemy is attacking. The gun is in my hand before I get to my feet. The safety catch releases. Without hesitation, I squeeze my finger on the trigger.

But the enemy hasn't attacked. The scene before me is like nothing I'd expected. Artem and Jamil aim their snipers at Iain, who is poised for the fight. It's a three-way faceoff. The two men exchange a look of solidarity willing to fight Iain to the death to get their way.

Bent on inflicting pain, Artem's high cheekbones and long narrow nose are contorted in a hideous rage. I once had envisioned this young Russian as a dashing hero of a romantic adventure, not a rogue killer spoiled by war. But he holds his sniper like a coldblooded mercenary.

The slant of Artem's eyes betrays an unspeakable evil. He points his weapon at Lily. "You need to go!" he says to Lily. His tight lips curl in a callous smile. And to demonstrate his intentions, he kicks hot embers with his boot. Cedar chips and bark fly in the air.

"Stop it!" I shout. "What—is—going—on?"

The evil in Jamil's heart intensifies his dark eyes. Sadly, his classic handsomeness is but a glassy surface betraying cruelty. His rage could easily change him into a cold-blooded murderer.

"You brought the Plague here," Jamil rants viciously. He seizes my jacket and clutches my throat. "I'll kill you."

In one fluid motion, Iain raises his fist and punches Jamil squarely in the mouth. He drops to the ground like a bag of rocks.

"Touch her again, and I'll kill you," says Iain in a deep voice, an empty, dead sound that frightens me. In his left hand, he holds an automatic weapon. "Get behind me, Jo."

"What are you doing? Put that sniper down!" I scream, my rebuke an echo of Captain Jack's raspy Marine voice. "Have you lost your mind?" I shout, waving my gun and accidentally shooting off a round. My shot goes wild, but gets their attention. They lower their weapons, but their yelling gets louder.

I want to shame them, but that will escalate the conflict. How do I save friends pulled by a riptide into an evil underworld? Whatever happens though, I will protect Lily.

"She's not diseased!" I cry fervently. "Look at yourselves. It's the killing. Stop this fighting."

Last semester I had a health and psychology course. The digital digest defined trauma induced symptoms as angry outbursts, hysterics and crying. Agitation. Irritability. Rage. I know the fight on the Warrior course was bad, but this is much worse. I don't know how the boys feel, but deep in my gut, a minute particle winds itself tighter and tighter in a spiral of ellipses, sending tremors throughout my body. The others must feel a similar overwhelming madness.

No one notices when Zebenjo tosses aside the blanket. He rises unsteadily to his feet and steps backward without uttering a word. He smiles slowly, an odd gesture given our dilemma, while his head and shoulders bob wildly like a horse ready to bolt. Time may heal his pain, but for now Ben turns and wanders aimlessly down the hillside.

"Where's he going?" Isaac asks, rubbing the sleep from his eyes. "I feel like crap. Got any morphine?" he asks. Despite his injury, Isaac seems in good spirits, but his eyes widen with alarm. "Hey, what did I miss?" he asks. He puts on his GoBot cap and inspects his bandage.

Freja frets with the buttons on her jacket. One pops off and lands in the dirt. Her fair skin is sunburned. Tears roll down her face, and she wipes them away, smearing dried blood and grime on her cheeks. "We're going to die. We're all going to die out here."

Juan Pablo moves about confused and restless, swinging his arms in wide frantic gestures like the Jibbterbug he demonstrated at dance practice. His outsized personality fuels his outburst. "They had horses and wagons with supplies." Juan Pablo rubs the front of his shirt as he speaks. "Let's go get them. We can ride all the way to Kings Mountain."

"It's too dangerous to go back," Iain says.

Uncertainty darkens Juan Pablo's face. Will he go with Jamil and Artem, or stand with Iain? As usual he chooses the wrong side and joins Jenna Slate where she stands behind Artem.

Cyrus, with a calm detachment, checks the magazine in his sniper and casually walks around Jamil and Artem. He takes a drink from the canteen and ambles his way over to Iain. "Whatever you want done," he says in a dispassionate tone.

Jamil is anything but calm. Sweat pours off his face, and he pounds his fists against his thighs as he paces back and forth. "We're done with you, Peone!"

By my side, Tala snarls and springs toward Artem and Jamil who back off and lower their weapons. I call her back into submission.

Jenna keeps her distance from Tala, but makes no small effort to attack me. "You're insane Jo. Bringing that girl here!" she yells, lifting her snub nose. "This is all your fault! Those Marines are dead because of you. We shouldn't be here. Even Iain thinks you're crazy!"

"That's not true, Jenna!" Iain shouts, straightening his posture to an imposing six foot three. "It's what I did," he hesitates. "The ropes course and fighting at dance practice. We're all to blame."

❈

Not so long ago, all I wanted was to kill Jenna Slate. Here's my chance. My hands tremble terribly, but I give Iain the handgun. "I can't do this," I murmur softly.

Most of my existence, I have lived within the depths of troubled waters underneath an iceberg. My essential self was immersed behind a cold, impenetrable stone. People saw an invention of Marie-Joëlle.

I've never been popular at school. While other girls are outgoing and beautiful, I was pulled by undercurrents into the depths of self-loathing, and ached for a reason to live and wondered—why me?

Why don't I belong? My skin could be orange or pink or purple. The color is not the problem. The curse I suffer is living in isolation with my pain. I hate to see my friends tormented with the same agony. Now I know why the visions come— to be a Spiritbinder for others.

"Stop it, Jenna. We're beat up," I state simply. I calm myself, but I know this fight is far from being over. I stare into her wide blue eyes.

Jenna's natural beauty is a smokescreen for a vindictive spoiled girl. Artem, Jamil and Juan Pablo encircle her like a crew of blind seafaring sailors enticed by the siren's song. They will follow her as they did on the Warrior's course.

"What's your problem, Jo?" Jenna taunts, stepping around Artem to provoke me. I recoil from her and the hatred in her face. The sun highlights her blond hair like the halo of a fallen angel that is bent on sprinkling human blood in a dark ritual.

"You're the problem," I snap, unable to control myself. I squeeze my fingers into fists. I'd like nothing more than to pin her down and smack her. "You've always been the problem. So shut up and sit down."

"Your dad's a drunk, and your mother abandoned you!"

Her bodyguards visibly flinch with embarrassment at her brutality. Positive self-talk is rubbish when someone calls you out and exposes your pain. Jenna's stupid talk forces my hand. What else can I do, but strike back and defend myself?

They say slander pierces the soul. Does not revenge ease the shame of bullying? Her smile mocks me and triggers my rage. An imaginary retaliation plays out in my head. The flash fiction comes fast and furious. Frame by frame, I witness Jenna's destruction. A room in my mind is the stage where I pin her to the floor and pound on her.

The hitting is abusive and cruel. My fists strike soft spots in her stomach. Jenna struggles beneath me. She is heavier than I am, but I'm much faster and restrain her with my legs, pulling her blond hair and grasping her neck in a death grip. One snap could so easily break her neck.

An exhilaration pours through me, a heady feeling of absolute power. This illusion is the rampage of a lost child. I am not that child. What doesn't kill us will heal us. For truly, I channel power from my gut, not the disorder of my head.

My hand upon Iain's arm is an anchor, and he holds me in a fixed place beyond the rage. First, I forgive myself for hating Jenna Slate and all the times I wanted to punish her for hurting me. The Spiritbinder is born of forgiveness, and the holy presence eases my suffering.

"Done. No more," I avow, thinking the storm is past, and my way is calm and steady.

"You're a coward," Jenna says, taking a sniper from Artem's hand. "We're taking over, and that girl is not coming with us!"

"What? You think Jenna is such an angel-girl?" I cry out, venting the remnants of pain. "Do you want to know what she does to little girls? She tied me to a tree, so tight the ropes left marks, and she cut my hair, taunting and spitting at me."

"She's lying!" Jenna exclaims. The secret is no longer mine, but the humiliation is hers. "She'll say anything to get you guys on her side." The midday sun lights her face with disgrace. She cannot escape the public exposure of her ugly act.

"You won't survive an hour out there on your own," I reply, spent of all emotion, but feeling clean and revived.

Wei and Dev walk Zebenjo back into camp, and they stand with Iain and Cyrus alongside me. Isaac decides to join with us.

"She's right," Ben says, slipping his hand into mine. "None of us will survive without Jo's help."

These are his first words since Lieutenant Kurt's death. Zebenjo

Tongogara was not born to raise his hand against another in violence. Though his stance is one of caution, he will defend me in a showdown. I'm relieved to see the adorable twinkle in his eyes has returned.

"Go ahead and leave," I say with bitterness, letting go of Iain and Ben. I drop down beside Lily and Tala. "I don't care what you do."

"You've said enough, both of you," Iain says angered, rubbing the side of his face. "We need to fight together. Isaac, put out the fire. Ben, pack up camp. The rest of you, we need to talk." Iain's brogue thickens when he's upset and worried. "We've no choice. I reckon it's time we make ourselves a plan for killing."

Iain takes the men aside where they talk war strategy and devise a course of action. The one who worries me is Freja. Withdrawn, she sits by herself in the cleft of a boulder. Freja refuses to be touched, but Jenna makes her come out and wraps an arm around her shoulder.

Staying at higher elevations works only if we find fresh streams. Despite the arguing, everyone is weak from lack of food and adequate rest. We can survive a day or two without water, but we'll need to stay hydrated to ward off hypothermia.

My father taught me that if you can't find water in the mountains, then head downhill and look for animal tracks. Solitary tracks don't mean much. It's best to follow converging tracks in close proximity. A primary water source will be in the area, but you have to watch for the larger, predatory animals. Clear flowing water is the best. Purification tablets, fortunately, are in my pack. Water down in the valley is the only option.

I've read about hunting, but I've never killed an animal, much less skinned and cooked one. Right now, the idea sounds ludicrous. Lily pretends to sleep. I know she heard the hate-talk about her.

Rolling the tent into a square, I push it down into my pack. "Hey, sleepy head. Time to get up," I say in a singsong voice. Tala responds with a high-pitched howl.

Lily hurdles herself over Tala's bulky form. She cuddles beside me. "I want to go home," she says, throwing her arms around my neck.

"Where's home?"

❆

"I dunno."

I offer her the energy bar Ben gave me. "Hungry?"

"Why do they hate me?" she asks sadly.

"They're afraid."

Lily holds the uneaten bar. "Where's yours? Can we get real food?"

"Food, how?"

"You're silly," she says. "Forage for nuts and berries. Set traps."

Iain sits down with us in the dirt. His wavy hair is loose about his shoulders and a two-day shadow covers his unshaven face. "Ye build traps?"

"They taught me," Lily says in a small, but firm tone.

"Traps, ye say," Iain repeats, pondering the concept thoughtfully. He looks as though he has discovered the secret to alchemy.

A five-inch long lizard races across the dirt. Lily snatches up the green Carolina Anole and holds its slender body in her hand. She pets its flat head with her fingertips. Her smile passes from Iain to me.

"You're funny," she says. "Soldiers not knowing how to hunt."

Iain and I exchange a look of embarrassment. In catching a baby lizard, this child has shown us that she is more adept in surviving than twelve world-class polymaths.

"Tell me everything ye know about catching wee baby lizards and trapping critters," Iain says eagerly.

Lily carefully places the baby lizard into Iain's large hands. "First, respect all life," she says astutely. Staring into his bright hazel eyes, Lily perfectly imitates his Scottish brogue. "And kill only when ye must."

❆

CHAPTER SEVENTEEN

Grandfather Mountain

"**D**ON'T EVER PEE on your trap," Lily says, shaking her finger at Iain. Her eyes give him a silent reprimand although I have to wonder how a small child managed to escape the firestorm. A knot clenches my stomach. All those dead were left unburied in the valley. How did Lily survive the massacre and who are her people?

Iain shrugs casually and replies, "Aye, we'll get to traps, but I've a few questions first."

The bully-four along with Juan Pablo separate themselves and sit in their corner of camp speaking in low, indiscernible voices while occasionally glancing our direction.

Zebenjo's face is full of life, which is an encouraging sign that he's feeling better. "No peeing?" he asks scooting closer to Lily. "What bait do you use for fishing? This area must be good for trout fishing and turkey hunting. I read that whitetail deer..."

"To mask your scent," Lily mumbles, fidgeting with the wrapper from the bar. She folds the crumbled paper into a neat square and drops it in my hand.

Unlike the twelve of us, the child seems to know how to live off the land. Maybe, she's familiar with local landmarks. Clearly, we won't be rescued. We must save ourselves and find the way out of the highlands through enemy lands. Even now, human predators could be tracking us. The irony is she could make the difference in whether we live through another day and reach Kings Mountain.

Iain opens his fist to free the squirmy lime-green lizard. It poses loftily, surveying its few options and flashes a red tongue before it projects itself like a missile from Iain's fingers. Nimbly, it evades Tala's paws and scurries into the brush.

Unfortunately, the real-life threats of the Blue Ridge outweigh the frivolity of playing with lizards. We share a sense of urgency to glean what facts we can. Lily catching the lizard infuses Iain with a modest rise of enthusiasm though short-lived.

"Now, about these mountains, what can you tell us?" Iain asks huskily, leaning forward with an unnerving menace in his expression.

Lily says nothing but moves into the circle of my embrace. She stares down at her dress, and her fingers play with lose threads from the checkerboard pattern.

Nothing in Iain's face resembles the boy who escorted me through the romantic gardens at Hotel Hohenzollern. Fearless and formidable, he's adapted to the wilderness of the Blue Ridge Mountains. Iain is the epitome of a formidable questing bear. Bushy thick eyebrows and disorderly red hair. Strong broad shoulders and a lean muscular frame.

I force a smile from my lips. Luckily, Iain's attention is on the girl. I rock Lily in my arms, hoping to ease her fear. "Don't be afraid. He's quite friendly once you get to know him. Do you know where we are?"

"Near Grandfather Mountain," she replies.

"Your grandfather lives here?" Iain asks. "Right, that's good."

"She means a place called Grandfather Mountain," I correct him, content to serve as interpreter and not upstage Iain as interrogator.

"Aye, fine," Iain says with a slight irritation. "Are there villages?"

"You're a soldier," Lily says. "You have guns. Why are you afraid of the bad men?"

My arms tighten around Lily. I rest my chin on the top of her head.

❖

Iain lifts his eyes to my face and stares intently, conveying a clear message to me. Time is a luxury we don't have.

He gives me an imperceptible nod. "I promise to keep you safe," I say, encouraging her gently with a kiss. "Who are the bad men?"

Lily buries her face in my shoulder and cries. "I dunno. I ran. Then you came."

"We know that!" Jamil exclaims, making his way into our group. He takes a spot between Isaac and Cyrus. His eyes are luminous in a frantic sort of way. "I say we go back for those horses!"

"Stop it. You're scaring her," Iain says firmly, ignoring the quizzical frown on Lily's face. "We've come six miles, but it's not safe to go back."

"I don't understand," I begin confused. "Who were you fighting before we found that camp?"

"Not now, Jo. The villages," Iain repeats.

"Those horses...," Zebenjo says tentatively. "It's too risky and..."

"Yes, horses!" Jamil argues vehemently. "We'll get to the mining camp in a few days. We've got ammo..."

"Is it worth going back?" Isaac asks. "We're safer in the mountains." A makeshift sling supports his injured arm.

"They could be tracking us," Cyrus says. "We've got no idea what we're up against."

I lean forward looking intently into Lily's face. "Is there water at Grandfather Mountain?" She nods, playing with the folds of her dress. "Can you take us there?"

"Back down?" she asks.

"No way!" Zebenjo says, "It's too dangerous."

"How about the cave?" Lily says excitedly. "We hid there."

Using a twig, I draw in the dirt three-square wagons, the lake and the mountain we climbed. "This is your camp. Where's the cave?"

She shrugs her shoulders. "Behind the waterfalls."

"It must be north of the reservoir. We'll have to chance it, and go back the way we came," Iain says.

"We can get the supplies. Whatever we can scavenge," Jamil says.

"No, it's not safe," Iain says sharply. "Jamil, talk to Artem and

Jenna. We have to work together."

"I agree," Cyrus says. "We evade the enemy, not hang around in their backyard."

Jamil stands up and stretches his hands above his head. He flexes the muscles in his arms as a show of force. "Tell them yourself, boss-man. I'm not your boy!" He spits in the dirt and goes to sit beside Freja.

"The cave is shelter where we can get our bearings." I speak calmly to reassure Ben. "You can hunt. We gather food. Isaac needs to recover. We all do."

"Jo's right," Iain nods. "Besides with these snipers, the locals are no threat. We post guards. Once their bellies are full, Jamil and the others will see things our way. Ben and Isaac, help Jo with the wee girl. We're going to Grandfather Mountain."

"Don't eat the berries," I instruct the group. "Some are poisonous. Look for birds circling overhead. Water will be near."

Iain and Wei set a fast pace, keeping the muzzles to their weapons up and ready to shoot. They cut a diagonal trail down the incline of the mountain to the northeast ridge far from the crash site. Ben carries Lily while Tala races ahead with Iain. We risk detection in the daylight, but we have no choice. After half a day of hiking down to the valley, we enter the old-growth forest of Grandfather Mountain.

"You guys, stay here," Iain says, "Wei and Dev come with me."

"I'm coming," Jamil says, not waiting for Iain's objection. "Artem, follow me." They march through the forest away from the main group.

Iain calmly watches as they make a footpath through the dense bushes trampling down young saplings. While most men would be threatened by rebellion, Iain laughs at Jamil and Artem who stop and look around, then decide to keep going and disappear into the foliage.

"Like they know the area, right?" Iain says in a light tone. His eyes capture the sunlight, sparkling like amber and burning with feeling. "Dev, will ye stay? Wei and I must save those fools. They're headed the wrong direction."

The four men eventually combine forces, moving with the grace of predators in a deadly game of kill or be killed. Their forest green camo uniforms match the leafy foliage and woodlands, and they blend into the undergrowth. We wait in the distance. Iain and Wei put their heads together whispering for a few minutes, then the four are gone to range the area.

A short time passes. Wei reappears and waves to us that the way is clear. An enchanted glade awaits us. Secluded in the cedar grove is a sun-drenched pool. A three-tiered waterfall cascades over boulders and rocky outcroppings into the mouth of a river.

The clear water could be healthy, but still we use the purification tablets in the canteens just in case. We climb up the steep slope to the highest lip of the hillside. The widest part of the watercourse plunges into a vertical white-capped falls.

The cave is hidden behind a thunderous waterfall. The barrier separates the safe haven from the outside world. We stow our gear and backpacks near the entryway. Zebenjo, Lily and I take a flashlight to explore a long narrow tunnel leading into a sizable limestone cavern where we find a pool of fresh water. Within the hour, Ben has caught fish from the pond. He cooks over a small fire and the group eats our first meal since leaving Castle City two days ago.

Cyrus and Wei wash their faces in fresh water before standing guard for the afternoon shift. The rest of us discard the filthy jackets, heavy socks and the mud-caked boots we've worn for days. Iain leads the men outside. They swim for the better part of an hour. Then they head out to defend the perimeter and give the women privacy to bathe.

Our shirts and pants along with Lily's freshly washed dress hang on a red spruce to dry. Tala sleeps on the shore basking in the sunlight. Jenna and Freja stay in the shallow water while Lily and I swim across the pool to a place of our own.

Upon inspection, Lily is fair-skinned with a birthmark on her shoulder. She is a healthy, intelligent little girl. Most importantly, she shows no sign of illness. My friends and I have been inoculated with modern immunizations. Still we can't risk contracting the Plague.

Bathing is a serious business, but truly a pleasurable task. I dive headfirst beneath the surface of the cold bone-tingling water. I scrub

❄

my skin with the grainy soil from the riverbed, washing off the dirt, grime and blood as though I could erase two days of death and frantic running through the woods.

Freja swims across the pool with her head and shoulders above the surface to the riverbank where Lily and I wade in the shallow water. Jenna sleeps beneath the shade of an old hickory.

"Do you mind?" Freja asks warily. "I meant, I'd understand if you hate me after the marts."

"That's behind us," I reply, though her words hold no apology, not that I'm expecting one. "What matters now is getting home. Are you feeling better?"

"Not really," she answers, removing her t-shirt and wringing out the water.

Modesty aside, I discard my soaked t-shirt and lay it flat on the ground to dry. "We'll sleep better tonight with shelter and food."

Freja has washed away the orange and green temporary dye from her hair. Her natural color is a honey-mist auburn. Exposure to the sun has darkened the freckles on her nose and cheeks. Without make-up, her face is bright with a natural radiance.

Lily's hair is a tight weave of leaves, briars and dirt clods much like a bird's nest. I pick at the knots and scrub her scalp with my nails. Then begins the work on my mass of tangled brown curls.

"You look different," Freja says. "Like you belong here."

"Spit that out!" I say harshly to Lily. Her cheeks are bloated with water and her eyes bigger than normal.

Lily swallows the water. "Why?" she asks, putting her face in the pool. She drinks another mouthful and gulps it down.

"You'll get sick."

"Why?"

"Microbes live in water. They make us ill."

"Not me," she replies, getting out of the pool to run with Tala.

"Stay here, Lily, where I can see you."

I step out of the pool and put on my damp shirt and pants, then help Lily with her clothes. Freja dresses quickly. We find a spot in the

❄

virgin forest of white pine, oak and birch. Wildflowers dot the hillside, and birdsong lulls us into a calm reprieve.

"Jenna hates you even more because you shamed her in front of Artem."

"Too bad. Why are you friends with her? You're nothing alike."

"I can be myself with Jenna. Girls hate me at school. Everyone said I'd win the Medallion Pin. Jenna was the first girl to like me, even with my orange and green hair." Freja's face is open with soft gray eyes, a bright smile and a bright light upon her face. "That's my mini-history. Not very pretty, is it?"

"It's not much different than mine. Why do you do what Jenna says?"

"From day one, we clicked, and the boys like her. I thought they'd like me," Freja replies. "Besides, who else was there?"

"Boys aren't worth it. I mean if you have to pretend to be someone you're not. Besides, take some credit for being who you are."

"Who taught you that?"

"What?"

"To like yourself."

"I don't like myself. I hate myself for fighting with Jenna. Losing control was...," I stop to think, "like slipping out of my body. I felt split apart. I couldn't stop. That's how rage is. Once it's out, you're empty and more vulnerable than ever."

"You know things I've never thought about," Freja says. She rolls on her side then sits up. "Can I braid your hair?" she asks Lily.

"Only if you're nice to Jo," she replies, playing with a pile of rocks stacked like a cave for her flower dolls, dandelions with long green stems and lemon-yellow faces.

Freja's smile is a peace offering. "Okay. One braid or two?"

"Two. Where do you live?" Lily asks.

"Oslo. It's in Norway."

Lily plays with Tala's ear and moves the dollies onto her back. The orkwolf plops her chin upon her paws and lets out a contented sigh. "Can I go?" she asks with wonder in her face.

❄

"Maybe," I answer.

I consider Lily's future after we reach Kings Mountain. Do people in the outback adopt orphans? It's not like dropping off a lost cat. Lily is like a stray kitten, helpless and homeless. I wonder who she is and where she came from.

The soothing heat quiets my mind like a summer day by Lake Coeur d' Alene. I can imagine Lily living in Idaho with me. The future fades from my mind. For now, the wilderness gives us a safe harbor, restoring our strength and healing our wounded warriors.

I AWAKE TO FIND Iain beside me, softly humming a Celtic tune. I rub sleep away and wipe a trace of drool from my mouth. Iain grins at my discomfort. How totally embarrassing.

The sliver of a moon rises in the eastern sky and casts a subtle light upon the glen. Stars sparkle a brilliant white. A cool mist rises from the silver-lit waterfall, and the night is alive with mystery and Mother Earth's power of rejuvenation.

Wet leaves mixed with dead bark from felled timber provide a rich, organic and life-giving soil upon the forest floor. The fragile compost, the natural decay of mulch beneficial to growth, nourishes the living roots and newly birthed saplings.

Often at home, I walk in bare feet upon the wet ground just to feel my oneness with the forest. The humblest of things bear away the greatest pain. Jolan taught me that not so long ago. Not since the night in the basement of Hotel Edinburgh has my mind been clear and my body completely relaxed. I feel regenerated resting in a bed of fragrant leaves, knowing Iain is beside me.

"Sleep well?" Iain asks, plainly pleased with himself, lifting his thick eyebrows and widening his silly impish grin.

"Yes, extremely good," I reply, sitting up and flexing my arms.

The heady scent of pine needles is strong and tangy. The air is charged with negative ions, crisp and clean before the approaching storm. "Where's Lily?"

"Cooking with Ben. She wants to surprise you."

"How long was I asleep?"

"Since sundown. Snoring loud enough to scare away the old hoot-owl overhead," he laughs.

"You're not funny, Iain. Wait until I catch you sleeping," I scold, scooting closer beside him. I want to know about Captain Jack and Lieutenant Kurt. "Do you dream?"

"No, no dreams," he says, but he looks away, not lying as much as avoiding my question.

I decide the best approach is a direct one. "What happened with Captain Jack?"

"I'd rather not...," he begins, "not to rehash that."

"I need to know."

"I need you not to know."

"It'll always be between us," I whisper, touching his warm hand. We lock fingers, and he squeezes tight. "Tell me what you can."

"I never knew my parents. They died in a crash. I always believed it was my fault."

"You were just a baby."

"They never told me how they died. Children make things up, I suppose. Lily will never know her mother's love or father's instruction. I was wrong to send her away. We must care for her, otherwise we're as evil as those who killed her people."

"Who?"

"We stumbled into a skirmish, and her people were outnumbered. Captain Jack, aye well, he dinna know who killed those poor Marines. Their bodies were stripped of uniforms and lying in the bushes."

"Oh, no. He ordered you to kill them all."

Iain hits his fist against his thigh. "Yea," he says, wiping a tear from his face. "I think we murdered some innocent men. But I swear we didn't kill those women and children. They were dead before we found them."

"Why were they fighting?"

"I dunno," he replies. "They would have shot you. Boomer took a hit then Andy. Wei, Dev and Cyrus stood their ground and killed the others."

"You tackled me to the ground."

"Aye, or you'd be dead." I hear no weakness in his open confession, but rather a fiery appeal in his words. "Lieutenant Kurt ordered the others to run for cover. He shot two coming up behind us. The evil in their faces was like nothing I've ever seen."

"I'm sorry, I—"

"At the Warrior's course. I saw that same look was in your eye."

"I can't talk about that."

Iain's gentle tug prevents me from leaving. I turn my face away from him so he can't see into the dark rage I feel for Jenna Slate.

"It'll always be between us," he says, using my words against me. No, not against me, but to comfort me. He pulls me onto his lap and rocks gently. To console himself or me, it really doesn't matter.

Whether it's his words or his arms holding me, I cannot say, but my body quivers and I want to yield to him. Still, I resist surrender and push him away with my anger.

"I'm ashamed. Is that what you want to hear?"

"I understand the rage. But it will hurt you more than her. And you're a healer. Ye must be stronger than Jenna."

The beauty of this place, the death of this place. Dare I admit this is my all fault? My vendetta toward Jenna splintered our team, forcing the men to choose sides, and Babbage punished them for my mistakes.

Off to Camp Lejeune for "real" life lessons in leadership and team building. Well, we sure got that. It doesn't get more real than the last two days. The weight of death is hard to bear, the dead Marines, the dead villagers. Our own death if we fail to survive this ordeal.

❈

"As a boy, I dreamed of being a warrior, not a bloody scientist. I read everything I could on Highlander history. Our lost history."

Iain sits beside me. He uses his sleeve to wipe away tears I didn't know were there. I hold my hand over my mouth to keep from crying. That old familiar void touches me, dragging me into a dark place. The tenderness in Iain's words saves me from the darkness.

"Our dance that night," he continues, "I wanted to kiss you in front of GAP and the world."

"You didn't though," I speak softly. I've wished for this since I first saw the boy with the flowing red hair and the ancient Celtic face.

Iain leans over and cups my face in his hands. His lips are soft and warm, but urgent for a response. I kiss him back with the same urgency.

"Ummm...," he says, "that's what I thought."

"What?" I ask disconcerted, pulling away to check his expression, which is something like smugness and delight. "You didn't like it?"

"No, I mean, yes..." he says smiling. "Kissing you is...well, I don't want to stop with just one kiss."

"I didn't imagine it like this," I reply, giving him a precious piece of myself in the revelation.

"You've been thinking about kissing?" he asks amused. "Our first kiss."

"You're distracting me," I answer, avoiding the longing in his eyes. "From all this."

"Aye, and it's working, too."

"Yes, but..."

Iain stares intently. "Don't punish yourself, Jo. I hate to see you torture yourself. I wish you'd believe me. This isn't your fault. Babbage meant to send us away, no matter what you did."

"You sound so sure. What do you know?"

"It was me. I discovered how my parents died," Iain admits, halting in mid-sentence. "They tried to escape Scotland when I was young. Jo, GAP wants my codes to the River. They'll do anything to..."

Someone is coming toward our secluded spot tramping through the woods and making no attempt to conceal himself. "Iain, where are

❄

you?"

"We'll finish this later," he says to me, standing up and aiming the flashlight toward the glen.

Wei appears and looks tired like a shipwrecked sailor, bruised and battered after being washed ashore. "They're gone," he says. "Jamil, Artem and Juan Pablo."

Dev comes up beside him. His face is like that of a man twice his age. He pauses in the shadows for a moment, his eyes aglow with an accusation. "We thought they were with you," he says. "Guess not..."

"They've gone to that camp," Iain says.

"That's crazy," Wei says, "and taking Jenna and Freja."

"The girls?" I ask startled. Frantically, I roll on my socks and lace up my boots. My clothes feel damp from lying on the ground. I throw my jacket on and stand beside Iain. "We've got to find them!"

"They'll come back," Dev says, though without much confidence.

"We've got no choice now but to fight," Iain says. "Let's go. We gotta get our weapons and follow them."

I make my way up the slope behind Iain. Inside the cave, Zebenjo, Isaac and Lily are asleep. My gaze falls upon Iain, the seasoned warrior, but whose kiss warms me from the inside out.

"Alright," Iain says. "What's our ammo?"

"Thirty rounds for hand guns. Only two clips for the snipers," Wei says, passing the weapons to Dev, Cyrus and Iain. They talk in hushed voices.

"Ben stays here. No more fighting for him," Iain replies. "Isaac is too weak."

Sitting down on the damp ground, I search my bag, all the while running through various virtual war games that I've played for years. One truth remains. It's kill or be killed.

"Pack up. Let's head out," Iain says.

"Where's my gun?" I ask.

"Your gun?"

"Yes, gun," I repeat, standing up and buttoning my coat.

"You're not coming."

"I am."

"You're not."

"I have to go. I can't wait here!" I turn to Wei for support. "Give me a weapon."

Iain paces back and forth then stops in front of me. "Haven't ye seen enough killing? You want to watch men die, their eyes wide with shock?"

"But..."

"They won't stop until we're all dead. It's either them or us."

"Isn't there another way?" I ask.

"They're hunting us," Wei speaks softly. "I didn't want to tell you."

"Hunting?" I look from Iain to Wei. "How many?"

"I'll talk to ye in private," Iain says, walking outside and expecting me to obey.

I follow Iain around the boulders that conceal the cave entrance. I gaze down at the cascading waterfalls. Wei is right. We won't survive, except with war games. Iain catches me by the arm and pulls me against him. We embrace until he releases me and stares down into my face.

"You won't be fighting, do ye hear?"

"I have to save Jenna. I need to set things right."

"Aye, I know. To redeem yourself. But you'll wait here."

"I can't, Iain."

"Ye've a mind of own, and you're as stubborn as an ox. That's why I...well, I respect you."

"So, what's the plan?"

"You worry me, woman. Whatever happens, you'll do as I say, and I'll do the killing."

❋

CHAPTER EIGHTEEN

War Games

MIRACLES COME IN SMALL ways like rain. It washes away our footpath from the cave and any signs left along the way. The rain helps, but we are soaked to the skin with teeth chattering. It does give us an advantage and the element of surprise along with the precious flash grenades.

An hour passes as we spy on the enemy's makeshift camp. Two men guard the camp while others sleep, unaware of our approach. Eight lie under a tarp secured by poles staked to the ground.

One guard at either end of camp disappears into the shrouded darkness. Cyrus and Dev kill one, Wei the other, their knives a silent, sharp edge spilling blood and making a path of safety for Iain and me. The downpour covers our approach to the shelter where our friends huddle. Juan Pablo rolls over and sees us creeping toward him out of the rain. His face is contorted with terror until he recognizes us.

Iain rushes in and clasps his hands over Freja's mouth to keep her from screaming. He whispers a warning. The others awake. Iain and I cut their bindings. We give Jamil, Artem and Juan Pablo handguns.

"Let's go," Artem says.

"Where's Jenna?" I ask.

"Wait." Iain holds them back using his body as a shield. "Cover your eyes."

He shoots off a round as a signal for the attack to begin. Men leap from their blankets with guns pointed, unsure from which direction the blast came. The first flash grenade goes off. Like an orchestrated line of dancers, we move in unison into the forest. Rapid gunfire follows us, and then the next flash of grenades illuminates the woods for twenty seconds, then we're plunged back into darkness again. The flashlights help but not much in the pouring rain.

"Keep going," Iain says. "Get them to the cave. I'll get Jenna."

My instinct is to follow him. I do not. Both badly beaten, Artem and Juan Pablo use flashlights to lead the way. The going is rough. The ground is slick with drenched leaves, and gunfire chases us through the night.

We make little progress. Freja cannot walk on her own because of her sprained ankle. Jamil tries to help, but he struggles from the bad beating he took. They sit on a log, broken and beaten, with their heads bent in defeat.

"Artem, can you carry Freja?" I ask. She seems fragile, almost frail compared with the robust, young woman from yesterday. "Juan, guard the rear, will you?"

Each time we stop jeopardizes our safety. Each stop increases the risk of detection. Dev and Cyrus catch up with us, but not Iain, Wei or Jenna. I help Jamil back on his feet, slipping my arm around his waist. "Lean on me," I offer, taking his weight on me. "It's not that far."

Back at the cave, the hours while I wait for Iain are arduous. I look through a glass darkly, face to face with the madness of my hatred for Jenna. And I feel responsible for Jamil and Artem's misguided scheme.

Warfare. Conflict. Death. Nothing prepares you for war, for the fear of losing friends, or the noticeable change on their faces afterward.

I stand at the cave's entrance wanting to believe in the Great Spirit. Why doesn't the One World Church teach us to believe in the beyond?

I utter words aloud, hoping some invisible force might hear me. "I'll do anything, just let Iain be alive. Keep them safe."

❄

Unnatural sounds and distant inhuman voices alert Cyrus and me of movement through the woods. Something or someone is coming fast. Cyrus positions himself behind the boulders. Wei is first in the glade holding the flashlight. Iain follows carrying Jenna toward the waterfalls. Quickly, they scale the hill. I leap aside as they rush into the shelter of the cave.

A bullet is lodged in Jenna's back. Someone will have to remove it. The words like a mantra echo in my mind. *A bullet is lodged in Jenna's back. Someone will have to remove it.* Training in my medical courses has prepared me to treat a gunshot victim. A cruel twist of fate puts Jenna's life in my hands. The prospect of her death horrifies me.

Dev volunteers to help. "Hold the flashlight steady," I tell him. "The bullet is between her shoulders left of the spine."

Jenna releases a low groan. "Jo, I have to tell you—"

"Later. Stay quiet. You're going to be fine."

Dev is skilled as a medic. He sits to my left, with the med kit and spreads out a layer of gauze, organizing bandages, vials of antibiotics, a portable IV, surgical tools and other items needed to remove the bullet and keep Jenna alive.

Dev cuts Jenna's uniform with a pair of sterilized scissors and peels off the bloody material sticking to her skin. Using a small pair of tweezers, I lift pieces of camo from the puckering and enflamed flesh. The skin surrounding the entry wound is a cherry red hue. The bullet missed her spinal cord and lungs, or she would have died instantly. Congealed blood stopped most of the bleeding. The belt they used as a sling stabilized Jenna's arm and saved her life.

"Start the IV with the morphine," I say to Ben. He looks dazed, but I need his help. "She'll be okay. I can remove bullet, but we have got keep the fever down. Can you do this?"

"Tell me what to do," Ben replies, settling down beside me.

"Morphine through the IV will control pain and reduce the risk of shock." I wash the bullet hole with saline solution.

The flesh is warm beneath my surgical gloves. Jenna is very hot with fever. I press the wound not too hard, but to feel if the bullet is lodged near the surface. Fortunately, my fingers find the shell in the soft tissue of Jenna's upper back.

"What happened?" I ask, searching Iain's face for reassurance.

Iain turns away and speaks to Wei. "Stoke the fire."

Wei puts firewood on the dying embers. Sparks scatter and the specks of light briefly lift off like miniature spaceships skyrocketing into the dark hollow space. Lily hides beside Tala, but fear mars the delicate features on her face.

Dev and Ben move close to Jenna's side to keep her from moving. The morphine is working. Jenna relaxes. As soon as I clean the wound, she lapses into unconsciousness. My fingers dig in the hole to locate the bullet. I hold open the incision and squeeze hooked forceps to pull the bullet out and then rub an iodine swab into the area.

"Give me the needle, Dev, and check her pulse."

Quick Clot is a white powder used to stop the flow of blood. I apply it into the wound and hold several layers of gauze on the area, applying pressure to stem the bleeding. Skillfully with a needle and thread, I suture the incision. At last, I'm finished and use tape to secure the bandage.

"Start with the antibiotics," I say, setting aside the instruments and soiled materials. "We need to cool her down and fast."

The likelihood of Jenna surviving isn't good. Fever, infection and other complications are common after a shooting. I plead to the spirit guide from my visions. *Please, let Jenna live through the night.*

Ben bathes Jenna's face with a wet cloth while I tend to the others. No nightmare can come close to the damage inflicted on Juan Pablo, Freja, Artem and Jamil. Assessment and triage. No broken bones. No internal bleeding, but black and blue contusions and injuries from blunt trauma. Nothing could have prepared me for this.

Their chips were cut out, their wrists slashed with a knife. I give the wounds a proper cleaning with saline solution and antibacterial ointment then suture the incisions and apply bandages. Dev rubs a healing salve over their other abrasions and administers morphine where needed. Ben wraps Juan Pablo's abdomen because he suffered a

❧

bruised rib. Artem's nose is broken. Their faces are badly beaten. Dev administers antibiotics, painkillers and fluids. For the most part, it has been devastating, but they will heal with time.

"The stew is hot," Ben says, noticeably tired. He hands me a bowl of seasoned stew. I sip the broth savoring the tangy taste of rabbit.

"Did you cook this?"

A black pot simmers over the flames in the fire pit. Tin plates, cups and utensils are laying on a canvas alongside dehydrated food packets and an assortment of dried packages. To the rear of the cave are bundles of clothes, jackets and blankets.

Ben's voice lacks any inflection, and his face is blank of expression. "No, Iain and Wei carried all this stuff and the pot of stew already cooked."

"They had to kill those men," I say, offering no excuses. I look into his dark eyes, taking his hand and holding it tight. "Zebenjo, we'll get through this."

A sparkle suddenly shines in Ben's eyes. "Better watch it," he says with a sly smile. "Iain might think I'm putting the moves on you."

"Yeah, but he won't be back till morning."

"Where is he?"

"Gone," I answer, choking down my tears. Alone, Iain walks the night where he can regain his sense of balance, but I know he's near enough to warn us of danger.

Freja and Lily sleep on top of a pile of blankets. Lily whimpers in her sleep burrowing deeper into Tala's warmth. Her dreams are those of an orphan. Freja awakens and stares up at me as I lean against the cool, limestone wall.

"I knew about their plan. I should have said something. Those men shot Jenna."

"Try not to think about it. You're safe now."

"They're dead. I mean, all of them in that camp."

"I know. Shall I stay until you sleep?"

"I wish we'd talked before."

"It's okay. Soon, we'll be in Paris, maybe even get travel privileges

❀

to go to Europe or Asia and shop with Jenna. Imagine me modeling hats."

This gets a chuckle from Freja. "I've had enough of traveling."

"Sweet dreams, Freja," I say, clasping her hand.

The effort of speaking in a perky voice is exhausting. I shut my eyes, rolling my head and stretching my shoulders to ease the tension and stiffness. In a few minutes, Freja falls asleep. I crawl on hands and knees to Jenna and touch her forehead, which is so hot. There is a vulnerability to the curve of her feverish face and a softness to her lips.

The specter of death touches its hand upon Jenna, waiting for her last breath. Fear like a snake spirals around the vertebrae of my spine, slithering upward and squeezing my heart. The cobra with black eyes is devoid of light like Dr. Babbage's sunken eyes.

I could easily become like Babbage. Had it not been for the crash, I would be the evil cobra with black eyes holding dead organs.

EXHAUSTED I LIE down on the blanket beside Lily. What must she have felt when we brought back our bloody and battered friends? I snuggle with her and Tala, savoring their radiant heat and feeling the strain leave my body. Someone moans, tossing and turning until he settles back to sleep.

Shadows move through the cave. The blazing firelight summons demons dancing on the walls who stretch their eerie forms high to the ceiling. The crack—sizzle—pop of the wood gives off a curl of smoke, which snakes it way out the cave entrance. I can't sleep. I want to hold Iain and give him what solace he can accept. Tala lifts her head and watches me.

Quietly, I move about the cave checking on Artem, Juan Pablo and Jamil who slumber by the fire pit. Hunkered down in a corner, Dev sleeps by himself. Isaac is strong enough to stand watch with Wei and Cyrus.

The raid gave us weapons, ammo, backpacks with Marine survival gear plus heavy coats, fishing rods and hatchets. Fresh game, a rabbit, and some pheasants and packets of dried goods, and enough food to last several weeks. Three horses are stabled and secure somewhere in the woods. There is nothing to do but wait for morning.

I cannot settle down. I take a flashlight and follow the winding curves through the long narrow tunnel into the deepest region of Grandfather Mountain. I turn off the light and throw aside my clothes and then dive head first in the pool. I hold my body under dark waters until my chest feels like it will explode. I surface gasping for air.

The cave is a thick blackness that disorientates the senses. Which way is up, which is down? Had I not been buoyant in the water, I would be lost. But I am lost, truly lost in a wasteland. I'm a heap of images of the broken girl I once knew. I fear what I might become if not saved.

Guilt is a strong emotion, and like a knife cuts into your heart and scars your soul. To know wrong and do it anyway is the worst feeling in the world. My vendetta against Jenna. I broke faith with all that is good and kind and selfless. I broke faith with myself, denying the good in me.

I float on the surface of the pool, letting the water rush over me. The seductive power of gravity pulls me into the darkness. It is cold in the void, so cold a chill rattles my bones, and even deeper, a chill grips my soul. How do I escape the abyss of a darkness unmatched by the blackest night?

I can understand the violence between men who kill at any cost despite the righteousness of the cause. The burning need for self-preservation and the struggle for control. Is there such a thing as a just war? Making war to find peace is insanity.

The insanity of humanity, but we do it. Is violence the only way?

❉

Use words not fists, but sometimes we battle the forces of evil. The good will conquer and win, but what price do we pay? The innocence of soldiers is forfeit to defend the weak from evildoers.

My hands reach the edge, but I search with blind eyes for the flashlight, and I fight a panic attack—not from the suffocating cave—but from a loss of self. I recall Dev in honor's class quoting someone called Gandhi. *The best way to find yourself is to lose yourself in the service of others.* I have no idea of the man's identity, but take comfort from his words.

My fingers find the flashlight, the life giving, soul saving light. It filters across the grotto and casts apparitions against the walls. When a child, my dreams often ended with feverish nightmares. I remember my mother coming in my room. She would lay a hand on my forehead and stay with me while I cried. The terror of losing yourself is worse than any physical torture. Orphaned so young, Lily says nothing of her pain.

Right now, all I want is to hold Lily in my arms. I dress and walk through the tunnel and into the main cavern with slow steps so as not to wake anyone. Iain lies folded in a tight ball. Curled into himself, he sleeps near the fireside. In repose, his face is lined with age and a harshness I never noticed because it wasn't there before tonight.

I grieve for his loss of innocence and run from the cave past Cyrus and Wei. They call my name, but I don't stop, and they don't follow. I run until my chest hurts, and my knees buckle beneath me. The agony keeps pace with me. I hit my fists into a fallen tree, feeling nothing but the ache in my chest.

I am to blame for my team being in the Predator when it crashed. But the voice of a boy echoes through the night. Two children walk toward Castle City a lifetime ago.

"Mindfulness."

"How?" the girl asks.

"Keep the clouds behind you. Let the rain showers cleanse you. Keep your eyes free of tears."

"No problem. I never cry," she says with an awkward laugh.

❋

"Not that, it means empty yourself with crying, and find your true nature. Your true self, free from illusion. Your eyes clear with truth."

A palpable grief overwhelms me. I cry for Lily, for lost innocence and for the pain my friends suffer. I cry tears of regret, tears of shame. I cry tears that bear away all pain.

My voice rises higher than the towering trees. My throat is raw with truth. Not one tear is withheld. The tears for yesterday's secrets and tomorrow's lost dreams. A flood of tears uplifts me. Everything that rises shall converge to witness the soul touching the heavens.

The night sky is clear of clouds. A breeze whispers from the trees above. *Be gentle with others. Be gentler still with yourself.* I cry myself to sleep in the presence of saints and the arms of angels.

The morning raucous of a blue jay jeering at a crow disturbs my dreams of Iain and Lily walking with me to Beauty Bay. I slept in the forest all night, but I awake with an insulated blanket laid over me, and Iain sleeps beside me. Tala rests against him.

"Can I share your covering?" Iain asks. His breath is visible in the frigid dawn.

"No choice, I guess," I mumble, but smiling and making room for him in the warm enclosure though he hardly needs it. Iain generates a heat of his own, an internal combustion of perpetual light.

"Did ye cry yourself dry?"

"What?"

"Calm eyes. Quiet mind," he says, kissing my forehead. "I'm glad for you. Jenna's fever broke." Iain takes something from his pocket and drops a tiny bag in my hand. "I meant to give you this sooner."

The tiny pouch of multicolored fabric is a Mexican design. I untie a thread and seven miniature wooden stick dolls fall into my hand. "Lily will love these."

"Worry Dolls. A reminder to keep the faith."

I kiss Iain lightly on the lips and look into his eyes. "I've nothing for you."

"Your eyes tell me enough."

I bend my head down, looking at the worry dolls to hide my

feelings. Iain holds me in his arms and tightens his embrace.

"I meant to tell you, long before now. I was ten when my uncle left me at a church near Edinburgh though he promised to return in the morning. He told me I had to stop ragin' over my parents' deaths, or I'd be lost.

"That night in the chapel on my knees before the altar, I learned humility. I cried myself empty. Come dawn a light flooded the nave. It was the fall equinox. A red light shined through a small triangle in a lovely rose glass stained window. The beauty of the place captivated me. The mystery is not in cryptic green men or fantastical symbols. But in the holy presence."

"You believe?"

"Better to forfeit your life than lose your faith. When everything you know is false, the one thing left is faith. It does not come from what ye see or hear. It is deep inside. An indescribable place where we truly are whole. The world is real, but the invisible is more tangible if ye can hold tight and don't let go."

I want Iain to understand my belief. "I asked my father to let me walk the vision quest alone. I nagged him for months before he agreed. For a week, I camped at Mica Bay, not a familiar place but one where I belonged. One night I slept in the open end of a downed tree trunk, most of which was rotted and hollow.

"I learned you can discover simplicity in nature. A tree is a tree. The animals know the secrets of the Great Spirit. My totem is the Bear, a strong spiritual presence protecting me. The Earth doesn't need man. The natural world is so perfect, even a child knows such an incredible creation must come from a higher power."

"What did ye see in your vision?"

"I found a place where I can stand outside of the chaos, but I've failed so often. The challenge is to live in the moment. But I suppose each breath is a new beginning, one moment to the next, a lifetime of chances to do better."

"Well said, Jo! But we'd best get going. Those clouds are about to burst."

❄

Tala runs ahead of us as we make a hasty retreat in the rain. We reach the cave just before the first clouds burst with lighting, thunder and a deluge of rain.

Everyone is awake. Subdued and quiet, they sit around the fire pit eating leftovers from the pot. Freja and Lily look up from the game they play with paper dolls. Artem feeds Jenna a warm broth. Jamil leaves his spot by Freja and takes a couple of steps forward to face Iain.

"You killed for us," Jamil says forcefully. "I owe my life to you."

"Aye, well, you'd do the same," Iain replies, grabbing Jamil by the forearm and pulling him into a guy-hug. They shrug it off and smile at each other. "Friends?"

"Oh, yeah. Friends for life," Artem adds, shaking hands with Iain.

"What's done is done," says Iain. "Together, we survive. Together, we fight our way to Kings Mountain."

"We protect each other, but first we protect the innocent," I add, looking from one to another. I lift Lily into my arms. "This child is my own flesh and blood."

"Battle takes illusions from our eyes," Iain says, stepping beside me and taking my hand. "Friendships are forged in the exigencies of war. I pledge my life to get you home."

Jamil takes Iain's hand and stands beside him. "I pledge my life to get you home," he swears solemnly. The others come to stand with us. Artem holds Jenna in his arms. One by one, each pledges his life and speaks the oath.

"I pledge my life," I finish gravely. "By all I hold true, I swear you will see your families again."

❈

CHAPTER NINETEEN

Shadow Play

A N UNCEASING DELUGE has blotted out the sunlight. Dark heavy clouds obscure the sky, and sheets of rain pour down as though a flood covers the Earth and keeps us from venturing outside of the cave. Even over the force of the waterfall, the howling winds and rumbling thunder can be heard day and night.

Two days ago, an upsurge of water gushed down from the cliffs of Grandfather Mountain, and much like a tidal wave poured into the cave saturating our meager possessions. We moved into the deepest part of the mountain for shelter using flashlights when needed in order to conserve the artificial light.

Severe weather disturbances like tornadoes, flooding, hurricanes, and high winds are common phenomena in the year 2216. Science is inconclusive as to the causality of these conditions. Thunderstorms can last as long as a month occurring frequently in summer.

Dev and Cyrus rotate with Iain and Wei guarding the cave, while Ben helps me care for the injured, dressing wounds and cooking and serving meals. Nearly recovered, Isaac cleans the guts and bones from fish he caught in the lake. We've consumed all the fresh meat and used the last purification tablets. The torrential rains have lasted three days, and have prevented us from exploring the woodlands for food.

A cave can be either a prison or a safe harbor. A lifetime in this cave could lead me to believe in shadow selves. The light can be an indirect sunbeam shimmering through the waterfall, or the nighttime flames of the wavering firelight. Day and night, distorted shapes dance across the cave walls, harmless but still captives among us, not ghosts or ghouls but perceived forms of real people.

The shadow self is a host for distortions of the mind. Most of what happens to us has little to do with truth, but more to do with what we believe is truth. I suppose the shadow is part of the whole.

These days we live somewhere between the dimness of a black aurora and the distant star of hope. We hope to make it to Kings Mountain. However, hope is fragile.

I believe the holy presence asks you, not to fear the shadow, but to embrace this part of yourself. This is the way to mend broken pieces of the soul. The aftermath of the crash has taught me. Rage is a granite wall we hide behind; crack the stone and light emerges.

By the fourth day, the skies are clear and the sunlit forest reappears. Daily chores become routines, and the men guard the area while the rest of us emerge from the cave. It seems as though we've crawled out of the belly of a beached whale onto an abandoned shore to dry our clothes and soak up the sunshine.

We make our way above the cave to the rocky encasement. Isaac leads us to a grassy swell and spreads a tarp on the grass. Freja limps beside Jamil, and Juan Pablo leans on Zebenjo for support, and Artem carries Jenna.

I toss a stick into the open grass. Tala chases the stick, and Lily chases Tala. "Don't go far," I call to her. The little girl and the orkwolf play tug of war. Their silliness lightens the mood and brings smiles and laughter. Dev and Cyrus stand close, armed with snipers, listening to our conversation. They look like seasoned Marines.

The clash between the bully-four and the rest of us is forgotten. The past fades into memory. What began as divided loyalties between Jo Peone and Jenna Slate is now an open space filled with the spirit of

※

fellowship. None is more deserving than each one of my friends to drink in the sunshine and breathe the heady forest scents.

The one constant is nature in perpetual motion. Nature in repose brings us solidarity. This day promises a slant of sunlight so exquisite its hurts the naked eye. Its fragility can awaken the tender places of the heart. Such musings comfort me in the realities we face. Iain and Wei climb the slope to join us. We sit perched like eagles with a bird's eye view of the valley yet invisible to locals passing through the territory.

"Another week, then we can leave this place," Iain says, sitting down beside me. "We'll follow the valley, not the ridges."

"But we're safe here," Freja says fearfully. "Maybe a rescue team can find us."

"None of the beacons survived the fight," Wei replies. "For all we know, the Predator's computer didn't send a signal. They don't know where we crashed."

"Three horses are stabled in a hidden place," Iain says. "We can make a flatbed to carry Jenna. Tala can pull our gear. We found a GPS and a tablet. The battery is good. Wei broke the password and found a map. I'm working to decrypt other files."

"We're bound to come across people," I say, watching Lily build a house made of sticks and stones for the worry dolls. "What about our uniforms? Anyone seeing us will think we're Marines."

"We'll wear stolen clothes," Jamil says. He points to freshly washed garments drying in the sun. "We ditch the camo and wear those."

"Local color," Wei says with a smile at Ben. "Like hunters."

"Hey, I'm in," says Ben, stepping over to select a shirt. The white and black checkerboard suits him although the shirt is too large and the pants baggy.

"We'll set traps and hunt," Iain says, taking a drink from the canteen.

The men have been talking nonstop about a hunting expedition. They are ready for anything after a week of hiding in the cave.

"Take Tala," I suggest. "She'll love to hunt."

"I was thinking the same thing. Hunting with the orkwolf just made my day," Iain replies, taking a shirt from the clothesline. "Lily, what do ye know about traps?"

Lily rubs Tala's belly. "Bigger is not better," she answers. She laughs at Tala rolling on her back. "A deadfall is for rabbits or squirrels. Not for a deer."

"A deer?" Ben grins, a sly smile on his lips. "It couldn't hurt to be ready. In case, we come across one. What do you think, Iain?"

"We can't shoot guns," Iain answers. "There's another way. We can cut branches and make spears."

All afternoon the men make traps though what they really want is to chase down a deer. I doubt they can. It's the foolish play of cave dwellers hunting with homemade spears. They look the part with unshaven faces and eagerness in their eyes.

The next morning, they play a game of rock-paper-scissors to see who stays behind. Disappointed, Isaac and Cyrus will take guard duty. At the last minute, Juan Pablo, Artem and even Jamil with his limp decide they are strong enough to join the hunt. An hour later, the band of merry hunters take off with spears, traps and Tala traipsing alongside Iain. As always, they carry weapons, a very real reminder of what may await them down the mountain.

Outside in the sunshine, Freja sleeps soundly while Jenna and I lounge on the tarp. Lily decorates us with flowers and braids Jenna's long blond curls, weaving in delicate petals and purple violets. She threads the green stalks of daisies into my thick brown braids. I put strands of white cupped lily of the valley in her hair.

"I can't keep my eyes open," Jenna says, yawning and stretching out lazily in the sun. The antibiotics are working. Her face and skin glow with health.

"Another few days and you'll be walking on your own. You'll have a scar to show your bravery," I reply.

I rest against the tarp and cover my face with my arm. The ground is rocky and hard. I roll onto my side, opening my eyes and blinking against the harsh glare. Sunspots appear in my vision.

I turn my face to the sun and feel its radiant heat. For the first time,

I can envision a future with my friends at the university.

"They said only one from our SG would attend the D.C. Academy. Just one," Jenna says in a low voice. "You were the best student in every way. I didn't know I'd win a placement in California. I was desperate that day."

Lily gives me a startled glance. She watches Jenna as though expecting fur to fly between two alpha wolves. I tighten my arms around Lily and kiss the top of her head. She looks into my eyes, then plays with her grass dolls, a tight weave of green stems with dandelions heads.

I keep my eyes on her dollies and then lift my gaze to Jenna's wide-open blue eyes. She gives me a tremulous smile.

"You should hate me," she says nervously. "We sabotaged you the first chance we got. At Castle Coeur d' Alene, we knew you took hikes on Tubbs Hill. No excuse though for what I did."

"We all make mistakes," I reply cautiously. "I was terrible to you at the marts."

"I deserved it," she says with tears on her cheeks. "You saved my life."

I shake my head refusing to take credit. "I did nothing."

"I wish I could make it up to you."

"I know. I feel the same. I was so angry at the marts. And the ropes course—I wasn't myself. I couldn't stop the rage. That sure backfired. How do you feel?"

"I'm exhausted. But I feel good like a weight is off my chest. Jamil and Artem shouldn't have taken off. None of us should have. They wanted to prove they were better than Iain. So did I. That's why I went with them. I'd be dead if not for you."

"It's behind us."

"We're alike, you and I. More alike than different, you know."

I bite the inside of my mouth unsure what to say. What can she be thinking? No two people are more different. We are exact opposites. A bubbly white woman and a dark skinned, moody loser.

"I panicked on Tubbs Hill. It got out of hand."

I shrug my shoulders and consider her with a speculative eye. I want to ask how tying someone up happens, much less cutting my hair and leaving me in the woods. I've never been a person who lets others off the hook. I hold a stone against those who hurt me. One by one, the stones become a wall, but today I let it go for the last time.

"How alike?" I say, my curiosity aroused.

"I'm your shadow, Jo."

I look at Jenna in surprise. "You're always in the spotlight. All the interviews, all personality and popular at Kickoff."

"You've no idea, do you? I watch Iain and the others," she begins. "They respect you, even Jamil and Artem. They trust you. When you blow it and get into trouble, they want to be like you because..."

"Because I grew up on the reserve. So what?"

"You protected Lily when we wanted to send her away. I think you are the best of us. You question everything. I saw that in honors class. Dr. Julius recognized your gift and abilities. You speak the truth. Speak it aloud despite the consequences. I don't know how, but you are different."

"Jenna's right," Cyrus says. He turns halfway toward us and looks down over his shoulder at me. "I want to know about my ancestors. What was their religion before the famine? They pretend to honor our cultures, but GAP buried our history."

"Why follow me? I break rules. I accessed encrypted data that got me into trouble."

"That's what we need to do. GAP is lying to us," Cyrus says. "They said the dead zones couldn't sustain life, yet here we are living off the land. Drinking the water. Breathing clear air."

"And Lily," Isaac says, coming to join us. "She makes me believe people can survive out here." Usually, his boyish smile show dimples, but today Isaac's features harden with resolve.

"They're lying about everything," I say sadly.

"Well, we're the enemy out here," Cyrus says. "GAP citizens. We fight to survive or die trying."

❈

THE PLEDGE OF LIFE spoken solemnly that night has changed everything, sealing our fates into one destiny. For our friendship is an unbroken circle like the infinity of a promise ring. Once sealed it has no beginning or end. The misfortunes we've survived have forged an emotional bond born of suffering, but teaching us compassion. The GPS will direct our footsteps, but someday our moral compass shall guide us to a place even more important than Kings Mountain.

This all becomes clear to me late that night when the men return jubilant from their hunt. Something of their innocence is renewed in their boyish expressions. Hunting has been a rite of passage and an ennobling endeavor more suitable for teenagers than soldiering. They enter the cave carrying their bounty with pride on their faces.

What's most exciting is the buck with an eight-point antler they brought down with the help of one orkwolf. Zebenjo recounts how Tala cornered the deer in a dry riverbed. In its haste to flee, the buck stumbled over rocks, and broke its leg in three places becoming fair game.

Ben stands taller with pride. "I've read about skinning a deer," he explains. His face is that of the boy who told silly jokes at Kickoff. The goofy boys grow into loyal men. "First, we hung it up. Then we drained the blood. I cut out the entrails."

"Stop, Zebenjo. We really don't need the gory details," Freja says, grimacing with distaste. "Is the meat clean? That's all I care about."

"Hunters field dress their game before hauling the meat home." Ben recites words as though reading from a book. He keeps talking as though Freja is as thrilled to hear his story as he is telling it. "Tala trapped that deer. What a dog!"

Jamil and Iain kneel side-by-side cooking over the fire pit. Their past differences have ceased to matter. "How about a little credit for us?" Jamil laughs, cutting off a juicy slice of meat.

"We helped a wee bit," Iain says, "carrying the carcass for ye." His comical frown elicits laughter from all of us. "You've earned a hefty slice, my friend." Iain stands up and serves Ben a plate full of food.

"You should have seen it," Wei says elated. "Zebenjo, the boy hero. He knew exactly what to do! You'd think he'd hunted all his life."

"It took three of us, it was so heavy," Dev says, smacking his lips and taking another bite. "We couldn't keep up with Tala charging that buck."

"Enough," Iain says. "Ye put us to shame in front of these girls. We did trap these little critters, didn't we?" He opens a bag holding the skinned animals. Three rabbits, a possum and a squirrel.

Iain looks surprised by the round of applause he receives. "Alright," he says embarrassed. "Who's turn for storytelling?"

Each evening after dinner, we fill the eerie silence with fables or imagined tales of magical hero quests. Some of us made up Teutonic fictions of ancient battles, while exaggerating some parts for the sake of good storytelling. We recreate what could have been real people and their lives with embellished facts shrouded in the mists of time.

"So tell me, Iain, where are ye from?" Lily imitates his brogue with precision. She waves her short, stubby finger. "Ye promised."

Another burst of laughter catches Iain off guard. He gives Lily a good-natured smile. "Well, my dearie," he says, tickling her until she squirms out of his arms.

"A good story," she begs with anticipation in her face.

"Home is a village," he says. "Moray."

"And Jo?" she asks.

"Oh, nowhere as romantic as Scotland. I was born in Idaho."

"And Tala?"

"My father gave me this pup for my birthday," I add, brushing my hand across Tala's back.

"And the cities, are they beautiful?" she asks.

"Here, let's do this properly," Iain says, clearing his throat. "Once

❊

upon a time, a gallant lad named Arthur met the very pretty Indian princess Genevieve in a faraway city of castles."

The half-recited, half-made up version of King Arthur and the Knights of the Round Table entertains the group. Iain then gives us a parody of Kickoff week. His quasi-modern spoof is a cast of twelve oddball candidates. He playfully recounts our activities, our meeting in honors class and a ludicrous mock battle during the Warrior course.

His elicits our laughter while he aggrandizes prom night and the theatrical kidnapping by sinister racketeers. Jenna and Artem insist they weren't involved. I believe Jenna. Iain includes Tala absconding with Mrs. Thalhammer's fur coat and Jolan lifting him off his feet in a scuffle to redeem my honor.

Iain shrewdly teaches us that we are fools in our own drama. Then Ben breaks the mood when he lets out a low, deep chested burp. Not to be outdone, Cyrus and Isaac out best him with loud belches, which incites another round of chuckles.

Jamil pokes Zebenjo in the arm and grasps him in a kid friendly headlock. Dev rolls over on his side as though in the throes of pain and farts. We all dissolve into a fit of giggles. The release of pent up emotions deepens our newfound camaraderie.

"Jo," Lily says. She watches me with trust in her eyes.

"I don't know." I fidget with the buttons to my shirt.

Lily wiggles out of Iain's lap and comes to me. Considering the short time together, Lily is very sensitive to my moodiness, which goes unnoticed by others. I think of her as my sister. I would die to protect her. I want Lily with me always. I want to take her back to civilization.

"You promised."

"Yes, I did."

I've heard Native American oral storytelling creates a real world beyond the physical plane. Speak the words aloud, and they manifest as reality and bring truth, but I cannot teach others what I don't know. What if they don't understand my truth?

So much of this uncertainty must show on my face. Iain stares at me with his wide grin. He encourages me to share what's buried in my heart. And so it begins...

"In the time of the ancestors...when the real humans of the earth moved from the flatlands to the mountains...and to the lakes and to the forests...they followed the spirit of the great white buffalo to the clean rivers and open spaces...the children played chasing around the campfire...one day a girl fell face first into the flames...she lives with scars. They call her Burnt Face. The children make fun of her, calling her names and throwing stones as she passes. There is no place among the people for Burnt Face.

"The people pack their belongings...it is a season of change... for leaving homes behind...to follow the curve of canyons...to places where the real humans gather before the moon of freezing rain...but the girl cannot go...she knows to go north to the mountains...where the eagles soar and the black bear roams free...she takes from her mother an urn of water, a bag of food and an extra blanket to ward off the cold.

"Tears from her mother's sad eyes touch the girl's face...they say goodbye...Burnt Face leaves her people and walks among the high grasses and climbs the steep mountain to the ledge where all the land can be viewed, from the sun to the west and the moon in the east...she watches the dance of stars in the night and waits.

"Burnt Face waits many days and nights...fasts and prays and looks to the Great Spirit...but she hears nothing, sees nothing. Faint of heart, she cries...and reaches her arms to the sky...and sings a prayer and moves her feet to the sound of her beating heart. 'Open my eyes that I may see, clean my ears to better hear...speak to my heart that I might know the ways of the ancestors.' The night is still...not the wind nor the crickets or the scurry of a mouse make a sound...the girl cries herself to sleep.

"In her dream, a Woman in White appears...her face is creased but beautiful...her hair is long and white, the buckskin dress is heavy with beads and feathers, her dark brown eyes wide and full of truth. 'You are Walks With Grace. The bear is your totem. The spirit of the wolf protects you. Go to your people. Tell them not to return to the white camp but leave...come to the mountains. They will hear and follow you.'

"The girl wakes...the Woman in White has left three gifts...a black bear's claw, an eagle feather and the pup of a female wolf. Walks With Grace puts the claw in her medicine bag, the feather in her hair and the pup in her coat. Many days pass before she finds her people...she enters camp...men and women whisper...children hide. The old ones ask...can this be the girl with scars...she walks so tall and the spirit of the bear walks with her.

"Walks With Grace warns her people to flee to the mountains where the Great Mother waits. Now the tribe is the Bear People. This is how the real humans found their way home and escaped the cities. In the mountains of the northwest...all the tribes came and survived a season of loss."

At first, I do not understand why no one speaks or moves. Did they come with me to my sacred place where I often go when the world confuses me? They watch me with a keen interest. My cheeks flame with embarrassment. I feel the need to break the spell and free them from the dream-making of my words.

Something occurs to me. I have suffered from migraines all my life. I haven't had a headache since the night of the crash. Not only am I healed of migraines, but also the black void no longer envelopes me.

"I felt like I was the girl," Freja says timidly. "I wish I knew more about my ancestors."

"I wish the white buffalo was alive," Zebenjo says wistfully. "To chase those burly animals. Have you seen pictures? They're huge."

Isaac takes off his much beloved GoBot hat and stares intently at me. "A few priests who live in Jerusalem tell of ancient texts."

"I was alone in the woods," I reply. "I had a dream or maybe it was a memory, I'm not sure. I wandered from a camp Jolan visited. I fell asleep under a tamarack. I think a black bear touched me. Jolan chased the bear away. An elder told me that no matter whose blood flows in my veins, I am one with the bear spirit and a member of the tribe."

Zebenjo takes a knife from Jamil. He stares intently at it. "How about we all become blood bothers? I read in the old days they had a ritual. They drew blood and..."

Iain pats Ben on the shoulder, but a grim look darkens his face. "No need to shed blood to prove our trust."

"Where did you learn this story?" Jamil asks. "I must know."

"It's what I imagine," I reply. "I can't explain. I speak the words, and the spirit world becomes real. Some believe sharing the sacred circle makes it weak. I believe if you speak the truth, your spirit grows stronger. The circle of my storytelling calls forth the spirit world."

The hour is late. The spirit world of dream-making calls us to sleep. Freja and Jenna fluff up their blankets beside the fireplace. Jamil and Artem are well enough to take a shift and guard the cave. The others settle down in their makeshift beds.

I take Lily to our blankets and lie down, cradling her with my body. Tala sleeps on her other side. Lily drops off into a sound sleep. I feel Lily's breathe on my face, and my heart swells with tenderness.

Tala lifts her head, waiting for my touch and relaxes with a long dog sigh. Iain comes over and kneels to kiss me good night. He cocks his left eyebrow and leans forward to whisper in my ear. "And to think, ye didn't want to share. What a loss had you not. Thanks for taking a chance on us."

"I love you," I confess.

I speak the three little words without thinking and immediately regret them and feel embarrassed. Iain grins like a foolhardy drunken Scotsman and kisses me lightly on the lips.

"Good night, my fair lady," he says and laughs. He ducks in time to miss my fist, thrown at him in all fairness. I said the "L" word, and he did not.

Tala hesitates, unsure whether to follow Iain outside or stay with me. I watch her leave with Iain who walks the night before finding his rest. A few minutes pass. I forget about Tala. I drift into dreams of Iain Sinclair with his face alight with a love meant only for me.

❋

PART III

The Mission

CHAPTER TWENTY

Valley of Bones

TWO WEEKS HAVE passed since that the night I removed the bullet from Jenna's back. This morning Freja and I pack up our meager possessions as my friends and I prepare to leave the safety of Grandfather Mountain.

Rested and in good spirits, Jenna lies upon blankets piled on a travois, a wooden frame tied to poles and attached to a black gelding. Iain has tied a harness around Tala's head and shoulders for her to pull a smaller flatbed packed with clothes, packets of dehydrated food, fresh game, pots and pans and fishing gear. I keep a backpack filled with the med kit, a canteen, dried meat and an assortment of nuts and fresh berries.

Wei decoded the password to the stolen tablet and has plotted a southerly route through the valley, a very real risk but also unavoidable. The men carry the handguns, not the automatic weapons. Those stay hidden beneath blankets for quick retrieval. They keep ammunition in their jackets, and the Marine uniforms are packed out of sight.

Our grubby, ill-fitting outfits are those of refugees. We hope to be inconspicuous, not be seen as an invasion of armed commandos intent on storming the territory. Should the enemy find us, our plan is to convince them that we have escaped from D.C. However, I doubt the local residents very often meet twelve teenagers carrying weapons and hiking with an orphaned girl, three stolen ponies and an orkwolf. I keep the fallacy of our plan to myself.

Ahead of the others, Iain and Wei take the forward watch. Artem climbs onto a gray mare holding the reins to the black gelding transporting Jenna. Jamil helps Freja into the saddle of a third horse, and I lift Lily up into Freja's arms so they ride together. Isaac along with Cyrus and Juan Pablo take the rearguard.

Too soon we reach the lower mountain range. No one speaks, but some linger for one last look at Grandfather Mountain where the cliffs and waterfall can be seen rising in the distance. Dev and Zebenjo and I share a quiet moment full of regret at leaving this place.

For a time, the wilderness has given us a secret hideaway. The old mountain has taught us what we'd never learn elsewhere. Grandfather Mountain will always be the one place where our hostilities yielded to enduring friendships and our common goal to reach Kings Mountain. An urgency infuses the group with the fortitude to face the dangers of traveling out in the open.

Day after day we descend from the Blue Ridge Mountains to the gentle rolling slopes, hiking the rocky terrain ever downward until we reach the fertile bottomlands. The heat of a blistering sun forces us to stop early. The high temperatures linger late in the afternoon, making it impossible to go far.

The magnificence of the mountain peaks is far behind us, and the Piedmont of rolling hills and flatlands await us. After ten days of tramping through the woods, we cut a path directly south and follow a network of streams. The elegant S-shaped valley snakes its way through a hollow and marks an easy trail for us. From the crash site, we have traveled all of thirty miles.

This morning Jamil and Artem returned from their scouting trip having discovered a forgotten highway. Once a four-lane freeway, the footpath is broken asphalt amidst overgrown trees. Weeds and bushes grow through cracks in the pavement. The path disappears in places,

❋

but the men easily find it among dead trees and rockslides.

They guide the horses over the rocky terrain to keep the flatbeds from tipping over. Dev helps me climb over the masses of debris, often difficult to cross. Lily wants Iain to carry her through the worst areas. At times, we take dangerous switchbacks, but always converging back to the forgotten highway, always heading southward towards the safety of Kings Mountain.

Occasionally, Lily will leave my side, racing ahead with Iain to pick flowers. She collects small treasures along the way and runs with Tala like little girls her age should. Lily rarely ventures out on her own, so I am happy to watch her play.

Toward noon, the forgotten highway veers to the west, circling around another ridge. The bypass deviates from our route a couple of miles. We wade through waist high grass and a meadow of wildflowers before discovering an airport landing strip three thousand feet in length.

While not in good condition, the strip was wide enough for small planes to land and takeoff at some time in the recent past. Abandoned mining equipment and rusty bulldozers clutter the area. Bordering both sides of the airstrip are four flattop knolls with narrow dirt roads winding upward along the contour of the hillsides.

Approaching the airfield, we stopped waiting for Lily and Tala join us. She stands beside me holding my hand. "White mountains like elephant backs," Lily says, picking a flower. She places the petals in the pockets I sewed on her dress. "I saw them in a book."

That surprises me. Where did Lily read a book? She refuses to talk of home no matter how subtle my questions. Each night we cuddle with Freja and Jenna telling stories to help Lily fall asleep. After several failed attempts, I have decided she'll share her past when she is ready.

"Elephants in North Carolina?" I reply, teasing her with a mock frown. But I know.

I know why the hilltops are dead, mutilated and forever a lifeless gray white. "Strip mining on steroids," I explain, shocked at the vivid contrast between the distant green wilderness and the dead hills, the color of aged bone.

Iain stands several feet away talking softly to Wei. He nods his head absentmindedly. "We'll take a break," he says to the group. "For fifteen minutes."

Jamil helps Freja dismount and hands her a canteen. "This place gives me a bad feeling. Why leave all this equipment?" he asks.

"Mining in the twenty first century was brutal and decapitated the mountaintops," I explain. "They used explosives to clear the trees. There were other ways, but they wanted a fast profit."

Dev is beside himself with excitement, practically jumping up and down. Exhilaration brightens his face. "Look, Ben, it's a D575A Super bulldozer!" he exclaims. "16 feet wide, 10 feet tall and made in Japan! We studied all about this in a hydrogeology course."

"Unreal!" Ben says, laughing and throwing his arms in the air. "I studied geochemistry, but nothing on this machinery."

"What about that other one?" Juan Pablo asks, his voice rising in eagerness. "That looks like alien technology."

"That's a Bagger 288, built by Germans," Dev says stupefied. "See that bucket wheel excavator. It's huge."

Before Dev can share its history, they race like five-year-old boys down the airfield claiming their vehicles. Artem hesitates, but stays with Jenna. Isaac and Cyrus look at each other and sprint at full speed down the asphalt. The GoBot hat goes flying in the wind as Isaac leaps onto the bulldozer, and they compete for control of the Bagger. Cyrus and Isaac combine forces and tackle Dev and Ben, playing around and throwing them off the dozer.

Juan Pablo and Ben climb across the extensions while Isaac and Cyrus jump down onto the platform and vie for king of the dozer with Dev running hot on their heels. They yell at each other, pretending to be workers and make imaginary sounds of machinery digging through the soil, stripping the land of minerals and coal.

I can easily imagine the mining crew from two hundred years ago operating the equipment. The Bagger 288 is a killing-machine with its extended mechanical arms and could have belonged to aliens from another planet because it does steal natural resources and annihilates the Earth.

Iain takes my hand. "Let's see what's on those hilltops."

"Jenna, watch Lily for me," I say, tossing my backpack down on the ground. Tala plays in the meadow, sniffing gopher holes and hunting whatever animal will give her a chase.

"I wanna come," Lily says, pointing at Iain. "I want him."

Iain grins and lifts her into his arms. "Alright, my wee gràdh."

"What's that?" she asks.

"It means 'my love.'"

Wei and I walk alongside Iain and Lily. We head for the elephant's back with Freja and Jamil not too far behind us. Excavation required a road to reach the hilltop. Erosion has washed away most of the dirt that was once a series of terraced strips cut into concentric circles. The topsoil is gone, and the surface is more a moonscape than anything we have seen in the Blue Ridge Mountains.

I envision the virgin land as it was before explosives blasted deep fissures into the body of Mother Earth and ripped old growth forests from the ground. Canals for fresh drinking water stay buried forever under tons and tons of rock and dirt.

The summit is not so high. The land has perished, death by strip mining and here we find the dead, the victims of the Millennial Plague. Human bones fill trenches the length of the airfield. Skulls, leg bones, full skeletons lying side by side like discarded carcasses. Thousands and thousands of bones stick up in the dirt scattered across the flat surface. Bones bleached white by the hands of time and two centuries of exposure to the sun, wind and rain.

"Shut your eyes, Lily!" I choke out the words, releasing a desperate cry and pulling on Iain's shirtsleeve. He presses her face against his shoulder.

Wei stares horror-stricken. "They were buried once, right? They wouldn't just leave them." He wipes away tears. "Do you think there are mass graves in China, too?"

"Yeah, they were buried," Iain says in a chilling tone.

❄

"Babbage said—but seeing this," says Wei, his voice breaking off. He doesn't try to hide his tears. The boy from Castle City, the one I imagined as an ancient ruler, now openly sobs. Some of his vital life energy drains from his inner core.

"Mass graves," Iain says, his face devoid of emotion. "They had no choice."

Math gives meaning to my life. How many corpses did they dump in these trenches and those on other hilltops? Millions and millions and millions of dead are the forgotten victims of the Plague.

Vertigo overwhelms me. I need to hold onto something physical before the vision comes. I reach for Iain's arm, but it is too late. I've lost all sense of gravity. A swirling sensation buzzes around my head like a swarm of mosquitoes.

The whirlpool of decay lifts me out of my body and carries me to the bones where thousands of black angels guard souls of the dead. Hanging weightless in the air, they hover over trenches where human remains once decomposed in open graves. Tall figures, both male and female in flowing garments with black wings, gaze my direction as though recognizing me. They are beautiful with thin veils covering their faces, and their hypnotic eyes glow bright with an all-pervading power over me.

Though I feel a gentle breeze, I suffocate as though dying in an enclosed tomb where the black angels sing of death with a bittersweet refrain. The melody echoes in the chambers of my heart.

One angel glides toward me and reaches out to me. Her touch is warm and inviting. She opens my eyes to a metropolitan city, which appears before me as it was before the Plague. People wander down the streets. Automobiles stop at a traffic signal. Bombs drop from the sky and explode killing the innocent.

I block the angel from my mind and force the pain down into a dark place. By the sheer force of will, I try to destroy the second sight and banish the visions forever. It doesn't work, and there is no escape from this valley of death. The bones sing louder. Spirits of the dead hovering over the skeletons rise up and move toward me.

✻

I can't breathe. I fall to the ground and vomit. The dry heaves tear my guts out, and my throat burns. I stay down with my hands upon the dirt as though touching their spirits. Nothing stops their song, or the sound of human suffering.

The angel's eyes gaze upon me. I surrender to her power. *Behold, I have set before you a task. These souls cry for justice. Only one can save them.*

They call my name. "Marie-Joëlle. Marie-Joëlle."

Freja's scream snaps me out of the maelstrom. Jamil pushes her down the road and away from the summit. The men have abandoned their games and race up the hill to see what's happening.

Wei pulls me to my feet and lifts me into his arms. His soulful eyes look into mine. He says nothing while he carries me down the hill and puts me on a horse. Jamil rides with Freja on her mount where she sits distraught and crying. Jenna tries to comfort her from the flatbed, but she cannot help Freja.

There is no time to explain. We have stayed too long in the Valley of Bones. Iain lifts Lily up to ride with me. His face is pale, white with shock and smooth as polished stone. Pinpoints of light blind me. I keep my eyes on Lily as if her innocence can save me.

The day is a wearisome trek although no one complains when we don't stop. We travel as fast as possible through the flatlands. Every mile is an escape from the Valley of Bones. Every hour shortens the distance to Kings Mountain.

We follow a watercourse known as North Toe River. Sunset comes late in summer months and lengthens the afternoon. The strain of the last twelve hours slows us down. But Iain pushes us another five miles.

Very soon the forgotten highway will lead us to Black Bear Cove. Whether we find bears or not, we need to replenish our water from the lake. Then onward to the abandoned town of Marion, the halfway point to the Piedmont of North Carolina and to Kings Mountain.

We turn southwest and break a trail up a low mountain in hopes the plateau will be visible. For the last hour, I have been walking with Iain and Wei scouting the area. Freja keeps Lily. I don't want Lily to know how frightened I feel after the vision at the Valley of Bones. The others follow at a safe distance. Cyrus and Isaac scout the area ahead.

We scale the peak as the last rays of sunshine sink over the horizon. The boundaries of sky and open space blend into a bottomless blue green forest. Hundreds of miles of wilderness stretch before us. A landscape of humps and escarpments lunge precipitously below us in a series of undulating slopes and rocky cliffs. The view is breathtaking and heart-wrenching. This foreign otherworldly place entraps us in its relentless grip.

"Oh, no. It's hopeless," I say, venting the despair I have felt all day. "Will we ever get out of these mountains?"

Iain takes my hand and squeezes it. "Mile by mile. One day at a time."

"I'm so tired."

He reaches out and pulls me into his arms. "Stay strong. We're halfway to Kings Mountain," he says softly. "Together, we can do it."

I glance back for the umpteenth time at the weary group. "I think we've come far enough, don't you?"

Iain swipes at a giant hornet buzzing around his head. His nose and forehead are sunburnt. "Aye, let's make camp," he readily agrees. "Wei, can you get them settled for the night?"

Wei keeps his hands in his pockets and turns slightly to the right. "Yeah, they're ready. This morning was unreal." The emotion is gone from his face. He backtracks a short distance to set camp.

These days Iain does not let his guard down. His emotions would expose his vulnerability. He devotes his attention to his leadership. Every hour he continues to protect us. Fascinated, I watch how the sunshine brightens the yellow specks in his hazel eyes.

My feelings for Iain Sinclair are a mad medley of pleasure and pain. I've fallen in love with him while he has been fighting for our lives.

Iain glances at me with raised eyebrows. His wavy red hair shines with copper highlights and his arms are tanned from days in the sun. He stands before me so strong and fearless.

"Well, I feel I've neglected ye. Something is wrong. This morning, what did ye see? Those bones held something evil."

"You mean back at the valley when you called me Marie-Joëlle?" I can't explain the visions. No way will Iain believe me. He might think I have lost my mind. Why do I feel detached from my body?

Iain takes a step closer. "What did ye see?"

I didn't think I could ever open up to Iain. "Things, not physical, I mean. All my life I've heard a voice and known things. The Indians call it a spirit guide, but I wasn't taught this. That's my secret."

"Uh, visions, ye say? Maybe, it's the stress or hallucinations?"

"I am not delusional," I protest. "It's something tangible. I thought my migraines caused them. But I'm not having migraines here. I hate this place."

"I love this place," Iain says firmly.

"Suffering and death?"

"Truth, not lies."

"I can't do this. I want—" I cry softly. My tears turn to sobs.

Iain comforts me without making me feel weak. "To go home."

Tears come easy these days, and I can't find the right words. I fear I may never see Océane and Jolan. "I never cry. Now I can't stop. I'm a mess."

Iain brushes the hair from my face and speaks in a voice soothing enough to calm the fears of a child. "Aye, I agree, you're a lovely mess, but I've no complaints."

"Boyfriends aren't supposed to be so agreeable," I reply feigning indignation. I push him away, but Iain closes the distance between us and tightens his arms around me.

His grin widens and he tilts his head slightly to the right. "Uh, is that what I am now, your boyfriend?" He doesn't wait for an answer.

Iain kisses me with a fierce urgency and then just suddenly releases me. His nose is too long, and his hair is unkempt. The lines on his face relax into a smile, lasting a moment then disappearing. Sometimes, he seems ready to share his secrets. I don't think I want to know them, not if they are as bad as my visions.

Branded in my mind are thousands and thousands of haphazardly

❄

exposed bones. I have told no one how the Valley of the Bones haunts me. I cannot stop the death song playing in my head.

"What a pair, you and I, with our secrets."

"What did ye mean?" Iain asks soberly.

"Your secrets, and my—well, vision power I can't explain."

"Never mind. I think we make a fine couple," he says tenderly. Iain takes my hand and kisses me again. "Time for a well-deserved dinner. They will be wondering where we are."

We backtrack along the trail through the darkening woods. A low fire in a pit wards off the chilly night air. Someone had the good idea of digging a hole and lining it with several rocks, which makes our fire undetectable from miles away.

Iain sits on a stump sipping a cup of steaming hot ginseng tea, a local native root, and safe for consumption. "Tomorrow, we need to make ten miles."

"We saw a campfire to the south," Juan Pablo says. He straddles an upturned log, digging his heels into the ground and stirring the loose gravel.

"Aye, a hunting camp, maybe." Iain scratches his head, a routine habit we have all acquired living outside with bugs and crawly things. "Strange, right out in the open. All the more reason to get out of here."

Dev accepts a plate of dehydrated mashed potatoes, dried nuts and freshly picked berries. "The road is in good condition," he says. "I'll have more tea."

Jamil pours hot tea into Dev's cup. "We're traveling through..." Jamil glances up at Freja, "we don't know what."

The others listen to Iain. His face is bright with confidence. "You're right, Jamil. From now on, we travel with everyone armed."

Jenna, Freja and I pack the supplies and makeshift kitchen. The moon is high in the sky, but no one wants to sleep. The twelve of us with Lily sit around the campfire. Tala sleeps at Iain's feet.

"Today is Jo's birthday," Lily says suddenly, looking up from her make believe village of worry dolls.

"Yep, July fourth," I confess, embarrassed at letting the entire day

❄

pass without telling anyone, except Lily.

"Ye could have told me," Iain says insulted.

"Colony Day," Lily says, putting her dollies in a wicket house made of bark, moss and twigs.

Iain turns his full attention to the little girl. "Colony is a village?" he prompts carefully. His voice is casual, and yet he eyes study Lily with speculation.

She glances up when no one speaks. To Lily, adults not talking signals trouble. Afraid, she drops her dolls and climbs into my lap, burying her face in my shirt. She plays with my braids before peeking back at the men.

"How about a story?" I suggest, rocking her in my arms. "Can you tell us about colonies?"

"I dunno." Lily is sucking her thumb.

"Maybe tomorrow is better," I murmur. My only concern is Lily.

"How about a chain story?" Jenna asks. "Each adding a part." Her idea lightens the mood, and Lily nods her head smiling.

"Good," I agree reluctantly. "Who starts?"

With a timid smile, Lily points her finger. "Him."

Iain digs his nails deep in his beard and scratches like a burly bear. "Okay, in my village, I sometimes wear a kilt."

"A kilt?"

"That's something like a skirt a wee girl wears." Lily's jaw drops in disbelief, which sets off a soft ripple of laughter. "Boys in a skirt?"

"In India," Dev grins shyly, "men wear a dhoti."

"Dhoti," Lily repeats. "Jo's Indian, but she doesn't wear a dhoti."

"I'm American Indian."

"Like Cherokee?" Lily asks.

"Cherokee is a colony?" I ask surprised. Do the tribes live nearby?

Lily shakes her head and pulls both my braids kindly. "I dunno. They didn't tell me."

"Your parents?" I probe tentatively.

"They said we were going to Black Mountain, then to Cherokee."

"All these mountains," Iain says with mounting frustration.

※

Lily picks up her worry dolls and parades them across my lap. "I dunno. They said grandfather protects orphans."

Iain looks perplexed and mildly impatient. "Her grandfather?"

"I don't know," I reply unsure. "Someone is expecting her."

"You're thinking we should find him. It's a bit risky, Jo," Iain says resolutely. "Alright, love, what's your grandfather's name?"

Isaac smiles at Lily. He takes his GoBot cap and places it on Lily's head. She puts both hands on the cap and twists it around with the visor in the front as she's seen Isaac do.

"I think Simeon."

"Simeon, what?" Iain asks gently.

Lily shrugs her shoulders.

"Who were those men with you?" Isaac interjects eagerly.

"I dunno," Lily says. "Can we go to bed now?"

Jamil leaves Freja's side to join Iain and Wei. "Whoever they were, we're headed right into their backyard. How do we play this?"

Crossing his legs and leaning back, Iain uses a knife to remove splinters from his hand. "Aye, tis a problem."

No one speaks. Iain often talks to himself when solving problems. "Tomorrow, we scout. Jamil, Artem and Wei. Just us." Iain leans back and crosses his arms. "We'll take her along. Then trade weapons for food. Learn what we can."

"You need a woman to come along."

"No," Iain replies, not bothering to look at me.

"You need me."

"Tell me something I don't know," he says, but his laugh doesn't soothe the building tension. "What's your point?"

"A woman isn't a threat," I add defiantly.

The men exchange subtle glances, and then they start to leave the fire pit. They recognize the storm brewing between Iain and me.

"Stay here," Iain says. Silently, the men obey and sit down.

"I'm going."

Iain shakes his head. "Just walk into a settlement asking for this man Simeon? I won't risk your life. You are not coming."

❄

"I'm afraid you don't have a choice," I reply, feeling triumphant, but at the same time horrified.

"Uh, and why is that, Jo?"

"Because Iain..." I lift my eyes and look at a hooded man standing behind Iain. "Because someone is pointing a gun at your head." Swiftly, Iain pulls a handgun from his pocket.

"Slow and easy. Hand it over." The bearded man's mouth twists into a crooked smile as he takes the weapon from Iain.

The shadow of death passes over Iain's face. One single tear hangs on his lower eyelid. His eyes hold sadness and regret. The man aims the barrel of his gun precisely at the crown of red curls, his finger visibly tightens on the trigger, and a shot echoes through the night.

❆

CHAPTER TWENTY-ONE

Bottleneck

A BLAST OF GUNFIRE rings through my head, but Iain's brain was not the target. Shrouded in the shadows, the marauders and madmen overrun our camp. All that can go wrong swirls into a flurry of motion. Fast. Cruel. Barbarous.

The world erupts and breaks into a thousand pieces spiraling out of control and vanishing into a black bottomless pit. We don't stand a chance. With bloodcurdling shrieks, they brandish their weapons and attack us like ravenous man-eaters.

My eyes never leave Iain's face. His expression hardens with hate, and I wonder if I will ever again see the boy from Scotland I love. My vision glazes over. However, on the periphery, I witness the enemy descend upon my defenseless friends, their terror giving way to fury.

Bodies tumble and roll in the dirt. I catch a glimpse of Wei leaping sideways and snatching a sniper from the travois as two men tackle him to the ground. Artem and Jamil pull out their blades and start hacking.

Paralyzed, I shrink into myself, closing my eyes and retreating into a corner of my mind. The sounds are unimaginable. Primitive. Savage. Hissing snarls. Deep, throaty growls. The sickening sound of fists smacking flesh. Bone crushing bone. Foul curses.

I feel a gut wrench listening to the distorted voices of my friends. I cringe inward when I hear their low, throaty grunts and guttural cries. Without looking, I know they bleed from the merciless beating. And I can do nothing to stop it.

My eyelids flutter open. Iain's eyes burn a liquid gold fire. His full lips tighten into a thin line and form one word. "Run!"

I want to obey but can only watch helpless. Iain moves with the agility of youth. The bearded old man doesn't expect Jujitsu from Iain or the vicious blows that knock him off his feet. Breathing heavily, Iain kicks the man squarely in the groin, and then he spins around into a crouched position.

"Run, Jo!"

His words break the mind spell, but I sit very quietly unable to move. A tingling fire at the base of my neck crawls its way down my shoulders like a column of red ants stinging my flesh. Someone is behind me.

He makes a coarse noise way down in his throat. "Get your hands where I can see 'em." His words are like bullets, firing into my back and squelching my urge to run.

I do what he asks and lift my hands. I look over my shoulder at the one-eyed man towering over me. He leers down toward me with one grayish blue eye, the other one covered with a black patch.

What strange sounds I hear. The crackle and pop of embers from the fire pit. Crickets chirping. The vibrating pulse of a primeval forest. A fleeting thought crosses my mind. *This is not how I envisioned my death. I will die an old woman in Iain's embrace.* Then the knowledge comes to me that once they get our chips, we are as good as dead.

I turn my attention back to my soul mate. Iain subdues his attacker with an arm lock, but not for long. From out of nowhere, someone comes along and slams the butt of a gun into Iain's skull. He drops weakly to his knees and falls face first to the dirt barely missing the campfire. It is over in minutes. Almost over.

An indistinct object catches my eye. Breaking through the tree

❀

line is a blur of fur. In the dim firelight, the orkwolf is a lethal weapon with round yellow eyes and white deadly fangs. Tala sprints in my direction charging the man. She lunges with her jaw wide open, her sharp fangs aiming for my assailant's jugular vein.

My first impulse is to leap up and knock the man down. I fling my body between him and my dog, but he is a very good sharpshooter. The one-eyed fiend takes aim and fires his weapon. One bullet stops Tala in midair.

With a high shrill yelp, she drops forcefully to the ground. I fall to her side and cover her with my body. She quivers with tension and lies limp beneath me. An unearthly wail echoes through the woods. Can that feeble cry be my roar in the night?

"Not Tala. Not Tala." The two words reverberate in my head. I cannot let go of her. I must save her. She can't be dead. Not like this. It can't be true. Not my Tala. *Tala.*

The one-eyed man advances on me with a lecherous sneer. I kick frantically to evade his hands. He lifts me to my feet like Raggedy Ann. "Hey, Logan, lookie what I got. Ain't she somethin'? Trying to save me from a wolf. Whatcha make of that?"

I spit in his face. "Get off me, you scumbag!" He slaps me hard across the cheek. The punch knocks my head back and rattles my teeth. He smells of unwashed body and foul gum disease.

"Earl, you bonehead. It was the dog, not you," Logan says. His voice is grainy like his throat is full of coarse grit. The bearded leader walks with a slight off balance gait, but handles himself with an air of authority. "Put her with the others. As for you," he adds, digging his fingers into Iain's scalp and lifting his head from the ground. "Try that again and I will shoot you."

Iain gives the man a half-formed grin wiping dirt and blood from his mouth. "Ye can count on it."

Logan kicks Iain in the ribs. "That's for the nose." The man uses his sleeve to wipe blood from his upper lip. He might be thirty and stands taller than Iain's six foot three. "I mean it. Don't try anything."

Lily crouches fearfully with Freja and Jenna. She hides her face in

Jenna's lap. Freja's gray eyes are full of terror. But I wonder how much of our conversation these outlaws heard before coming into camp. I count ten, but more will be guarding the woods.

"Do what they ask," I whisper fervently. "But say nothing."

Logan and his men waste no time confiscating all our weapons, sorting through our backpacks and discovering the Marine uniforms, snipers and ammunition. All this time, the guards move restlessly, stalking the night, tense and alert as if they expect an attack.

In our poor condition, exhausted and hungry, we are no threat. It has been days since we have eaten fresh game. Wearing filthy clothes, we stink from poor hygiene and sleeping in the wilds. Every head and beard is crawling with lice and who knows what else.

"Roy. Ira. Get over here," Logan orders. "Cut those chips out." The men have pocketknives, and they would eagerly slice our wrists.

"No, wait!" I shout. "Let me. I know how." I appeal to Logan the only way I know how. I drop to my knees and beg him to spare our lives. "Please, let me do this," I cry, pleading and whimpering helplessly. "Infection can be deadly."

Logan draws his eyebrows into an annoyed frown. His face is a patchwork of deep lines and wrinkles. "Make it quick before I change my mind."

Jenna helps me. We work rapidly removing the microchips from seven of us. They allow me to use the med supplies to numb the skin, sterilize, suture and bandage the wounds. All said and done, this takes less than one minute per chip. Not a bad day for shopping technology.

Logan takes a seat on an upturned log and leans forward, elbows on his knees with a gun in his left hand. "I got no time to waste. I want answers," he demands. "Who's in charge?"

"I am," Iain and I say in unison. We stare at each other dumbstruck with mouths gaping open.

Iain's face is swollen badly, and his lower lip is bleeding. Despite the terrible beating, or maybe because of it, Iain rears up on his knees as obstinate as ever.

I will not risk Logan inflicting further damage to Iain. I must convince Logan of my leadership. As if on cue, Iain and I repeat louder and stronger, "I am."

"I'll get the truth from them," Earl boasts, so much like Blackbeard the pirate he should be wearing a captain's hat to match his black patch.

Logan puckers his lips repressing a loathsome smile. His shrewd eyes narrow with speculation. "Shut your trap, Earl. Go with Willard. Pack those supplies."

Another man who could play the part of a scarecrow with his thin frame and gangly arms and legs hurries to the fire pit. He whispers something to Logan. "Alright, Cal, go. Check it out." Logan's deep voice rises with irritation. "Now, what's your name?"

"Sinclair," Iain answers, touching his jaw and grimacing in pain. Already patches of dark bruising cover half his face. The other half is a thick, russet beard.

"I want the truth about the crash."

"What crash?"

"Don't lie to me, boy. I kill liars and thieves."

Logan wears a dubious scowl, and his face is lined with creases, aged from exposure to the harsh elements. His brown eyebrows are arched over beryl green eyes. He studies us with a dark expression.

"I'll ask once more. Give me a straight answer or you die."

"You intend to kill us no matter what," I object, staring down my nose at Logan. His dark scrutinizing gaze burns through me. Like a mind reader, he anticipates my words before I speak them.

"Why shouldn't I kill you?"

"We've done you no harm," Iain yells. "We're nothing to you. At least, let the girls go free." Emotion chokes off whatever else he wanted to say.

"Don't you know about the war? Your kind kills my kind." Logan leans toward the campfire and rubs his hands over the heat. "We hide and evade," he says forcibly, "but we never engage the enemy. We are different from your patrols. I haven't killed you, not yet."

"We can help you," Wei says, standing somewhere behind me. His voice is overconfident. "Give you tactical advice and all that we know about the military."

Logan unties a red bandana from his neck, wiping sweat from his face and drinking from a canteen. His clothes are brown and dusty from the trail. "I doubt you know more about your military than I do."

"Patrols won't stop, no matter where ye take us," Iain insists with a grimace. A deep cut on his forehead needs stitching. It will surely leave a scar. "They'll come," he finishes stubbornly.

I wave my hand motioning for Iain to shut up. Why make a bad situation worse? "Iain, stop antagonizing him." I stare at Logan while formulating an argument that might save us. "We can barter for our freedom. You'd like our passwords and codes, and how we hack into the Network."

"Yes, go ahead and tell him, Jo," Jenna says, nodding her head with encouragement.

I look back and forth between Logan and Iain. "We're candidates."

"Oh, are you, now?" Logan says sardonically. "Owned by GAP. Tell me something I don't know."

"What I know? How can I?" I exclaim, mildly out of control and taking him literally. Feeling giddy but ramped up, I let him have it. "You beat us. Threaten to kill us!"

I don't glance over at my dead dog, for fear I will lunge for Logan's jugular. I do not want to think about Tala, so I blow off steam that has been boiling for days.

"What's to tell? We crash. Run for our lives from human predators. Endure brutal thunderstorms and get attacked by nasty, bloodsucking bugs. And let's not forget, you want to slice and dice for our chips. Oh yeah, no matter what, you plan to kill us!"

"Marie-Joëlle," Iain says tolerantly. Something in me melts at the sound of his voice and the way he speaks my name. "Kindly, shut up!"

Flustered and profusely perspiring, I try to calm down and think through the problem. "What? Of course, they will kill us. We know their names and faces."

"Aye, but don't give him more reasons to murder us. Besides, he has the patience of Job to tolerate that thrashing."

❄

"You killed my men," Logan says in a low, coarse voice.

"They were already fighting in a battle when we came upon them. Um, which men were yours?" Iain asks hesitantly.

"It was fight or die," Wei adds with conviction.

Logan drops his voice lower. "I sent eight to meet some refugees. They didn't make it back."

Iain hangs his head low. "We came onto two groups who were fighting. Those who stalked us were the same men who slaughtered the women and children..." he stops abruptly.

A red blush suffuses his face with a fierceness I have never seen. He clears his throat and expresses the regret we all feel. "I'm sorry. By the time we found them, no one was alive, except the girl. Those men were hunting us until we rescued our friends and killed them."

"Hunters?" Logan asks clearly startled. "No, not my men. Likely bounty hunters. Dressed in Marine uniforms, you were easy targets for ransom or sport." Logan stands up and stretches his long legs. "Killing you would surely bring patrols to our doorstep. Easy targets, though, twelve stranded candidates."

"Aye, well, ask what ye want," Iain says, hunching his back and almost bowing in submission. "We'll be on our way."

"No doubt to Kings Mountain. To tell 'em what you know?"

"Nothing," I insist, my throat tight and choking off my breath. "We know nothing."

As odd as it sounds, I see no cruelty in Logan's eyes, though I lower my gaze under his scrutiny. I glance away searching for my dead dog. But Tala is gone. If she's not dead, then she is seriously wounded. Earl gave me no chance to check her wound.

"Like the girl said, you know our faces," says Logan. "You're right, Iain Sinclair. Patrols are looking for you. All this time. What choice do I have? Kill you and the patrols come. Free you and they still come."

"What now?" Scarecrow asks, pointing one of our own automatic weapons in our direction.

"We make sure they get found," Logan says. "Back on the Blue Ridge, near the crash site. Let 'em find twelve dead candidates."

❈

AN OLD MAN STEPS away from a tree where he has been watching us. His face is creased with deep folds and heavy wrinkles. A jagged scar winds its way along his jawline and up the side of his face. The deformity doesn't diminish the raw power of his imposing presence.

"So, you've finally made it back to the Blue Ridge. Simeon Justice, you're one stubborn old man. I'm glad to see you, my friend." Logan shakes hands with the grim-faced man.

Simeon Justice walks with a limp and leans heavily on a tall crutch made of burled wood. The long cloak he wears is an earthy dark brown with dark pants and shirt. His hair and beard are a pure colorless white.

"No killing tonight, Logan!"

"Well, Simeon, it's my way of getting rid of them," Logan says. His tone is condescending though benign. "And we don't have time for twenty questions. Better to leave them dead. Better for all of us."

"Dead, you say? You're a fool!" Simeon chastises him summoning the latent powers of his warrior past. "You are right about GAP not stopping until they find these children. But what risk to our people to kill them? Hundreds of patrols will avenge these candidates."

"I'll deal with this!" Logan insists. "Tie 'em up. We're moving out."

Simeon Justice raises his cane shaking it and nearly hitting Logan. "These children are under my protection. I claim rights as elder of these lands!"

"An elite force of Marines and these children murdered my men," Logan says in a steely voice. "A life for a life the Good Book teaches."

"I'll know the truth before another life is lost. Go on now, Logan. You know what we need to do. I need only ten minutes."

"Good luck with that," Logan says, spitting his chewing tobacco in the fire. "I say killin' is best."

"When we started this, you agreed not to harm them. I'll get what you want, but we do this my way."

"For you, old man. But make it fast." Logan pats the elder on the shoulder and turns to his men. You three," he says to the woodsmen, "watch these tough guys."

"I need one man," Simeon says, staring down at us. "As we know, they failed miserably on their own."

The old man smiles but behind his facade is a seasoned warrior, clearly hardened by decades of killing. Simeon reaches into his brown coat. To my surprise, he pulls out a modern pocket size Smart pad.

"Calvin, take this," he orders, handing the pad to the lanky, tall scarecrow guard. "Record our conversation."

One by one, Simeon asks our names, where we were born, where we live and the names of our parents. We recite passwords, codes, data encryption and describe Network protocols. Anything he asks we freely give hoping to buy our freedom.

"We monitor communications," he says unconcerned. "We knew you crashed, but not where. Unfortunate timing for everyone, except the orphan."

Good at concealing his feelings, Iain sits quietly giving Simeon a stony glare. He slumps forward with the weight of the world on his shoulders. "Lily's parents," he asks, "did they die in the fight?"

"No. She never knew her parents."

"Then your Lily's grandfather," says Iain.

"No, I'm not her grandfather. I spearhead a rescue project. It took over a year for the refugees to reach the Blue Ridge. The child was born elsewhere, but learned to survive in the wilds."

Iain straightens his posture with resolve. His wide shouldered frame and tousled red hair are once again that of a brave Highlander. "The Grandfather Project?"

"You know of this, I see. We rescue orphans from an unspeakable place. That is all I can tell you. You did well, Iain Sinclair, saving her life. The other children who died in the valley, well, we can only grieve for them." Simeon speaks in a low-pitched but menacing tone. "The

❋

brave warrior clasps a sword in one hand and a child in the other."

"What about Bottleneck?"

"Bottleneck?" Simeon asks startled. The old man looks at Iain with curiosity. "I underestimated you, young man. But then again, you are the architect of the River."

"The River," Zebenjo says with amazement. "It is the newest logic programming language. The most powerful one ever created. Yeah, you didn't get to present at Kickoff."

"Later, Ben. Right now," Iain says, a challenge in his eyes, "why does GAP systematically eliminate human populations?"

"It's an old story of power and corruption. Not ethnic cleansing, but population control. Ten billion people inhabited the globe before the outbreak. Climate caused a radical decrease in food production. Projections were bad. How would the planet sustain so many?"

"The Plague was intentional?" I ask horrified.

Simeon watches us with a contemplative expression. "Forgive me. You don't know your history. Yes, we suspect an engineered virus was released on third world countries. It got out of control. Mutated into the Millennial Plague. Malnutrition weakens the immune system. The famine was deplorably inevitable and unstoppable."

"The Heartland of America died," Zebenjo says as though reading from a book. "Extreme weather, floods and droughts. World markets collapsed. Russia's Farm Belt and China's food economy became dead zones. Crops failed worldwide."

"How do you know, Ben?" I murmur, shocked by his words.

"Hacking," he replies, staring down at his hands.

"You must be very good," says Iain, studying Zebenjo carefully.

"Enough sadness for one night," Simeon says, rising to his feet and leaning on his staff for support. "We must leave this place. Too close to enemy territory."

The guards separate us into four small groups. Our captors bind my friends' hands and herd them toward horses and mules. Stripped of weapons with no means of escape, we have no choice but to obey. Wei, Iain and I remain with the old man.

❈

"Follow me," says Simeon, but abruptly turns around with a knife in his hand. He is nimble for a cripple. "Don't try anything," he warns. "I'm very good with this."

"Will our friends be safe?" I ask boldly, stepping beside Simeon, surprised at his agility and fast gait. His limp does not handicap him nor slow his movements.

Simeon glares at me. "Your friends are under my protection. None will dare question the authority of an elder. But I don't expect you to understand. In your world, none hold such a position."

"Where are we going?"

"You attend the Crystal Cathedral," he says, not as a question but more a statement of fact. Simeon gives me a sidelong glance.

I feel uncomfortable that he knows so much about me. But I nod unsettled by the wild look in his eyes. I wonder whether this old man is slightly crazy.

"To gain your freedom, you must swear an oath. It is time you bear witness to the destruction of Bottleneck on the world. After a night in the Holy Sepulchre, then you'll know what truth may come."

CHAPTER TWENTY-TWO

Chimney Rock

DAWN TO DUSK we travel nonstop through miles and miles of wilderness. The long trek takes more than two days of riding in the harsh summer heat. Simeon Justice rides a white gelding while we follow behind him on three good mounts at a fast trot.

A woodland footpath turns south and away from Black Mountain, and immediately the terrain changes. The valley gives way to rugged mountains. Steadily, we climb upward giving the horses free rein to find their way through thick timberland.

We trail behind Simeon in a single line up the rocky slope and over the back side of the mountain until descending into a narrow gully bordered by steep cliffs and barely wide enough to give us access. For fifteen miles, the horses step upon stony bedrock, dry of water and leading ever deeper into the canyon. We begin the laborious ascent up another mountain. The horses walk slowly along an ascending trail, so high it seems we will never reach the top.

All my life, I have been fighting mountains like those in the Blue Ridge, only to find one more insurmountable obstacle. My world is more broken than I imagined. Something, maybe a spirit guide, has always pricked my heart with deeper truths. I reflect upon the battle with my shadow self at Grandfather Mountain. I wish only to return home into the safety of my father's arms and tell my mother I love her.

We dismount at the summit to appreciate the rugged landscape and the narrow gorge we traveled. I breathe deeply of the clean air and realize that I have conquered the mountain and come to a holy place.

The panoramic view is breathtaking, for the divine touches me as I stand in this sacred place of Chimney Rock. Tears slowly roll down my cheeks. I am so high above the broken world that if I lift my hands and reach for the heavens, I could touch the face of God.

"Iain, take the horses," Simeon Justice says. "Take them over in the grove. You'll find a lean-to and pen. Unsaddle and feed them."

"We're here for the night?" Iain asks, taking the reins to my sorrel and waiting for Simeon to speak. He glances at me in concern. "Will ye be alright, Jo?"

"Yes," the man says in a low-pitched whisper. "We'll wait for you before going on."

"Let's go, Wei."

Iain leads the horses away with Wei following with the two mares. They disappear into the shadowy woods. The air is brisk and cool. A cloak of darkness is falling quickly.

Simeon settles himself on a felled log near the edge of the cliff. I follow and sit beside him. "Tell me about your research," he says with interest.

"I—it's..." I consider how much to reveal. "Complex." I study the creases along on his forehead, the curvature of his cheekbones. The irregular angles of his face tell a history of their own. "What of yours?"

"Hummm, one night won't be enough," he says provocatively, "but we'll try to answer that."

I am more convinced than ever that Simeon Justice is a seasoned warrior. Whether his warfare was on battlefields or with cybernetics remains a mystery to me.

"Where did Logan take my friends?" I ask urgently. "We won't help you, not if you hurt them. You must tell me where they are!"

Simeon sits very still and refuses to answer my question.

❄

"Why are we here?" I ask, softening my tone.

Simeon shifts his position to gain a better view of the panoramic view, which spans hundreds of miles in the distance. "I thought you'd guessed why. To build trust. You need my protection. I need your obedience."

"Why would you trust us?" I ask, realizing that I really shouldn't challenge him, but unable to stop my scathing accusation.

"You could say this is my home. I swear your friends are safe. But you must hear me out. After tonight, I think we will trust each other."

We lapse into an intimate silence, intentional and comfortable but without looking at one another. I know without checking. He watches me. I feel no embarrassment or disquiet. I wonder if an oath of silence is all that Simeon Justice will expect.

The cave he leads us into encompasses a large cavern, more like a cathedral with a high dome and expansive walls. The men build a fire in the pit. The soft glow reveals a few items in the corner, a feather bed lying on the ground, a trunk and a small wood table and chair.

"Iain, you seem troubled," Simeon says, taking a bite of beef jerky from his saddlebag. "History tells of many conflicts. Valor earned in fighting evil."

"'The brave warrior clasps a sword in one hand,'" Iain recites back to the old man. "'And a child in the other.' What did you mean?"

"I pose a more pertinent question. Who are the evildoers and who the saviors?"

"I've had all I want of killing!" says Iain, his words sounding like a harsh reproach to Simeon Justice. "I've done enough killing for one lifetime."

"And Lim Chang Wei, will you battle the forces of evil?"

"Recruiting, are you?" I ask angry, preventing Wei from accepting the old man's call to arms.

I pitch the dregs of brewed tealeaves from my tin cup into the fire. I stand up to face Simeon Justice. I know Wei has passed the test of bravery and will heed Simeon's battle call. I wonder how Wei and Iain, or any of the boys, will settle into the university after killing the men in the valley and those who hunted us.

"Is this how you gain our trust, old man?" I ask, feeling resentful. "We're students, not medieval knights, here to do your bidding! To fight your war!"

Simeon gives me a half smile. His eyes widen with approval. "Did I say war must be physical combat?" His voice is a hushed murmur like a breeze through aspen leaves.

What did he say? I sit back down. Iain takes my hand. "You said 'the sword in one hand,'" I recite back to him. I consider his words and marvel at the light in Simeon's weary eyes. Memories of my mother flash through my mind, of things she tried to teach me, but I refused to accept.

"The sword of spirit," Simeon says, his words evoking invisible things into the physical plane.

His words resonate with my feelings, and his voice floats upon the air like an echo through the cave, louder than any war cry. His physical appearance is that of an ancient spirit, and he breathes a life-giving vibrancy into the cavern.

I feel my soul responding fully to Simeon Justice. His words flow through me. "The word of truth," I say with reverence.

"Yes. The evolution of consciousness. Ours is an oral history," he says. "They call me the messenger. But I'm a simple storyteller who possesses the memories of our ancestors for five hundred years."

"What about other places?" Iain asks with mounting excitement.

"The ancient Scots settled these lands," Simeon explains. "Patriots traveled Victory Trail and fought at Kings Mountain. They defeated those who threatened their lives and families."

Wei sounds as captivated as Iain does. "What of China? Were my people ever free?"

"Not in the way you wish they were," Simeon replies. "But they're free now, freer than before the pandemic. History is not shrouded in darkness. Some books survive." Simeon stands and takes a flashlight from a shelf nearby. "Come, learn your past."

We follow him deep into the innermost part of the cavern. The

❋

length of the cave extends three hundred feet back from the main entrance. The ground is smooth with hard-packed soil. The air is clean, cool and moist and comes through a vent in the cave's roof, which provides for ventilation in the enormous space.

Twenty cedar lined oak chests line the wall. Simeon opens the lids. Books, photographs and a horde of documents are sealed in airtight, waterproof stainless steel containers, and fireproof time capsules hold data drives.

"Much was copied onto archival paper. Some protected with acid free covers. Many survived two hundred years." For the span of two hours, Simeon teaches us the past and then shows us a page from an old newspaper. "US Eighteen Trillion National Debt," he reads the headline.

I reach for a worn, leather-bound book. "*Project Bottleneck* by William Justice. A relative?"

"Perhaps," Simeon replies coyly. "You may read it."

"After Project Bottleneck?" Wei asks, reaching for a book from the opened trunk.

"Controlled growth and genetic cleansing." Simeon knows GAP's initiatives, or maybe he developed the science.

"To engineer disease-free genes," I prompt him, hoping he will divulge what he knows. "Who are you?"

Simeon Justice stares in our direction without seeing us. His eyes cloud over, envisioning a past I can't even imagine. "The evolution of a new species. Stronger, healthier and more intelligent humans? You should investigate these things once you return home."

Despite our protests, he will say no more of this. Instead, he speaks of mystical things. For several hours, we listen as though transported into an alternate reality of our world. Simeon Justice teaches us sacred truths from the lost books, ancient texts and forgotten manuscripts.

His revelations weigh heavy on me. I feel the walls pressing the air from my lungs. I place a book back in the trunk and leave the men behind. I walk back through the tunnel needing a private place to sort through the day's events. I keep walking outside until dropping down onto the ground at the edge of a cliff.

Darkness falls swiftly in the North Carolina wilderness. The sun is long gone. The air is cold. The first stars appear overhead. I rub my eyes and dry the tears as someone approaches.

Simeon sits down beside me. He possesses an uncanny ability to gather the power of silence and the potency of memory into simple words, but he speaks with ancient wisdom. "'We do not see the world as it is, but as we are,' from the Talmud."

"You have a copy?" I ask intrigued. Simeon's use of quotes reminds me of Julius, whose confidence reassured me at Castle City. Suddenly, I realize how much the young Frenchman's friendship helped me.

"Ask your friend Isaac. He is Jewish, yes?"

"I don't know. I mean, I guess," I answer, looking inquisitively at the old man.

Simeon stares into the distant night. I study his stern profile, the hooked nose, his high cheekbones and wizened dry skin. The breeze rustles his white hair. The song of a nighthawk echoes in the canyon.

"You risk a lot bringing us here."

"Actually, I can see into you," he says cryptically. "You saved Lily's life."

"What about her?" I ask, suddenly comprehending his meaning. Simeon Justice holds her future in the balance as he holds mine. "Where did Logan take her?"

"She'll be adopted into the clan," he says softly.

"Why bring us here?"

"You must convince your friends not to betray us. You are the one. I wanted to open your eyes to the truth."

"Your truth?" I feel dangerously close to exploding at him with accusations.

"No, my dearest," he replies lightly, "your truth." His kindness is disarming, and his humility compelling proof of his sincerity.

Hot tears sting my eyes and choke off anything I could hope to say. Iain is calling to me. I stand up and brush the dirt from my clothes. I leave Simeon outside and crawl through the narrow opening of the cave. I walk straight into Iain's arms.

"I think we can go home," I whisper, feeling his arms tighten about me. I rest my head on his shoulder, breathing in his manly scent. Iain kisses me lightly on the lips.

"What did he say?"

"It's what he didn't say."

Wei sleeps near the firelight. His face in repose reminds me of the boy I met at the Taste of Culture luncheon. Who could imagine the same twelve candidates, from small talk, ending up in North Carolina?

Iain leads me to the feather bed where I lie down. He covers me with a blanket. "Let's call it a day. Sleep well, Jo."

"Stay with me."

"Are you sure?" he asks surprised, pulling the blanket around his shoulders and holding me in his arms.

I feel shy and very fragile. "I don't want to be alone."

"Jo, you're not alone," Iain whispers. He strokes my face and kisses me with ardent desire. "On my life, I swear to love you. Don't be afraid."

"But those bones. I saw things, horrible things," I cry, touching his face and wishing for more than he can give. To help me understand.

"Aye, those dreams can't hurt you. Tis okay," he says, sighing and content with the intimacy we share without crossing unspoken lines.

I lie in the comfort of Iain's solid body. He rolls over, and I snuggle against his back. I know when he drops into sleep because his muscles relax and a moan escapes his lips. I stay awake a long time watching the firelight dance upon the walls.

The images evoke a forgotten tribe of people with blackened faces and long spears performing a war dance. The light conjures the spirit world drawing forth those who pray for power and the black angels praying for the souls at the Valley of Bones.

A cascade of emotions sweeps over me. I could easily lose myself in shame. Indirectly, the citizens of my world bear the blame for the patrols who hunt women and children like animals brought to a slaughtering house. GAP citizens perpetuate the ongoing genocide.

We are twelve superior polymaths, but truly only young fools. A dreadful feeling threatens to overwhelm me. Do my parents know about Bottleneck? Why did they never tell me about the war?

And it seems that falling in love with Iain in the majestic land of North Carolina has clouded my mind. How did I fail to put the pieces together about Iain when it was so obvious? Iain Alexander Sinclair is a man with secrets and the architect of the River. He can control the crisscross of SASS computing.

The same wise blood that runs through Iain's veins also gives life to Lim Chang Wei, a cyberwarrior with every right to challenge his allegiance to GAP. Who will stop the madness? Whose war if not ours? No wonder Iain and Wei are tight buds. One is the code master and the other is game master. Does Logan plan to use both Iain and Wei to strike back against GAP?

Suddenly, my need to learn Iain's secrets and crack the man code is not such a good idea. He has reminded me of this often enough. He withholds secrets to protect me. I no longer begrudge him for that. Rather I feel relieved of the burden weighing him down day and night. A man of virtue and honor, he strives for truth and asks the hard questions.

What retribution can there be for the bloodshed of Bottleneck? For the war crimes against the innocent? Simeon said the Grandfather Project rescues orphans. Likely, there are other underground efforts within the cities to aid refugees in escaping.

The wind howls incessantly in the distance. Iain tosses and turns in a broken dream finally uttering a deep groan and finds his peace. Wei snores softly. Simeon Justice does not return to the cave, at least not while I am awake. Perhaps he seeks a solace in his own visions as I do.

Eventually, I close my eyes and travel to the spirit world, a place of my own making where memories and imagination blend stardust into sunlight. Too soon, ethereal voices draw me away into dream-making. Much later the darkness yields to the rush of dawn. I cannot hold onto the truth in the dream message, but I awake feeling better.

Breakfast is a meager selection of beef jerky, corn fritters and hot tea. The morning sun lightens the atmosphere in the cave. Simeon does not seem in a hurry to hit the trail. He putters around a shelf, organizing small bottles and jars and finally opening a drawer.

Iain, Wei and I wait patiently, sitting around the dying embers of the fire pit. Simeon comes to me. Without asking, he moves my braid aside and secures the clasp of a necklace. His touch is cool upon my neck. I finger the pendant of a bronze cross hanging on a thin rawhide string.

"It is the Occitan cross," Simeon explains. "Four keys and twelve spheres, one for each of you."

"I can't accept this," I object, starting to unclasp the chain. "It's too precious."

"A remembrance," he replies, waving aside my protest. "To honor your bravery in the face of adversity. Please, wear it in remembrance of your night in the Holy Sepulchre."

Iain throws dirt into the fire pit to extinguish the embers. He brushes his hands against his pant legs. "Won't they ask where she got it?"

"She can tell them it's a graduation gift from a friend," Simeon says with a twinkle his eyes.

I finally give voice to the ache inside me. "What about Lily?"

"I know a good woman who will raise her with other children. She'll be educated and well cared for."

"Will you travel with us to Kings Mountain?" Wei asks, rolling up the blankets and putting them back on the feather bed.

"I find my way to many places. Best not to say too much."

Simeon leads us out of the cave with Wei behind him. "You have an organized military?" he asks.

"Stop it, Wei," I snap fiercely, but regretting the rebuke though he deserves it. Wei won't drop the subject of warfare in the wilderness. "I won't let you stay behind to fight. We pledged to get home together."

"Wei," Iain says, placing his hand on the young man's shoulder. "We're going home—all of us. This isn't our war."

Wei knocks Iain's arm away and takes a step toward Simeon who

❖

stands leaning on his staff. "Whose war is it?" Wei asks passionately. "You think we can go back and pretend we saw nothing?"

"That's exactly what we'll do!" Iain says aroused. "Patrols will hunt these people. Retaliate. We say nothing."

"Time to find your friends. We've a long ride," Simeon says. "Go saddle the horses. We'll wait here."

Simeon remains quiet until Iain and Wei head toward the small corral. "Marie-Joëlle, one more thing." We walk to the clearing and wait while Iain and Wei saddle the horses.

Here it comes, the moment I have been expecting all morning. "What do you want from me?"

"Such cynicism from one so young." He takes my hand and clasps it in his own. "If nothing else changes for you, promise to learn about your people and their origins."

"Why is that important to you?"

Simeon laughs for the first time. "Not me. You. You will find yourself in their history. The ancient history in mythology."

"Myths and old legends?"

"In signs, symbols and simplicity, we find what's often concealed." Simeon smiles, however, his eyes glisten with tears. "So few care these days."

"I promise, but you must keep Lily safe."

"I will protect this child with my dying breath."

I surprise myself when I rush into his arms crying and embrace him. He has touched something in me that I do not understand. I cannot explain, but I know my life has changed forever from a night with Simeon Justice, elder of the Holy Sepulchre.

❄

Shadowland

SIMEON CHARGES AHEAD at a reckless speed and his white gelding's hooves kick up dirt in his haste to leave. We push the horses hard, galloping over rolling hills and fording shallow creeks. We travel nonstop, riding northwest late into the night, then resting for a couple of hours until dawn. Finally, on the third day, Simeon turns directly west, and we keep riding well past sunset.

Under the cover of darkness, we enter a deep depression in the earth, riding by oddly shaped steel structures and twisted arches, and we pass through a wasteland that has been reclaimed by the wilderness. This is a dead city overgrown with flora and a vast timberland within a deformed forest. The remnants of buildings lie buried under fallen concrete, uneven asphalt and stacks of decaying ash.

"This was the city of Asheville," Simeon Justice states simply. That he discloses our location strengthens a tenuous bond between us.

This is Shadowland, a ghostly place with thousands of deformed columns with metal frames and misshapen buildings. The demolished skyscrapers have fallen to the ground. The ruins of antiquity surround us though the damaged foundations still retain a measure of glory. But a gloomy atmosphere possesses the once-thriving city that is forever an otherworldly land of death.

"Twenty thousand fell sick with the Plague. Eighty thousand died in one day of bombing."

"That's impossible. They wouldn't," I object, but fall into silence. "They killed an entire city?"

"One day of nap-bombs and chemical drops."

"On healthy people," Iain adds despondently. He leans forward with his shoulders dropping as though resigned to the bleak reality. "I know about this from hacking the Network core."

Another one of Iain's secrets. I don't want to know how his River penetrates the core, or might change the course of human technology.

The old man cuts a path alongside the towering brick walls of an edifice much like a Spanish villa. What stands is nothing more than the damaged ramparts of a church. Structures in the area are lost in the black night. Guarded by a haunted forest, this eerie metropolis is a refuge for lost souls who want justice. Specters of a ghost city follow us although the others don't perceive their wraithlike forms as I can.

Simeon dismounts and bends down to the ground and snags the handle of a trapdoor hidden by a synthetic canvass, the camouflage matching the surrounding foliage. Concealed beneath the canvas is a large flat entrance wide enough for us to walk with the horses down a gradual decline into inner earth. Simeon makes sure Iain closes the trapdoor shut behind us.

The dark tunnel is an underground subway system with rusty tracks weaving its way beneath the old city and leading to an extensive labyrinth. Once a spacious subway, the subterranean cavern has been converted into an underground bunker. We walk several minutes toward a chamber resembling a stone temple.

"A military outpost," I whisper, watching the glow of the flashlight as it casts shadows upon Simeon Justice's somber face.

He lifts his finger to his lips as though we are conspirators hiding a well-kept secret. "You mustn't speak of this," he cautions. "Tether the horses."

Wei ties the reins around large chucks of asphalt. Iain slips his

❈

hand into mine. We walk side by side. His presence protects me from visions I have fought off for days.

We stop at a solid iron door, heavy enough that both Iain and Wei struggle to open it. A dim light illuminates a passageway. Somewhere down the hall, the dead call to us for help. Their cries echo, not in my mind but truly aloud. Fear overwhelms me. I tremble uncontrollably and step away from the door.

Iain pulls me to him startling me with his strength. "Snap out of it. It's our friends, not ghosts!" he says, but reassuringly. His body is extremely hot, and I cling to him for warmth. "I swear, Jo. I'll keep you safe."

We follow the voices searching for our friends, down one hallway after the next, each one leading us further into the maze. Finally, we find them locked in a dark room. Their hands and feet are bound with rope. Iain unties them as I light several candles. Artem's left eye is black and blue. Ben, Dev, Cyrus and Isaac all have cuts and bruises on their faces, and Juan Pablo has a bloody nose. Jamil has a busted lip and walks with a slight limp.

"Wait!" I cry panicked. "Where's Lily?"

"She'll be gone by now," Simeon says, "to the clan."

"I wanted to—" I choke off a sob, "to say goodbye."

"We must get going. Wei, keep us moving," Simeon says. "Take the flashlight. That way through the bunker. Plenty of fresh water and food down in the next section."

The supply room houses not only food reserves but also weaponry and shelves of ammunition. Jenna and Freja distribute bottles of water and assorted packets of dried goods. Jenna takes a bag from my hands and gives it to Freja to put in a backpack.

"I didn't get to say goodbye," I cry softly.

Jenna gives me a hug. "I'm sorry," she murmurs. "Lily knows you love her. But she couldn't stay with us, could she?" Jenna asks, trying to comfort me. I stare into Jenna's blue eyes and think of my mother, and all those times she never understood me. Jenna understands me.

Artem reaches for a handgun, but Simeon stops him with a light touch of his staff against Artem's forearm.

"Not so fast, son. Give me the gun," Simeon says, eying Artem and Jamil with speculation.

Jamil takes the weapon from the lower shelf. "I'm not leaving here without a gun." He fills a backpack with ammo.

"He's right," Juan Pablo readily agrees, following Jamil's example and arming himself. "Logan threatened to kill us."

"Several times," Artem says, taking a flashlight and putting ammo in his pockets. "I'm done with these outlanders."

"Continue on this path," Simeon speaks in a deep resonating voice, "and I cannot help you. You won't live to see the sunrise."

"I'll guarantee that!" Logan shouts, with a weapon pointed at our backs. "Put it down," he says before Jamil can take aim.

Iain makes a fast move toward the door, but Simeon prevents him from challenging Logan. "No fighting tonight, Logan. I thought you'd be halfway home by now."

"A change of plans," Logan says. "Your orphan is sick."

I push my way through the men until I stand nose to nose with Logan. "Where is she? Where?"

"My men are bringing her," he says in a hoarse voice. "None too soon, I'd say. Old man, I told you something like this would happen. You should have followed protocol and quarantined her. This is your fault."

"She was perfectly fine before you took her from me," I yell at Logan, frantically and fighting a panic attack. "Where's my pack? I want those antibiotics."

"That's a fine thing to want, missy," Logan says in a condescending tone, "but we need those medicines."

"You have no right," I cry, trying to compose myself.

"You have no right!" he yells back, roughly clutching my arm. My friends rush Logan, but five henchmen fight them into submission.

Logan releases my arm and turns away, and Simeon follows him. The guardsmen force us into the room and lock the door. I collapse into a chair, trying to sort out the options left to us. Once again, we must rely on the providence of elder Justice to protect us from Logan.

Zebenjo offers me an energy bar and kneels beside me. "Where did the old man take you?"

"We almost broke free last night," Jamil says frustrated, stomping back and forth. Artem, Iain and Wei stand together in the corner. "Just two guards. We tried again this morning but they overpowered us," Jamil says, pacing like a trapped animal.

Iain steps in front of him and blocks his way to get his attention. "Did you see patrols? I mean, back where they captured us. Simeon said we were in enemy territory."

"No, but they had to be close," Jamil answers, leaning against the wall and crossing his arms. "We can take these guys. What, Logan has like seven men, maybe?"

I walk over to the door and rattle the doorknob. Locked, of course. "Stop that talk! They will shoot us. Besides, Simeon promised to get us home."

"That senile old man," Jamil says. "This is his fault."

Iain pats Jamil on the back and turns around to face the group. "A lot has happened, my friends," Iain says thoughtfully. "Things we saw and what we learned."

"What?" Freja asks shyly. "Something important?"

Iain holds himself upright against the concrete wall. He lifts his chin and smiles. "We'll get out of this. Simeon Justice is an honorable man. He wants us to change things. Things that would—"

A guard swings the door open. Earl gives us a cold glare with his one eye. "You, come with me," he orders Iain. "The rest of you, Logan says get some sleep. You're going to need it."

Earl points his gun at Iain's back. They walk out leaving us all dismayed. Someone bolts the lock on the other side of the door.

"What's that all about?" Wei asks with a bewildered frown.

"Yeah, why take only Iain?" Isaac says, giving Cyrus a worried look. Somehow, Isaac has managed to keep his GoBot cap. Except for the cap, he is all woodsman with long black hair, heavy beard and intense brown eyes.

❊

Zebenjo looks on with a wide-eyed stare. "Do you think they plan to execute us?" he asks. "Starting with Iain? I once read…"

"Please, Ben, not now," I plead. A small stool sits in the corner. I grab it with both hands and slam it with all my might against the door. "Hey! We want out of here!"

"That's a lost cause, Jo," Dev says sedately, taking the stool and setting it on the floor. "Calm down. Iain can handle himself."

The one thing I would avoid I must ask. "Did Lily have a fever?"

Jenna lifts her eyes to meet mine. "Things got crazy. It happened so fast."

"The little girl was so scared," Freja says. Her feeble effort to comfort me fails.

Jenna puts her hand on mine. "Lily will be fine, Jo."

"Why are they questioning Iain?" I ask desperately.

I rest my head against the cool wall. Despite the churning doubts in my mind, I believe Simeon. Attached to the rawhide string is the bronze cross with twelve spheres. I must trust Simeon Justice for Lily's life, and for him to defend Iain Sinclair, my soul's protector.

The hours stretch late into the night before Iain returns from the negotiations for our release. "We're free to go. In the morning, we ride south," Iain says, grinning while reassuring our friends. He curls into himself at my side while everyone talks over each other with questions.

"Logan will ride with us," he says. "It's three days south. We swear an oath, and they leave us near the mining camp. Then we're on our own. Dressed in uniforms, we can pass as Marines and not get shot by Patrols."

"Maybe it's a trick, Iain," Isaac says. I watch transfixed as his dark eyes turn inward discerning truth as I often do. Does he possess a gift like mine? "I don't think we should trust them," he adds.

"Yeah, because of some old man," Cyrus says. "Those jerks took the last of my gum. What's his name? Daryl, the one-eyed butthead?"

"It's Earl," Dev corrects him. He kicks his foot against the wall to scare off a large rat eavesdropping on our conversation. "We don't have a choice," he adds.

❄

Artem scoots across the floor and leans toward Iain. "Speak in whispers, in case the room is bugged. How about we make a plan? We outnumber them. We wait for just the right moment, and beat them senseless. We can find our way out of here."

Iain leans back and casually stretches his arms over his head. His hooded eyes betray nothing. "No fighting. They have no choice. They know the patrols are searching for us. But we swear an oath, or no deal." He holds my hand in a tight clasp and kisses me in front of everyone. "At Grandfather Mountain, I swore to get ye all home. That's what I'm doing."

I notice something I have not seen in weeks. Iain is doing that thing with his face. His eyes are bright with excitement, but there is that ridiculous impish grin. He is lying about something important.

Zebenjo leans forward and asks timidly, "Tell us about the Holy Sepulchre?"

The group listens as Iain and Wei explain Project Bottleneck and war crimes. Sacred texts and hidden truths. The air is charged with adrenaline much like the aftereffects of Shout Out and the debriefing with Julius. Except today, the rage is tempered with a mystical power.

The spirit of the sepulchral settles upon us. Everyone sits in silence stirred by our words as Simeon Justice predicted they would. The power of our conviction convinces them, even Artem and Jamil, to swear the oath. We talk all through the night rehearsing our story, a version of truth. Whatever GAP threatens, we stick to the plan.

"What about GAP's interrogation?" Zebenjo asks anxiously. "I'm not very good at lying."

"The best lie is based on facts. As much as ye can, tell GAP about everything. But say nothing of the last few days," Iain says, as though schooled in the art of deception. "Hunters found us. They beat us, but we managed to kill them and escape."

"Uh, what about the chips?" Juan Pablo asks astutely. "Easy to say how our chips were removed. How about you?"

"Tell them we removed the chips," Iain answers, "after we rescued you, to elude predators."

❊

"This doesn't make sense," Dev says, clearly doubting Iain as much as I do. He presses his lips into a tight sober line. "Why do they trust us?"

"They don't trust us, but I gave my word," Iain says evasively. He looks drained and extremely tired. He keeps hold of my hand, not letting me leave his side. "I told Logan everything."

"Everything? You told them about—" Wei pauses appalled, "the River?"

Various thoughts flit through my head to explain Iain's treason. Brainwashing? No, there hasn't been time. Torture? Maybe, he does look beat up. I recall the military basics of evade, resist, escape. But we failed to perform all three. I concede we should not resist but to reveal the River. That leaves one explanation.

"Have you lost your mind?" I ask, standing up and pacing the floor.

Iain gives me that look, the one when I amuse him and the one I find most insulting. "Either the truth, or be shot."

"What were you thinking?" I ask, sitting down with a thump.

"As I started to say, Logan shoots liars."

"Then what else happened?" Artem asks, voicing the concern that shows on all our faces. Jenna lays her head on his shoulder.

Iain takes another swallow from his cup. "Lots of questions about the crash and technology. Ten years ago, Logan escaped the mines at Kings Mountain. He was fifteen and said it's a shameful place."

"Sounds like you found a new best friend. What are you drinking?" I ask, taking Iain's cup and sniffing the brew. "No wonder you told them about the River. Logan got you drunk."

"Aye, well, we're alive, aren't we? That counts for something," Iain adds, reaching for his cup but falling off his chair. He gives me that comical look again, too endearing for me to be angry. He reminds me of my father.

"Oh, one more thing," Iain says as Wei and Dev help him to his feet. "GAP is lying. Logan says the Plague died out a hundred and fifty years ago. They use it as an excuse to make war on these people."

"A hundred and fifty years ago?" Zebenjo asks.

❈

Jamil hits his fist into the wall and spins around to face Iain. "Do you know what this means? Do you?"

Artem drops his hand onto Jamil's shoulder. "Yeah, they'll use our research for—who knows what?"

"What does it all mean? What of Lily?" I ask fearfully.

"She's with Simeon," says Iain.

"I need to see her."

"No, Jo. He's caring for her."

"What symptoms?"

"Nausea. Maybe a low-grade fever," Iain replies with a yawn. "We should rest before morning."

I drift asleep, but jerk awake before I feel myself falling fast from the sky into a black sun. Twelve stars are dancing, singing and praying. I awake to a kingdom of muted colors and a cacophony of sounds. A string of dissonant notes floats in the air. The howling wind blows withered leaves in circles. Round and round they go, where they stop nobody knows. Native drums one by one beat loud and strong.

Holding a skull in my lap, I sit beside a desk with tattered books scattered around me somewhere in the heart of the Holy Sepulchre. Simeon's bottles and jars and potions are broken on the ground. I fly away riding the back of a black winged horse, three others stallions following and Tala running alongside to a city of castles.

I wear a purple gown and sit upon a throne. My mother calls my name. She yells for me to run away from Dr. Babbage and Mrs. Thalhammer, who imprison me with ropes of golden thread and promise me a sugar castle in a kingdom of Marines.

"Marie-Joëlle. Marie-Joëlle. Wake up."

The remnants of my dream and the Woman in White fade from my mind. I am lying on a cot in a small concrete room separated from my friends.

"Lily," I call, hardly able to speak for the painful sore throat.

I touch Lily's forehead. She is slightly warm. The contagion she carries infects my body. I never thought it was possible for me to be ill.

Lily lowers her chin and closes her blue eyes. "I didn't think you'd ever wake up," she says with puckered lips. Tears and dirt stain her face.

"Are you okay?" I ask with an audible croak. Lily nods her blond head and climbs onto the cot with me.

The air is damp from the underground moisture, but I am hot and uncomfortable. The backpack with the med kit is nearby along with the Marine uniform I discarded days earlier. I quickly change into it, tie my boots and sit down to drink water from a canteen. My lips are parched and cracked.

"How long did I sleep?"

"I dunno," she replies, sitting on the cot and swinging her legs. "Can we go? I don't like it here."

"Where's the old man?"

"He told me to wait here."

"When?"

"A long time ago," she says, her eyes wide with worry. "They didn't want me," she whimpers pitifully.

"I know. They don't want to catch your cold." A harmless cold, I hope. It's the one word I can manage to say, not wanting to consider an illness more serious. "Are you hungry?"

"No, are you?"

"No," I laugh. "Don't worry about me, Lily."

"Do you worry about me?"

"Let's find the others," I suggest lightly. I lift the pack onto my back and tie the straps around my waist. The room is spinning round and round like a merry-go-round. I catch myself leaning against the wall to stay upright. The weight of the bag pulls me back down onto the cot.

"What's wrong with me?"

"Sick, they said."

"I've never been sick."

"We haven't any time to waste," Simeon Justice says, coming into the room and helping me to my feet. "We must get you treatment."

"Am I contagious?"

"I've no instruments. No way of knowing what it is. Our best chance is Kings Mountain."

I lift Lily up, but I am too weak to carry her. Simeon takes her into his arms and leads the way through the long corridor. In minutes, we are back in the network of tunnels headed up to the surface. I lose my footing. Simeon catches me despite using a crutch and holding Lily.

"Where are my friends?"

"Waiting for you."

Quickly, we exit the outer door and a blast of light blinds me. I stumble and hit the ground with my hands and knees. Strong arms enfold me and lift me onto a horse. Iain sits in the saddle behind me and holds me tight. "We're going home, Jo."

"Lily?"

Sweat is pouring off Iain's face. The concern in his eyes worries me. "Riding with Wei."

"Aren't you afraid of me? Of catching this?"

"Never."

I lay my head against his chest and feel the horse's rhythmic gait, the gentle movement rocking me to sleep. "What have you done?"

Did I speak aloud, or only imagined myself uttering the words so close to my heart? Dev's voice reverberates in my head like a trumpet sounding the alarm. *Why do they trust us?*

A soothing voice answers. *Fear not, for I am with you and will comfort you. Iain must stay behind.* I try to object, but my words fall into empty space. Jamil and Artem are right. We should fight Logan, not lend aid to the enemy.

Logan instructs his men to keep an eye out for patrols. "We'll take the southern route through Biltmore Forest and Horseshoe Valley," he says. "Once out of this basin…" A strong gust of wind carries his words away.

We begin the long trek from Shadowland to the world of GAP. The morning sun filters through the canopy of trees, but shadows follow us. I no longer fear the spirits of the dead. A chill moves over my skin, and I shiver not with fear, but with fever.

"Try to rest if ye can, Jo," says Iain. "Soon we'll be on the highway

❋

with room to gallop. Maybe make fifteen miles before dark."

It is well past midnight by the time Logan stops. They use fallen boughs, a pile of leaves and forest debris and blankets to make a bed for Lily and me. They build a lean-to above us by propping up cut limbs covered with another blanket.

Jenna bathes Lily's face with a damp cloth. "They say another day or two and we'll be there."

"Almost home," I croak. "My voice sounds funny."

"Yeah," Jenna says. "Drink this. Simeon said it'll help you sleep."

Lily drinks first and lies back down without complaining. Every bone and joint in my body aches. "Am I going to die?" I ask drowsily.

"I believe Simeon," Jenna replies. "I believe in you."

Weak as a newborn kitten, I smile up at Jenna. "You'd only say that if you thought I was dying."

Freja snorts at my dark humor. Jenna nods, but her smile fades and her bright eyes shimmer. "Yeah, then make me wrong, Jo Peone. Fight this. You're strong."

I squint and try to clear my vision. Sapped of strength, I surrender to the heat wave consuming me. How do I fight this? My white blood cells attack an invisible enemy invading my system. It could be bacteria, and easily cured with antibiotics. In any case, it won't matter. In my world, the weak and diseased simply vanish without a trace.

❄

CHAPTER TWENTY-FOUR

Tears Forever

IT'S BEEN THREE DAYS since we left Shadowland. The Green River flows into many tributaries winding through gentle rolling foothills until reaching South Carolina. The Piedmont is French for "foot of the mountain," and vastly different from the higher elevations where the X29 Predator crashed. The ninety-mile route south of Asheville was a fairly easy stretch on the old paved highway 74, but required a substantial detour to evade patrols.

Over evening meals of rainbow trout and catfish, the militiamen recited local history, satisfying Zebenjo and his avid curiosity. He would keep the men awake late into the night with a multitude of questions. Not once did any of my friends avoid either Lily or me. The infection has wreaked havoc in my frail body, leaving me weak and disorientated. Simeon Justice administered healing treatments from a bag he carried inside his cloak.

Delirium brought desperate cries for my mother and fitful dreams, some dark and frightening, while others were exquisitely beautiful. A vision revived me each morning from the long hours when the fever raged, and I was lost in a sheen of light and chaotic madness.

But one truth comforts me. Perched on Chimney Rock, the Holy

Sepulchre reaches out, infusing me with light and opening a thousand windows, each one equally magical in nature.

I try to explain to Iain, but words fail me. My time in the Valley of Bones and the haunted Shadowland imparted to me a vague sense of the occult, not a haunting but an awakening, not as the good daughter or the ambitious candidate, but a solitary soul searching for meaning.

I wonder if archaeologists feel the spirits that belong to unearthed skeletons excavated in forgotten places from millenniums past, or only even two hundred years ago. Simeon encourages us to honor the dead and keep their history alive.

The days of carefree camaraderie on Grandfather Mountain are far behind us while the adversities of surviving in the wilderness have matured us. I have grown into a woman who must reconcile divided loyalties between two enemies—the outlanders and GAP.

I exist in a world of blind men who make war fighting to protect their citizens while killing the innocent. Does one choose a side and fight? I don't have the answers, only the confusion and moral dilemma. How can generation after generation bequeath to their children such a broken world?

What is my mission but to save the children? But what justice is there for the dead? Simeon Justice refuses to disclose more about the Grandfather Project although he teaches us the world suffers from spiritual amnesia, a death worse than the physical, because the soul wanders lost through this life and the afterlife. At least the whirlpool within the bottomless, black void no longer threatens me. Something else of a spiritual nature has expanded my second sight.

A fixed light anchors me to solid spaces and earthy footholds. I have found myself while living in the Blue Ridge Mountains of North Carolina.

To avoid patrols, Logan and his men ride ahead of us, heading east along the shallow clears waters of the Broad River. No force of man or nature hinders our progress. Once again, we follow another detour along a watercourse going north and zigzagging our way toward the mining district. Our journey will end today when we will reach the outlying zone of Kings Mountain.

Cautious, Logan keeps us moving at a slow, steady pace. I ride in the saddle with Iain on a bay gelding. He gathers me in his arms while holding the reins and letting the horse find its way over a rock-strewn riverbed.

Lily is worse, much worse. Her body does not have the resistance to infections like mine does. She's never had immunizations, vitamins or supplements to strengthen her immune system. Antibiotics can help, but Dev administered the last vial two days ago.

Wei rides ahead of us holding Lily on his mount. The horses walk slowly. The rhythmic clip clop of the horses' hooves hitting the dry riverbed catches Lily's attention. She smiles briefly before burying her face in his shirt.

Just five miles south of Kings Mountain is Patterson Springs. The woodlands are where we stop to rest. The twelve of us with Lily will walk the final leg of our journey up Buffalo Creek.

Iain helps me dismount and carries me to a canopy of trees where shade provides relief from the scorching sun. We sit beside a pond fed from a waterfall flowing over a large collection of boulders. Freja and Jenna care for Lily, cooling her hot skin with wet compresses and forcing her to drink small sips of water to ward off dehydration.

Iain has stayed by my side since we've left the underground bunker. He holds a canteen to my parched lips. I swallow the cold refreshing water. "Your fever is back," he says, dipping a cloth into the pool and placing it on my forehead.

"Almost home. What will they do with us?"

"I don't know," he says. "Can't even imagine."

The promise of a man is fulfilled in Iain's poised stature and self-assured movements. I realize the raw power emanating from him that once made me feel uneasy is the source of his manhood.

These weeks he has fought to save our lives. The boy with the rough-around-the-edge looks and burly bear-like frame is now the warrior he always dreamed of becoming.

For all his manliness, the play of light in his eyes and flecks of

❄

brownish gold amber still fascinate me. "Will you go to Edinburgh after quarantine?" I ask, dreading the unknown and what waits for us at Kings Mountain.

"No," he replies emphatically, leaving little doubt he won't return to Scotland. That surprises me. All I can think about is going home to my parents and Idaho.

"You'll be declared healthy. Won't your uncle want to see you?"

"I don't want my uncle or kin involved in this."

He pauses for a moment in thoughtful repose, and speaks in such a gentle manner that my heart suddenly beats off kilter. "Wherever they take you, demand to see Julius. I wish we had more time. I should have told you things."

He won't make eye contact with me. Iain turns his attention to Logan who orders two militiamen to ride ahead and scout the area.

"Told me what?"

Iain looks at me with a steely expression. He squeezes my hand and appears visibly shaken. "GAP is evil incarnate. Kickoff was never about jealousy over the Medallion Pin. It was the River. I possess the key. No one else. The River is powerful enough to bring down the Network core."

"I know. It's okay," I reassure him. "We'll find a way. Together. Right?"

"Traitors," he says.

"What?" I ask. What is he trying to tell me? "You said missing people go AWOL like the professor Zebenjo saw with file .dc2 on his console."

"They escape through underground efforts. Others are put into camps," Iain says. "A year ago I used the River and broke into the core."

"I know, but it doesn't matter now. All that matters now is that we stick together."

He swallows hard before the true confession. "I work for Jove with cyber warfare."

"Cyber warfare? That can't be," I cry alarmed. A capital offense and punishable by death. "Iain, what is Jove?" I ask, not really wanting

Iain's honesty nor wanting to know his secrets.

"Wrong question."

"Who is Jove?" I whisper, bracing myself for his truth. My head is swimming with fever and confusion.

"That's the right question."

I tremble gazing into the face of a man I don't truly know. "It was you! You spycammed me. You emailed me file .dc2." I wipe away tears.

Iain rubs his hand against the back of his neck and wipes the sweat from his forehead. "The night in Sandbox, Jove wanted Babbage to monitor you, then I could—follow his instructions."

I feel as though I am hallucinating. "You used me," I say weakly. I want to accuse him more forcefully, but haven't the strength. I fell for Iain with all his lies and deceptions. "It was never about me. It was you and Jove. Who is Jove? Tell me—"

"Jo, I'm sorry. At the beginning, it was for him—and then I fell for you and—"

"The prom?"

"I wanted to tell you then," he replies. "I tried walking back that night." A look of regret darkens his eyes. "I told your father everything. About my parents. The River and Jove. He was going to help me get away to Coeur d' Alene."

The disorder swirling through my head clears as I comprehend the implications of his words. "I was a red herring. No wonder Babbage tracked my violations, not yours."

The agony in Iain's face defuses my anger. Still, I feel pained by his betrayal. "How is my father involved?"

What is Jolan's role in all this? My father was a new man. Youthful, handsome, no longer silent and brooding, but driven with purpose and restrained elation. Not a reconciliation with Océane. I wonder whether Océane knows about Jolan's true loyalties. But loyal to whom?

Iain shifts uncomfortably and slides close to me. I pull away and refuse his touch.

"No, Jolan doesn't work for Jove," he whispers. "Your father hates Jove with a vengeance."

❄

"Julius, he works for Jove?"

A kaleidoscope of memories flash before my eyes, the Frenchman with a dazzling smile, so noble, fine looking and trustworthy. What were those subtle clues I missed?

The fugitive looks between Julius and Iain. Their secret meeting after Shout Out and their reactions to Jolan. My father was the instigator. Of what? A conspiracy to overthrow GAP? Defeat Jove?

"It's complicated." A stoic expression hides Iain's thoughts, and he withholds more secrets from me. Truly, the Machiavellian drama I accused my father of that night.

"My head hurts. Please, stop."

"You need to know. I have the key, and Jove wants it. By now, GAP knows about the break-in. They know everything I did at Kickoff. They will kill to get the key."

"Who will?"

"GAP," he says, "and Jove."

"The kidnapping wasn't Jenna or your friends. Who then?"

"I don't know. They botched the job and had to dump us in the forest. I think it was Jove's men, trying to get me out of Castle City."

"Against your will?"

"I refused to give Jove the key. I want nothing to do with him."

"Prom night. You and Jolan on the balcony. Don't tell me you were defending my honor. I won't believe you. Tell me how my dad is involved!"

"I can't."

"Why tell me all this now?"

Iain holds me unbearably tight. I lean my head on his shoulder. "Trust no one," he says urgently. His warning strikes fear in me. "I think Julius can help you, but he didn't tell me much."

Calvin and Earl gallop hot and fast into the shaded area. Logan talks to them in private. The younger men gather around Simeon. Iain helps me to my feet. He gives Wei the backpack he has carried for several days.

Logan calls everyone into a circle. The strain of traveling so near

❄

patrolled areas marks his suntanned skin with a heavy worry.

"You kids head north. Four miles up Buffalo Creek, you'll come to three strip-mined hills. They use 'em for dead workers." Logan grins at Iain. "Time to say goodbye to your girlfriend."

Like trained killers, Jamil and Artem's swift attack catches Calvin and Earl off guard. Dev and Juan Pablo take on the other guardsmen, plowing into them and fighting hand-to-hand. The mayhem keeps up until Logan, Iain and Wei separate the mass of bodies rolling around in the dirt.

Red-faced and sweating, Logan hits Jamil in the stomach, and then takes a step backward and catches his breath. "I'd shoot every one of you if I had my way," he says with malice. He scowls with fury in his eyes. "Tell them, Iain, before we all get captured and shot."

"I agreed to stay in exchange for your release." Iain kisses my forehead and forces me to look up. "I'll be executed if I go back."

"You swore to get us home. You said trust you." Tears choke off my accusation and my grief.

Iain pulls me into a hard embrace and holds my shaking body. His decision does not surprise me. Nothing Iain Sinclair says or does will ever surprise me again.

"Whatever it takes, lass," he says, his accent thick with emotion. "Aye, well, that's what I'm doing."

"I'll stay. We'll find a way together."

Yes, I am angry with him, but my love forgives all his lies. When Iain shakes his head, I pound my fist on his chest.

"I will stay," I shout. A grief too deep for words hits me in the gut. A dull ache deadens my soul.

"Lily will die without medicine. And you need treatment."

Logan's men mount their horses preparing to depart. They train their weapons at us. Logan admonishes us with a hard stare. "You can't tell anyone Iain's alive. He is dead, do you understand? Otherwise, patrols will come looking for him. They hunt and kill traitors, and I can assure you if that happens, Iain Sinclair will die by my own hand."

"Tell them I died at Grandfather Mountain," Iain says, "during the rescue of the five."

Wei steps forward with determination on his face. "I'm staying, too. Take both of us as hostages." He clearly wants to heed to the battle call urged upon him in the Holy Sepulchre.

"We can take them, Iain," Jamil says fiercely, leaning forward with an intimidating expression. His good looks have matured into those of an imposing and brilliant man, his eyes intense and full of feeling. Once an enemy, Jamil will fight to the death to save his friend.

"No, don't!" Iain says. "Wei, lead them north. Take Marie-Joëlle and Lily. Get them treatment. See them safely home."

"I should be the one," Wei says with remorse. "I want to fight on their side." His face is open with every emotion revealed in his smooth confident demeanor.

"They want only me," Iain says, releasing me and moving toward the young men.

I turn away from Iain as he bids farewell to his friends. Jenna and Freja pack our meager belongings into backpacks. Lily sleeps soundly for the first time in days. I check her pulse, and her eyes flutter open. Zebenjo comes to carry her. Lily groans softly resting her head on his shoulder.

These moments pass too quickly. Simeon Justice embraces me. "Heal Lily," he says. *Bring her back to me.* Did he speak the words aloud, or did I imagine them?

"I will protect Lily with my dying breath," I reply, my voice an echo of Simeon's promise. Lily is crying as Simeon walks away.

For the last time, Iain takes me in his arms and kisses me hard on the lips. The intensity of unfulfilled love rivets my senses. "I can do this, if ye go now," he says harshly, but with tenderness in his eyes.

I lean against Iain and feel myself falling into him as though some supernatural force is re-creating us into one physical body, one ageless soul to endure what is to come. His touch gives me the strength to leave him and travel back to my world, while he remains a prisoner in a forbidding wilderness.

Will we meet again? Desperately, I reach inside my mind listening

❄

for the spirits, but no answer comes. I cannot see what will happen in the future. I hear Iain's words again. *I can do this if ye go now.*

"I can do this if you go now," I repeat back to him. I slip the worry dolls in his pocket. "The med team will only take them during the exam."

Iain's face holds no fear of the future, or germs or impatient men with guns. He steps into the saddle and pulls the reins tight to the nervous gelding. Iain rides off at a fast trot behind Logan and Simeon Justice, disappearing down the slope and through the woodlands.

Faced with the responsibility and duty of leading us north, Wei gives the young men a strategy for our approach to the mining camps. Skilled as a gamer, he will outwit and outmatch any foe attempting to harm us.

Dev notices my distress as I sway unsteadily and reach out for him. He lifts me in his arms before I faint. But nothing can stop the sickness ravaging my body and mind or the changes in my brain chemistry that started in the wilderness of North Carolina.

I fall into a world spinning off its axis and spiraling out of control into a cold, bottomless netherworld of no air, no light, no escape.

This is the beginning of an endless dark night of the soul, the loss of self beyond anything I could have imagined or possibly foretold.

CHAPTER TWENTY-FIVE

Orphanet

THE MINING DISTRICT of Kings Mountain looks like it took a hit from an atomic bomb. The basin is an enormous crater in the earth that spans thirty miles to the south. The layered surface with wrinkled ridges could be stepping-stones for giants to use and climb down into the bowl-shaped pit.

The deformed depression is a dumpsite where the tailings are full with waste rock. The hillside is asymmetrical where embedded toxins and heavy metals reside along the slopes. The extraction of mineral has left the soil ash white, an almost colorless dust.

Behind an electrified barbed wire fence are the active mines and armed guards. The military base is not too far from the large refinery and power plants. The basin is a busy beehive with similar equipment like we found at the Valley of Bones. The D575A Super bulldozer and Bagger 288. Off in the distance, the blast of explosives can be heard, the first phase of shattering the bedrock and preparing the ground for excavation.

Wei takes charge, and we follow his instructions "Jamil, Artem, Juan Pablo, go and bring help." They walk off at a fast pace down the slope toward the patrols guarding the fence.

I lie back and shut my eyes while the boys talk about the mining operation. Their words float on the breeze and drift through my mind. Geologic resources, lithium and Mica Mines, all of which I've studied in the production of the mineral deposits. Refined lithium is highly unstable, reactive and flammable. Every digital device on the planet requires a rechargeable battery. Fusion fuel is necessary for nuclear weapons and earth metals for technology.

Within forty minutes, a Special Ops team from Camp Lejeune lands on the long airstrip, and they section off the area into units of containment. The first unit is the sixty Marines who aim weapons at us to protect a hot zone, a five-hundred-foot perimeter demarcation line between us and everyone else. They keep the medical teams from the hot zone where the twelve of us sit in a circle outside the electrified fence.

A short time passes, but the biohazardous alert is swift, and the second unit behind the Marines is the exchange station. Hazardous First Responders (HFRs) talk with security teams, and the last safety unit farthest away from us has portable sterile tents equipped with modern technology.

Personnel are wearing body armor, canary yellow biosuits with hazmat gear and rubber gloves and black boots. On their heads are white hoods like helmets with a mask and an air hose that connects to an oxygen-purifying respirator. A fully, self-contained, well-ventilated and protected environment although I fail to understand why all this is needed when the Plague died generations ago.

Dressed in protective suits, a man and woman quickly approach us. "I'm Dr. Steven Grant. We're here to help."

"I'm Dr. Malum. Can you walk?" the woman asks me. The mask muffles her voice.

"Yes, but Lily," I say weakly. "She's very ill."

Dr. Grant speaks into his I-Doc med device and then talks to my friends. They are all asymptomatic. The doctor motions toward the contact station. Five HFRs walk toward us. "Let's get them scored and secure," Dr. Grant says. "Packed and ready to go."

❄

They divide us into pairs. A female worker takes Jenna and Freja into an isolation tent. Another takes Wei and Ben who disappear into a larger tent. Dev and Juan Pablo stay together. Artem and Jamil. Cyrus and Isaac.

"The two of you will come with us," Dr. Grant says emphatically.

I carry Lily and walk alongside him into a med tent. Two HFRs are waiting for us. One lifts Lily onto a table with connectivity to a console.

"Take a seat," the older woman instructs to me.

"Keep all samples," says Dr. Malum. "Examine them and prep for transport to Orphanet."

"We're not equipped to do much out here," the older nurse objects.

"Document everything," Dr. Grant says. He looks back at me. "Dr. Malum will take care of you."

Dr. Grant is abrupt and to the point. He takes Dr. Malum and the nurses aside. They speak in low voices. Within a couple of minutes, Dr. Grant exits the tent.

"I'm Nurse Sharon. Answer my questions in a loud voice. What's your name?"

Lily states her name. She doesn't know her age or last name or the place of her birth. The nurse undresses Lily and deposits the clothing into a bin labeled toxic waste. She puts Lily in a lightweight gown.

Taking a black marker, Nurse Sharon writes on a strip of adhesive tape and attaches it to the side of the bin. Two words: Orphan Lily.

They examine the little girl, her eyes, nose, throat and ears. "No rash, abrasions or cuts. No external bleeding," says Nurse Sharon.

Dr. Malum stands to the side, observing and speaking softly into her I-Doc.

Finally, Nurse Sharon asks about symptoms. "Any vomiting?"

Lily shakes her head.

"Speak out loud."

"No."

"Hiccups?"

"No."

❋

"Diarrhea?"

Lily shakes her head. "No."

Nurse Sharon takes Lily's temperature. "Does your stomach ache?"

"No."

"Temperature normal, but moderate dehydration. No signs of Hemorrhagic Fever."

"Right, Mandy, let's get her packaged," Nurse Sharon says. The younger nurse lifts Lily off the table. "Start an IV drip with antibiotics in case of MRSA."

"What does that mean?" I inquire while Nurse Sharon takes my temperature. I want to ask why all the precaution when the Plague was cured years ago. But I don't.

"Bacterial infection, the Superbug."

"No, I mean packaged?"

"Dressed in personal protective gear."

Lily stares wide-eyed with her mouth agape in surprise. "I get to wear that?" she asks.

"Well," the woman says, "I have a special one for you."

Lily undresses and takes her first ever health care shower, an on-site portable wash-up kit. A warm mist covers Lily with the scent of eucalyptus. Mandy uses a sanitized towel to dry her body and dresses her in a biomed gown, gloves, booties and a breathing mask.

"Marie-Joëlle Peone," Nurse Sharon speaks into the console. A miniature hologram matching my description appears like a six-inch twin sister hovering on the table. "Get undressed."

"How do you know my name?"

"Our team's been prepared."

So prepared they had a suit ready for a child? Perplexed, I toss my uniform, underclothes, socks and boots in the open hazardous bin with my name labeled across the front in black letters. I slip into a gown and slide onto the table.

"The opening should be in front," Nurse Sharon says.

I remove the gown and turn it around, tying the strings into a bow, a feeble attempt at modesty.

❄

"Remove your jewelry."

"I want this back," I demand, giving her the Occitan cross.

"We'll keep it for you." I watch the nurse drop it into a sanitized bag. "Put this cap over your hair." She examines my eyes, ears, nose and throat. "What happened to your chip, Marie?" She disinfects the area, removes the stitches and puts a clean bandage on my wrist.

"I cut it out," I reply casually.

"Pause examination," Dr. Malum says. "Why?"

"We all did, just in case."

"Why?" Malum demands. "Why in such unsanitary conditions would you risk infection?"

"Is that so important?"

"Things will go better for you, Miss Peone, if you cooperate." Dr. Malum says tersely, "Continue exam."

"No rash or abrasions. No external bleeding. Any vomiting?"

"No."

"Hiccups?"

"No."

"Diarrhea?"

I shake my head. "No."

"Does your stomach ache?"

"No."

"Temperature moderate, and moderate dehydration. No signs of Hemorrhagic Fever."

"Anything else?" Dr. Malum asks.

"Fever, body aches," I respond. I try to keep my voice calm so as not to scare Lily. "Do my parents know I'm alive?"

"Lie back and put your feet in the stirrups."

"No," I object, scooting off the table and looking frantically about the tent. "Why?"

Dr. Malum and Nurse Sharon exchange a meaningful look. "You lived for several weeks in the wilderness with nine men."

"Nothing happened. We didn't do anything wrong."

"We believe you, Marie," Dr. Malum says. "But protocol requires

❄

a complete examination."

"I want to see my parents."

"You're in a restricted GAP quarantine. And even if your parents were standing right outside, you couldn't see them, not for thirty days. Do you understand the trouble you're in?" Dr. Malum asks austerely.

"There was a crash—and we," I hesitate. "My parents think I'm dead."

"Calm down," Nurse Sharon says. "This won't hurt."

Dr. Malum takes me roughly by the arm. The mask she wears reveals very little of her face, only her auburn brows and wide green eyes with large black pupils.

"I'm here because San Miguel Bueno is your patron. But for him, you'd find yourself without treatment."

"I want to see Dr. Julius."

"Outlanders aren't eligible for treatment," she adds. "Do you want Lily to get better?"

I consider the implications of her threat. "Do you swear that Lily can stay with me?"

"I can't make promises," Malum says. "But I'll do my best if you behave."

I nod and smile at her, but at great cost to my pride.

"That's a good girl, Jo. Take Lily outside," Dr. Malum tells Nurse Mandy. "Marie will be there shortly. But you prefer Jo, right?"

I lie down on the sterile table and imagine sitting with Iain in the cave at Chimney Rock while watching the firelight flicker against the granite wall. "Where are you taking us?"

"There's a fleet of emergency vehicles here from Camp Lejeune," explains Nurse Sharon.

"A healthcare facility," Dr. Malum adds. "Someone's relieved to know you are here."

"Dr. Julius?"

"Archbishop Babbage."

The examination is over. A single tear rolls down my cheek as I stand in the healthcare shower, letting the warm spray wash off Nurse

Sharon's touch from my skin. I dress in the biosuit with gloves, slippers and mask.

Outside biomed trucks line the road. None of my friends can be seen. HFRs walk me up the ramp into an emergency truck converted into a chamber fully equipped and with trained staff.

Lily waits for me. We remove our masks. The attendants give us energy bars, but Lily nibbles only a few bites. I force myself to follow what they designate as HP Series protocol, high-electrolyte beverage, nutrient enriched health bar and protein along with Vitajuice.

Sinking into the cushions, I snuggle alongside Lily beneath warm blankets. The attendant places a mask over my nose and mouth. I close my eyes, feeling relaxed, drifting toward sleep. It is too soon for me to regret leaving Simeon Justice and to grieve for Iain Sinclair.

Too late to refuse the oxygen that is a powerful sedative putting us in a deep slumber where we can do nothing but acquiesce to whatever diabolical experiments they have planned.

WHEN I AWAKE, A CRACK of light makes its way past my heavy eyelids. I blink and shut my eyes against the brightness. I can't lift my head or move any part of my body. I am naked and feel exposed under a cool sheet. I drift in and out of consciousness, one moment craving the dreams, the next moment fleeing the nightmares.

I am not lying on a bed, but upon a cushioned flat table. A Smart machine hovers over my head. It puts off a whirling sound. Embedded in my left wrist is a new chip. The skin is irritated. My body is slowly assimilating the device, but the electrical pulse is interfacing with my nervous system.

My brain is numb and feels like a knife slices lines through the gray matter into four distinct segments. I hear the buzz of eighty-six billion brain cells, or neurons, which produce all my thoughts and emotions. A series of electrical shocks pulse across the temporal lobe on the left side. I can feel a narrow band of energy like frigid artic water stream through my brain as they stimulate and steal my memories.

Someone watches me, someone whose voice is familiar, Dr. Julia Malum. "San Manuel Bueno approved the procedure. Interface with her AURA. Scan subject and display results."

The hologram I have known all my life materializes though I hardly recognize Gladys. Her glaring eyes startle me as she projects a hot beam that captures my energy field while stimulating chemical reactions. She remains stationary and doesn't acknowledge me with her usual upbeat voice, or my pet name Mudpie.

They have corrupted my precious Gladys by deleting the complex programming designed for human compassion. The one-of-a-kind grandmother betrays me. Her eyes are a lackluster colorless hue.

Now, the instrument of evil, Gladys speaks in a monotone, almost robotic and callous. "Activating deep brain scan."

The three-pound organ in my skull lights up like an explosion of fireworks. The probe like a needle delves deeper and deeper to initiate brain communication, or brain hacking. Gladys scans me with a subtle light that encompasses me and activates chemicals that awaken images and projects them as holographs through networking software.

"Where's Iain Sinclair?"

Modern technology can probe the mind and steal the truth. What have I told them while unconscious?

"She's resisting. Increase dosage."

Someone sticks me with a needle. A cool wet sensation like liquid ice races through my veins. Relentlessly, they question me.

"Tell us what you know about the River."

It's not so bad being examined and locked in a cell made of mirrors without reflections. This is a superconductor Smart room and fully equipped for medical examination and interrogation.

❈

The drugs are having the opposite effect. Rather than weakening my resistance, they help me find a place inside my mind safe from the brain hacking.

"The important castle is what's inside you."

"Julius, is that you?" I ask, reaching out to touch his sleeve.

He sits beside me under a willow tree at the end of a drawbridge. It leads to a diamond-shaped castle, or more like a multifaceted crystal quartz stone.

"You'll make yourself crazy like this," Julius says, taking me by the hand and helping me to my feet. "Remember what I told you."

"St. Teresa of Avila. The castle is inside me."

"Perhaps it's time you read her devotions."

"Who was she?"

"A sixteenth century holy woman. A woman in a man's world. A saint disciplined in the practice of prayer and compassion."

"She wrote about castles?"

"*The Interior Castle*. In renewing herself, she brought about radical reform. Go to the castle. The seventh castle will protect you."

"How does that help Lily?" I ask irritated. "Dr. Malum took her."

"Enter the castle and pray. Prayer is not an abstract idea. It focuses you on the righteous way. Discipline teaches you to fight for a just cause and compassion to endure suffering for others."

"I am suffering, Julius. Help me!"

"Every moment you're here," Julius says sadly, "I see a little more of you disappearing. Fight them! For Lily. For us all."

"I'm trying."

Julius fades away into the shimmering sunlight. I step on the drawbridge. A heavily scaled, red dragon the color of fire and blood approaches with outstretched wings and the head of Charles Babbage.

Tattooed across his chest is a large, gold popish cross. He opens his mouth and a horde of black demon bats flies out. Is death my only escape? Demons dance and angels weep. The Occitan cross on the chain around my neck protects me from evil and renews my strength.

"Try stimulating those optical implants. Oppenheimer ordered them during her medical exam at Castle City." Gladys's dispassionate voice totally creeps me out.

What implants? Does she mean the medical patches that cured my migraines? No, living in the wilderness healed me.

"Something has triggered all this brain activity. I've never seen anything like it," says Dr. Malum.

I want to ask about Lily. Where is she? I cannot speak.

"She said something about visions. Her brain holds the key. Yes, stay with that image. Track it and save to the Network."

I must get inside the castle.

"Fear not. I am with you," says the Woman in White. She is grace and the essence of purity. "They can't harm you, Jo. Enter the castle."

I walk across the drawbridge, and the dragon withers and dies. I manage one small step at a time as I pass those I trusted. Lieutenant Kurt pats me on the shoulder. "The brave warrior clasps a sword in one hand and a child in the other," he says.

Jenna Slate smiles and claps her hands. Océane embraces me and kisses me gently. "Where's Iain?" she demands, but in Dr. Malum's voice.

Below is a wide moat filled with beautiful white bones bathed in crystal clean water. A song rises from the human remains into heaven.

"Honor the dead," Simeon Justice says, walking beside me to the archway where he kisses my cheek. "You must succeed in your mission."

My father waits for me here. No longer broken with despair, Jolan is a tower of strength. He is dressed in camo. He pulls me into his arms and refuses to release me.

"Things aren't always what they seem. We must fight. The only way to freedom is war."

"Daddy, help me! I'm scared," I cry, clinging to the hope he will stay with me. "What are they doing to me?"

"You are a healer, the Spiritkeeper. They want your second sight. The wolf protects you. The bear is your totem. Find Iain. Now run, Jo, run as fast as you can."

Crystal stone battlements and conical spires rise high above me. I

❄

leap up the staircase of a circular tower connecting to a wall. I stand upon a platform made of crystal. From my vantage point, a whiteout opens my eyes.

I rise above the Earth and see into the heart of darkness. Pure love can save the world. What comes from the holocaust, but a new world created in the wake of a storm. I'm safe in the crystal castle. The chaos calms. My fear subsides.

I don't know how many days pass. An IV with tubes attached to my body provides nourishment. Each time the needle pierces my arm, it means I am alive and strong enough to evade the mind probing. My waking and sleeping and running into the interior castle take on a monotonous routine. After each session, the drugs knock me out until Dr. Malum pushes the limits of my mind.

"This is not working," says Gladys. "She's not like the other ten. Something is blocking access to her mind. We don't want permanent damage."

"Stop the test, Gladys," Malum says. "Save all data to her Orphanet file. Label it 'Lena' and passcode it 'Malum'. I can wait. I know another way. I will get what I want. It's only a matter of time."

❄

CHAPTER TWENTY-SIX

Forgive Our Sins

I GUESS DR. MALUM doesn't want to kill me. A data technician removes the IV, releases me from the flatbed and helps me into a wheelchair. The glass hallway curves in and out, fast and furious like a crystal carousal. Everything is white, and the light hurts my eyes. The sound of children's laughter follows me. Is Lily with them?

Strong hands lift me into a warm bed, but a needle pricks my skin. It hurts like a bumblebee sting, but thankfully, I drop into a dreamless sleep. Too soon I awake and return to the land of the living. Frantically, I cling to my sanity and the corporeal reality of my weak body.

"One more bite. Come on now, you need your strength."

Julius wipes a wet blob of oatmeal from my chin and lifts another spoonful to my mouth. I gag on the cold, chunky gruel. Now that I am physical, I haven't the willpower to resist anything they want.

"Where's my mother?" My throat is dry, and my voice crackles from not speaking for a month.

"They're treating you for a mental breakdown brought on by the illness."

"I'm not crazy! It's the drugs."

Julius inhales a deep breath and looks me straight in the eyes.

"Today there's to be an exit interview. That's why I'm here." The self-assured mentor is a man stressed to his limit. Agitated, Julius looks as nervous as I feel. "Agree with them—with everything they say."

My voice is barely audible. "You're with Jove, aren't you?"

"My benefactor is San Manuel Bueno, a high-ranking official."

"I want nothing to do with Jove."

The pain of losing Iain is an open wound. I don't understand his betrayal. Malum's questions about cyber espionage and the River echo in the corridors of my interior castle.

"I want my dad. Where is he?"

"He went to the crash site. He hasn't returned."

"What? He'd never abandon me. Where are we?"

Julius wears a black wrinkled business suit. His dark unruly hair is longer than the last time I saw him. His face is drawn with deep lines I hadn't noticed before now. Dark circles under his bloodshot eyes are a sign of insomnia.

"I don't know. They blindfolded me on the plane. Someone on board said Orphanet."

I study him with a critical eye. But Iain said I could trust the young Frenchman whom I romanticized as noble and aristocratic.

"They're hurting me. You should have come sooner," I accuse him with a weak attempt at anger. The small rebellion is feeble and all I can manage given how shaky I feel.

The disconcerted frown upon his brow shames me. "Jolan and I flew to Camp Lejeune the night of the crash. They wouldn't let me join the search parties." Holding himself with a quiet reserve, Julius stares down at me with a weary frown upon his face. "I've been down the hall since you arrived," he replies with raw emotion.

The ball of anxiety in my chest eases considerably as I realize how much he cares. "The entire time?" I ask meekly, offering a timid smile as an apology for my outburst.

"I felt responsible." His confession is heavy with remorse. "I mean, letting Babbage send you off. I should have stopped him."

Of course, Julius is here because he's Océane's friend. However, he fixes his eyes upon me with something more than worry. I see what lies beneath his cool aloofness, an infinitesimal glimpse of tenderness for me. Iain often gives me that same look. A shade falls over Julius's face, and he resumes his role as my mentor.

"What's important is your exit interview," he says with renewed confidence. "We'll have a long talk when this is all over. Maybe then, I can finally get some long overdue rest. You need to get dressed. I've brought an outfit."

I place my bare feet on the ice-cold linoleum floor and wobble on spasmodic legs. Julius keeps me from falling. "I'm glad it was you, Julius, who came for me."

I kiss his cheek and shyly reach around grasping the loose folds of the hospital gown.

"Can you manage, or should I call a nurse?"

"I need help," I answer feebly.

Julius places his finger on his S-pad and requests a nurse. A few minutes later two young women walk through the door. One takes me by the arm, the other carries the garment bag and shoebox from the chair. They help me take a menthol shower and blow-dry my hair.

I inspect the personal items and the outfit they want me to wear and feel disheartened. I wore the same uniform as a student. But I'm mistaken.

The white blouse and brown skirt are quite different. The blouse has a V-neckline with a fitted bodice trimmed with lace and delicate embroidery. The skirt is a rich velvet brown perfectly tailored for my height and slim waist. The length in front falls slightly above my knees, and the back flares out with a full train touching the floor. The box contains black leather high heel boots reaching up to my knees.

Despite my confinement, my dark skin glows with a healthy shine from weeks of living in open spaces. I examine the determined curve of my lips and a new quality of gentleness, not there before the crash.

I am no longer the girl who won the Medallion Pin two months ago. Gone is the misfit friendless freak who raged against life. I don't recognize my eyes. The soulful brown holds ineffable truths yet to be

❄

understood. I gaze into the full-length mirror and see the reflection of humility.

Julius walks into the room shaved, groomed and attired in an expensive black Dior suit. For the next hour, he drills me for the exit interview. He prepares me for the courtroom interrogation with the same questions, each time he phrases them slightly different. I practice giving consistent and truthful answers.

"According to official records, the child you found doesn't exist," Julius says hesitantly. "Lily was never at Kings Mountain."

For the fifth time, I refuse to accept what he's telling me. "You're wrong. I swear they examined her," I insist, wishing Julius could take me home. "I saw the nurses input data into a console. Dr. Malum was there."

"I believe you, Jo. I can't explain where she's gone." His voice is thin, and his words come faster and faster as he talks. "They won't tell me anything. Nothing about Malum, or your friends."

"Use your password. I need two minutes at a computer. Maybe I can find Lily. I need to know." I think she's down the hall, but I can't focus my thoughts. My throat tightens until I can't breathe.

The pain of losing Lily gets worse each day. The world is a cold place with no escape from the indescribable sadness. I stare wide-eyed and unblinking, challenging Julius to explain what is happening to me because he works for GAP.

"Listen, this interview is—" he begins, but I interrupt him.

"More interrogation?" I cry softly, not even trying to disguise my fear. "I can't endure more tests!"

"No, Jo," he says, sliding his chair closer and taking my hand. "They want to know what happened to Iain Sinclair."

I don't like the way Julius watches me with doubt in his eyes. "I told you. He's dead," I reply harshly, letting the tears flow unchecked. "It's true." But the more I argue, the less convincing I sound.

I've weighed the morality of lies to save lives. Is there such a thing as a righteous lie? No matter what, I will protect Iain. But in truth, he is destined to an ill-fated life and lives as a ghost in the Shadowland of

❧

forgotten places with invisible people—dead and alive—the peoples of the Earth. Iain Sinclair is dead to me.

"I can see this upsets you," Julius says. He reaches into his pocket and offers me a handkerchief. "I'm sorry."

When it comes to Iain, the best way out of this mess is one giant lie. He must stay dead, and so must my memories of loving him.

"I didn't see it."

"Are you sure he's dead?"

"I wasn't there. Wei and Dev told me."

"Good. That's consistent," Julius says relieved. "Exactly what you told me earlier. I'm sorry about your dog."

"What—Tala?" I catch myself before blurting out something I might regret.

"I assumed she was killed?"

"Yes. I mean, I don't know what happened to Tala."

"Listen, this is very serious. You need to focus. I don't know if you are telling the truth or not."

"I know how serious this is. They've practically burned away every brain cell I have. I don't feel well. It's the drugs."

"They won't harm you. They want Iain and the River. Obviously, you passed their tests."

Julius uses a comb to untangle my hair. He places a white lace veil upon my head held with a comb made of mother of pearl.

"The final touch. A mantilla. Humility, modesty, contrition."

"An old fashioned custom?" I ask defensively.

"Your patron San Manuel Bueno requests you wear the mantilla. You'll be seen by GAP and religious officials. They want confession and contrition. Short answers. Just yes or no will do."

"I'm afraid. What if my friends and I disagree?" I ask, trying to stay calm. "They must be here, too, being tested."

Julius stares with hooded brown eyes, so unlike the sophisticated Frenchman I met at Castle City. "That's good. They want you to be afraid. They won't look you in the eye, but be humble and don't ask questions. I managed to get this back." He holds the four-pronged bronze cross on a plain necklace.

"The Occitan cross," I murmur, recalling Simeon's words. "Four keys and twelve spheres, one for each of us." My voice fades away as if the life seeps from my body.

The faces of Iain, Lily and my friends appear before me, and I feel a gut-wrenching sorrow. I feel pressure in my chest, and my heart is heavy. Did my friends survive the brain hacking and stick to the plan? Stick to the truth we agreed to?

"May I?" Julius asks tentatively.

I lift my hair so he can clasp the necklace. I finger the cross as I did so long ago, and I hear Simeon's voice in my mind. *A remembrance to honor your bravery in the face of adversity.*

"I promise," I say aloud.

Julius looks at me with an odd expression. "Pardon?"

"To find meaning in the simple things."

"Where did you get this?"

"A graduation gift from a friend."

"Do you know its meaning?"

"No."

"It was the cross of a people known as heretics. The Cathars lived in southern France." Julius takes my hand and holds it upon his arm. "So it begins." He gives me a reassuring smile though it doesn't reach his eyes, or soften the deep lines on his face.

An attendant holds a wheelchair for me. I keep my eyes front and center, ignoring the nurses at their stations. The automated door opens, and we exit the glass reception room and head down the long corridor. Wherever Lily plays with those children, she is beyond my help. The orphan I adopted is lost to Orphanet experimentations.

Julius walks alongside the attendant who wheels me through the lobby toward an elevator, which transports us several floors beneath ground level. Our final destination is an empty and sterile room made of mirrored walls and virtual technologies.

For my entire life, I have feared GAP. Now I do understand why people escape to the wilderness, and traitors simply disappear. Eyes front and center, I remind myself. *Front and center.*

The young attendant comes around the wheelchair and looks down at me with a warm expression on his handsome face. I reach for his extended hand, and he takes mine and kisses the back of it.

"I am Damien. Think of me as your representative. This interview is to reinstate your privileges as a citizen. I promise, it will be brief. Activate Peone-GAP session," he says into the panel on the wall.

The empty space changes into a holographic reality, a hospitality suite large enough to accommodate one hundred spectators. Some are dressed in white robes while others wear business suits. I sense the dark inhuman shapes hovering far in the background.

The space is light and airy with a vaulted ceiling depicting a fresco of colors, an authentic rendition of Michelangelo's Sistine Chapel found in Vatican City. The setting reminds me of a museum with rare works of fine art and Greek and Roman marble statues and with lavish gold furnishings and original masterpieces.

Damien helps me to stand up and walk to a witness stand situated before a platform. Where usually clergy sit are five men enthroned in ornate chairs in an elevated semicircular alcove.

"I'm Trace Conti. You look much better today, Ms. Peone." Trace Conti was the speaker from opening ceremonies. His eyes sweep over me from head to foot, blatantly appraising my appearance. Then he acknowledges me with a condescending smirk. "Finally, we meet," he says.

I nod and resist the urge to smirk back.

"It's my honor to introduce Gregory Albrecht, Adrian Ellison, Raymond Walton and Lucius Koch," says Mr. Conti genteelly.

The five-headed beast is not as fiendish as I'd feared. The world leaders are younger than I had anticipated, possibly thirty years old, not wearing military uniforms but silk suits, so dissimilar to the coarse militiamen from North Carolina.

Their hairstyles are a modern length, touching their shoulders, neatly trimmed and decorated with jeweled barrettes. They could be Vogue fashion models on display. Expensive rings adorn their fingers

❋

with manicured polished nails. Powder on their faces, blush to their cheeks and gloss on their lips.

A sixth man sits in a wheelchair. San Manuel Bueno is the elegant but elderly man with the Spanish accent who greeted me that night at Edinburgh Castle and who loves a Basque Bertsolaritza.

"You needn't fear us," Mr. Conti says nonchalantly. "I assure you, we are quite civilized. We were once candidates like yourself. Young, idealistic, ambitious. We are not the villains here. We save humanity."

Kill humanity. But I've lifted the drawbridge to my interior castle, and nothing they can do will touch me. None of the events following the crash happened. Not the night with Simeon Justice at Chimney Rock, and not what I saw at the Valley of Bones. To reveal what I know is to admit treason. Heresy is a capital crime.

"Damien, you may begin," says Conti.

The young man promptly takes from his pocket an I-Med device. "Eye scan and DNA to monitor your responses," says Damien sedately. He gives me a sympathetic expression no one else observes. I look into the scanner and place my finger on the I-Med. "State your full name for the record."

"Marie-Joëlle Peone."

"Verified," Damien says. "Bring in Dorothy Thalhammer."

For better or worse, Mrs. T appears as a hologram. She is wearing her customary black pantsuit. Pinned to her sash are all those gold pins symbolizing her allegiance to GAP.

"Your service is commendable," Damien says. "You are here to account for your actions at Castle City. You were her liaison?"

"Jo has always been my special girl." Mrs. T looks confident and lifts her piggy nose with an air of condescension. "I trained her."

"You failed. Lack of supervision led to her violations. How do you explain this?" Damien challenges her.

"I complied with the rules." Mrs. Thalhammer's nose and cheeks flush bright pink. "How could I know about her unpredictable moods? Her parents failed to report the migraines. The team fell apart. I was responsible for Marie. I wanted her to shine, and she did!"

❄

"What do you know about Iain Sinclair?"

"Nothing. I never talked to him. My duty was to Marie."

"You make a fine argument," San Manuel Bueno interjects. "Five years ago I entrusted you with Marie-Joëlle. Under your tutelage, she succeeded."

Mr. Conti takes a sip from a wine goblet. "I'm satisfied with the results. I see no reason for further questioning. You are free to leave."

Mrs. Thalhammer visibly relaxes as patrols escort her from the witness stand. She makes no indication of having seen me sitting across from her in this virtual reality. Her hologram disappears.

A patrol officer ushers in the next witness. Damien proceeds with the interview. "I present to you Archbishop Dr. Charles Babbage."

The tall, thin historian is attired in the full black regalia suited to his position in the One World religious order. The man I consider the Prince of Darkness stands before the council dumbstruck with fear, but his dead-like eyes are full of light. Everything about the day is surreal and unnerving.

Mr. Conti acknowledges the rattled Archbishop. "You served as director of 2216 Kickoff. Three thousand polymaths this year. Quite remarkable."

"Thank you," Dr. Babbage answers. "Glad to be of service, sir."

"Babbage, what say you?" Mr. Conti asks, leaning back into a relaxed posture while giving the man his undivided attention.

"Sir, I'm happy to serve."

"So you said. The record indicates your esteem for Ms. Peone. You plainly respect her."

"I, well sir, hummm I—" Babbage chokes on his words and needs several moments to recover.

An attendant gives him a glass of water. He composes himself before addressing the council. To contradict a high-ranking corporate fellow is surely the worst career move ever. Dr. Babbage hesitates a moment before acceding his approval.

"I stand behind my report. I deem Marie-Joëlle to be the finest student of all candidates in the class of 2216. A brilliant young woman, and no one would disagree with me."

"More to the point, Babbage, I find it quite reprehensible that you managed to monitor an insignificant schoolgirl studying medicine while Iain Sinclair, a technician linguist from the Defense Language Institute, went unsupervised all week. Why monitor her and not the boy?"

A red flush suffuses Dr. Babbage's pained white face. Crimson blotches break out on his hollow cheeks and long neck. "Her behavior. Fighting with teammates. That ropes course fiasco and hacking the Network," Babbage stammers, noticeably shaken. The contradictions between his statement and his report don't help.

Trace Conti lashes out with a scathing judgment. "You've failed. Iain Sinclair is a traitor. He escaped because of your foolishness," says Conti with disgust. "The council finds you guilty as a co-conspirator. What say the members?"

A strangely beautiful sound rises up like a church choir singing. The volume swells until I realize what it is. The one hundred members pass their unanimous judgment with the chant of a death song.

"Off with his head! Off with his head!"

I shut my eyes and murmur softly. I quote Shakespeare, and only Julius hears. "'Woe, woe…! Not a whit for me; For I, too fond, might have prevented this.'"

No responding quote comes from him, but Julius places his hand on my shoulder and squeezes gently. "Steady, Jo," he whispers into my ear. "Remember, I always win. Together, we'll get through this."

Océane Peone takes the stand. Fear dulls her vitality though she holds herself still and erect. I feel the strange co-mingling of love and hate. Unconditional love for Océane and righteous hatred for GAP. Never before have I been so proud of my mother.

"You chose to separate from your husband. While unorthodox, we tolerate your decision because of your elevated status. Why did you leave Jolan Peone?"

"San Manuel wanted my daughter in D.C., and I travel for my job."

"Jolan Peone is an enemy of the state. He killed five patrols when he escaped into North Carolina. What do you know of his treason?"

"I've always known how we differ in our political views," Océane replies bravely. Her eyes are clear of tears, and the sparkle returns. I watch in fascination as my mother fights for her life. "But do you really think I'd actually betray the man I love?"

"As her patron, I can attest Océane speaks the truth. She is my loyal employee." San Manuel addresses the assembly. "Océane Peone is a faithful citizen with a spotless record as a diplomat. She would not jeopardize her daughter's life."

"Jolan broke the law. When we capture him, he shall be executed. What say the council? Océane Peone. Guilty or innocent?"

I shrink from the proceedings into a gray cloak and hide away in the dungeon of my interior castle. Dr. Malum damaged my mind, and GAP has trespassed upon my soul. My family is torn apart. When life destroys what you cherish most, forgiveness seems impossible.

The Woman in White materializes right in front of me though no one else can see her. Hundreds of black angels who guard the Valley of Bones stand nearby and comfort me with a terrifying simplicity. An invisible realm reaches across the invisible divide to protect me from these proceedings.

"Innocent!"

This one word spoken from the assembly pulls me back from a threshold of fear, and then the Woman in White disappears. When I open my eyes, the hologram of Océane is gone.

Mr. Albrecht speaks up for the first time. "Your performance at Castle City inspired students around the world and earned us millions. We were amused by you and the horses and that dog of yours." He laughs. "Quite the show. Who came up with this brilliant concept?"

"I knew you'd enjoy it," Pépé DeMolay says. He stands behind San Manuel Bueno, another minion of the ubiquitous man manipulating my life. Not vain today, Pépé wears a classic black suit. "Meant for your entertainment, of course."

"Quite right. Our members loved opening ceremonies. The best ever, Pépé."

❄

"Let's get down to business," Mr. Conti says, dropping all pretense of cordiality. "Miss Peone, you are an erratic, capricious young woman, unbelievably beautiful and a rare genius. You may address the council."

"Thank you," I reply with a bowed head. My nervous stomach churns with turmoil.

"The findings of the last thirty days are inconclusive. Your friends have strong minds, but Dr. Malum gathered general data. Several of them confirmed that Iain died at the hands of rebels. One claims an outlaw Logan killed him. Another insists a buffalo killed Iain.

"Some sort of symbiotic bond exists between you and your friends, a fascinating and measurable psychic connection. Adversity builds friendship, which we deem necessary for an effective team. What Babbage failed to accomplish, you achieved with your leadership. You built a solid unit of polymaths."

"I'm so thrilled."

What did I just say? The brain hacking and the drugs make me feel like I'm disconnected from my body and floating above myself. They want to know if Iain is alive.

"You will begin courses at L'Université de Paris. We've approved your team's project. You will crack the code and gain control of the River. You twelve will be monitored. Failure is not an option. Not only that," Mr. Albrecht adds, "but Dr. Julius will replace Iain Sinclair and supervise your team."

"I'm so very pleased." I force the words out with a glorious smile, hoping that I can be excused to go somewhere soon and barf my guts out. Bitterness rises in the back of my throat. "I absolutely love Paris. My mother will be so happy."

"That being understood, one question is pivotal to our decision. Tell us about the night you spent in the woods with Iain Sinclair."

Somehow, I keep smiling. I knew Iain would be the target, but I didn't expect the memories to hit me like a blow to the heart. "Which night?"

Which one of the star-filled nights in North Carolina? Our first kiss at Grandfather Mountain, or the moonlight strolls through the mystery and magic of the woodlands? *Get a grip on yourself Peone.* Which night indeed!

"Which night did you have in mind?" Trace Conti asks, smiling like a satisfied Cheshire cat playing with a trapped mouse. Julius seems a caricature of himself. I've never seen such fear in a man.

"I'm embarrassed," I speak softly, regaining my equilibrium. "The night at Hotel Hohenzollern."

"What happened?"

"I'd rather not say for propriety's sake." I lower my eyes feigning shyness and to give myself a moment to gather my thoughts. Focus. Mindfulness.

"Actually, you will say. Iain Sinclair is a traitor." Mr. Koch finally introduces the purpose of the session. "What's your relationship?"

"He was a team member."

"Can you identify the kidnappers?"

"It was a practical joke. Iain's friends from London. They wore black masks."

Mr. Ellison leans forward with a hardened expression on his face. "During your time in the wilderness, did Iain Sinclair share passwords or encrypted codes? What did he tell you about the River?"

"You probed me for weeks. I know nothing about the River!"

"You kept saying Shadowland. What is this?"

"A song by the band Mercy Me."

"Did Iain try to recruit you?"

"No."

"What about the JOVE website?"

"I didn't talk to anyone about it."

"It's an infraction, but not too serious," Conti declares. "And those violations. Nothing but pranks. Your sins are forgiven. However, your AURA indicates you are lying. We have punishments worse than the death penalty. Miss Peone, tell us the truth. What do you know about the River?"

"I had a crush on Iain. He's the first boy—I ever kissed." I sound like Zebenjo Tongogara rambling endlessly and blubbering insistently.

❄

Tears stream down my cheeks. I don't hold back the sobs. The grief pours out of me for the first time since losing Iain, Tala and Lily.

"He made me laugh with that stupid lopsided grin. He killed to save me. He saved us all. I fell in love with him. Now, he's dead!"

"The penitent Marie with tears of contrition," Mr. Conti says magnanimously. "Very good. The council reinstates you."

The men rise and exit into an adjoining room where they break out cigars and brandy. Damien offers me a refreshment. I sample the bread of angels and sip the sweet grape juice, avoiding the young man's scrutiny.

Julius puts his arms around me. "I'm so sorry, Jo. I had no idea."

"I want—I can't do this." Crying, I lean into him seeking comfort. "I so screwed up."

"No," he whispers. "Your tears prove your innocence."

"I don't understand." I hiccup several times, resisting the urge to throw myself like a helpless female into his arms.

Julius makes no effort to mask his emotions though he blinks away tears. "The heart of a beautiful woman," he says, "always weakens a man's good sense." He is a GAP member like my father, but I know he is not truly one of them. He helps me back to the wheelchair.

"I don't feel well," I moan, holding the empty plate in front of me.

Julius's eyes widen when I reach up to cover my mouth. "Where's the bathroom?" he asks Damien urgently. "Like, right now!"

"Down the hall." Damien wheels me out of the room. "One more thing. Dr. Malum implanted a special device in you, Marie-Joëlle. She can track you anywhere on the globe. Remove it and an electric current will stop your heart."

❄

Epilogue

Jove

THE FIRST THOUGHT that crosses my mind is my mother's betrayal and Jolan's treason. My father is my deepest pain. He is a hunted man. I wonder for the umpteenth time if Iain is still alive and safe with Logan.

I wish I could just stay in bed with the pillow over my head. I feel numb. Losing Lily is an unspeakable anguish, and until I delete the spyware, I am afraid to reboot Gladys from her backup program.

I climb out of the large canopy bed onto a decorative carpet soft beneath my bare feet and enter the self-care room, which is hugely expansive with whitewashed walls, intricately designed floor tiles and windows open to the sea breeze. I want an ergo bath. I step down into the sunken tub full of hot water and sparkling bubbles.

Seven days have passed as I've listened to my mother finally speak her truth. Océane never had a choice. Her loyalty to Jove takes her from home as an intelligence courier, an ideal cover with her security clearance as an international diplomat. I have never understood her. I understand her less since learning Jove is San Manuel Bueno.

My mother—the Jove spy. Jove uses file .dc2 to recruit unsuspecting candidates as undercover agents to enter the Network core and steal data inaccessible to him. Whimsical and carefree hardly describes my mother's double-agent life. Her travels bring her to San Manuel's fortress-like villa, the one from my mother's room that I saw in D.C. The town of Jove is one of many parishes in Gijón on the northern coast of Spain.

I sink beneath a luscious froth of bubbles fully submerged and relive that desperate night at Grandfather Mountain when I swam in the darkness of a cave. I hold myself down until my lungs beg for air. I surface with rapid, shallow breathing to ward off the tears as another day of Jove's revelations begins.

Océane, Julius and Pépé DeMolay are seated at the patio table and are waiting for me. A servant brings breakfast. Each day I force myself to consume nutritious meals. Gradually, I regain my strength.

I stretch out on a lounge chair overlooking a vast turquoise blue ocean. The rising sun reaches its zenith as I listen to my mother and her two accomplices.

Pépé and Julius confess to being the masked men who botched the kidnapping to get Iain to Spain where Jove could protect him. Pépé's arm has healed from Tala's attack, but required eighteen stitches.

Of course, Julius was the insider who gave Iain my password to use in Sandbox. Mentors at Kickoff have special access to the candidates' SASS computing. But I fail to understand my father's part in this, his subterfuge and secret meetings. I think Jolan was plotting how to rescue me from GAP, but Océane was too afraid.

They know Iain hacked the core and discovered that GAP killed his parents when they tried to escape. But they won't tell me what else he accessed. They explain that Kickoff was a week of extravagance, excess and espionage.

It was a ruse to bring together Jove's players for the first time since recruiting them many years ago, or five years ago in Julius's case.

Jove recruits candidates at Kickoff, but enlisted Iain when he was twelve years old because of his groundbreaking programming of the River. I had no idea Iain had been working on the River for so many years.

That was Kickoff. Nothing, however, could have prepared me for the real bombshell, the painful truth of my existence. How Jove has manipulated me, even before my conception. When did scientists become God, playing with engineered DNA and the genius gene and implanted embryos? Is this what I am?

I hate that I have advanced science with my tome, *The Human DNA Terminal, Cytoplasmic Nanites, and Enhanced GMR Notation*. The language of 0's and 1's and the manipulation of the human cell and reproduction bring disorder to my mind.

I listen as a multitude of words wash over me like white-foamed waves, crashing into a cliff made of stone. I dive beneath the crushing power of nature. In my crystal castle, I hear Cyrus Bashir's quote from a myth story he told one night in the cave. *He who knows himself knows God.* I don't understand why God lets evil rule the world.

"Don't trust anyone," Iain once told me, not even parents. Jolan and Océane did not separate because of my birth, but because of my paternity. No, I am not adopted. And yes, my biological parents are Native American and French. I do look like Jolan, but I did not inherit the sparkle gene from my mother.

The pureblood is not from the Salish, but from Océane's lineage. Moreover, Jove with his special cocktail, a unique blend of his DNA strands, included his genetic makeup into my mother's egg prior to my conception. How many parents do you need to create a baby?

Screening embryos is nothing new. The science of three parent babies piggybacked with the Human Genome Project. By 2020, many corporations promised parents disease-free babies by eliminating mutations. Progressive science will always lead to corruption.

Pépé DeMolay is the one who tells me these truths while Julius is noticeably subdued. He will not speak nor look me in the eye. I think he feels bad for his part in using me as a red herring. I don't blame him or Iain for their lies and deception. For that matter, it becomes clear to me that the people I trusted most are waging their own kind of cyberwarfare, while Logan's militiamen fight to survive.

Birth certificates and newborn DNA samples give GAP what they need to monitor citizens, not to ensure their health but to pool their genes. Only privileged citizens conceive with implanted embryos and genetically engineered DNA. The genius gene and disease-free lives. The majority of citizens belong to the working class. Of course, I understand how, but not why.

Pépé pauses to take a deep breath and then continues. "In 2050 Orphanet started collecting genes to offset the effects of population Bottleneck. Later they tested for genetic defects from chemical fallout. China was first to isolate alleles for intelligence. Then the new techno genetics rat race produced a progeny of geniuses," Pépé says, stopping his history lesson to gauge my reactions.

I stare in disbelief at the courtier of the royal court. No makeup, wig or silk stockings. He wears a casual white shirt opened at the neck and blue jeans and sandals.

"GAP doesn't suspect a fashion designer of corporate theft. Do you remember what I said? By all appearances you draw attention to yourself. In my ostentatious costumes, I can go anywhere undetected. Frivolous and amusing to those in power." Pépé smiles as charming as the first day I met him. "They overlook my other disguises, you might say." Score Jove, another polymath recruit.

"Brendan Frey used whole genome analysis and predictive models. What he called a deep learning machine. Advanced technology gave us algorithms. A superior race. Voilà—polymaths."

"Stop already." My feeble outcry lacks any real show of strength. "What about me and Jove? I mean, this man San Manuel?"

"All polymaths are conceived by in vitro fertilization at Orphanet. DNA splicing, the Gene factor for genius and embryo implantation," Pépé explains. "You, Jo, were born with something Jove's been waiting to see for a very long time."

"I'm an experiment?"

"No more than any of us are. "Océane removes her sunglasses and stares at me. Her eyes flash with intensity like the blue of an azure stone of antiquity. "All polymaths are implanted in their mothers' wombs," she declares frankly. "Believe me when I tell you, Jolan and I knew nothing about Jove's DNA until your birth. He manipulated all three of us. But Jove will explain."

"I don't care! I hate this world. It makes me sick. I want to vomit on all of you. Why can't you stop this? You can stop GAP. Fight with the militia!" The outburst exhausts me and shakes me to my very core. "What else are you lying about?" I cry drained of emotion.

"You know about the war?"

I recognize the voice without seeing the man, and a male caregiver pushes the wheelchair to where San Manuel can sit directly in front of me. He is mentally alert but failing in health. A gray blue pallor tints his skin. He breathes into an oxygen mask before setting it aside.

"You two may leave. Océane, I want you to stay. It's time this child and I to get to know each other."

Pépé and Julius walk down the path leading to the white sand beach. A stretch of deserted coastline is a private barrier guarded by security agents and armed patrols protecting Jove's dominion. I retreat into my interior castle where their words cannot reach me.

"The facts are quite simple," Jove says. "Your scan at birth showed a unique signature. I bought the patent. No other corporation knew. No one questioned me since I owned your parents' DNA."

"Something, we don't know what, caused your problems, Jo," my mother says rather pointedly. Can I ever trust her again? "A chemical imbalance caused your night terrors and the mood swings."

"Stress triggers the gene," San Manuel says speculatively, "and your migraines worsened at puberty. You changed in North Carolina. I sent Jolan to find you."

"You mean find Iain."

"Where is he?"

"I wish I could say he's alive." The numbness I feel has to be some kind of emotional shock. "But I can't."

I cling to the excruciating sadness because any pain is better than being so numb you can't feel any part of your body.

I cannot resist the temptation to imagine a younger San Manuel. His short gray hair would have been jet black and his olive-toned skin smooth and flawless. My hair is dark brown, but streaked with bold auburn highlights from days in the sun.

Though crippled with age, San Manuel is thick chested, broad shouldered and brawny, and nothing like me. What I inherited from him was the Gene factor for Einstein genius, and maybe more. I can't really know for sure.

"Is the Jove site yours? How stupid of me. I'm sure it is." I refuse to acknowledge Océane or the vulnerability in her face. For some reason I don't understand, I blame her for this and want to deny her as my mother.

❊

"GAP pushed me out. My protégée Julia Malum stole Orphanet from me. They perverted my experiments. I had Iain send you file .dc2. Malum's tests are inconclusive though, but something extraordinary is happening inside you."

"Playing God, are you?"

"My science stopped the Plague."

"Your science made the Plague!"

"Climatologists predicted our downfall. Ten billion people with limited water sources. A world famine."

"No, you can't blame nature."

"Technology seduced the world. Who could resist phone apps and interactive Smart walls for homes and the Internet? Why do you think corporations went public with the Network but to distract people with virtual reality and entertainment? No one paid attention to Ebola or the Superbug. It wasn't random outbreaks but at first slow methodical strikes. Things got out of hand, and the Millennial Plague mutated. It was an accident. Global Advanced Programs saved what was left."

"They don't save humanity. They exterminate humanity."

"2216 Kickoff achieved more in one week than I had hoped for. Three thousand perfect polymaths I designed almost seventeen years ago, and then the crash lost me the River. While Iain's disappearance is inconvenient, it won't stop me. Your team will crack his cryptology and get me the River to set things right."

"Huh, a moral scientist. What an oxymoron! How do you make right fourteen million people in mass graves?"

"Oh, this is extraordinary. Your ability to beat the brain scan. You lied to Malum and beat the test!" San Manuel exclaims.

He laughs, nodding his head while scrutinizing me. I feel as naked as I did on the flatbed at Orphanet. "How remarkable. You know, of course, Iain has an eidetic memory.

"You mean had."

"Your eyes betray you. Iain lives. You said you love this boy. It is mutual, I think. He will not stay away from you. You hallucinated during the scan. Spoke of second sight. Tell me about the visions."

"What do you want from me?"

"Your innate power can change everything, and you can make a difference. We are fighting a war. This is a turning point in human history."

"What, so you can rule the world? Haven't billions died already because of you?"

"My battle isn't with military forces. Our world cannot survive another war. My plan is to use cybertronic enhancements to overtake GAP without killing one life, or destroying another city. You are a miracle of science. I think your power, if allowed to progress, will make you immune to GAP's control. You are my final restitution to humanity. You will continue my science. You are my legacy."

"Listen to him, Jo," Océane says. Her urgent plea unsettles me. She reaches for my hand, but I pull away. "You're upset. I felt the same at your age. The law makes us who and what we are."

San Manuel takes the respirator mask and inhales several shallow breaths. "I tire so easily these days." Time steals his life force, but his mind is sharp. "I need rest. So do you," he says. "Take me to my room," he orders the caregiver.

"Wait. The little girl. Can you rescue Lily?"

"I will if you find Iain for me. A service is planned. You will attend."

"Why should I help you?"

"They believe Iain is dead. We must keep up appearances."

Océane takes a chair next to me. I refuse to let her off the hook. "I want to be alone," I say emphatically, looking the opposite direction.

"Let the child be for now," says Jove.

I listen to the distant crash of ocean waves. The white froth spills itself along the shore. Seagulls circle overhead. They flap their wings frantically against the strong currents of a windy day.

These confessions hurt me to the core. I have failed to stay safe within the walls of my interior castle. Tears cannot relieve my distress. GAP wants me to access the River, while Jove wants me to betray Iain.

Every choice we make has a ripple effect like dropping a pebble in

❄

a pond, a half hundred ripples, circles upon circles over time.

Black and white concentric circles. This is how the world of GAP is organized. The red bullseye is the Network Center where GAP's army protects the core. The farther away from the core, the less access citizens have to food and medicine. Those outside the cities live a far better life in the wilderness without technology.

All the dimensions of the physical universe fall into their place like puzzle pieces placed precisely together, only they create a fragmented and incomplete picture.

I wish Iain and my friends were here to help make sense of the insanity. The insanity of humanity. So many pieces are still missing from this chess game. I can't decipher what it all means. The endgame of Jove versus GAP stretches before me, winding its way through unknown mazes of light and darkness. Must I save Lily by sacrificing Iain's life? How can I possibly choose between the two?

SEVEN MILES SOUTH of Edinburgh Castle is Rosslyn Chapel. Its charm and antiquity have withstood the ravages of time and political claims of GAP. Although once part of the Scottish Episcopal Church, Rosslyn Chapel is owned by the One World Church.

The chapel retains its original interior without the virtual walls or the holographic heavenly host singing praises like that at the Crystal Cathedral. Its existence, like thousands of sacred places around the globe, no longer stirs the imagination of pilgrim travelers nor peaks the curiosity of conspiracy fans.

Rosslyn is a modest house of prayer, but a forgotten place used for infrequent services by local townspeople. The narrow but decorative ceiling of roses and stars is a steep rib-vaulted arch. At the east end of the chapel is the richly carved Apprentice Pillar. The Latin inscription reads, "Wine is strong, a king is stronger, women are stronger still, but truth conquers all."

The flamboyant Gothic architecture is a fair rendering of Melrose Abbey barely forty miles away. Every surface is etched with ancient images, some pagan and some Christian. The fertility and richness of the nature theme runs through the Master Mason's stone artistry. In the fashion of legends, some look upon the sandstone carvings and interpret meaning in the cataclysms of nature.

The one hundred "green men" are mutant figures amidst the lush greenery. Their barefaced grins remind me so much of Iain and his lopsided smile that I want to cry aloud. There is the altar where a ten-year-old boy once knelt and cried, finding mystery not in fantastical symbols but in the holy presence.

The altar is a reliquary for supplications from truth seekers. The movements of mind, while subtle give clarity. *When everything you know is false, the only thing left is faith,* Iain's words come to me. But faith in what?

The organ music fades in the background. A Scottish man dressed in the traditional kilt holds the great Highland bagpipe and begins piping an ancient tune, "Flowers of the Forest." The haunting notes to a simple but lovely melody vibrate through the chapel.

A veiled woman in a plain monastic gown takes her place at the front of the congregation. She speaks of *Revelations of Divine Love,* the writings of a saint who received sixteen visions on her deathbed in 1373. A plague and an uprising. The Dance of Death. The penitent suffers. Visions are a gift. The truth is that love does conquer all.

For the first time in my life, I utter a prayer to the holy presence in this sacred place. *Please keep my family and friends safe. Show me the Way.*

No divine light illuminates my mind nor does a vision convert me. Silence resonates with the passage of time. But a profound reverence for the invisible mystery does comes to me.

✻

And in that silence somewhere in my heart an echo of the divine speaks. *The brave warrior clasps a sword in one hand and a child in the other. They can't harm you. Enter the castle.* I can save Iain with my silence as he saved me in every way that mattered.

Now I understand the cost of valor earned in death battles. Iain and my friends sacrificed so much to save our lives. Am I willing to kill in order to rescue Lily and set free the children at Orphanet?

The memorial service lasts only thirty minutes. I have no chance to meet Iain's family seated in the front wooden pews. We exit the chapel. A thunderbolt like a sonic boom rumbles in the gathering darkness as we rush to the car. The wind whips rain into my face.

Had Julius not taken my hand, I would have slipped on the wet pavement. I slide into the backseat of the car. Julius slams the door shut against the blustery storm and a destiny taken out of my hands. Pépé and Julius converse, but the loud clap of thunder and heavy rain prevent me from hearing their words. I am glad for time to myself. I must consider a plan. Can I rescue Lily without betraying Iain?

Before returning to our suites at Edinburgh Castle, we stop at a well-known pub in Gilmerton known for its culinary delights. I'd rather return to my room and sleep. I lost my appetite days ago, but missing a meal won't help my state of mind.

I still feel off balance and unsure of myself. Our flight back to Spain departs at eight o'clock in the morning. I seethe with anger at Jove for many reasons, not the least of which is that he prohibited Océane from coming to Scotland.

I dread spending time with the old decrepit man, but it cannot be helped. Each day is an effort to accomplish simple tasks. How long before I regain my strength? In two weeks, my team will begin courses at L'Université de Paris.

A server leads us to a dining room reserved for elite customers. The prospect of spending an entire evening with Julius and Pépé is unappealing. I haven't been alone with Julius since Orphanet.

I excuse myself from the table and head down a long corridor in search of a bathroom. I feel nauseous and I need to throw cold water on my face and to settle my emotions.

Somewhere to the rear of the building is the washroom. I drag my feet and keep my eyes lowered, not interested in anything except eating dinner and going to bed. Maybe, I will sleep undisturbed until morning without the nightmares of Lily crying for me, or reliving the brain hacking at Orphanet.

I pass the kitchen and turn left into an adjoining walkway. The smell of sausage, pork and beef with fried onions is heavy in the air. I am tired and distracted until I make a wrong turn. A man blocks the narrow hallway. I pay him no attention until he won't let me pass.

"Excuse me," I say politely, but annoyed by his rudeness.

I sidestep him, but he mirrors my movement. When he grabs my arms, I struggle to pull myself free, but I fail pathetically. Frightened, I look up to see Damien, the man from Orphanet who represented me with GAP.

Damien's handsome features no longer reflect compassion. But he smiles with pleasure at capturing his victim. The dim light exposes his smug expression.

Fear triggers a toxic terror to the extreme. Needles and drugs and mind probing. What kind of diabolical experiments do they perform on living, breathing human subjects? On children?

What happens to them after the experiments? The horror of a sterile room and being subjected to brain hacking is beyond my worst imaginings. Dr. Malum has sent Damien to kidnap me, and this time no one can save me.

This time I won't escape Orphanet alive.

⚜

ACKNOWLEDGEMENTS

There are many people who have offered help in the researching, writing and publishing of *Jove's Legacy*. My husband and friend John Christopher Morgan gave me invaluable advice for the science and mathematics during long arduous hours with the world building of 2216. Together we discover the stories within and around us that give meaning to our lives and continue to shape our imaginings. Other family members either reviewed drafts and offered suggestions or reluctantly participated in book-talk at the dinner table. Thank you for the great dialogue. I used it in the narrative.

To my editor, Angela R. Conrow, I offer my appreciation for her expert advice, professionalism and friendship. Graphic artist Kyle Lantzy designed a wonderful book cover and kept working with me to get it right. Over the years are those who shared their faith in God and offered their encouragement: Kathleen Canepa, Tammy Sonnen, Vicki and W.C. Gilbert, the Carroll cousins, Emma and Riley Clark and also Lloyd Duman, a dedicated English teacher at NIC. A special word of appreciation must be given to David W., a spiritual counselor who helped me realize that truth can be found in a broken world even though one's eyes are not free of tears.

Attribution is extended to Internet Encyclopedia of Philosophy for quotes from Heraclitus of Ephesus http://www.iep.utm.edu and Open Source Shakespeare http://www.opensourceshakespeare.org.

Finally, grateful acknowledgement is made to Dr. Rodney Frey, author of *Stories That Make the World: Oral Literature of the Indian Peoples of the Inland Northwest*, and professor of ethnography and director of general education at the University of Idaho. I thank you for teaching me that "great stories will come" to those willing to walk the landscape of the ancient peoples and listen for guidance and their words whispered in the wilderness of a forgotten world.

AUTHOR'S NOTE

COEUR D' ALENE is my home and a suitable birthplace for Marie-Joëlle Peone in the narrative and in my imagination since I have lived here for twenty-three years. I hope her story has touched something deep inside you that compels you to know more about your interior castle and encourages you to understand your own life using the study guide I offer for your further reading and truth seeking.

I MENTOR WRITERS of all ages who aspire to become published authors. Particularly, I enjoy working with teen writers. Successful storytelling creates a memorable experience for the reader who will return to this book to decipher deeper meaning embedded within the tale that goes unnoticed through obscure details, or what I consider "shadow play."

AN ALLEGORY IS a complete narrative involving characters and events representing an abstract idea or message. A symbol, on the other hand, is an object that embodies the attributes of another object and its particular meaning.

NATIVE AMERICAN STORYTELLING, the speaking aloud of an account that transcends the printed page, transports the reader into a reality beyond the physical, hence the term metaphysical, the creation of a world. The soul of the story becomes a vehicle for the reader's own awakening and travels into spiritual realms.

OFTEN, I FOLLOW JO'S footprints along the shores of Lake Coeur d' Alene or hike to Mica Bay to marvel at the graceful flight of osprey. I feel the breeze. I listen. The mountain knows me by name. The Bear is my totem; the spirit of the Wolf protects me. I encourage you to begin your own quest for self-realization. Jo Peone's words echo through the chambers of my heart and mind and soul.

An Introduction to *Jove's Legacy*

Jove's Legacy was written in first-person, present tense narrative for the purpose of imparting to the reader the scope of one woman's vision quest to discover the forbidden truth of a world governed by the corruption of science and the misuse of technology. It is the redemptive story of a broken family and a displaced daughter, the story of a dysfunctional team and loyal friends, the story of enduring marital love and first love and the power of forgiveness.

Level One—*Jove's Legacy* for the General Reader

1. To what extent does the novel address overcoming personal obstacles? Do you have any experience dealing with a bully? What course of action could you take to overcome these social pressures?

2. Do you have stress in your life to achieve high grades in school? Are your parents and teachers expecting too much from you? Make a list of everything that makes you worried about school.

3. If you won first place or achieved a perfect score, would you feel better about yourself? Can you relate to Jo's concerns? She won the coveted Medallion Pin, but Jo values the Occitan cross. How did her self-confidence change in North Carolina?

4. Has one or both of your parents let you down? Stress triggers Jo's migraines. How do you manage the stress in your life? How would you describe your self-talk?

5. Jo escapes when playing the piano. When you feel alone and depressed, where do you go or what makes you feel better?

6. What do you do when feeling disappointed or faced with a problem? Jo feels threatened by Jenna Slate who verbally attacked her. What could Jo have done differently to confront

Jenna with words rather than fists? Do you think Jo justified fighting back, or just as responsible for the fistfight in the marts and on the ropes course? Why or why not?

7. Jo lives in a world of half-truths and deception. How does she and her team react after Shout Out and learning the truth about the censored past and the world according to GAP? Have you felt hurt when learning the truth or uncovering secrets in your family?

8. Jo questions her world, but she involuntarily participates in opening ceremonies and prom. Shocked by the execution, Jo feels as though the blade cuts her own body. She perceives the truth but doesn't trust herself. What is the significance of Jo's entrance to St. Vitus Cathedral riding four horses, which is a clear reference to the book of Revelation?

9. Jo finds it hard to obey rules and judges Iain, but she fails to see how similar they are. Compare and contrast Jo and Iain. Jo doesn't recognize how much she and Iain are alike. How is Iain reflecting back to Jo aspects of herself?

10. Jo convinces herself she stayed on the team because she met Iain Sinclair. But do you think Jo stayed because of meeting a boy, or because she truly wanted to pursue her mission?

11. Jo has low self-esteem, and she is always trying to prove herself worthy and to measure up to the expectations of her parents and teachers; however, she often fails because of self-sabotage. What advice would you give Jo?

Level Two—*Jove's Legacy* for the Critical Reader

On its most elementary level, the narrative may be interpreted as a commentary that interweaves the 2016 science of the three-parent baby with international corporations and governments presently competing in the marketplace for the exploitation of the genius-gene.

The critical reader may wish to research what in the story is science and what is science fiction. This narrative may be viewed as speculative commentary on what today's technology will unleash on the world two hundred years from now.

Underpinning the complexity and interplay of plot and subplots lie the fundamental disputations between science and God, corporate globalization and the endangered environment, religious patriarchal hierarchy and the mystical dimension of faith, and the delicate veil separating the physical world and the metaphysical experience.

Reading Questions and Topics for Group Discussion

1. The construction of *Jove's Legacy* is based on the story arc of the hero's emotional and an often painful journey from an orphan to the mature leader. Can you identify the elements of Jo Peone's vision quest? Where in the narrative does it deviate from the classical myth paradigm?

2. How did the portrayal of God versus science affect your views on modern technologies applied to genetic engineering? Did you examine your routine use of phones, computers and the Internet? Have you ever been the victim of cyber-abuse? How did you help yourself?

3. What emotions propel Jo Peone in her conflict with her teammates and the adults in her life? She lacks faith in herself and fears she is flawed. How much of her self-doubt is based on fact and how much on her own fear of the unknown?

4. At the very least, Jo has trust issues with adults and her parents

3

and also problems dealing with a bully. Can you relate to her problems, and how she eventually befriends Jenna Slate? You might consider reviewing chapters War Games and Shadow Play. Can you forgive those who have offended or hurt you?

5. Jo's naïveté could be viewed as a character flaw, especially because some might consider her gullible to the deception of her parents, the corruption of GAP, the betrayal of Iain Sinclair and the manipulation of Jove. On the other hand, you might want to consider her vulnerability as the source of her mystical gift. What do you think about her gift? What qualities do you admire in Jo?

6. Do you think Jo Peone is a credible narrator? The onset of migraines can distort her vision, for example. How would you describe her objectivity and habit of leaping to action without confirming facts? She accuses Jenna Slate of the botched kidnapping. What incidents can you find of Jo's judgment being correct or misinformed? Now that you have read the entire narrative and know about Jo's developing gift, you may wish to review her account of the summer of 2216.

7. The axis of evil as a dominant theme is predictable, i.e., light versus darkness, good versus sin, and yet often the imagery is juxapositioned. Can you find examples of evil represented as good and darkness revealing the truth? How does this literary device change your perception of the One World Church and the subjugation of history, faith and the candidates' personal experience of God?

8. Castles—the seventh castle in particular referred to as the Interior Castle—represent many things in the novel. What roles do the castles play in the world of GAP? What does the seventh castle seem to say about Jo Peone and her growth in self-awareness and her ability to see the truth in a broken world? Can you identify how this tale differs from most Cinderella stories?

9. One predominant theme threads its way through the novel—the idea of physical sight, mental insight and spiritual visions. Often, someone will urge Jo to wake up from sleeping or wake up to see the truth, and her perceptions of light can be clear or often distorted. Even her visions sometimes are not what you'd expect when she encounters angels who appear as black apparitions, not brilliant with celestial light. How do you explain the visions?

10. The novel carries multiple themes embedded in dichotomous symbolism and cryptic imagery. For example, the difference between the pectoral cross of an archbishop, the Occitan cross of a heretic or the Medallion Pin worn by a candidate. Can you identify in the text similar symbols, compare and contrast their meanings, and how they are used to advance the characters and plot?

Level Three

BEYOND THE SCOPE of this study guide, the novel pivots a wide range of themes, issues and preoccupations of the American landscape. In the same mode a multifaceted diamond captures light, *Jove's Legacy* offers you, the reader, a fascinating study through the explication of characters and their names, different places, objects and symbols that signify varied meanings across religious, historical and mythological realms.

To apprehend the subtext embedded in the narrative, pay close attention to the juxtaposition of various symbols. In other words, the reader will want to study context for unusual names and places, even numbers or colors can hold deeper meanings. Jove, for instance, could be a man, or a scientific journal, an Internet website or a location in Spain. Also, Jove refers to Jupiter, the god of sky and thunder and king of the gods in Ancient Roman religion and mythology.

TO RECEIVE YOUR FREE eBook, Jo Peone's *Revelations of Love: Dreams, Visions and Imaginings*, contact the author today at kimemorgan3@gmail.com. This special edition comes from Jo's personal journal of Grandfather Mountain, Chimney Rock and Castle City that discloses her most intimate revelations about Iain Sinclair, her teammates and her private reflections on her spiritual mentor Dr. Julius, not included in *Jove's Legacy*.

Revelations of Love:
Dreams, Visions and Imaginings
By Jo Peone

MOST IMPORTANTLY, THREE Crystal Keys unlock the secret mysteries hidden within *Jove's Legacy*. Don't wait to contact the author for an exclusive eBook containing the Crystal Keys at kimemorgan3@gmail.com. You can follow Jo Peone into the esoteric initiation she has encoded in her narrative.

VISIT www.kimemorgan.com today.

Meet Kim E. Morgan

Kim E. Morgan is an award winning poet, lecturer and retired English and TESOL professor who teaches creative writing to teens and adults. She lives with her family in Coeur d' Alene, Idaho, the landscape that inspired her to write *Jove's Legacy* and explore the sacred paths to the *Interior Castle* of St. Teresa of Avila. She divides her time between writing and traveling and is currently working on book two in the Jove Chronicles: Children of Destiny series.

To schedule select readings, lectures and writing workshops, please contact the author directly at kimemorgan3@gmail.com or visit www.kimemorgan.com for more information.